The Waymﬁete Trilogy

VOLUME 3
A Pyrrhic Victory

N.E. Miller

Clink Street

Published by Clink Street Publishing 2021

Copyright © 2021

First edition.

The author asserts the moral right under the Copyright, Designs and Patents Act 1988 to be identified as the author of this work.

ISBN:
978-1-913340-25-4- paperback
978-1-913340-26-1 - ebook

Acknowledgments

Firstly, my thanks to David and Annie Welch, who evidently saw worth in bringing one woman's story before the public gaze and helped in every way to bring it to fruition.

Secondly, in alphabetical order, I would also like to thank the following: for their interest and encouragement in getting this book off the ground, I would particularly like to thank historians Baiba Berzins, Mickey Dewar, and Peter and Sheila Forrest; for giving me inspiration and help in ways of which they may not be aware, I thank CDU lecturers David Carment, Clayton Fredericksen, David Mearns, Alan Powell and Dennis Shoesmith. I am similarly grateful to CDU staff members Judith Austin and Linda Cuttriss. Museum professionals George Chaloupka, Christopher Chippindale, Mike and Anne Eastman, and Pina Giuliani, instilled in me a more percipient depth of feeling for rock art and understanding of Aboriginal culture for which I thank them. Thanks to Yvonne Forrest and members of U3A, Darwin, who bore with my talks about the early days of Cooinda and other adventures and spurred me on to get it all down on paper. Grateful thanks to my Uni colleagues, Julie Mastin and Ron Ninnis, for their help in proof-reading and suggestions to clarify meanings of certain wartime terms which they believed were unfamiliar to modern day readers. Special thanks to Jeff Gillies and all the staff at Gagudju Lodge, Cooinda, for their hospitality during my recent visits to the area. Thanks likewise to Helen Rysavy of Storm Front Web Design for her valued assistance in setting up my Web Page. I would also like to pay tribute to my dear wartime companion, the late Kay Watts, and her family, for helping me keep alive so many memories of those WW2 days.

I must especially note and give thanks to the staff at the Territory Wildlife Park. Their more recent kindness and consideration in permitting me access to the Rock Shelter site – part of my Meditation Trail – during the period of a reconstruction program of the area was much appreciated.

My deepest thanks, of course, to my own dear sister, Julia, and brother-in-law, Anthony, who have always been there for me.

I must not fail to mention the three men in my life who have offered me, in my Uni days and beyond, so much in terms of the helping hand of friendship, in both academic support and later assistance in the publication of my book.

My never-ending thanks go to Associate Professor Harry Allen of Auckland University who pulled me out of the doldrums when I began to think I was an academic failure and who, by his wisdom and encouragement, succeeded in getting me back on track.

Enormously grateful thanks must go to Dan Dwyer, my one time office mate, whose friendship I hope will continue far into the future. He could be relied upon to lighten the load of life with a good giggle at some gag or other, and was always ready to verbally spar with one on more abstruse ideas – such as the purpose of life!

And thanks indeed to Trevor Le Lievre, a fellow PhD candidate, for not only steering me through the intricacies of the electronic preparation of my thesis for publication – a task somewhat beyond a typewriter mentality, but also for his contribution to the readability of my autobiography. His interest, encouragement and friendship were indispensable in producing this book.

Judy Optiz
Darwin, December 2008

Acknowledgements

Nothing about computer viruses or spyware could have been built into this story without the help of Ed Skoudis, author of "Malware: Fighting Malicious Code" and "Counter Hack Reloaded" (Prentice Hall). I also owe a debt to the countless people who made my many Internet searches so interesting and informative.

The map of Bali and neighbouring islands is from Wikimedia (https://commons.wikimedia.org/w/index.php?curid=204498). The map of the Hawaiian Islands is from the US Geological Service website (https://www.usgs.gov/media/images/hawaiian-islands). The schematic lifecycle of mosquitoes was taken with permission from the website of the Plymouth County Mosquito Control Project (http://www.plymouthmosquito.org/hproxy.php/life-cycle.html).

The author

Norman Miller is a doctor and medical scientist. In the 1970s, he and his brother discovered the link between 'good' cholesterol and protection against heart disease, their paper on which became the most cited ever published in The Lancet. This important discovery was to form the bedrock of a distinguished research career in the UK, USA, and Australia.

He was the scientific adviser and presenter for two award-winning documentaries on the prevention of heart disease, and was an expert consultant to the biotechnology company that developed the first gene therapy to be approved for human use in Europe.

He turned to writing fiction when a Visiting Fellow and Waynflete Lecturer at Oxford University's Magdalen College.

He is a Fellow of the Royal Society of Medicine and Royal Society of Arts.

Chapter One

Pacing the length of his spacious office overlooking Magdalen College's St John's Square, Sir Quentin was in no mood to have another tricky decision on his plate at such a busy time in the academic year.

"Quite frankly, Giles, what you're suggesting is so exceptional, involving yet another lengthy period away, I'm really not sure what to do. It's undeniable your exploits these past years have brought us many benefits. I'm very conscious of that and appreciate all you've done, not just for the College but for the whole university – and, indeed, for science in general. I hope you know that?"

Sir Quentin turned to look for a reassuring nod.

"But it *has* given me a few headaches," he continued. "The problem's that some of your more pernickety colleagues have been complaining about the extra workload on their plates. Only the other day, Daniel Shelton was nagging me about it over a pint in the Eagle and Child, and you know what a pain in the arse he can be. They all exaggerate, of course, but it's something I do have to take into account."

Glancing through one of the leaded windows across the lawn, Sir Quentin spotted Fiona sitting on the doorstep of the nearby Grammar Hall, waiting to be called should Giles think her presence might do the trick. The rumour going around that Sir Quentin had developed a soft spot for her was not to Giles's liking, but he was certainly prepared to take advantage of it should the need arise.

"What does Dr Cameron think about it?"

"She's all for it, Quentin," replied Giles. "And, one thing's for sure. I wouldn't go without her. She'd be essential. At times, she puts me to shame with her perceptiveness and powers of deduction."

Sir Quentin turned to peer over his glasses from the far end of the room, and smiled for the first time since the beginning of their meeting.

"If that wasn't coming from Professor Giles Butterfield, I might take it with a pinch of the proverbial salt! Not many men would use perceptiveness and powers of deduction as the justification for jetting off to a South Sea island with a pretty and charming young lady."

Sir Quentin slapped the back of his hand in self-rebuke.

"Sorry, that was out of order! Everyone knows the two of you are 'serious', as they say. Word had got round long before your Jane spilled the beans about the two of you sharing that hotel room in Rome."

"She let *that* out?"

Sir Quentin raised his hand again, this time to hide a glimmer of a smirk.

"Oops! What have I done? No going back now!"

"She seemed to take great pleasure in it, I'm afraid, Giles. It was the night before that Middle Eastern chap of yours packed his bags and went back to wherever he came from. He was standing right behind her at the time. Looked quite upset; went very quiet, anyhow. About twenty minutes later, he left the room without a word, and that was the last I saw of him. If Nathan Willis hadn't bumped into him on the coach to Heathrow the next day, I wouldn't have known where the hell he was. Quite extraordinary! I sent that email to you in Indonesia the moment Nathan called me about it. Judging from what Dr Cameron told me at High Table one evening – I invited her as a special treat when you were in Leeds, by the way – I didn't imagine he was a great loss. But I *was* rather concerned about what he may have said to Professor Yamani about our staff having affairs. I was fearing it might be the end of the cosy relationship between the College and his institute. Then, lo and behold, only a week later that huge donation from MECCAR arrived in the College's bank account."

Sir Quentin paused for a moment and looked at Giles over his glasses.

"I've never asked if you heard from him. Did you?"

"You mean Aram, our research fellow?"

"Yes."

Giles nodded pensively. "While we were in Indonesia. He'd already scarpered from here by then. Said he'd had to return home because his brother had been taken ill. That was it. Nothing else. Haven't heard a dicky-bird since."

"I see. Nevertheless, still very odd."

"He always was unpredictable…" replied Giles, "and rather strange. Bit of a problem. Fiona breathed a sigh of relief when I read his message to her. During the flight back from Jakarta, she was praying he wouldn't return. She'd never trusted him. Reckoned he was dishonest; that he was up to something."

"Anything in particular?"

"Nothing specific… just things he'd got up to in the lab. I used to tell her she was paranoid."

Giles reached for his glass of sherry from Sir Quentin's desk to take an unusually large mouthful. As he did so, he considered the other possible reasons for Aram's disappearance that had been troubling him.

"I can see you're beginning to enjoy my 'cheap Californian piss', as I gather you once put it, Giles. Jane let that one slip out, too, I'm afraid. I'd noticed you were in the habit of leaving most of it, of course. But never commented. I knew you'd grow to like the stuff eventually. Everyone does. Has a special nutty flavour with a subtle hint of apricots you don't find in any other sherry. Grows on you, doesn't it? I'll send you a crate when the festive season's upon us."

Giles smiled weakly. "Thank you."

"My pleasure, Giles! Only too glad I persevered. Well, to get back to where we were. I don't want to get Jane into too much hot water, but I'm afraid it *was* pretty obvious Aram was upset by the thought of you and Fiona having a Latin love-in. Put him in an awkward situation, I suppose. It *is* a complication, of course, no doubt about that – you and her, I mean. But I'm prepared to tolerate it as long as it doesn't interfere with your work. Apart from which, she's a delightful girl. It's nice to have her around."

"Obviously, you were present when Jane blurted it out?" said Giles.

"Yes. It was during one of my sherry parties. As always, it was a full house. She was standing by that cupboard over there, glass in hand, flushed and giggling like a schoolgirl on her first date. She also mentioned, by the way, that you'd asked her to find the identity card of 'an olive-skinned French lady' who'd attended the Sorrento meeting, and to send it to you as soon as possible by courier. Her interpretation, announced with gusto, was that Dr Cameron must have accused you of an infidelity during the symposium – although, I can't imagine what the card was supposed to prove, other than she was a bit of a corker. Jane went public with that one, too."

"What… that she was pretty?"

Sir Quentin nodded sombrely.

"Afraid so, Giles."

"Good God! I gave Jane strict instructions to keep the business of that identity card strictly confidential… for ever. I'll be having a very serious talk with her in the morning."

"Blame it on my sherry, Giles. So, was it true… about you, her, and Fiona?"

"No, none of it. As usual, Jane's speculations were a million miles off the mark."

"But you *did* ask her to send you that card?"

"Yes."

"What was it all about?"

"Pardon?"

"I asked what it was about."

"Er… let me think…" Giles rubbed his chin briefly. "Oh yes, that's right… The lady's university had asked for it. They said they'd noticed her name wasn't in the official programme, and needed to check she'd actually attended the symposium.

As the booklet had announced I was to be the society's next Hon Sec, they thought I'd be the best person to ask. I said her name wasn't listed because she'd registered onsite, not online in advance like most of us. So they then asked me to provide her card as proof. Simple as that."

"Bit odd, wasn't it?"

"Was it?"

"Well, I would have thought they'd have taken your word for it."

"Around here, yes, of course. But everyone has their own rules, don't they? And you know how difficult the French can be."

"That's true," said Sir Quentin. "Couldn't Jane have sent the card directly to France, though?"

Giles paused while he collected his glass again and topped it up from the cut glass decanter Sir Quentin always kept on the cabinet under the window.

"My! You're right about this sherry, Quentin," he oozed, holding the glass under his nose. "It certainly does grow on you. Definitely a hint of blackcurrants, as you said."

"I think you mean apricots, don't you?"

"Er… yes, of course. What did I say?"

"Blackcurrants."

"Did I? Sorry. Too many things on my mind these days. Where was I? You see, I can't even remember that."

"You were about to tell me why Jane couldn't have sent it to France."

"Ah yes, of course. It… er… just so happened that the lady's head of department was in Rome… to give a lecture."

Leaning with his elbows on the mantelpiece, Sir Quentin studied Giles's reflection in the mirror.

"Are you okay, Giles? You seem very fidgety."

"Yes, I am a little. I suppose it's because the favour I asked of you is so important to me. After spending the last few weeks in Indonesia helping INDOMED set up their new labs, I'd love to accept their invitation to return for a sabbatical. After so many years of cancer research, I'm chomping on the bit to return to my old stamping ground of virology. Don't get me wrong. Cancer's been very rewarding. And you've been very supportive from day one. But nothing beats viruses. I find the little buggers as fascinating as ever."

Sir Quentin moved from the fireplace to flop into the easy chair by the bookshelves.

"Ah, that's better! My back's been playing up this week. Yes, I understand how you feel about it, Giles. I remember the joy when I had the opportunity to swap magnetism for nuclear physics. However, with the best will in the world, it's impossible for me to give you an answer on the spot. I'll have to put it before the Senior Common Room for a collective decision. Democracy and all that! You've just returned from one trip to the tropics, and now you want to go on another. I have to tread very carefully. Between you and me, my inclination is to say 'yes', and let the two of you get on with it. But I don't want any accusations of preferential treatment. Trust you understand?"

"Why on earth should they…?"

"Money, Giles, money. You must be the most successful money-raiser in the College's long history. You're like a magnet to the stuff. First there was the *Marchese*, then your Russian friend, and now Professor Yamani. *One hundred million pounds!* Just like that – out of the blue, no explanation. At first, I thought it might have been to compensate us for Aram's sudden disappearance. A gesture to keep us sweet ahead of the study leave that Professor Yamani wants to spend here. But when I telephoned, he said it was for all the support you'd given MECCAR. That's a hell of a lot of money, though, just for nailing Stephen Salomon. You don't think it could be a sort of bribe, do you, to ensure you keep nominating him for a Nobel? After all, you've had a few unsuccessful attempts. He might be worried you're getting tired of the damn business. If so, he's not the only one!"

Giles shrugged his shoulders. "Anything's possible, I suppose."

"Or do you know something the rest of us don't, Giles? Does he have any skeletons in his cupboard?"

"What makes you think that?"

"Nothing. Just wondered, that's all. Have you done him any other big favours: saved his marriage, covered up a sex scandal?"

Giles shook his head.

"Well, no point brooding over it, is there?" said Sir Quentin. "We've got the cash. Let's thank our lucky stars and make the most of it." He paused for a moment. "By the way, now we're on the subject, how's MECCAR doing? Any more life-saving genes rolled out?"

"Not to my knowledge, Quentin. But my guess is their discovery of *Achilles* was just the beginning. As you may recall, had Ahmad Sharif given his press conference after fleeing to London from Sorrento, he'd have predicted a revolutionary AIDS vaccine was on the horizon. And he was right. What's more, I've heard MECCAR's going to give the secret of the vaccine to any company that will donate unlimited doses to Africa for the first five years, all subsidised by MECCAR."

"Wonderful! What a fine example. And what did you and Dr Cameron think of the new INDOMED centre while you were in Indonesia? Is it up to the same standard?"

"Definitely. The building and facilities are stunning. Although designed as a sister centre to MECCAR, everything is geared to the study of infectious diseases. How they constructed it so quickly, I can't imagine. Can you believe, they actually bought a small island off the coast of Bali called Nusa Ceningan, and built it in the centre, complete with its own helicopter pad?"

"How do you get there?" asked Sir Quentin. "You don't have your own helicopter yet!"

"There's a suspension bridge connecting the island to its larger neighbour, Nusa Lembongan," Giles replied. "It's been there for years, an iconic yellow structure. But that's the only connection between the island and the outside world. And, like Wadi Rum, it's a really beautiful spot. There's always been a small tourist industry on the island, mostly young Aussies surfing and snorkelling, and that created a few contractual problems at first. But it was all sorted out. A little piece of paradise, really. The Indonesian government is very happy."

Giles took another sip of his sherry before continuing. "And it's an absolutely ideal place to study mosquito-borne diseases. They have three programmes in development: one to find a vaccine against malaria, another to find much-needed new antibiotics, and a third on arboviruses. It's all very ambitious. But, with their money, I'm sure they'll succeed."

"You've mentioned those arbovirus things before," said Sir Quentin. "Tell me about them."

"How much time do you have?"

Sir Quentin reached for his pocket watch.

"Let's say ten minutes. But before you start, one quick question. Although most Indonesians are Muslims, Bali's an exception, isn't it? I think Hinduism is the main religion there. If the same is true of those smaller islands, is that going to cause friction?"

Giles shook his head.

"Not at all. The relations between Hindus and Muslims on the islands are very good, just as they are between all religions throughout Indonesia."

"I see."

"Okay, a brief rundown on arboviruses. They're quite a large group of viruses, about five hundred species, all carried by blood-sucking creatures like mosquitoes. They're important because they cause about twenty different illnesses, mostly in tropical and subtropical regions, but also in parts of the US. You've probably not heard of any of them, apart from yellow fever and perhaps dengue fever. However, in many countries, they're a huge public health problem, and one that's growing due to global warming.

"To give you an idea, there are now four hundred million cases of dengue fever each year worldwide. It's only the female mosquitoes that bite and transmit disease. Normally, both sexes feed on nectar and other plant juices, but when females have mated they need blood to provide protein for their eggs. Birds and small mammals, like squirrels, are the usual source, especially birds. When they bite, viruses can move both to and from the victim. So, mosquitoes give the viruses to birds. Birds give them to mosquitoes. And so it goes on. In this way, birds act as a permanent reservoir. In *some* mosquito species, infected females also transfer certain viruses to their eggs, and, as they usually lay hundreds at a time, it can be a major cause of the spread of a virus within a species. The West Nile virus, for example, is one that can be spread this way."

He paused for a moment. "Not boring you, am I, Quentin?"

"Pardon?" Sir Quentin responded, jolting slightly. "Er... no, of course not, Giles. It's fascinating. Please go on."

"Okay, good. Now we get to the nitty-gritty. Along with horses, we humans are what are called dead-end hosts. We're different from birds. When we catch one of these viruses from a mosquito, it multiplies inside us in the same way it does in birds, but in our case not by enough for us to pass it on to an uninfected mosquito that might bite us. Hundreds of millions of people get infected with arboviruses every year. Fortunately, in most cases, we don't even know about it. The rest, about twenty per cent, develop a flu-like illness with a temperature, headache, muscle and joint pains, that sort of thing, which passes off in a few days. However, in a few people, it progresses to meningitis and inflammation of the brain, called encephalitis. And that's serious, very serious. In fact, it can be fatal. Fortunately, this happens in less than one per cent of cases. But, when you consider the huge number of people who get infected each year, it adds up."

"There must be jabs against the blighters, I presume?" said Sir Quentin.

"Not so, I'm afraid. With the exception of yellow fever, there are almost no vaccines. And that's where INDOMED comes in. They have an ambitious plan to develop a vaccine that would protect us against every single type of arbovirus in existence. And that's why the centre's new Director, a chap called Teuku Shihab, is desperate to identify the virus that recently caused a devastating epidemic on a tiny Pacific island called Ni'ihau."

"Which, in turn, is why he wants you to go back... to help him?"

"Yes."

"Where is this Ni'ihau?"

"It's one of the Hawaiian Islands. Very small, the most northerly. As I thought you'd ask, here's a map."

Giles withdrew a folded sheet of paper from his inside pocket to show a photocopied map of the islands that Fiona had prepared.

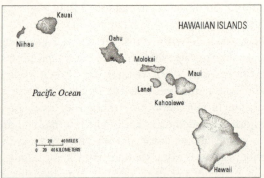

Sir Quentin raised an eyebrow as he studied the map.

"Keep going."

"Nobody knows exactly what sort it of virus it was," said Giles. "But what we do know is that it was carried by a host of mosquitoes that suddenly appeared from nowhere, and that everyone who was bitten died in a matter of days.

"It's unheard of. There's never been anything like it. And Teuku's frantic to be the first to get the answers. He sees it as a golden opportunity for INDOMED to make a big splash, like MECCAR did with *Achilles*. But, despite all the sophisticated lab equipment at his disposal, there's not much he can do without outside help. Teuku's a world expert on antibiotics, but doesn't know much about viruses, and he doesn't yet have a top virologist on board. And that's where I come in. He reckons I'm the ideal person to help him out. It seems Rashid Yamani put my name forward as someone they could trust."

"What do you know about him?" asked Sir Quentin.

"Teuku?"

"Yes."

"After graduating in medicine at the University of Jakarta, he emigrated to join the Centers for Disease Control in Atlanta, where he remained for about ten years. A series of jobs in industry followed, mostly on the West Coast, ending in a biotech company in Oregon. And that's where he was when he was headhunted by INDOMED's search committee. He was trying to find new antibiotics in endophytes at the time."

"I really should be moving, but this is interesting," said Sir Quentin, looking at his watch again. "What are *they*?"

"They're unusual bacteria and fungi that only live inside plants, and there's hope they may be a goldmine of new drugs. In fact, they've already been found to produce a valuable anti-cancer drug."

"I see."

Giles paused for a moment.

"A remarkable career, considering Teuku started life in Jakarta's Jembatan Besi slum. He's clawed his way to the top –

and, of course, he wants to stay there. If he can discover what happened on that island, he's made for life. He's desperate to beat the Americans to it."

Sir Quentin got up from his chair. As he meandered around the room, his thumbs tucked behind his belt in his usual posture when deep in thought, Giles sensed he was making real progress.

"Very interesting, Giles, very interesting indeed. Well, it's been good to have this chat. I do understand your position. But, as I said, I need to consult your colleagues. And right now, I also need to nip to the Bodleian."

He nodded towards several stacks of paper and open books on his desk.

"And then I have to return to that lot with a deadline of eight o'clock tomorrow. I've also several overseas calls to make. Denise was gesticulating behind your back a few minutes ago to tell me it'll soon be too late. So, as I said, hold fire for a few days, and I'll be in touch."

Chapter Two

It had been a little more than two years since Giles and Fiona had returned from their fateful meeting with Virginia Brandolin in Rome. Back in their routine of lab work and tutoring the students – punctuated, in Giles's case, by the chores of committee meetings and university administration – Fiona had succeeded in getting the grant she needed to ensure the continuation of her appointment for another three years. Helped by Giles's timely intervention, her new ideas on antibodies and cancer had been published in a reputable journal, and, with the pressure of insecurity off her mind, her work in the lab had blossomed.

Over the summer break, Gunnar Eriksson and his wife had spent a week at Giles's cottage in Little Compton, when the four of them had got on famously. Bill Eccles had followed on their heels from Majorca with his new girlfriend, from whom Fiona had taken the opportunity to learn some Catalonian recipes. The visits had made Giles's Sundays, so often spent alone pruning and weeding in the garden while Fiona remained in Oxford for her Italian lessons, more than worthwhile. Meanwhile, in Cape Town, Conrad had been awarded a bonus by Southern Security Systems for his role in exposing Stephen Salomon, an achievement that had brought the company much good publicity, making his long-cherished ambition to buy a second home in the Drakensbergs' Champagne Valley a reality.

The one person about whom there had been no news in all that time was Stephen Salomon. Even Hank Weinberg, now the CEO of his own biotech start-up in Dallas, had little information. All anyone knew was that, soon after leaving the National Cancer Institute, Steve and Marie-Claire had gone their separate ways under a cloud of acrimony. Always anxious to protect the reputation of a pedigree that included a congressman, a three-star General and a captain of industry, Marie-Claire had been unable to come to terms with her husband being at the centre of an international scandal. Although he'd repeatedly denied any wrongdoing over *Deidamia*, sticking to his claim that his only motive had been to make what he'd assumed to be the Bedouins' DNA switch available to the world, suspicions of intellectual property theft had been too widespread and entrenched for him to be offered another position of leadership, academic or industrial.

Giles was one of the few who'd been inclined to give Steve the benefit of the doubt, although he did wonder if this was merely because he himself had transgressed on so many occasions. From his raid on Steve's office in Bethesda, to his failure to tell Virginia Brandolin in Rome about Brigitte Dubois Yusuf, he had crossed the line whenever he felt he could justify it. In which case, how would he have behaved had he been in Steve's shoes if something of such inestimable value to humanity had fallen into his lap under similar circumstances?

A rumour that Steve had been offered a job in Canada had circulated for a while, but nobody knew if it was true. What was known for sure was that he had sold the family home for a knock-down price after Marie-Claire's departure and moved in with his daughters in La Jolla Shores, the smart residential community just north of San Diego. He had not left a forwarding address, and Giles had received no replies to his many emails and telephone messages. Steve's absences from congresses around the world, normally essential events in his agenda, seemed to confirm he'd dropped out of academic life altogether.

Meanwhile, Giles had slowly become adjusted to being a minor celebrity. No longer fearful of journalists or of being the star of school prize days and Women's Institute garden parties, he had grown to reluctantly accept his unsought status. Recognition of more lasting value had been bestowed when the Swedes had made him a *Commander Grand Cross of the Order of the Polar Star* for protecting the reputation of the Nobel Prizes. Jordan had soon followed suit with the *Grand Cordon of the Order of Independence* for his role in protecting MECCAR's interests. Less grand, but more appealing to his instincts, had been his appointment to the official list of Nobel Prize nominators, announced by Gunnar Eriksson on the cottage terrace in Little Compton one summer evening. To Giles's great disappointment, the nomination he had rustled up for Rashid Yamani after returning from Stockholm had been unsuccessful, the Assembly voting instead for a Japanese expert on stem cells, the undifferentiated embryonic cells that can be transformed into any other type, from heart muscle to nerve cells, by tweaking their genes. The knowledge that he would no longer have to round up support for Rashid's future nominations, but simply fill in a form and take it to the nearest post office, had taken a great weight off his mind.

It had been around the time of Bill Eccles' visit to the cottage that Giles had been invited to help Teuku Shihab set up his virology laboratories in MECCAR's new sister centre in Indonesia. As an expert on antibiotics with little experience of viruses, Teuku had agreed with the Advisory Committee that it would be good if someone with an international reputation in the field could help him get the virology labs off to a fast start. With Sir Quentin's blessing, Giles had accepted the invitation and travelled to Nusa Ceningan with Fiona. Though brief, the visit had been a great success and they had returned to Oxford pleased to have played an important part in INDOMED's preparations for the future.

Sir Quentin's email to Giles informing him of Aram's sudden departure from Oxford had arrived just before he and Fiona had attended INDOMED's official opening celebrations in the Batu Karang resort on Nusa Ceningan's close neighbour, the much larger island of Nusa Lembongan. By then, Fiona had adjusted to the prospect of Aram being in the laboratory for a few more years and had set up a system to protect her files from his prying. But she had remained uncomfortable in his presence nevertheless, finding it difficult to discuss her work openly in the lab or leave an experiment running when out for a cup of coffee or a visit to the library.

Consequently, the unexpected news had been more than welcome. But it had also been a puzzle, and a troubling one at that. Perhaps she'd been keeping too close an eye on him, she had feared, to the extent he'd suspected she was onto his undercover work for MECCAR and taken flight to alert Rashid Yamani of the fact. Giles had thought that highly unlikely, preferring to believe Aram had probably left for family reasons. When Aram's later message had arrived to say his brother had been admitted to Qatar's Al Amal Hospital for emergency heart surgery, that had seemed to be the answer. But, after discovering the hospital was a cancer centre, Fiona was no longer convinced. Giles's reassurance that heart muscle can be affected by tumours just like any other tissue, albeit rarely, had done little to settle her mind.

Though enthralled by her first experience of the tropics, Fiona had found Indonesia's climate a tad too hot and humid for her liking. There had been days when she had longed to feel Scotland's cool breezes on her skin, its misty drizzle on her face. Apart from the occasional walk to Nusa Ceningan's west coast to feel the sand between her toes at the Le Pirate Beach Club, or farther south to listen to the pounding of the surf at Mahana Point, she'd spent most of the time in the air-conditioned laboratories of INDOMED's top floor. When not working there or in her office, she would usually be found reading or writing on the terrace of the villa that Teuku had provided for the duration of their visit.

It had been while she'd been dozing on the terrace one late afternoon, after finishing Murphy's classic account of the yellow fever outbreak in eighteenth-century Philadelphia, that Giles had skipped up the wooden steps from the garden with news that was to change their lives.

"Fiona! Wake up! I've been talking to Teuku in the library. Had a long chat. It's really important."

Fiona had wiped her eyes, her book having fallen from her lap. Stooping to pick it up, she had gathered from the state of Giles's shoes that he must have taken the shortest route from INDOMED's main building.

"I can see you've been in a hurry. What is it?"

"He's been telling me about a mysterious epidemic."

"Near here?"

"No, thank goodness. On one of the Hawaiian Islands."

"When?"

"Last month."

"Serious?"

"Extremely."

Fiona had pushed the leather Ottoman on which she'd been resting her feet in his general direction.

"Go on, I'm listening. Sit down."

"Thanks. It was on the smallest and most westerly of the islands, a place called Ni'ihau. It's got… or, I should say, *had*… a total population of barely two hundred, all native Hawaiians speaking their mother tongue. A really unique spot. In the space of twenty-four hours, most of them went down with the same illness. In each case, it started with one or more ulcers, usually on an arm or a leg, or on the neck. Then a high fever developed, followed by multiple organ failure—the liver, kidneys, heart, brain, all at once. Everyone who went down with it died. It was devastating, unprecedented."

"How awful! What was it due to, Ebola?"

"No. Ebola's nothing like that."

"So?"

"That's the big question."

"Nobody knows?"

"Yes and no. The previous evening, a swarm of mosquitoes had arrived from nowhere, and most of the victims thought they'd been bitten where their ulcers had developed. Now, as you surely know from your youth in the highlands and islands, mosquito bites cause itchy red bumps, never ulcers."

"Except that part of Scotland doesn't get mosquitoes. It gets tiny little midges. But never mind. Go one."

"Really? Anyhow, the patients were rushed by helicopter to The Queen's Medical Center in Honolulu. The medics there had never seen anything like it. After scratching their heads, they did the obvious thing. They took blood samples and tested them for as many mosquito-borne viruses they could think of. And what they found was staggering."

"What?"

"Most of the patients started producing antibodies to the West Nile virus."

"Never heard of it."

"It's a virus that's carried by some species of mosquito in many parts of the world – Europe, India, Africa, USA, for example. But it's *never* been known on any of the Hawaiian Islands. Not only that, but its effects are normally completely different. Many people get infected every year. In the USA, about two per cent of the population do at some time in their lives. But the vast majority don't even know it. They don't develop any symptoms at all, and soon produce antibodies that kill the virus. And that's that. Over and done with. The rest, about a third of those infected, develop an illness that's a bit like a mild attack of influenza – a temperature, headache, aches and pains, and so on. And that's as bad as it gets. Only in a very small number, about one per cent, does it produce serious complications."

"Such as?"

"Meningitis and infection of the brain."

"Do those people die?"

"Only about one in ten. So that's a tiny percentage of the total infected. And they're usually old or already ill for some reason."

"And these Hawaiians had been young and healthy?"

"Exactly. But what's also important is that, even in the very worst cases, West Nile virus *never* produces an ulcer at the site of the mosquito bite. So, the whole thing's bewildering. The blood tests seemed to be saying it was due to West Nile virus carried by the mosquitoes. But, clinically, it couldn't have been that at all. It was something else, something completely different."

"Now I understand why you said it was a mystery! Why is it called West Nile virus, by the way, Giles? Was it originally discovered in Egypt?"

"Not exactly. It was first identified in Uganda before the Second World War. And that's where it seems to have stayed until the fifties, when it turned up in Egypt. Then, in the nineties, it spread to the Mediterranean region, presumably carried by birds."

"Why not by humans?"

"Because, once we've caught it from one mosquito, we can't give it to another one; nor can we infect anyone else. Horses are the same. We're both what entomologists call 'dead-end hosts'. But birds are different. When they're infected, they either get sick and die, or the infection becomes chronic. In either state, they can pass it on to any uninfected mosquito that bites them. In this way, birds act as permanent reservoirs of the virus, and can carry it from country to country."

"Interesting."

"So, to get back to where I was," Giles had continued. "The first time it appeared in the USA was in 1999, when it turned up in New York. And from there it gradually spread across the country to the west coast."

"How on earth did it cross the Atlantic Ocean?"

"They think a mosquito must have hitched a lift in an aircraft or a boat."

"Which is presumably also how it got to Ni'ihau?"

Giles had shaken his head.

"No, I think we can definitely exclude that one. First, there's no airport on Ni'ihau, only a helicopter pad for a service to and from the neighbouring island of Kauai. And the only boat service also goes between the two islands. There are no tourist boats. Ni'ihau is privately owned, and you need a permit to set foot on it. The locals call it 'The Forbidden Island'. Anyhow, as I said before, West Nile virus has never been known on any of the Hawaiian Islands. Hawaii and Alaska are the only two states of the USA where it doesn't exist. So, wherever it came from, it wasn't from another part of Hawaii."

"What about a cruise liner?"

Giles had shaken his head again.

"Nope! They don't call into Ni'ihau. It's not particularly attractive. Unlike the other islands, it's not tropical. It's very dry. In fact, it has so little rainfall, its lakes sometimes dry up."

"So, what's the answer?"

"Teuku reckons some infected mosquitoes must have been blown across the Pacific. Either that, or the virus arrived in a migrating bird, which then infected a local mosquito, and its eggs... they lay hundreds... were also infected."

"So, when a mosquito gets infected from biting a bird, any eggs the mosquito lays are infected, too?"

"It can happen with the West Nile virus, yes. But not in all species of mosquitoes... only some."

"Do migrating birds call into Hawaii?"

"I don't know, Fiona. It's certainly a long way from anywhere, isn't it? We need to look into it."

"Where did Teuku get his information from? I've seen nothing in the news or journals about it."

"That's something else I don't know. He said he'd tell me more when we next meet."

"Which will be when?"

"Tomorrow. Our regular weekly session over lunch in his very smart personal dining room."

"How posh!"

"It's certainly a puzzle, isn't it? D'you think you could fetch me some of that iced tea you brewed earlier, dear, while I think it over? It's so muggy today!"

While Giles was in the kitchen, Fiona had closed her eyes in the hope of coming up with a plausible answer to the mystery. Obviously, there must be one, she had thought. It was just a question of thinking of it. She'd always been of the opinion that, if you're worth your salt as a scientist, you should be able to formulate a working hypothesis to explain *any* set of observations or events.

As Giles was returning with the tray, her face had lit up.

"I've had a few ideas, Giles. Here, quickly! Put that on the floor. There are two questions. No, wait a minute, three. Why was the virus so lethal? Where did it originate? And how did it get to… what was it called?"

"Ni'ihau."

"Thanks. Starting with number one, do you know if the genes of the West Nile virus are made of DNA or its close relative, RNA?"

"RNA."

"Good! Because RNA viruses, like the AIDS virus and flu, tend to mutate easily, don't they? That's why it's so difficult to produce effective vaccines against them. So, perhaps a normal West Nile virus somewhere in the world mutated into one that was much more vicious. Yes?"

Giles had nodded. "Certainly a theoretical possibility. Even though it had mutated, it might still be detectable by the same blood tests, of course."

Fiona had smiled as she stretched to pat herself on the back.

"And I had another idea, Giles. It might have been a *normal* West Nile virus, but it had such a terrible effect because native Hawaiians have never been exposed to it before, and therefore never acquired any natural resistance. Don't forget how a host of infections – syphilis, measles, smallpox, tuberculosis, and others – devastated the Hawaiians when Europeans arrived in the eighteenth century. Historians think the population was reduced to less than a tenth of its original size."

Giles had agreed.

"I suggested that to Teuku, actually, but he said modern Polynesians don't seem to be any more susceptible to arboviruses than the rest of us. Surprising, I know, but that's how it is. Apparently, outbreaks of dengue fever, due to a related virus, have occurred on both Hawaii and Tahiti, and in neither case were the indigenous people seriously affected."

"Then I'd put my money on a mutation. What sort of tests did the medics do? You mentioned they'd detected antibodies in the patients' blood. Anything else?"

"Not really. By the time they'd obtained those results, all the patients had died. Serum from clotted blood samples had been stored in a freezer, but as there wasn't much and they were afraid to waste it, they decided to leave them alone while seeking the advice of the Centers for Disease Control in Atlanta. However, before that happened, somebody left the freezer door open over a long weekend."

"And the samples were ruined?"

"Every single one."

"Was there no temperature alarm?"

"It didn't go off. It failed."

Fiona had stared at him in alarm.

"Oh my God! This is a real emergency, isn't it? If that virus spreads, we could be the next dinosaurs. What about the mosquitoes? Were any caught?"

"No. Once they'd got the positive blood tests, a team of entomologists from the University of Hawaii at Mānoa set up a few mosquito traps on the island, but they didn't catch any. They'd either died before the team got there, flown off somewhere, or been blown away. Whatever the explanation, the scientists don't even know what species they were."

"How many species are there?"

"On the Hawaiian Islands, only a few. But, according to Teuku, there's more than three thousand worldwide. But not all of them can carry West Nile virus. Here, drink your tea before the ice cubes melt."

"Thanks."

Fiona had adjusted the cushion in the small of her back as she prepared for a quiet hour while the sun was setting behind the thicket of acacia trees that bordered the garden. Finding the pouf not to his liking, Giles had pushed it under Fiona's legs, before fetching the rocking chair from the living room.

"Oh, look!" she'd exclaimed on his return, pointing to the garden. "There's the pair of spotted doves we saw yesterday. Which makes me wonder. Did anyone think of testing the birds on Ni'ihau? Perhaps some of them got bitten by the same mosquitoes?"

"Yes, they did, albeit rather belatedly. They erected some nets among the trees. But, again, no luck. Plenty of birds were caught, but none was infected."

"How about horses?"

"There were a few on the island. But none became ill, it seems, and there were no signs of bites on any of them."

"I can see I'm not getting very far!"

Rising from her chair, Fiona had poured her tea onto one of the potted guava bushes that stood at the top of the terrace's short staircase.

"Hope that doesn't hurt them! Don't be offended, Giles. It was very nice, but I'm not in the mood for caffeine right now. My brain needs soothing. So I'm off to make one of my herbal teas. By the way, a couple of days ago I discovered a new one to add to the supplies I brought here from Oxford. It's called *kratom*. A man in the market recommended it to me. He said it's made from the leaves of a local tree."

"I'd look it up if I were you, Fiona. I think I've heard of it. Might be addictive."

"Really? Okay, I'll stay with Moroccan mint for now. Care for a mug?"

"No, thanks. This Yorkshire's doing me a power of good."

Fiona had returned to the terrace to find Giles sniffing the flowers of a bush that overhung the wooden railing.

"Aren't they gorgeous?" she'd exclaimed. "Apparently, it's called *ylang-ylang* and it's indigenous round here. The housemaid… a surprisingly well educated one, I must say… told me in her almost perfect English… well, perfect, apart from that twang she'd picked up as a teenager in Boston… that oil distilled from those yellow petals is one of the ingredients of *Chanel Number Five*. She also said it wasn't Coco who invented that concoction, by the way. She was offered ten mixtures of oils by somebody, and the one she liked most just happened to be the fifth. Isn't that a hoot? Who'd have guessed that?"

"Or that she spied for the Nazis."

"What! Never did like the stuff anyhow."

The next day, Giles had been busy all morning lecturing to INDOMED's new laboratory staff, before joining Teuku for lunch in his penthouse dining room on the tenth floor of the building. Decorated with traditional Balinese wooden sculptures and Javanese batiks, and with glass walls providing a panoramic view of the neighbouring islands, it was a place to which Giles was always happy to return.

During their previous lunches, always on a Friday, Giles had developed a liking for his host. The bond had not been as swift to develop as in Rashid's case, but Teuku was a very different person. His true character revealed itself more slowly. By nature, he was less confident and more self-critical than his opposite number in MECCAR. Perhaps for this reason, his style of leadership was also very different. While Rashid would invariably attempt to cover up his shortcomings after finding himself in unfamiliar territory, hastily bluffing his way out of trouble or changing the subject, Teuku would openly admit to his ignorance of a topic and never hesitate to seek the advice of others.

The habit had served Teuku well in industry, and he had no reason to change it now. In fact, his new team welcomed the approach. It gave them confidence that INDOMED's journey would always be guided by a consensus based on facts and experience, not by the diktat of a single person distorted by prejudice or pride. They also loved the way his office door was always open, figuratively if not physically. The moment someone entered, no matter how junior, he could always be counted on to push his papers to one side, shut down his computer, and return his Conway Stewart to its alabaster stand. Whether it was a senior faculty member or a cleaner, they were all treated with the same consideration and courtesy. The body language he'd acquired in the southern states, coupled with his regular attire of leather sandals, jeans, and a cotton T-shirt, would at once put them at ease, whether to discuss the complexities of enzyme inhibition in malarial parasites or the difficulties of cleaning the exterior of his office windows.

When the offer of INDOMED's top job had landed on his desk in Portland, Teuku had been reluctant to consider it. He'd been enjoying his work, and he and his American wife, a senior partner in a law firm in Cascade Locks, to the east of the city, had just moved into a large house overlooking the Columbia River, and were in the process of decorating their skiing lodge near Montpelier in Vermont. They were relatively affluent and content with their daily routine, with a son and a daughter doing well at a local school, and friends who could be relied upon. The thought of leaving it all and returning to Indonesia after so many years had held few attractions. Although his elderly parents were still living in Semarang, an eight-hour drive from Jakarta, he'd been able to visit them annually – and, by good fortune, they were still in good health. Pulling up the anchor and accepting the insecurity and unfamiliar responsibilities of directing a new research centre on Bali's doorstep had been a daunting prospect, despite the attractive salary and the promise of working conditions equal to those in MECCAR.

After delaying his decision for several weeks, the scales had been tipped when Rashid Yamani made a courtesy visit following a lecture tour in California.

"How will anyone take seriously a new research centre on a tiny tropical island, in a country with no history whatsoever of scientific achievement?" Teuku had quipped. "Your situation was completely different, Rashid. The glorious history of Islamic scholarship is all around you in Wadi Rum. The creation of MECCAR was like a dormant bud springing to life from the desiccated remnant of a once magnificent Cypress, a fountain bursting through the sand to nourish the minds of fellow Muslims and scientists everywhere."

"Very poetic!" Rashid had scoffed. "Perhaps you missed your true vocation! But poetry is for poets. We're scientists. We have our heads on our shoulders, not buried in the sand. Open your eyes, Teuku. The world has changed. Islam needs world-class research centres, and you and I are the sort of people to make them happen. With your talents and experience, I've no doubt INDOMED will be just as big a success as MECCAR."

Rashid's only advice had been to waste no time setting up the virology laboratories.

"Your forte is discovering new antibiotics, Teuku. Wth the latest equipment that INDOMED will provide, I'm sure you'll race ahead of the field. No problem. Same with the malaria programme. As you know, the search committee has appointed a real high-flyer from New York, who'll be with you soon. It's the third programme, the one on arboviruses, that you might need help with. Unfortunately, the committee still hasn't found the right person. And that's worrying. With global warming on the rise, insect vectors of disease are also on the rise. Soon, mosquitoes, ticks, and the rest will be invading new territories, taking their infections with them, passing them on to the local animals… and, eventually, to us. And there are virtually no vaccines. We're going to need some very soon. The field's going to be hugely important. And the Americans will be competing for the laurels. You'll need to move quickly, very quickly. Get someone here you can trust, and then grab any opportunity to make a breakthrough."

At this point, Rashid had thumped his fist on the desk in a gesture Teuku would never forget.

"I did it with the *Achilles* gene, didn't I? Now it's your turn."

When Giles had entered the dining room for their regular weekly chat, Rashid's parting words had been at the forefront of Teuku's mind. Once they'd shaken hands and sat down, prompting the waitress to open their silk napkins and serve *soto ayam* soup from a ceramic pot, Giles had sensed that something special was in store. Normally laid back and spontaneous, there had been a clumsy hesitancy about Teuku's body language, his movements oddly out of sync with his words, as if his thoughts were somewhere else. Resisting his usual habit of leading the conversation, Giles had waited to see what was on Teuku's mind.

"Good week, Giles?" Teuku had opened, his eyes fixed on his soup as he tucked his napkin into the neck of his T-shirt.

"Yes thanks, Teuku. No problems. Very good progress, once again. Thanks to Fiona's hard work, we're still on track to have everything up and running on time."

"Great! I don't know what I'd do without you Brits. Rashid certainly gave me good advice when he suggested I entice you here for a while. He's a very big admirer of yours. Knows we can trust you."

"That's nice to know. As a matter of fact, I'm a great admirer of him, too."

"Yeah, he's a great guy, Giles. I agree. Very sharp, boundless energy. Pretty daunting, really, the prospect of trying to compete with him."

"Is it necessary to look at life that way? You're in a very different field, Teuku. Why the competition?"

"Well, you know… he got off to such a flying start with MECCAR, everyone will be expecting me to do the same. With the facilities, equipment, and funding I've got, they'll think I've no excuse. It's a huge amount of pressure on my shoulders. It's almost as bad as having a Nobel Prize winner as your father. God, I couldn't cope with that one!"

"I think you need to be more philosophical, Teuku. People have to understand that what we discover, or don't discover, as scientists isn't just down to how clever we are. As you know, there's much more to it than that. Luck comes into it, too – what field we're in; what pops out of our experiments; whether what we discover turns out to be important. These are things we've little control over, no matter how bright we are or how many hours we put in."

As Teuku reflected on his words, Giles had recalled the chat he'd had with Conrad on the same theme in Cape Town.

"Yeah, of course, you're right, Giles. Nevertheless, it has become a bit of an obsession with me. Getting off to a fast start, I mean. Making a breakthrough of some sort. I feel I owe it to the organisation to keep up the momentum, to justify the faith they've put in me. I'm praying for an '*Achilles* gene' of my own, so to speak. Sounds stupid, I know. But that's the way it is."

Teuku had paused for a moment and then focused on his soup.

"Anyhow, let's eat before this goes cold. It's a very special chicken soup in these parts. Don't be alarmed by the chunks of black meat floating around. They're not rotten or burnt. It's a rare type of Indonesian hen called *ayam cemani*. They're jet black everywhere, and when I say everywhere I mean *everywhere*: feathers, skin, organs, meat, beaks, even the bones. I almost said teeth! It's due to a mutation that affects the distribution of melanocytes. We rear our own down by Blue Lagoon on the south coast. We've also got an organic veggie plot there."

Teuku had lifted a celery leaf to his nose. "Ah! Gorgeous! That's where this came from. You can't beat organics."

"Absolutely."

"Giles, to change the subject, I need to finish that Ni'ihau story I was telling you about. May I?"

"Please do. I'm all ears."

"Thanks. Just before we broke up last time, you asked me how I'd got all that information about what had happened, considering there's been nothing about it in the journals or TV."

Pausing with his spoon in his hand, Teuku had glanced at the waitress and nodded towards the door. Once she had closed it behind her, he had whispered across the table.

"I heard it from one of those Alhazen research fellows. I gather from Rashid you've got one in Oxford?"

Giles had nodded.

"Well, this one's called Mouktar Souleiman, and he's from Djibouti. He was given a fellowship in the Pacific Center for Emerging Infectious Diseases Research in Honolulu. That's where The Queen's Medical Center sent the blood samples from the Hawaiians for analysis. And it was Mouktar who did the lab work as part of his research project. He was the one who detected the antibodies to West Nile virus. At first, his chief, a bastard called Oscar Robinson, didn't believe him. 'How could a serious illness like that have been caused by such an innocuous virus?' he said. 'It's not possible.' Accusing Mouktar of sloppy work, he made him repeat everything.

"Anyway, when the lad got the same results again, Robinson still didn't believe him. He got one of his favourite techs to repeat the tests a second time. It took her a while, as she needed to order new reagents and wasn't familiar with the procedures. But when she eventually got it done, her results confirmed what Mouktar had been saying. By now, a lot of time had been lost. So much so that all the patients had died and their bodies returned to their relatives. Not knowing what to do with what remained of the blood samples, and not wanting to waste any, Robinson decided to ask the CDC people for advice. Not a bad idea, of course. The only problem was that, while the CDC was waiting for key members of its staff to return from a congress, some clown left the door of one of the lab freezers open over a weekend. And…"

"Don't tell me. It was the one containing the samples?"

"How did you guess? The freezer had been installed the previous week, and nobody had checked it. All the samples were ruined. When none of the technicians owned up, the blame was dropped on Mouktar. Without any evidence, Robinson simply assumed it was his fault. Mouktar was adamant he had nothing to do with it. He said he was working at home on the Friday before the weekend in question, and didn't return to work until the Tuesday. A few days later, Mouktar was handed a letter from Robinson accusing him of gross negligence and forbidding him from entering the lab until further notice. His stand-in was the same girl who had checked the antibody assays… who also happened to be Robinson's mistress… or so everyone reckons."

"And you're satisfied this Mouktar is telling the truth?"

"Absolutely. His record is pristine. I've spoken to him several times on the phone. Sounds like a first class guy. He's devastated. There's no doubt in my mind he's a scapegoat. After all, he's easy prey, isn't he? He's new; he's very young; he's an Arab; and he's from a small country hardly anyone in the USA, never mind in Hawaii, has ever heard of. So, as you can imagine, he's pretty sore. In fact, more than that – he's vengeful, which is why he decided to leak everything to me. He also sent me copies of his test results. He wants to move to INDOMED to try and determine the precise nature of the virus. He wants to outdo that Robinson beast. And I can't blame him. He's a bright kid. He had a bright future. And then this happened. It could ruin his career."

Teuku had ladled more soup while waiting for Giles's response.

"You haven't met him, Teuku?"

"Not yet."

"So, how do you feel about it? Are you going to take him on?"

Teuku had nodded energetically.

"No question. He needs help. And he's a good guy. But I have to be honest, Giles. There's more to it than that. It's not just Rashid and MECCAR I'm going to be compared with during the next few years. That Robinson guy and his fancy-named centre in Honolulu are just as important. In truth, they're probably my biggest competitors. Listen to this."

Teuku had pushed his bowl to one side and stretched to take an iPad from the bottom shelf of the dessert trolley.

"Okay… I'm looking at their website here. After describing the place as… wait for it… a 'multi-disciplinary centre of excellence', the splurge goes on to to say the focus of their research is 'new, emerging and re-emerging microbial threats of regional concern and global importance.' And, if that isn't enough, it goes on to say… and this is the crucial bit… they're aiming to develop *effective low-cost treatments and affordable vaccines for tropical infectious diseases…*' which, of course, is *exactly* what Rashid and the rest in Jordan are expecting me to do. Enough said?"

Giles had taken the iPad from Teuku's hand.

"Have you checked their recent record, their publications, and so on?"

"Yep, and they're very impressive, Giles. If I could beat them to solving the mystery of that Ni'ihau epidemic, and then develop a vaccine, it would put INDOMED on the cover of *Nature* or *Science* at a stroke… even *Newsweek*. It would show the world what we're made of. We'd have the Americans, the Brits, French, Germans, Japanese, the whole lot in the palms of our hands. Why? Because we'd have saved the world. Those skeeters and their killer viruses might have disappeared for now, but my bet is they sure ain't left the planet. One day, they'll be back."

Teuku had pulled off his napkin and tossed it across the table.

"And if they turn up in the USA, or Asia, or Europe, instead of a tiny island in the middle of nowhere, they'll make the Black Death of mediaeval times look like an outbreak of nits in a kindergarten."

"But this is pie in the sky, isn't it, Teuku? What can you do, with or without Mouktar? Even with the best labs in the world, you can't do anything without blood samples to work on. And there aren't any, are there? They were all ruined, and the patients are dead. So…?"

With an affected wink, Teuku had rubbed his hands before looking around uneasily.

"These glass walls make me nervous, Giles. Finish your soup. Then we'll go outside."

After he and Teuku had shared a bottle of local beer in the relative solitude of INDOMED's gardens, Giles had not returned to the villa. Instead, after sending Fiona a brief text message, he had walked to the *Bakung Hindu* temple near the yellow suspension bridge that connects the island to Nusa Lembongan. His intention had been to sit on the temple's steps and mull over the implications of what Teuku had disclosed. However, finding the place populated by a coach-load of tourists, he had crossed the water to the *Sakenan Lembongan* temple, and from there followed the road bordering the mangrove forest on the eastern shore as far as the temple of *Empu Aji*. Knowing how Fiona would be fascinated by the buttresses and aerial roots of the plants, he had stopped *en route* to take a few cuttings for her pots on the terrace. The stillness of the forest, with no sound but the calls of unseen birds among the branches and leaves, had been captivating.

On reaching his destination, Giles had found a religious ceremony was underway and had stopped to watch the process, using the stump of a nearby Sukun tree as a stool. It had been the early part of the *Shodasha-upachara Pooja*, when the faithful, on this occasion fifty or sixty women in brightly coloured traditional dresses, embark on the sixteen stages of worship of their elephant-headed deity. When it had seemed that the offerings, bathing, anointing, and chanting would never cease, a young girl had left her mother's hand to run towards him, frantically waving a stick and screaming.

"Hati-hati! Kobra! Ada ular kobra di belakang Anda!"

Giles had recognised only the single repeated word. But that was more than enough. Jumping up, he had run towards the road as fast as he could manage, not stopping to look back until he had reached the safety of the fractured bitumen, weeds, and pebbles. By then, the girl was with her mother again, waving to him with a broad smile on her pretty face. After making his way towards her, stepping gingerly between the clumps of grass and bushes as he went, he'd removed his watch and presented it to her. As far as he had known, it was the only time he had owed his life to another.

He had arrived back at the villa at around five o'clock to find Fiona stretched out on the bed with her open laptop balanced on her abdomen.

"Hello, Giles! You look as if you've been through a bit of an ordeal. Are you okay?"

"Yes, thanks, just about! I'll get you up to date later. Now's not the best time. Been doing some research?"

"You know me! And I have some interesting news for you."

Raising herself, Fiona had tucked her feet under her bottom.

"I looked into whether those mosquitoes could have flown across the Pacific Ocean to Ni'ihau from the coast of, say,

California, and taken their infection with them. But it's a non-starter, as most species can fly only a few miles. So then I looked into air currents across the ocean, to see if they could have been blown there. I got quite excited when I learnt that the Trade Winds provide a steady flow of air from North America to the Hawaiian Islands at an average speed of about fifteen miles an hour. Given that the distance is about two and a half thousand miles, it would take about a week for an insect to be blown from one to the other. As this is shorter than the average life span of a mosquito… usually about six to eight weeks for a female, one or two for males… I thought that's what could have happened. *However*, I then learnt that, when producing eggs, which is the only time they suck blood, the females need to feed every two or three days. So, they would have arrived either *very* hungry or very dead. And I think it's safe to assume it would probably be the latter. Also, the idea of being blown across begs two questions."

Fiona had paused for a moment to take a sip of water.

"First, if they'd come from the western seaboard of the USA or Mexico, why hadn't there already been a similar epidemic there? And second, why had they landed only in Ni'ihau, the most westerly of the Hawaiian Islands, and not a single one, as far as we know, on any of the other seven islands they would have passed over? So, I think we can forget about that scenario. Agreed?"

"Agreed. Is there more?"

"Yes. Next, I'll tell you what I've learnt about migrating birdies. But first, you tell me your news."

"Okay."

After dusting the seat of his trousers, Giles had joined Fiona on the edge of the bed. Having decided he would leave the best part until the end, he'd started by telling her what he had learnt from Teuku over lunch and then described his visit to the temple, avoiding any mention of his time with Teuku in the garden.

Preferring not to contemplate what might have happened at the temple, Fiona had questioned whether there really had been a cobra. After all, he hadn't seen it, had he? Perhaps the girl had played a trick on him, she'd suggested, to ensure he didn't hang around for the rest of the ceremony? The truth was he'd been an unwanted intruder. But Giles had been adamant. The look on her face had said it all.

"Now, if that wasn't enough for one afternoon," Giles had continued, "get ready for what came between the black chicken and the snake."

"I'm ready."

"After lunch, Teuku herded me outside to a quiet spot in the azalea plot, where he confided that Mouktar Souleiman had offered *much* more than mere information. You see, when the blood samples were sent from The Queen's Medical Center to the Pacific Center for Emerging Infectious Diseases Research, Mouktar was given the job of unpacking them, pipetting the serum from each one into clean tubes, and putting them in a freezer. Unknown to his boss, he actually did more than that. He also transferred a small amount of each sample into a separate tube that he popped into liquid nitrogen, the temperature of which, as you know, is much lower than in a freezer. Nobody had asked him to do that, and nobody else knew about it. But, having been taught good habits during his previous job, he'd decided to keep some samples in reserve. He'd also had in mind the possibility of doing some experiments with them, ones that would need ultra-deep frozen serum. And he is still the only person... apart from Teuku, me, and now you... who knows these extra samples exist."

"And...?"

"He's offered them to Teuku."

"They're coming to INDOMED?"

"Yes."

"Wow! But how will he get them here? I thought you said before that he'd been banned from the lab?"

"He has. But Robinson's secretary has a soft spot for him and warned him what was coming. So, in the dead of night he transferred the tubes from the liquid nitrogen into a box of dry ice, and took them to his flat, which is where they've remained ever since."

Giles had shifted to a more comfortable position on the bed.

"With those samples, of course, INDOMED will be the only research centre in the world that has any chance of discovering the true cause of the epidemic. Teuku sees it as a golden opportunity to make as big a splash as MECCAR did with the *Achilles* gene. If he can beat everyone else to sorting it out so a vaccine can be developed, INDOMED will probably have saved the world from a huge disaster. It could even mean a you-know-what. And, of course, Mouktar would be more than happy to see Robinson humiliated."

Fiona had looked at him and frowned.

"But Teuku isn't in a position to analyse the samples yet, is he? He has the labs, the equipment, lab techs, bags of money… but no expert virologist who could take it on. It might be months before he can do anything, by which time it might be too late."

Giles had got up and walked to the bedroom door, before spinning to face her.

"All of which would certainly be true, if there was nobody who could stand in to provide the necessary expertise at short notice. But, of course, if there *were* somebody, or even better *two* somebodies, Teuku's problem would be solved… wouldn't it?"

"You're saying he's invited us?" Fiona had gasped, slamming her laptop closed. "He's asked *you and me* to take it on?"

Giles had nodded as a broad grin swept across his face.

"Gosh! I can hardly believe it, Giles. And what did you say?"

"That I'd think about it, which is what I did for the rest of the afternoon… between swatting flies and running away from cobras."

"And…?"

"On my way back, I called him on my mobile to say I was very attracted by the idea, but would have to consult with you. And then, if you were in agreement, we'd have to ask Sir Q for another period of study leave."

"Of course I'm in agreement!" Fiona screeched. "It's a no-brainer! Why did *you* need to think it over? Is there a problem I don't know about?"

"I'm not sure how Sir Q will react. I was wondering how best to go about it. Obviously, I can't be totally open and tell him everything."

"But you *have* decided?"

"Yes."

"So, why not call him here and now, and just tell him we need a few more weeks? What's the time? Oh yes, sorry... of course... your watch!"

Fiona had re-opened her laptop.

"Okay," she continued, it's about ten-thirty in the morning there. He'll probably be in his office. Perfect!"

Giles had shaken his head.

"Unfortunately, dear, I think we'll have to return to Oxford to ask him. It would be too easy for him to say 'no' on the phone. He's much more likely to agree to it face to face. I know him too well. On the blower, it can be: 'Terribly sorry, Giles. Would love to help. But just not possible. Will explain later. Must go now. Bye.' But in his office, with a glass of that ghastly sherry in his hand and his eye on the mountain of work that's perpetually on his desk, he almost always gives in. That's something I learnt pretty quickly when I first arrived in Magdalen."

"Okay, if we have to, let's do it. When would Mouktar get the samples here? Did Teuku say?"

"No, only that he'll bring them in his baggage, addressed to INDOMED and marked 'for medical research' with a letter attached from Teuku to show the customs people. The usual sort of thing. Then, once they're safe and sound, Mouktar will resign from his position in Honolulu. Teuku's giving him a job. He'd work with us in the lab."

"Wonderful!" said Fiona, clapping her hands together. "But there is something that worries me a wee bit. Who *owns* the samples, do you think? Are they the university's property? And, if so, is Teuku entitled to give them to INDOMED without permission? What if it's theft? Where would that put us?"

"Very good question, to which I'm afraid I don't have the answer. I don't know if Teuku's thought of it. I certainly hadn't."

"I'll look into it. Meanwhile, let's get ready for dinner. We're supposed to be eating in style at The Palms, aren't we?"

"I almost forgot!"

"I'm going to wear my new dress. And, on the way there, I'll tell you all I've learnt about bird migration."

As Fiona had walked towards the bathroom, she'd paused at the end of the bed, dropping her eyes to the bamboo rug with its intricate pattern of entwined snakes.

"That's the last time I'll fall asleep on that terrace! I don't suppose there are many words in Indonesian that sound like ours. Thank God 'cobra' is one of them. Otherwise, you mightn't be here now. The other day, the gardener told me cobras have enough venom to kill an elephant."

Chapter Three

Ignoring the approaching clouds, they had left the car, provided by INDOMED for the duration of their stay, in the villa's drive, and walked the mile or so to the restaurant, just long enough for Fiona to complete her account of her day's work.

"Now, let me tell you what I learnt about the chances of a virus having got to Ni'ihau in an infected bird," she continued, rubbing her hands together in anticipation. "Can I?"

"Of course. Fire away!"

"Well, the first thing is that no migrating birds fly to the Hawaiian Islands from either the east or the west – in other words, not from the US, Mexico or Central America, or from Asia. There are no flyways, as they're called, along those routes. Not surprising, when you think about it, considering there wouldn't be much point. *However*, there is a regular route north and south between Alaska and New Zealand. It's called the Central Pacific Flyway. And, believe it or not, there's a bird called the bar-tailed godwit that does the entire six and a half thousand miles non-stop. Other, less heroic, species land in the Hawaiian Islands to recover before setting off again. There are even National Wildlife Refuges there to protect their landing sites. However, as you've said, it seems the West Nile virus has never been found in Alaska, and there've been no documented cases in New Zealand, either. So, if the normal virus doesn't exist in either place, clearly there couldn't have been any there to mutate and then hitch a ride on a bird to Hawaii. So, it seems we can exclude migrating birds as the source of the virus."

"So what are we left with?"

"Basically, nothing. There seems to be… STOP!" Pointing at something in the ground, Fiona stopped in her tracks and held Giles back from walking onwards. "What's that in the grass? Stay still… completely. Oh, thank God for that! It's one of those plantain squirrels."

As she spoke, a small creature had scurried from the long grass and sped away. "I was terrified it might be another you-know-what."

She'd taken a deep breath before continuing.

"Okay, back to normal. Where was I? Yes, that's right… there seems to be no way in which the virus could have got to Ni'ihau by natural means, either in a mosquito or a bird. And, as it seems we've already excluded boats and aircraft, I thought long and hard."

Sensing she was about to come up with another one of her great ideas, Giles had stopped walking. They had just reached the crossroads where the route south leads to the Villa Trevally resort and Secret Beach. A strong wind had picked up, tossing the trees wildly, causing Fiona to hold on to the Victorian-style bonnet she'd knitted in Oxford. Apart from occasional flashes of lightning, the sky was now ominously black.

"I don't like the look of this, Giles," she said, pulling him by the hand. "Let's hurry."

As they continued walking, Fiona had carried on with her speculation.

"If you think about it, there can be only one explanation. What would a tiny privately owned island, thousands of miles from the nearest continent, and out of bounds to visitors, be an ideal place for?"

Giles had shrugged his shoulders. "A nudist camp?"

"Very true. But I wasn't thinking of that. Try again."

"A monastery?"

"True again, I suppose. But also, again, not what I'm thinking of."

"I give up," Giles sighed. "And in more ways than one. Let's slow down. To hell with the rain. It might never happen."

"As I keep saying, Giles, you should meet me in the gym every now and then. Anyhow, the answer is… a germ warfare lab."

Giles had stopped in his tracks again. "*A germ warfare lab?*"

"Yes. What if the US military has a secret lab there for developing nasty insect-borne viruses as weapons? If it's underground and among the trees, nobody would know. Despite being very dry, there *are* some trees on Ni'ihau, many of which were planted by the owners. It wouldn't need to be a very big facility for this sort of thing, just one lab for the gene work and another for the insects. And then… what if there was an accident that allowed some infected mosquitoes to escape? It could explain everything."

Giles had frowned, deep in thought, while listening.

"Think about it, Giles. Why hasn't there been anything in the media about the epidemic? There's been nothing in the newspapers, medical journals, television. If it hadn't been for Mouktar, even Teuku wouldn't know about it. So, obviously a lid was kept on it for some reason. Presumably, even that horrible Robinson man doesn't know."

Fiona had paused for a moment, and then gasped.

"And now I've just had another thought. Oh, my God! It's even possible those mosquitoes didn't escape *by accident* at all. For some reason, this hadn't occurred to me…"

"What?"

"Perhaps they were *deliberately* released as part of a field test. Who better to act as unknowing test subjects than a small community of poorly educated natives living on a small, isolated island forbidden to visitors?"

"I need to chew on that one," Giles replied. "Let's get moving before we're soaked. We're nearly there."

By the time they had reached The Palms, the first heavy drops of what was to be a torrential downpour had fallen. With no possibility of dining on the deck by the water's edge, they'd followed a group of German businessmen and a Japanese couple from the reception area into the restaurant. Covered by a high timber ceiling, but open on three sides, it was the perfect place to shelter from the storm while still enjoying the sounds and the smells of the sea and forest.

After choosing a table and settling into the heavy wooden chairs, Fiona had remarked on how the patter of rain on the roof and the roar of the surf reminded her of when she used to camp overnight on the small beach near Kylerhea on the Isle of Skye, before crossing the strait on the first ferry the next morning.

"Fortunately," she'd laughed, "we never experienced anything like this! Do you remember the last time we got caught in a storm?"

"Could I forget! Do you still think I made the right decision on the Spanish Steps?"

"Of course you did. The proof's in the pudding. From what Rashid confided in you not so long ago, MECCAR's already on the verge of an HIV vaccine, isn't it? And INDOMED certainly wouldn't be here if you'd gone running back to Virginia Brandolin. It was a really courageous decision, Giles… and the right one. Though, I must admit, I wasn't *totally* convinced when you first told me."

"Thanks, dear. Your opinion's so important, Fiona. Always is. It's a strange feeling, the fact we're the only two outsiders who know the truth about what happened in Sorrento, about how the *Achilles* gene was discovered, and what's going on between MECCAR and all those Alhazen fellows it planted around the world."

"You can say that again. It's also a bit frightening, don't you think?"

"Why's that?"

"Fear of the unknown, I suppose… what might be waiting round the corner. If the only secret we knew was MECCAR's method of beating everyone else to the breakthroughs, it wouldn't be quite so bad. But it's the rest that worries me. It puts us at risk."

Fiona had taken a sip of her wine before continuing.

"Is there any way Rashid could learn of our suspicions about Ahmad's death, do you think? What if he'd somehow got news of our meeting with Virginia? Perhaps there was something in the Roman newspapers? There must be an Alhazen fellow or two in Rome. And, don't forget, there's a European Molecular Biology Organisation centre just north of Rome in Monterotondo. It's a small chance, I know, but it still makes me jittery. And what about our one and only Aram? There's no chance he could have found out about what happened in Rome, is there?"

"How?"

"I don't know. Just wondered."

"The only person who knows about our visit to Rome is Jane," said Giles.

Fiona had turned to look at the surf as a huge flash of lightning lit up the restaurant.

"Okay, let's place our order."

Ever since arriving in Nusa Ceningan, Fiona had been in awe of the enormous variety of Indonesian food. She'd tried every dish that had come her way, making notes and taking photographs of her favourites. On this occasion, she'd decided to treat herself to a *nasi campur* served on a bed of rice with a side bowl of chilli sauce. Somewhat predictably, Giles had limited himself to a simple stir-fry of tofu, shallots, and green beans.

As soon as the chatty Sumatran waitress had served the dishes, Giles had returned to Fiona's theory.

"To get back to that idea of yours, dear…" he'd said. "I've been thinking. It's not crazy at all. There have been several occasions in the past when islands have been used for the testing of biological or chemical weapons. The Americans used to have a big biological weapons programme. It started in 1942. The army set up a lab in Maryland and a few field test sites, one of which was Horn Island off the coast of Mississippi in the Gulf of Mexico. Then, in the fifties, they set up a facility on Plum Island off the coast of New York. And the Americans are not the only ones to have used islands. The UK used Gruinard Island, off the west coast of Scotland, to test an anthrax-based weapon. The whole island had to be quarantined for about fifty years due to the presence of spores in the soil. And the Soviet Union used to use an island in the Aral Sea."

"This is getting interesting!"

"And it gets even more so. Some of the American field tests during the Cold War involved spreading germs in public areas. In the sixties, the New York metro was deliberately contaminated with a bacterium that simulated anthrax. And, in another incident, some black Americans were intentionally exposed to *Aspergillus* spores, a fungus that can cause a fatal lung disease, to see if they were more vulnerable than whites. So, not only would the use of an island be nothing new, nor would using ethnic minorities as unsuspecting guinea pigs. You may have hit the nail fairly and squarely on the head."

"Have there been any accidental releases?"

"I don't know about the Americans or Brits, but the Soviets certainly had a major emergency once, when some smallpox viruses escaped."

"When did you learn all this stuff, Giles?"

"During my Liverpool days. They tried to seduce me into the UK's biological programme at Porton Down, and fed me with all this sort of information during a site visit I made. But I wasn't interested. I only went to see what goes on."

"Has anyone ever thought of using insects as attack vehicles?" Fiona asked. "Sort of airborne hypodermic syringes. Or would that be a first?"

"Yes, they have. The usual approach was to disperse the organisms in 'bomblets' or aerosols, but I can think of two programmes that used mosquitoes to carry viruses. In one case, it was yellow fever and, in the other, Venezuelan Equine Fever, which is quite similar to the West Nile virus."

"My! We *are* getting close."

"Care for a cup of *kopi tobruk* to wash your meal down, dear?"

"What's that?"

"Teuku introduced me to it. They take something like a beer mug, add coffee grounds, then add water just on the boil, give it a stir, leave it for three or four minutes… and that's it."

Fiona had grimaced.

"But there'll be a big sludge in the bottom, won't there?"

"You don't drink that."

"Am I allowed to add sugar?"

"Plenty. Most people do."

"Then I certainly shall. Giles, if you already knew all this about germ warfare, the islands, and so on, why didn't the same thoughts occur to you?"

"Probably because germ warfare has been illegal for many years now. In the seventies, an international convention was drawn up outlawing all biological weapons, of which the USA was a signatory. But now, I'm thinking that might not be relevant. To be honest, I don't think the US cares a toss about international law. What with Guantanamo Bay, Bay of Pigs, the Iraq war…"

"Now you've told me all that, Giles, I bet that's what this is all about. If there isn't a germ warfare lab hidden on that island, I'll wear a haggis round my neck for a week. Either those mosquitoes escaped, or they were deliberately released as a field test. And it wouldn't surprise me at all if it was number two."

"I doubt it could have been intentional, Fiona. To deliberately release insects carrying a virus as deadly as that would have been a step up from anything anyone's ever done before. I think it *must* have been an accident."

"So, where does it leave you and me?"

"Assuming Quentin gives us the green light, I think we should go for it. This is an emergency, and if *we* don't do something, who will? If nobody who is truly independent takes it on, the military and the politicians will simply keep their heads down, sit tight, and wait for it to blow over. And when those mosquitoes or thousands of their offspring turn up somewhere else, it could kill millions of people. And the World Health Organisation will assume it was all due to a natural mutant. As Teuku said, somebody needs to discover what that virus was so a vaccine can be made."

"You're right, Giles. And we need to move quickly. If the Pentagon gets to know of those samples, they'd never see the light of day again. Which takes me back to my question about the legal ownership of the samples. Do we just ignore it, forget about it, or look into it?"

"What do you think?"

"I think it's too serious for legal considerations to get in the way. It would be nice to know where we stand, of course, but that's as far as it goes. I'm not worried about the Pentagon being angry about their programme... their murderous, reckless, and illegal programme... being exposed to the world. It needs to be. It's not as if we'd be spying on them. We'd simply be doing our job as responsible scientists. And if, in the process, we stumble across illegal activity, that's their problem, not ours."

Fiona had paused to take a sip of her drink.

"No, what worries me is whether any person or organisation claiming to be the owner of the samples could sue us for financial loss. For example, might the University of Honolulu seek compensation for losing the opportunity to develop a test for the virus or a vaccine, either of which could be worth many millions? I read once that the Gates Foundation had put the potential market value of an HIV vaccine at three or four billion dollars a year. This might be in the same league."

"Agreed. We ought to know what we might be getting ourselves into, but we shouldn't let the answer put us off. You look into it, dear, and when you've done that let's see if we can find any clues as to what might have happened to those mosquitoes. That's what *really* worries me."

"Me too. I mean, how could they have just vanished?"

Chapter Four

Throughout a restless night, disturbed by the incessant drip-drip of rainwater outside the bedroom window and the intermittent flapping of a shutter in the wind, Fiona's mind had drifted repeatedly to the question of who might be the legal owner of Mouktar's samples. This was such unfamiliar territory that she had hardly known where to start.

It would have been the same for virtually any medical researcher. Normally, questions about the ownership of blood samples didn't enter their minds. The general attitude was that they didn't actually *belong* to any person or institution. Rather, they were the property of medical science. It was only their value as a source of knowledge and benefit to mankind that mattered. Responsibility for their safekeeping, the uses to which they were put, and their eventual fate rested with the leader of the research team, the so-called Principal Investigator. If another researcher later requested some of the samples for his or her own study, the most that might be demanded in return would be co-authorship of any article describing the work.

That sort of trading of biological material for publication credits went on all the time. Though ethically dubious if the giver was not to be involved in the second piece of research, it was nevertheless widely practised as a way of increasing one's list of publications, a lengthy bibliography being essential for success in the competitive world of academic medicine. Epidemiologists were particularly disposed to indulge in the habit. When taking samples from many people, perhaps thousands, for population studies, they would often collect more than was necessary in case some measurements needed repeating, storing the surplus material in a freezer. More often than not, some of this would end up in other laboratories, not uncommonly in several different countries. Although on occasions it might be necessary to request the volunteers' permission to use their samples for a purpose other than originally intended, this was usually no more than a formality. Questions of legal ownership hardly ever came into it.

After rising at 6 am, Fiona had tried to forget about the issue while preparing for the day ahead. Knowing Giles was going to be busy for the next few days, putting together a lecture and talking to Teuku's staff, she had booked for herself a couple of nights at the Inna Grand Bali Beach Hotel near Sanur on Bali's south coast. Having been warned that the trip across the Badung Strait could be choppy, the cloudless sky that had followed the storm was a welcome sight through the kitchen's large windows.

She'd been planning to visit the beach on Denpasar's eatern seaboard ever since accompanying Giles on a visit to Udayana University a few days after their arrival. It wasn't that she was an enthusiastic swimmer – far from it, especially in water where she imagined sharks might be lurking. Nor was she one who could stretch on the sand for hours on end soaking up the sun. What had drawn her was the prospect of strolling with the warm sea between her toes as she added to her collection of shells and pebbles. There had also been the Balinese flora to photograph. Regretting she hadn't done likewise in the Cape of Good Hope, when she and Giles were visiting Conrad, she had been planning to create a portfolio of every leaf, flower, and fruit that caught her eye. And who knows? Perhaps Teuku would let her write an illustrated article on the subject for INDOMED's monthly journal.

After enjoying a cocktail of chopped guava, snake fruit, and longans that she'd prepared the night before, accompanied by a slice of the maid's home-made *lapis legit*, now her favourite cake, Fiona had browsed a travel magazine in the hope of keeping her mind off the burning question of the moment. But it hadn't worked. It didn't matter that the answer would have no effect on their course of action. She just needed to know what it was.

Pulling her laptop across the kitchen table, she'd surfed as many websites as she could find that touched on the ownership of blood samples, printing the most interesting to take with her. By the time she was on her third cup of tea, she'd reluctantly concluded that the official international guidelines she'd assumed would be available did not exist. All she'd found were the opinions of lawyers, discussions among academics, and the seemingly arbitrary conclusions of judges that had little or no relation to ethics, common sense, or morality. Just about everything in the USA seemed to depend on case law, none of which mirrored the circumstances surrounding Mouktar's samples. Statutory laws of the sort laid down by governments were nowhere to be found.

"How is it possible," she'd muttered, "that nobody has been in this sort of situation before? And, even if they haven't, surely the problem could have been anticipated by lawmakers and some thought given to it?"

After reluctantly contemplating the prospect of continuing her research in the evening, it had occurred to her that it might actually be better this way. She and Giles could argue that the situation was far too urgent to delay while lawyers debated the matter, couldn't they? When thousands of lives, perhaps millions, might be at risk, they could claim they simply couldn't afford to waste time getting permission. They had to act. It would have been negligent, unethical, to do otherwise, wouldn't it?"

Upon returning to the bedroom to finish her packing, she had started to vacillate, wondering if it would be worth calling her cousin, the one who had advised her on the patentability of Steve Salomon's software. But then she'd remembered he was on vacation, rock climbing in Utah.

"I know," she'd said to herself. "I'll call Ros. Maybe one of the solicitors in her firm would give us an opinion. They were pretty helpful when Giles asked them about Steve's software, weren't they? I'll do it now. No time like the present."

As she was carefully avoiding Giles's outstretched arm to take her phone from the bedside table, she had realised her friend would still be in bed.

"Okay, it will have to wait," she'd continued. "And there again, it mightn't be such a good idea after all. Given it's all so confidential, it would probably be better to not talk to *anybody*, wouldn't it? Yes. That settles it!"

There were only two alternatives: either to forget about the legalities and leave it at that, or to read the printouts in Sanur, and confer with Giles upon her return.

It was time to turn to the much more pleasant task of deciding which of her new batik dresses she should wear. Expecting she'd have to wade through the sea to board the boat, after some deliberation she'd opted for a short orange and green creation with yellow bows on the bodice. After slipping into it and doing a few twirls before the mirror, she had put on her snakeskin sandals and chosen her jewellery for the occasion – a gold necklace with pink and white pieces of coral, matching earrings, and a jade and silver bracelet. All that was left was to drop her washbag, bikini, flip-flops, laptop, and a few extra clothes into her travel bag and wait for the 1980s Ford Escort that would take her as far as the yellow suspension bridge. Knowing that the bridge could accommodate nothing bigger than a motorbike, a second cab would transport her from the other side to Nusa Lembongan's Jungkut Batu harbour, from where a Snook Fast Cruise boat would speed her across the strait to Sanur, a journey of about an hour.

After pausing to give Giles, still sound asleep, a soft peck on the forehead, upon hearing the car arrive she had sped to the front door to greet the driver, a young Javan with a toothy grin and long, black hair. Taking her bag with a polite bow, he'd placed it on the rear seat and helped her to get inside.

Hoping to make the most of her time in Sanur, Fiona had attempted to have a quick look at one of her printouts on the way to the bridge, but it had proved impossible on the bumpy, twisting road. Feeling queasy, she'd opened a window as far as its makeshift handle would allow. The sudden influx of aromas from the plants and the sounds of the birds as the car sped among the trees impressed upon her how much pleasure a second visit to INDOMED would give, apart from the excitement of investigating the mystery of Ni'ihau. In the short time they had been there, the rich, natural world of Indonesia had already provided many memorable experiences: the flock of oriental white-eyes that had flitted among the branches in flashes of gold and white while she'd been strolling one morning; the almost surreal incandescent toadstools that illuminated the forest at night, like a picture in a book of nursery tales; the goliath birdwing butterfly that had settled on her bedroom window ledge, for just a few seconds, but long enough nevertheless to create an indelible picture in her mind. Even the huge rhinoceros beetle that had appeared from nowhere on the kitchen worktop, as harmless as it was ferocious-looking, had been a welcome guest.

***

After a breezy, but reasonably smooth crossing to Sanur, Fiona had checked into the hotel, and at once set off to the beach to make the most of what was left of the day. No longer in the mood for the carefree walk along the water's edge she had planned, and feeling peckish after the journey, she'd made herself comfortable in the shade of a leaning palm tree. Placing her printouts to one side, she'd opened the bamboo lunch box the maid had thoughtfully prepared and peeked inside. From the way Hana had smiled as she'd dropped it on the table, Fiona had been expecting something special. And so it was. Five very different, but equally delicious-looking, snacks, carefully arranged in three layers, were labelled with their names and recipes: on the top, three rice dumplings with a spicy chicken filling, labelled *lemper ayam*, plus an equal number of deep-fried potato croquettes, *kroket kentang*; below them, separated by a sheet of bamboo paper, two *terang bulan* pancakes, folded to enclose a mixture of condensed milk, cheese and ground peanuts, plus three parcels of pastry stuffed with chopped pork and minced shrimp, apparently called *pangsit goreng*. To finish it all off, at the bottom, were two slices of jackfruit wrapped in aluminium foil, a carton of coconut water, and a small bag of ice cubes.

Fiona hadn't enjoyed a snack so much for a long time. Once the box was empty, she'd tossed the crumbs in the direction of an attentive seagull and then stretched out on the warm sand to read the articles, writing notes in the margins as she progressed.

By the time she'd reached the last paragraph of the last article, the sun was setting and a cool breeze had got up from the sea. But she wasn't ready for the hotel just yet. There was too much on her mind. Covering her shoulders with the towel given to her by the receptionist, she'd gazed forlornly at the stack of papers and wondered if it would have been better to have left them behind, after all. A recent article by Monica Allen and colleagues, published in the journal *Clinical Chemistry*, had a sentence that seemed to say it all: "…there are no clearly defined regulations regarding the ownership of human tissue specimens and who can control their fate." She'd found the article again, and underlined the words with a red pen.

Rolling onto her back, she'd gazed at the swaying fronds overhead and listened to the soft swish of the waves. What should she tell Giles? How much detail? Everything… or nothing? To her mind, it was all painfully boring stuff, as different from scientific enquiry as it was possible to imagine. The telephone call would be long and tedious, she'd thought, and almost certainly lead nowhere. But she owed it to him, didn't she? Their return to Oxford was only ten days away now, wasn't it? Soon he'd be faced with the unenviable task of requesting Sir Q's permission for them to about turn and get on a plane again. He would need to have his answers prepared and his wits about him.

***

The balcony of the bedroom, overlooking the garden and swimming pool with the beach just visible above the trees, would have been perfect for what she'd originally had in mind – a quiet hour listening to her latest Mozart download with a Campari and soda before taking the elevator to the rooftop restaurant. But it was not to be. As Fiona arranged her printouts on the balcony's wrought iron table, her one concern had been that Giles might feel obliged to volunteer any information that she provided to Sir Quentin, notorious for worrying about the College's reputation and rushing off to ask his QC friends for advice. After taking a sip from her glass, she'd picked up the phone.

As usual, Giles had answered within seonds.

"Fiona! I was just about to call to check you're okay. Good journey? Nice hotel?"

"Yes, thanks. Everything's lovely. The only downside is I brought some articles with me about who owns blood samples and so on, and spent the afternoon plodding through them."

"Good idea. And…?"

"It's so confusing that, at first, I thought I wouldn't bother you with it all. But then I had second thoughts. My own opinion, before I start, is that we should do what we said: forget about the legalities, get on with the job, and deal with any problems down the road, if they arise."

"That certainly doesn't give me a problem, Fiona. We wouldn't have achieved what we have over the years if we'd let the law get in the way of common sense. If we consult lawyers on this one, thousands of people could be dead by the time they've made up their minds. Nevertheless, I am interested to know what you've learnt. So fire away."

"Okay. Here goes. Even though I realise it's only American law that's relevant, I'm going to start with some guidelines on the ethics of using blood samples that I found on a UK Medical Research Council website, since I imagine this is what Sir Q might use as a benchmark."

"Fair enough."

"The site says that blood samples collected from patients for making a diagnosis or monitoring their treatment are considered to be different from those taken for research. In the former case, they are used only for the benefit of the patient, while in the latter the beneficiary is all of humankind."

"I've heard that argument many times, Fiona. However, I think it overlooks the point that the patient is a member of humankind. So, any sample taken for research is potentially for his or her benefit as much as everyone else's."

"But not immediately. And, as you say, it's *potentially* of benefit. More often than not, it isn't?"

"That's usually the case, I agree," Giles had replied after pausing for thought. "But the results of the research could be to his or her benefit in a few years' time."

"Fair point… I suppose. Anyhow, Mouktar's samples fall somewhere between the two, don't they? Although they were originally collected for the patients' diagnosis, they're now of interest only for research."

"I'm not sure that's true, you know. We want to find the cause of death, don't we? Is that pure research, or the quest for a diagnosis? I think it's more akin to doing an autopsy. We want to do tests *post mortem* to determine the cause of death."

"I suppose that's one way of looking at it," Fiona had sighed. "But it's also true that, while the results may be of value to the rest of us, they certainly won't be to those Hawaiians. It's too late for the diagnosis to be any use to them, isn't it?"

"Er…yes, of course. Does that change things?"

"It might to a lawyer. The same website provides guidance on when various courses of action should first be approved by an ethics committee. It doesn't cover our situation, unfortunately. But the general message is that researchers are expected to apply to an ethics committee for approval to do any work that a patient hadn't consented to before a sample was taken."

"I'm familiar with that, too, dear. But I think we should ignore it. We can't just throw the samples away simply because the doctors hadn't said, 'Look, sorry, we don't know what's causing your illness, and we think it's going kill you. When that happens, will it be okay to use your blood to find out what it was all about?' That would be crazy. On top of which, valuable time… possibly months… would be lost applying to committees and waiting for them to sit, during which the virus could be multiplying inside mosquitoes somewhere. And this is ethics anyhow, isn't it? Nothing to do with the law?"

"That's true," Fiona had replied. "Okay, let's move onto the law. I'm not going to bore you with every article, but the next one I've got in front of me was published in the *Journal of Blood Medicine* by the President of the *Istituto Superiore di Sanita* in Rome. I thought it looked very promising at first, but it turned out to be mostly about the *commercial* use of samples, not research. Nevertheless, I thought it worth mentioning, because it says, and I quote, '…general guidelines valid for every situation are not feasible'. And later on it says, '…specific considerations should be applied on a case-by-case basis.'"

"I see. I'm getting the picture. What else have you got?"

"I found one article from the Office of the Executive Vice Chancellor and General Counsel of Washington University School of Medicine, which I thought might provide the answers. However, all it says is that just about everything depends on case law."

"You mean courts are guided in their decisions by what other courts decided, those earlier courts having used as guidance what previous courts decided, who have…?"

"Precisely!" Fiona had interrupted. "What's particularly interesting is a table summarising cases in which ownership of samples used for research was disputed. It covers several scenarios, including samples originally collected for the care of patients and then used for unforeseen research. In most of those cases, the courts decided that the patients did *not* retain ownership."

"Okay, so we can forget about the patients' relatives having a say in the matter?"

"Probably."

"Anything about transferring samples from one institution to another?"

"I was just about to come to that, Giles. Yes, and the authors concluded that when it's a gift, ownership is considered to have been transferred from the donor to the recipient, but when it is a bailment, ownership stays with the donor. As bailment was not a word I was familiar with, I looked it up. It's when property changes hands for an agreed purpose, but is then returned – for example, when a car goes into a dealer to be serviced, or a cloakroom in a theatre looks after your coat."

"But this doesn't make much sense for blood samples, does it? Once blood is drawn into a syringe, it either starts to clot or there's a chemical inside to prevent it clotting. In neither case is the sample the same anymore. It's something else."

"And you certainly can't return it to where it came from."

"Absolutely."

"The article also reviews a number of different cases," Fiona had continued. "One that's not very promising for us concerns an expert on prostate cancer, a certain William Catalona. When he moved from one American university to another, he wanted to take some samples of tissue with him. However, the university he was leaving said he couldn't do so. So he took his case to the District Court for East Missouri, which unfortunately for him sided with the university. When he went to an appeals court, he got the same answer. Even when he got thousands of people from whom the samples had been taken to sign a statement saying they *wanted him and nobody else* to have them, it made no difference. As they were no longer the owners, the courts said, their wishes were not important. Isn't that mad?"

"Totally. In fact, it's more than mad. I wonder how many people have died because his research was interrupted? He should have turned up in a truck in the middle of the night and simply carted them off."

He had paused for a moment.

"Does the article say anything about samples that are simply left over and no longer needed, as opposed to being kept in storage for a specific purpose?"

"Yes, it does actually. It says… hold on… 'currently, no laws or regulations exist regarding ownership of… leftover materials.' So, where does that leave us?"

"Just about where we started, I think."

"That's what I thought. I've lots of other stuff here, if…"

"I've heard enough, thanks, Fiona. You've done brilliantly. And I agree with you. We shouldn't waste time on lawyers. How they cope with that sort of thing, I can't imagine. We should just move ahead and get on with it."

"Will you mention all this stuff to *you know who* when we're back?"

"Quentin?"

"Yes."

"Not a chance! He's the last person I'd tell. I'd have to be mad. To change the subject, how's the beach?"

"Beautiful."

"Swim?"

"Not likely! Just lazed under a palm tree."

"Fair enough. Well, enjoy the evening, and I'll see you when you get…"

"Don't go just yet," Fiona had interrupted. "There's something else."

"What's that?"

"During the boat trip, I got thinking about those mosquitoes. As you know, the only ones that bite are females after they've mated. Normally, they live on nectar and plant juices, like the males, but they need blood to provide protein for their developing eggs. So, the ones on Ni'ihau must have included lots of females that had just mated. Now, as you also know, mosquitoes need water to breed. It's essential for their larvae to develop, even if it's only a puddle or a few drops in a hole in a tree. So, after biting the Hawaiians, they would have gone off looking for somewhere wet to lay their eggs. Presumably, some would have flown to the nearby trees, where they could very well have bitten a bird. I know you told me that when a few birds on the island were caught, none of them tested positive for West Nile virus. But so what? There could be several hundred there. Yes?"

"Presumably. Thousands even."

"Right. Now what if an infected bird had flown from Ni'ihau to the nearest island, Kauai? Ni'ihau is very dry, but Kauai is much wetter. It's tropical, with rainforest all round the perimeter. So it must have plenty of its own mosquitoes. If that happened, in next to no time the place would be a no-go zone, and the entire Hawaii Islands might need to be evacuated and quarantined."

"You're right, Fiona! All this assumes, of course, that the virus doesn't make birds so sick they can't fly, even though it's lethal to us humans."

"Perfectly possible. Think of the virus that causes Lassa fever in Africa – often very serious, even fatal in humans, but no effect at all in the rats that give it to us."

"Yes, unfortunately, the scenario you described is quite possible. It's a scary thought. But don't let it keep you awake."

"I'll try not to."

Chapter Five

The following morning, restless with so many questions and uncertainties on her mind, Fiona had returned earlier than planned, arriving at Nusa Lembongan, after a choppy sea journey, at around midday. Still queasy as she crossed the yellow bridge, she hadn't had the stomach for another taxi ride and opted instead to walk to the villa. Though her bag was laden with paper and her dress wet from the spray, she'd chosen the long way to make the most of the sunshine, keeping to the coast as far as Bias Munjul at the island's northern tip before following the road home.

As she approached *Pura Adi Sakti*, the junction near the centre of the island from which the newly constructed gravel drive led to INDOMED's residential compound, she had looked forward to seeing Giles on the terrace, perhaps planning their return journey or getting his thoughts together in preparation for his meeting with Sir Quentin. He was a great believer in planning well ahead, and Teuku's invitation had given him a real lift. It wasn't just the challenge of solving Ni'ihau's mystery that appealed to him. There was more to it than that – much more. The opportunity to return to virology, the field in which he'd forged his reputation, was just as important, his switch to cancer genes having been only to comply with the *Marchese's* wishes.

He'd not had any regrets. They'd done some solid work together and had a lot of fun in the process. But as she'd made her way down the drive, she had known he would jump at the chance of going back to his roots, and was desperately hoping Teuku's invitation would make it happen. After all, as he had said, he could still honour his agreement with the *Marchese* by studying cancer-causing viruses, like HPV and hepatitis C, couldn't he? The only downside was it would delay their retirement in Italy. But those plans had been premature, anyhow. It would be several years before the refurbishment of the old farmhouse near Cortona was completed. The architects had not yet even decided how to repair the balcony without damaging the old Wisteria that framed the view of the distant church. And goodness knows how long it would take to rebuild the garden wall out of the original stones.

Before the villa had come into sight from behind the banana trees at the drive's final bend, Giles had heard the crunch of Fiona's sandals on the stones and walked to the gate to greet her. After ushering her into the entrance hall, he'd taken her bag and hung it on the bamboo coat stand.

"You certainly caught the sun!" he'd quipped, removing her sunglasses. "You look like an owl!"

"Oh dear! Do I?"

"Kiss? Oops, now I've left remnants of my chocolate digestive on your cheek. Here, use my handkerchief."

"Thanks. Anyhow, what are you doing? You're supposed to be getting rid of that paunch."

"While the cat's away…"

"I see! Well, this moggy needs to rest her paws. I've walked all the way from the bridge, and the roads are so hot this time of the day. Could you bring my bag?"

Seated on the sofa, Fiona had proceeded to sift through the printouts she had taken with her, dropping them on to the floor as she organised them into groups.

"Ah!" Giles had sighed. "Now I know."

"Know what?"

"Why there was no paper in the printer for my lecture notes."

"Sorry, but it *was* for a good cause, wasn't it? As you'll have gathered from this lot, I didn't get much rest while I was away. I don't think the best lawyer in the world could help us with this mess. Every case is different: which part of the world you're in, what a judge's opinion happens to have been in a particular case, and so on. And I couldn't find any situation remotely similar to ours."

"But overall, that's probably an advantage, isn't it?"

"Absolutely! Gives us the perfect excuse."

By now, Fiona had found the summary she'd written the previous evening.

"Here, why don't you read this while I have a shower? I need one. I was up to my knickers in tiny fish and bits of seaweed when the swell hit me getting off the boat."

By the time Fiona had reappeared, Giles was stretched out on the sofa, having been through her notes a couple of times. Putting on her slippers and pulling her dressing gown tightly around her waist, she made herself comfortable at his feet.

Meanwhile, he had struggled to prop himself up with one of the cushions.

"My, that shower was good!" she'd enthused. "Not as good as the one in the hotel, but brilliant, considering where we are.

"Okay, Professor Butterfield, what you think?"

"Well, to précis your admirable summary, dear, the situation seems to be like this. First, according to US case law – and always remembering that judgments in one American state don't necessarily apply to others, plus the fact that a case like ours has never been heard in Hawaii – as soon as those blood samples were in their plastic syringes, they no longer belonged to the patients. They already belonged to the employer of the doctors or nurses who took them, in this instance The Queen's Medical Center. Presumably, this means that the patients' relatives also have no claim. Agreed?"

Fiona nodded.

"Second, since the medical centre later transferred the samples to the university, the next question is whether ownership of the samples was also transferred. As you say in your notes, it's very unlikely there was any sort of contract between them. And, as they were definitely not bailments in the legal sense, a judge might reasonably consider the samples to have been gifts."

"Agreed again. So… if the samples then belonged to the medical school, where does that leave us?"

"But *did* they?"

"What do you mean?"

"Did they in fact belong to the school? If Mouktar had already been given the responsibility of doing the lab work, which seems to have been the case, was he an *employee* of the medical school at the time, or was he a *visiting scientist*? It might make a big difference to who can claim ownership."

"Well, like our Aram in Oxford, Mouktar was funded by the Alhazen foundation in Jordan, wasn't he?"

"Yes."

"And Aram was appointed to the university's staff. Yes?"

"Yes."

"So…?"

"But I have a feeling the rules were changed, after an Alhazen fellow in Canada complained that McMaster University had been treating him unfairly. I'm pretty sure that ever since then, all new fellows have been given contracts with the Alhazen organisation itself, not with the host university. If Mouktar was on the payroll of the foundation, officially he would only be a *visitor* in Hawaii. And it seems from your notes that that might be important, *very* important."

"You mean, once the samples were in Mouktar's hands, legally they might have become the property of the Alhazen foundation?"

Giles had shrugged his shoulders

"Seems possible, if there was no contract and they were given to him directly with sole responsibility to look after them."

"Why don't we call Teuku and see if he knows?"

"Yes, why don't you do that, Fiona, while I hop to the loo? Too many cups of Yorkshire tea while waiting for you."

Fiona had stared purposefully at the empty bottles of rum and ginger beer that were now just visible behind the cushion.

"Or too many glasses of Dark and Stormy!"

When Giles had returned, the smile on Fiona's face had said it all.

"Called him?"

"Yes."

"And no words needed, I can see. So, if the worst comes to the worst, we could argue the samples were actually given to the Alhazen foundation, and therefore Mouktar was entitled to do what he wanted with them."

Giles had rubbed his hands in satisfaction.

"*Quad erat demonstrandum!* But why are we rabbiting on like this? We said we weren't going to worry about these things, didn't we?"

"Yes, we did. So what exactly will you say to Sir Quentin?"

"None of this stuff. Only that there's been a mysterious epidemic of a new mosquito-borne virus on Ni'ihau. That it's an emergency. And Teuku wants us to sort it out. That's all."

"And if he agrees, we plough ahead and take any flack that comes our way when it's all over?"

"Exactly. Where would we be now if we'd been afraid of flouting the law when we knew in our hearts it was the right thing to do?"

Giles's mind had drifted back to the hours he had spent agonising over whether it would be ethical to break into Steve's office in Bethesda, to infect his laptop in Stockholm with spyware – and, most of all, to not tell Virginia Brandolin in Rome about Brigitte Dubois Yusuf and her identity card. Their judgement had been spot on every time, hadn't it? There was nothing to regret or to apologise for. One day for sure, MECCAR's methods would be out in the open. And who knows how the world will react? But, between now and then, a huge amount of good will have been done. Thousands of lives, perhaps millions, will have been saved. In fact, thousands already had.

"Let's look at it this way," he'd continued. "What would happen if we dumped the whole idea, and told Teuku we couldn't do it? He and Mouktar would struggle on without us, wouldn't they? They can't afford to sit on it. And without outside help, they'd never get there. With the facilities INDOMED's got, in a year or two they're bound to have a world-class virologist on board. But they need to get on with this *now*. At best, their progress would be slow and strewn with errors. At worst, they would get nowhere, which would be a disaster, because once they'd used up the samples, there'd be no going back. That would be that. On top of which, nobody knows what's happened to those mosquitoes. We don't even know what species they were. They might have laid thousands of infected eggs somewhere. Even if some are hibernating on Ni'ihau, there's no guarantee spraying the island with insecticides would kill all of them. It might even make matters worse by causing the development of a resitant strain."

As Giles had paused to roll up his sleeves, Fiona had taken her opportunity.

"So, that's the final word?"

"Yes, I thought we…"

"Wonderful! I'm so happy, Giles. To be completely honest, when I was away, after talking on the phone, I was tempted to avoid raising the issue again in case you decided to talk to a lawyer. But then I decided I had to."

"Why was that?"

"Because, to be honest, it was impossible for me to look at it objectively."

Fiona had stretched to the coffee table to take a stem of *Mokara panni* from the cut glass vase, one of several orchid cuttings the maid replenished every week.

"Well, you know how much I love nature, particularly plants?" she resumed, holding the yellow flowers under her nose. "I don't know what it is about them, but I've always been like that, ever since dropping onto my knees as a five-year old to peer at the heather, mosses, and liverworts along the banks of the *Allt Dearg Mor* in Skye. You've seen it in me so many times – during our walks around the Cotswolds, that car trip we made to Shenandoah, the day at the Cape of Good Hope while waiting for Conrad to make up his mind. If it were just for the plants alone, I would want to return. Indonesia is teeming with so many that don't occur anywhere else. They knock me out... even to the point of keeping me awake at night... if that's not a contradiction! Wherever I look, I'm drawn to one. And the closer I look, the more I see, and the more I'm fascinated."

She'd stroked the flower's petals lovingly as she inhaled their perfume.

"I want to touch them, and smell them, again and again. But, more than anything, I want to understand them – why their leaves are this shape or that, how their aerial roots work, what pollinates them, why they glow in the dark, how the insectivorous ones sense their prey. And then there's the insects themselves... and the birds. The place is overflowing with so much nature it almost makes me cry. In fact, during my first walk alone, I actually did."

At the sight of a parrot in the garden, Fiona had got up to take a closer look.

"There's another example. Just look at those colours! Did you know that the birds around here, in Bali and further west, are *completely* different from the ones on Lombok, just twenty miles across the sea to the east? All the animals on this side of the strait belong to the Asian biogeographical region, while those on the other side belong to the Australasian one, which includes New Guinea and Australia. Although it's only twenty miles, they've never mixed and have evolved separately. Alfred Russel Wallace, the man who had the idea of evolution at the same time as Darwin, but never got the same recognition, discovered this. Apparently, it's because the strait is more than four thousand metres deep, and has been there for fifty million years. There's just one..."

"Okay, I've got the message!" Giles had interrupted, having approached quietly from behind and placed a hand on her shoulder. "Once you start on one of your nature trails..."

"Sorry!"

"No reason to apologise. I agree with you. It's staggering. And fascinating. But I'm a bit short of time... need to go and see Teuku soon. But before I do, there's something else I want to mention. It's to do with your germ warfare theory."

"Oh."

"Last night in the study, after your telephone call, I looked into it. And you'll never guess what I found."

"What?"

Giles had taken his notebook from his back pocket and found the relevant page.

"It seems Ni'ihau has been popular with the US government for military activities for many years. According to the *Boston Globe*, and I quote: 'The preservation of native culture and wildlife is not the only reason Ni'ihau is kept under wraps... the island has had a longstanding, little-publicised relationship with the US military, which has conducted special-operations training and research and development on top-secret military defence systems.' Apparently, the technology for the so-called Distant Early Warning Line was developed there during the Cold War. The US Navy still maintains a radar-surveillance installation on the island's highest point, and stages manoeuvres in the channel between the island and Kauai, where there's a ballistic missile facility, from which the radar is remotely operated. According to the article, income from military contracts provides revenue to support the residents and the general upkeep of the island.

"So, it looks as if your idea about germ warfare might have been spot on. And if the Americans are violating international agreements, the world needs to know about it."

"I can't wait to get back to Oxford and hear what Sir Q says," said Fiona. "What will we do, if he refuses?"

"I'll let you guess."

Chapter Six

As Giles stepped off the doorstep of the President's Lodgings into the sunshine, little more than forty-eight hours after their return from Jakarta, Fiona was sitting on the grass, her back against the Grammar Hall, feeding a few starlings with what remained of her *baguette* from Taylors. The two tiny islands of Nusa Ceningan and Ni'ihau had seemed so far away that she'd been pinching herself to come to terms with the purpose of Giles's conference with Sir Quentin. They'd heard nothing from Teuku since they'd said their farewells in Soekarno-Hatta airport. Nor had there been anything in the news about the mysterious epidemic.

As she watched Giles pass the young magnolia in front of the Lodgings, she tried to guess the outcome from his body language. But he was giving nothing away. Not until they were together did a smile and a wink say it all.

"He needs a little time," he whispered with an eye on a nearby group of students. "But I think he'll play ball."

"That's a relief. I'm still hungry. Shall we eat?"

"*Pierre Victoire?*"

"Done!"

"I'll fill you in on the way."

Several hours later, after sharing a bowl of *bouillabaisse* and a bottle of *Chablis* in their favourite *bistro*, seated on the back row in the College chapel, a habit Giles had developed after long trips abroad to 'inhale the smell of English history', new doubts were occupying Fiona's mind.

"We need to remain completely objective, don't we?" she whispered, not wanting to be overheard by a nearby solitary student. "We must forget about all the other reasons why we want it to happen: the thrill of another globetrotting adventure, the excitement of amateur detective work, the opportunity for you to return to virology, my passion for tropical plants. My God, there are so many! Otherwise, we could be heading for a fall. People round here expect a lot from us now. Ridiculous as it is, even I've acquired celebrity status. I was really taken aback by those invitations waiting on my desk: a talk to the Girl Guides in Jubilee House, afternoon tea with the Women's Institute at Boxford Village Hall, and a guest appearance on Desert Island Discs. I ask you! I'm terrified of the BBC. How many recordings can I choose? Do you know?"

"Eight."

"Are you sure?"

"Yes. My mother used to listen to it. She used to say how appropriate it was that you were allowed eight discs."

"Why?"

"It reminded her of Robert Louis Stevenson's *Treasure Island*, in which Long John Silver's parrot keeps squawking 'Pretty Polly! Pieces of Eight!'"

"Ha!"

"But why are you telling me this now, dear? I thought we'd made up our minds, and that was that."

"True."

"So, shall we go?"

"Not just yet. I like it here."

It was almost midnight. In spite of a cold draught from the wooden doors and the discomfort of the hard bench, it was as if a strange force was holding Fiona there. Perhaps it was the familiarity of the old stone walls, as different from the wood and plaster of the villa in Nusa Ceningan as it was possible to imagine. She looked up to admire the beautiful vaulted ceiling, the sight of which she never grew tired.

"Okay," she sighed. "I'm ready now. Let's go."

They hesitated while a plump, olive-skinned girl entered the Chapel and crossed herself before walking the length of the aisle and kneeling in one of the pews.

"Is she a student?" Fiona whispered. "I didn't recognise her."

"She's new, from Mexico," Giles replied, covering his mouth with the collar of his coat. "Met her this morning. A maths genius."

"You'd never guess from here," Fiona sniggered. "Sorry! That was out of order. To get back to where I was, I suppose we shouldn't jump to any conclusions about what happened on Ni'ihau, should we? Maybe there's nothing sinister about the news blackout. It might be just to protect the tourist industry, nothing more than that. After all, the economy of Hawaii would be ruined if the news spread."

Fiona peered into Giles's eyes inquisitively.

"Are you okay?" she asked. "You seem uncomfortable about something. You were the same in the restaurant, too."

"I'm fine, thanks."

"Have you told me everything about the meeting?" Fiona pressed. "Apart from the fact Sir Q needs to ask around, you didn't say very much about it, considering you were in there so long."

Giles glanced towards the Mexican girl before taking Fiona's hand and standing up to lead her towards the entrance of the tower's narrow staircase.

"You go first," he said.

"Okay."

In all her years in Oxford, it was the first time Fiona had ascended the city's most famous architectural feature. Upon reaching the top, after pausing halfway up for Giles's benefit, they were greeted by a cool, damp wind from across Christ Church Meadow. Fiona wondered why she had never made the effort before. But this was not the time to dwell on it.

Buttoning her tweed jacket and wrapping her scarf around her neck, she waited anxiously for what Giles was about to say.

"It's to do with Aram, Fiona. Quentin said his sudden departure from the College came just after he'd learnt from Jane, during one of his get-togethers, that you and I had shared a hotel room in Rome. It seems she announced it to one and all after too many of his sherries."

"So much for being your *private* secretary! Do you think that could have been the real reason for his flight? That he disapproved, and it had nothing to do with his brother?"

Giles shrugged his shoulders before turning to look into her eyes.

"Possibly. But there's something else. She also blurted out the fact I'd asked her to send me Brigitte Dubois Yusuf's identity card."

"WHAT! But you instructed her not to…"

"I know I did."

"Oh, my God! So now I know your problem. You're worried Aram might have already known the truth about Ahmad's death in Sorrento, put two and two together, and rushed off to tell Rashid Yamani we could be on to him. But is that plausible? I know MECCAR and the Alhazen foundation that funded Aram's fellowship are part and parcel of the same organisation, but is it likely someone as junior could have known the truth?"

"Not impossible, I suppose," said Giles. "Perhaps it got out somehow, and the news quietly spread among the Alhazen fellows. They're a very closely knit lot, I gather, a kind of worldwide network. As you know, they have a social event every year in Jordan."

Fiona stepped away to meander around the tower top in silence, before returning with a noticeably less anxious look on her face.

"Well…" she said, "if that *was* the reason for Aram's disappearance, presumably Rashid would have taken comfort from the fact that you seem to have done nothing about it. After all, it's well over a year now since we were in Rome. If you *were* going to let the cat out of the bag, you would have done so by now, wouldn't you?"

Giles nodded pensively as he scanned the city's horizon.

"Quite. I wonder if that could be why Rashid sent the College that huge donation… a backhander to thank me for keeping the lid on. The timing would fit. I haven't told you, but when Quentin called Rashid about it, he said the money was to thank the College for all it had done. That's all he'd say."

"That could mean a couple of other things, of course: what we did to expose Steve, and your nominating him for a Nobel. But they happened even longer ago, didn't they? If he wanted to thank the College for *them*, why hadn't he done so sooner? So, perhaps you're right, and it was for not revealing the terrible truth about Ahmad's death."

Giles turned in a complete circle, his hands thrust deeply into the pockets of his coat, his eyes fixed on the old stones beneath his feet.

"Now I'm more worried than ever," he sighed. "If it was a sweetie to ensure we continue to keep our traps shut, what if it's just a temporary measure, while Rashid's working on a more permanent solution?"

Fiona clasped her face in her hands, before grasping Giles's arm and drawing him towards her.

"Oh my God, yes! I think we need to be very careful, Giles. He's obviously a ruthless character, to say the least. If we do go back to INDOMED, we should watch our backs, and look out for any unexpected visitors, even if they do seem like *bona fide* scientists."

She took one more look at the cityscape below.

"And, while we're chewing that one over, let's go back to the lab. I've just remembered I left the lights on. You know what Sir Q thinks about wasting electricity."

Chapter Seven

As always on a Saturday morning, Fiona was doing her domestic chores when Giles telephoned at around ten o'clock to give her the news. Knowing he'd been due to meet Sir Quentin over breakfast in the College Hall almost two hours ago, she prepared herself for a huge disappointment. Had it been good news, long before now he would surely have been on the doorstep with a Bakewell tart from Queen's Lane Coffee House, his regular way of celebrating such successes.

"Hello Giles, bad news?" she said disconsolately, switching off the vacuum cleaner and pushing it one side with her foot.

Giles tossed his hat across the room and kicked off his shoes.

"To go straight to point, dear, I'm sorry to say he said it would be impossible."

"Why?"

"Too expensive, he said. And that was that."

"But that's ridiculous! Teuku would be paying for the tickets, wouldn't he?"

"That's what I said. But he said he didn't care whose money it was. Wherever it came from, it would be extravagant, wasteful, and therefore couldn't be justified."

"Extravagent?" said Fiona angrily. "Spending some money to save thousands, perhaps millions, of lives? What's he talking about, the old fool?"

"I tried my best, but couldn't persuade him. Sorry."

"So that's that?"

"Afraid so. There's no way out. We'll have fly all the way on Business Class… instead of First."

"What? Oh, Giles, you rotter!"

Pushing him onto the sofa, Fiona threw herself onto his lap.

"How could you be so cruel? I really believed you."

"Sorry, but you asked for it."

"What on earth do you mean?"

"You were saying the other day how much we seem to have lost our sense of humour lately; that we've been taking life too seriously. So I thought about it, and..."

"Fair enough! So when do we leave?"

"As soon you've tidied up the mess in the lab, we've packed our bags, and I've found somewhere to park the Van."

Fiona stared at him in disbelief.

"You've got a *van*? Why?"

"Not the sort with four wheels," Giles chuckled. "The type with four paws. The neighbour's housekeeper asked me if I could find a new owner for her cat, as she's about to move into a flat where she's not allowed to have one. As she was in a bit of a fix, I rather foolishly obliged. And last night it arrived. It's a Turkish Van, she said. Very cute. One eye's blue, the other green, apparently very common in the breed. It can swim, too, also quite normal for them... as I discovered after I'd fallen asleep in the bath with the bathroom door open."

Giles unbuttoned his shirt.

"Here's the evidence."

"Ha!" laughed Fiona when she saw the scratches. "Oh, sorry... I mean, how awful. I hope they don't leave scars. Male or female?"

"Male."

"Neutered?"

"Yes. If it hadn't been before it attacked me, it would have been by now... the slow, painful way!"

"It sounds gorgeous," said Fiona. "I'm sure Sue downstairs will take it. She adores cats. Said only last week how she'd like another."

That afternoon, after sending the good news to Teuku, they set off for the village of Biddestone, little more than an hour's leisurely drive away. Immersion in one of Wiltshire's prettiest spots was the best way they could think of to settle their nerves as they prepared themselves mentally for the coming adventure.

After dining on the village pub's celebrated meat pies, they took their glasses to one of the wooden benches overlooking the duck pond to consider an email from Teuku that Giles had opened while filling the Austin Healey's tank outside Chippenham. The news, that the medical school in Honolulu was on the programme of the next meeting of the International Society of Infectious Diseases, to be held in Mexico City in only five days' time, had come as a surprise. The title of the presentation in the session on 'Late-breaking Clinical Studies', devoted to results that had not been available until after the application deadline, had raised their eyebrows more for what it did not say than for what it did.

With so much competition for places on congress programmes, researchers were normally keen to make the outcome of their studies sound as interesting as possible. Common ploys were to choose a title that suggested an important or unexpected outcome, to pose a question guaranteed to stimulate interest or be provocative, or to make a claim that was highly controversial. However, "An outbreak of West Nile virus on a Hawaiian island" was not a title that was likely to fill the seats when a lecture on "Breakthroughs in anti-viral drugs" was in progress in the next room. It was as if the authors had deliberately created a title that would attract little attention. As summaries of the presentations were not available in the booklet that Teuku had attached to the message, they agreed they had no alternative but to abandon their fledgling plans for a stopover in India *en route* to Jakarta, and instead go the other way across the Atlantic so they could attend the congress.

"It'll be the first time in my life," Giles mused, as he tossed the crumbs of a pie crust to a black swan eyeing him from within a clump of water irises, "that I've travelled thousands of miles with the sole purpose of listening to a ten-minute talk. I hope it's going to be worth it. I can't say I'm in the mood for Mexico City. When I look at this peaceful rural setting, the trees, the sound of the birds, the fresh air on my face…"

"I suspect it will be worth it, Giles," said Fiona. "We haven't gone anywhere yet without it bearing fruit. India would be wonderful, but we should bite the bullet and go. I have relatives who are Turnbulls. The family motto is *Audaci favet fortuna*."

"I'm not sure this is going to take courage, except crossing the roads and risking Montezuma's Revenge!"

They admired the view towards the green with its simple war memorial as Fiona continued.

"Interesting, isn't it, how everyone uses Latin for mottos and so on? You never see any other language on a heraldic crest, do you? I mean, why on earth did my relatives' ancestors choose Latin in preference to Gaelic or Pictish? After all, the ancient Romans never even got to Scotland."

"I don't suppose there's any point having a motto if nobody outside Scotland can read it. Don't forget, in those days Latin was the language of intellectuals."

"True. On top of which, *Tha fortan a 'cur fàilte air an gaisgeach* would certainly be difficult to fit on your average heraldic shield!"

Fiona leant forward with the intention of breaking off a few of the yellow flowers at the water's edge, when she remembered that her flat would be empty very soon.

"Do you think Jane would like some of these?" she said. "No, never mind, she's got a garden, hasn't she? They're better where they are. On top of which, I'm not sure she deserves them after what she did."

She looked around her for a moment.

"What shall we do now? I feel restless with all this ahead of us, Giles. How about a stroll to the church? The landlord told me it's called St Nicholas, and dates from the twelve hundreds. He said it doesn't have a proper tower or spire. The bells are in something called a turret."

Upon entering the church and spotting an old lady sitting near the lectern, stooped as if in prayer, Giles led the way towards the font that stands at the top of the nave.

"Let's stay here a while," he whispered. "How about this for a plan? After attending the congress, we go to Honolulu. There must be direct flights from Mexico City. We stay overnight near the airport and meet Mouktar there with his samples. The three of us then travel to Jakarta together. This would kill three birds with one stone: we see the presentation; we get to know Mouktar; and we arrive at INDOMED with the samples safe and sound. I could ask Teuku to organise it all from his end. What do you think?"

"Sounds good," said Fiona. "Do you think we could also squeeze in a few days in Puerto Vallarta on the west coast? Ros went there a few years ago with that rich stockbroker of hers. Said it was fabulous."

"We'll see if we can fit it in. I'll give Teuku a call. Now, I'm going to study the carving on the lid of this font. Looks Norman to me."

As Gile removed his glasses and stooped to get a closer look, Fiona's eyes were drawn to the imposing bronze wagon wheel chandelier that hung from the ceiling, the stained glass windows, the roof timbers, the oak plank door.

"This is such a nice church, Giles. I'm glad I bumped into the landlord. Nothing spectacular, but interesting, and cosy. Just think how the world has changed during all the years it's been standing here, while day after day villagers have been coming and going through that door. In places like this… small, isolated, quiet, musty… you can feel history like nowhere else. It's as if the souls of the villagers are still living here, watching us."

"What's that, dear?" said Giles distractedly.

"Sorry! I can see you're in another world. I think I'll take a look at the war memorial plaque by the window over there."

"Of course. I'll follow in a tick."

When Giles caught up with her, Fiona was motionless, her hands clasped, her gaze fixed on the four columns of names in black letters enclosed within a simple wooden frame.

"There are seventy-nine names there, Giles. I counted them. Seventy-nine in such a tiny village. What would you say the population is these days?"

"Perhaps five hundred or so, at a guess."

"And so many seem to have been related – seven Bakers, five Wares, five Coles. What it must have been like here in those terrible days, I can't imagine. The sleepness nights, the waiting for news, the sorrow, the despair, the emptiness…"

She paused for a moment. "Shall we go?"

Giles took his handkerchief from his top pocket and offered it to her.

"Yes, let's. Suddenly, Montezuma's revenge seems so trivial."

Chapter Eight

Sitting in the lobby of the Gran Hotel Ciudad de Mexico, recovering from the previous day's long haul flight, Fiona was admiring the *art nouveau* ceiling when she caught sight of Giles waving his phone in her direction from one of the internal balconies.

"Teuku's sent a message," he mouthed silently so as not to disturb the flock of elegantly dressed guests who had gathered after a *matinée* at the Palacio de Bellas Artes.

Collecting the diary in which she'd been recording the week's events, Fiona hurried to the elevator.

"There's been a change of plan, Fiona," said Giles. "Mouktar's been recalled to Jordan to give his account of what happened, and has to be there in a few days. So our precious vacation is off, I'm afraid. Teuku's booked us an Aeromexico flight to Honolulu via LA. It leaves at…"

He looked at his notes, squinting.

"Let me see… seven forty-five in the morning the day after the congress ends, and it gets there around seven in the evening. We rest our heads in the Best Western at the airport, and the following morning drag ourselves to meet Mouktar in the lobby and collect his box of samples. Then we catch an All Nippon flight departing at… er… I really do need to change these damn specs… one o'clock for Jakarta via Tokyo, getting there at… five minutes before midnight the next day local time."

"Five minutes before midnight?" said Fiona. "I'm not going to ask how long it takes. I hope Teuku meets us."

"He will, but not immediately. He'll send one of his new research assistants. She'll be in the airport, and take Mouktar's box straight back to INDOMED. You and I will rest our heads at the Bandara International Hotel, a couple of miles from the airport, and we'll fly to Denpasar in Bali the following morning. Teuku will collect us there in a chauffeur-driven limo to take us via the ferry service to Nusa Lembongan island, and from there to Nusa Ceningan."

"A limousine! How about that for five star service!"

"Yes. Beats the socks off taking the bus from Oxford to London, and then the tube from Victoria to Hampstead, which I had to do the last time I needed to take some blood samples from one place to another."

"I don't remember that."

"Before you joined me. It was the only way in those days. No money. Thank God I bumped into the *Marchese* a few weeks later. What a difference money makes!"

"Anyhow," said Fiona, "despite the luxury of a limo, we're both going to be pretty pooped by the time we get there. I hope Sir Quentin doesn't imagine this is all one big holiday. Let's go to bed. When's the presentation on Ni'ihau?"

"Eleven-thirty, in the Centro Citibanamex. So we can have a late breakfast. And then, after the presentation, spend the rest of the day enjoying ourselves. Okay?"

"Och-aye!"

***

After a lazy morning that took in little more than a few cups of coffee and a quick tour of the Metropolitan Cathedral, just a stone's throw from the hotel, they took a cab to the congress centre, full of anticipation. The Centro Citibanamex, all white walls and glass overlooking a well-tended lawn and a pond and solitary palm tree, proved to be one of the more welcoming places they'd ever had reason to visit. Upon collecting their badges and programme from the "A - C" recepton desk in the lobby, they followed the floorplan to the *Palacio de la Canal*, carefully avoiding eye contact with any passers-by in the remote possibility they might be recognised.

Finding less than half the chairs were occupied, they chose two in the front row near the centre aisle, always Giles's favourite position, to be sure he could read the smallest print on the slides. The Japanese chairperson seated behind a desk in the front interrupted his quiet conversation with the projectionist to acknowledge their arrival with a smile, pleased to have two more faces in the audience. As Fiona turned to scan the room, she felt sorry for the upcoming speakers, knowing most would have spent many hours preparing their slides and rehearsing their talks before travelling long distances for the occasion. She had been through it all herself so many times. In fact, she could never make up her mind which was worse: to find a small audience and feel your work had not attracted much interest, or a large one and know there was likely to be at least one aggressive individual present who was intent upon criticising your work. How she longed for the day when she was confident enough to not care about such characters.

To their disappointment, the Ni'ihau presentation, given by a young, heavily made-up American girl, included little more information than what Teuku had imparted to Giles over lunch in Nusa Ceningan. After she had finished and the customary patter of polite applause had subsided, an elderly Mexican limped to the microphone at the rear of the room and cleared his voice.

"Thank you, Doctor err… very interesting. The story reminds me of an incident reported in one of our newspapers a while ago. A diabetic lady was suddenly taken ill on a liner during one of those cruises between the west coast of the USA and Hawaii. When the ship was touring the islands, she became very ill after developing a rather nasty ulcer on her leg. The ship's doctor gave her antibiotics, thinking she had septicemia, but she died a few days later. Her body was taken off when the ship docked in Ensenada on its way back to San Diego. After what you've just described, I'm wondering if it could have been the same illness. I'm not certain of the date, but it could have been around the time of that epidemic. If so, perhaps some of those mosquitoes flew on board, and she got bitten. Is that possible, do you think?"

"But if that were the case," the presenter replied, shrugging her shoulders, "surely more than one passenger would have gotten infected, wouldn't they?"

The professor paused while he adjusted his monocle.

"Not necessarily. The point is, given the terrible threat posed by such a virus, isn't the possibility, however remote, worth considering?"

"I suppose it might."

"Only suppose? But, if an infected mosquito had hitched a ride on the ship, a disaster could be brewing in this country or somewhere, couldn't it?"

"But it would have happened by now, wouldn't it?" the girl replied.

"Not necessarily. As others here are no doubt aware, mosquitoes can lay hundreds of eggs at a time. And the eggs of some species can survive for months under the right conditions. They might not develop into new mosquitoes until the ship was in dock somewhere."

The girl shrugged her shoulders and looked towards the chairpersons for help.

"I think my time's up, isn't it?" she said.

Before waiting for a reply, she stepped down from the rostrum and returned to her chair, eyes fixed to the floor, prompting Fiona to whisper in Giles's ear.

"Very odd she doesn't seem interested in talking about the potential dangers. I wonder why?"

"Perhaps they've something to hide that she wants to put to bed."

"More likely she's been instructed to do so *in bed*. Could she really be a virologist?"

"Perhaps she's the lab tech who's supposed to be the head of department's favourite? The one who was given the job of checking Mouktar's assays."

"That would fit."

After two further presentations about a mumps outbreak in Nigeria and a new strain of influenza in China, the chairpersons thanked the speakers and declared the session closed. Giles followed Fiona down the central aisle as they made their way towards the exit.

"Well, we didn't learn much from that, did we?" Fiona sighed. "What a long journey just for that. But we had to come. There was no choice. Did you read anything into it that I missed?"

"Not that I'm aware of," said Giles. "I don't think we'll hear much more about it. My guess is the Pentagon had no option but to let the medical school into what had happened, and gave them the go ahead to present their results in the hope that would be the end of it."

"No doubt after getting them to swear an oath of allegiance to the Stars and Stripes," Fiona sniggered, "and being told if they give the game away, they'll spend the rest of their days behind bars."

"Quite possible. Germ warfare's a very serious business."

"Shall we now try and forget about it for a while, Giles? It's a gorgeous day outside, far too nice to be stuck in here. I've got a suggestion. Why don't we get a cab as far as the *Bosque de Chapultepec*, which I've been told is the biggest park in the Western hemisphere. Then, after a couple of hours, we take another cab to the *Café de Tacuba*, and have a good Mexican meal. What do you say?"

"Sounds splendid. I can see you've been doing your homework, as usual."

***

Unable to resist the opportunity, Fiona asked the cab driver to drop them off on the *Paseo de la Reforma* outside the imposing entrance of the National Museum of Anthropology. At the time, the courtyard's vast roof, supported by a single massive bronze column surrounded by a torrent of cascading water, was the centre of attraction for a crowd of tourists.

"What do you think that fountain's all about?" Giles asked as they negotiated their way through the throng.

"It's obvious, isn't it?"

"Not to me."

"The fountain of life."

"Why is that?"

"Well, it's like a giant phallus in a never-ending orgasm."

"Jesus! What an imagination you have. Reminds me more of a mushroom in a tropical thunderstorm."

"Which simply proves you're getting old!"

Although their intention had been only to take a look at the Aztecs' famous 'Stone of the Sun' before walking through the park, once in front of it Fiona was unable to draw herself away. It wasn't so much the intricate carvings, the meanings of which she'd read about in the airline magazine, and which even archaeologists couldn't agree upon, but its sheer size and weight that held her. She'd imagined from the photographs that it was about two feet in diameter, not more than twelve. She wondered they had they chosen such an enormous stone, when a smaller one would have done the job just as well. There must have been a very important reason, she thought.

After several minutes, she decided that the general belief it had been lying flat on the ground might be wrong. After all, in that climate the intricate carvings and engravings would surely have become clogged with soil, mosses, seeds, bird droppings, and so on. Maybe it was designed to be placed vertically and visible from a great distance, and had to be so enormous for that reason. But if so, what could have been stopping people from getting closer? Was the ancient Aztec city on an island?

While she'd been contemplating such things, Giles had wandered off to look at other artefacts around the room. Normally, he'd be engrossed in the details of such exhibits, challenging himself to interpret their origins and significance without referring to the catalogue. On this occasion, however, he couldn't get his mind off the Ni'ihau epidemic, particularly the Mexican professor's concern about mosquitoes flying on board. Perhaps, subconsciously, it was because the Aztecs had also been decimated by an infectious disease.

When Fiona turned, expecting him to be at her shoulder, Giles was at the far end of the room chatting to a couple with a young boy. As she could see they were in deep conversation, she sat down on one of the many wooden plinths and returned to the nature and purpose of the stone. She reflected on how, just a few years ago, she would never have questioned the consensus of authorities in her own field, never mind those in a totally unrelated one like archaeology. But leaving Scotland had changed her – or, rather, working with Giles had done so.

During their first year together, he had supervised every aspect of her work. His line of research had been far too removed from her previous topic of research in Aberdeen for it to be any other way. When she'd applied for the vacancy, it had been with no serious expectation of getting the job. After all, a PhD on the genes of *Vertigo modesta*, a rare species of Scottish snail, had hardly been the perfect preparation for a career on the causes of cancer. Treating the application more as a practice run than anything else, she'd assumed there would be many applicants who were far better qualified. But, what she did not then know, but had since witnessed many times, was that Giles was more interested in a young person's mind than the number of publications or grants in his or her curriculum vitae. And, as far as he was concerned, letters of reference from previous employers or senior colleagues were not worth the paper they were written on. Shunning the traditional office interview, he would take applicants for a chat in the Botanic Garden, or, if the weather was inclement, to a local pub, and seek evidence of creativity, perceptiveness, and deductive reasoning. Enthusiasm and critical capacities were also important. The rest would come in good time, he believed. And so it had been with her.

During her first year, she had made good progress in the laboratory, but had been slow to acquire the self-assurance needed to publicly question other scientists' ideas or data. This had worried her, as she had known it was not possible for a researcher to realise his or her full potential with such an impediment. The ability to conduct experiments was not enough. Having the confidence to stand up in a packed auditorium and constructively critique the work of others was an essential attribute.

The transformation had occurred without warning one 'May Morning', that special day in Oxford's calendar when daybreak is greeted by the *Hymnus Eucharisticus* sung by boy choristers from the top of Magdalen's tower. After a weekend worrying about how Giles was going to react to her comments on his latest theory, the beauty of the ancient music filtering through the treetops outside her bedroom window had changed her for ever. Her eyes still closed, she had pondered how nobody down the centuries would have had the pleasure of what she was experiencing, had Benjamin Rogers been too timid to reveal his wonderful creation to the world.

The peal of bells as she walked down Holywell Street to the College had completed the transformation. Upon reaching the half-open door of Giles's office, Fiona had marched inside and dropped her notes in front of him with a flourish. And, from that day on, she had never looked back. Her approach to her work, indeed her entire approach to life itself, had changed. And it had been exhilarating. It was as if she had been liberated from bondage, all the more rewarding because it had been self-imposed and so senseless.

At last, she could feel herself becoming what she had always wanted to be – not just an assistant, with all that that title embodied, but a true researcher in her own right, with an independent mind and the potential to make a real contribution to her field by challenging the established view. Had it not been for that May morning experience, she would never have had the courage to submit her theory about the role of antibodies in cancer to a top journal.

Nor would she have had the self-belief to work with Giles's laptop through the night to discover what smoking guns might be lurking inside Steven Salomon's laptop, or the confidence to argue her interpretation of the note that Ahmad Sharif had written on the website report in the face of Giles's profound scepticism. Without those two breakthroughs, she and Giles surely could not have succeeded. She took pride in the fact that they were now genuine partners in everything they did together.

After Giles had finished chatting to the young family and was making his way back, Fiona jumped up to throw her arms around him and give him a kiss.

"What on earth was that for?" he gasped.

"To thank you for making such a difference."

"To what?"

"Never mind. Let's go!"

After walking a little way down the leafy sidewalk of the *Paseo de la Reforma* and then dodging the traffic to cross to the park, pausing in the central reservation to take in its oversized statue of a penny-farthing bicycle, they were soon within the welcoming tranquillity of the lake. Strolling along its bank, they admired the *Casa del Lago*, its white façade and blue awnings reflected in the green water. It was a colourful and happy scene, the lake alive with blue and yellow paddle boats, the chatter and laughter of the children mingling with the splashing of the fountains and the songs of the birds. However, the high note for Fiona was the elegance and maturity of the trees, some reputedly planted by the Aztecs themselves, that stretched in every direction. She had never imagined that Mexico City had such a vast expanse of nature at its heart.

Once they'd taken in the imposing exterior of the *Castillo de Chapultepec*, they made their way past the *Museo de Arte Moderno* to re-emerge from the clean air and peacefulness of the park into the city's more familiar traffic noise and pollution.

"Where shall we eat?" Fiona enquired, wafting her face with her guide book as a lorry clattered by at speed.

"The concierge recommended *Café de Tacuba*," replied Giles. "Very old and full of history, he said, and very good. Not far from the Alameda Central Park."

"Can we walk it?"

"It would be about an hour, I think. Another cab?"

"In that case, yes. I don't think I could make it in this heat."

***

Seated at a table under one of the restaurant's colourful murals, Giles studied the menu while Fiona went to wash her hands. By the time she'd returned, he was slaking his thirst with an ice-cold glass of beer.

"Sorry I started," he said. "I'm parched. The other bottle's for you, if you wish."

"No D 'n' S?"

"Didn't have the courage to ask."

"I'd rather have white wine, please, and some mineral water," said Fiona. "To help you choose, I gather L.A. Cetto is the Mexican winery to go for. I was reading on the flight that the grape vines were originally brought here by the Spaniards. How about that? Presumably, they didn't care much for the Aztecs' agave concoctions."

While Giles was attracting the waiter's attention, Fiona's eyes became fixed on the unlit candle in the centre of the tablecloth as she fiddled with her napkin.

"Giles," she said quietly, whispering for no obvious reason and stretching across the table, "a strange thing happened when I came out of the washroom just then. There's a large wall mirror outside the door. You can probably see it from where you are. It has a massive gold frame. Well, I stopped to do my lips, and, while I was at it, a man appeared from nowhere and stood at my shoulder to comb his hair. He was about my height, heavy designer sunglasses, and a bushy grey beard. Before he took out his comb, he placed the programme of the congress we're here for on the glass table under the mirror. I was just about to comment on the fact, when I noticed something. He had a big, dark mole on his left ear, flat like a coffee stain, about the size of one of these buttons on my dress. It made me think of Steve. He had one like that, didn't he? I only met him once, as you know, but it struck me. I thought it rather ugly."

"So did his wife. She was always nagging him to have something done about it."

"And he didn't?"

"No."

"There was something else, too," said Fiona. "This guy had a scar on his forehead, just above his left eyebrow. It didn't look as if it was from a knife. It was irregular, jagged, as if he'd banged his head on a piece of glass or rusty nail at some time, and it should have been stitched, but wasn't."

Giles thought for a moment.

"Well, if you're wondering if it could actually have been Steve, which I assume is what's going through your mind, the scar certainly doesn't sound like him – although, of course, he has had serious domestic problems since I last saw him, hasn't he? That could explain it!"

"Ha! Or, he could have had an accident," said Fiona. "There could be lots of explanations. From memory, that mole was just like Steve's, honestly. I know he didn't sport a beard and this guy was also a bit chubby, whereas Steve was the lean and fit type, but he could have let himself go. Wouldn't be surprising under the circumstances. He was certainly about the right height. It does make me wonder."

"Not impossible, I suppose. But all the evidence is that Steve'sdropped out of science. He's not been publishing or lecturing anywhere as far as I've been able to tell. Nobody seems to know where he is. And, of course, he was never into infectious diseases research. So, why would he…?"

"Oh, my God!" Fiona exclaimed, covering her mouth with her napkin. "Sorry to interrupt, Giles, but I've just seen him again. He's over there in the bar… look… the one wearing jeans and a light green shirt."

Giles was about to look over his shoulder.

"No, stop! Not now… he's looking this way! He's just taken off his sunglasses, and is chatting to another guy, who looks Mexican. Short, big black moustache. Can Steve speak Spanish?"

"Never heard him," said Giles. "And you know how much he likes to show off. But he might do. It's popular in schools over there. Can I look now?"

"Yes, it's okay. He's got his back to us."

Giles turned to take a quick look.

"Impossible for me to tell from here, Fiona. His friend looks pretty rough, not the sort I'd expect Steve to socialise with… unless he's really gone downhill."

"Might have done. With what he went through, he could easily have hit the bottle…" "Crikey!" she gasped. The barman just stopped his friend lighting a cigar, in return for which he got a full glass of red wine in his face. Now they're leaving. You stay here!"

Waiting until they'd disappeared behind a column, Fiona picked up her handbag and left in pursuit. Four or five anxious minutes later, Giles was relieved to see her reappear with a broad grin on her face.

"Phew! Sorry about that," she gasped. "They left the building and jumped into two expensive cars. While one of them was busy trying to extricate himself from between a couple of delivery vans, I took a few photos. Have a look."

Fiona pushed her phone across the white tablecloth.

"I see what you mean by expensive," said Giles. "They're Mercs. Curious that they're both the same model and colour."

"Perhaps they're company cars?"

"From their behaviour, they certainly didn't seem like top management to me. Hope they didn't see you."

"What are you thinking… drugs?"

Giles said nothing, only raising his eyebrows.

"But that can't be the case," said Fiona. "What about that programme he put on the table? A drug trafficker would hardly attend a medical congress."

"Confusing, I agree."

"Anyhow, I'm sure they didn't."

"Didn't what?"

"See me. Is there any way we can find out if Steve checked into the congress?"

"There's no official list that I'm aware of. You know how it is with some of these huge meetings. They're not like symposia. If they have a list, it might not be printed for weeks, just for the record."

"Okay. Let's order our meal."

Chapter Nine

Having discovered for the first time that a long-haul flight through multiple time zones could be an arduous undertaking, Fiona opted out of attending the congress the following morning and chose instead to spend the day window shopping in the city's *Centro Santa Fe* mall. She didn't have anything particular in mind to buy. Shopping for something specific was never relaxing in her view, and at worst could lead to disappointment and frustration. Browsing, stopping here and there, and buying on impulse were what she needed.

As Giles preferred to spend a few more hours in the convention centre, they said their goodbyes outside Fiona's taxi on the *Avenida 15 de Septembre*. His plan had been to attend a couple of morning sessions; however, on entering the lobby, he succumbed to the temptation to hang around for a while in the hope of spotting a bearded man in jeans and a green shirt. Collecting one of the many plastic chairs that were scattered around and a complimentary cup of tea from the bar, he made himself as inconspicuous as possible behind a journal from one of the display cases. Scanning the attendees as they flooded through the revolving doors to disperse down the corridors, up the escalators, and into the elevators, was tedious. But it was something he had to do.

When it became clear that the number of entrants was rapidly dwindling, Giles moved to a more comfortable chair in the now abandoned press room. There, in uninterrupted solitude, he waded through all 543 pages of the book of abstracts, the short summaries of each presentation, to see if he could spot Steve's name among the author lists.

By the time he had reached the last page, he'd found no evidence for Steve's involvement in any of the studies in the programme. The only lingering doubt was owing to the fact that five abstracts had had their author lists truncated to the stipulated upper limit of eight, each ending in the customary *et al.*

"But even if he hadn't been a co-author of any of the studies," Giles pondered as he dropped the book to the floor, "he could have attended the meeting just to keep up to date and network with other researchers, couldn't he? After all, that's what I'm doing, aren't I?"

Realising that the second session was now well underway, he decided that was enough for the morning and set off for the long walk back to the city centre. For the rest of the day, he would forget about Steve and mosquitoes, and relax in one of the parks while Fiona finished her shopping. They could then go for a meal before packing their bags in preparation for the journey to Hawaii and their meeting with Mouktar.

Chapter Ten

Descending over Waikiki towards a brilliant Pacific sunset on the approach to Honolulu International Airport, Giles gave Fiona a gentle nudge in the ribs.

"Quick, look out of the window, dear. There's Oahu's convention centre, where MECCAR first announced the discovery of *Achilles*. That takes me back!"

Adjusting the backrest of her seat, Fiona leant forward to get her first sight of the islands she'd been reading so much about.

"How strange it should be so close to Ni'ihau. Less than two hundred miles away." She paused to reach for Giles's hand. "You don't think there could be anything in that, do you?"

"What do you mean?"

"I don't know. It just gives me a strange feeling. When you think of all the places in the world those two events could have happened. Could you give me a glass of water?"

After doing as requested, Giles returned his hand to find hers cold and clammy as she held on tightly.

"Are you all right?"

"Yes, thanks… I suppose. It just seems odd, that's all. Makes me wonder if there's some connection between the two."

"Between the discovery of *Achilles* and the epidemic?"

Fiona nodded before taking her first sip, spilling some water down her dress in the process.

"Damn!"

"Here, let me wipe you down. How could there possibly be any connection?"

"I don't know. It's just a weird feeling that came over me. Makes me think of your experiences with the waning moon in

Oxford, and how we set off from Cape Town for Stockholm on the very day…"

"Pah! I don't think it makes sense to read too much into those things."

"You didn't think that at the time, especially when we were with Conrad."

"I know… but, in retrospect, I think we were over reacting. Anyhow, how on earth could what happened on Ni'ihau be connected with *Achilles*?"

"Can't imagine."

Sensing she was taking it too seriously for his liking, Giles proceeded to describe his experience during the congress, when the multitude of excited scientists had flooded down the staircase from the banquet; how he'd been swept along by the group of Australians to the hotel room and watched them scroll through the *Achilles* website in amazement; how Steve had been standing in the corridor with such painfully mixed emotions before giving his extraordinary combative delivery during the press conference.

Collecting his map and placing it on the small table in front of him, Giles pointed to the John A Burns Medical School. Smiling uneasily, Fiona thought she'd caught a brief glimpse of the very building below them.

"I wonder if Mouktar was watching from one of the windows as we flew past?" she whispered. "And I wonder what he's like? Better than Aram, I hope."

***

Given the look in her eye as she strode through the lobby after a stroll around the hotel's gardens, it came as no great surprise to Giles when Fiona gave him some unexpected news. He had just finished calling Mouktar about the arrangements for their meeting.

"He'll be here at around midday," he announced. "Suit you?"

"Yes, of course."

She sat down beside him and gave a deep sigh.

"The two of you will be able to get to know each other over lunch, then," she said, her eyes fixed on the ceramic floor tiles, "…while I'm away."

"Away?"

"Yes. I hope this doesn't upset you, Giles, but I won't be staying here. Knowing you wouldn't be needing me, I've organised a wee trip for myself."

"What! Where to?"

"To a fascinating little island not very far from here. I picked up the courage to charter a light aircraft."

Giles stared at her in amazement.

"How many propellers?"

"One."

"Sounds risky to me. Carry on!"

"The idea occurred to me in Mexico City, soon after you gave me the message from Teuku about meeting Mouktar. As I knew I couldn't afford it, I called my rich lawyer of a cousin. As you know, he's been very generous in the past. So I told him how much I wanted to make this particular trip and so on. And, quick as a flash, bless him, he gave me the details of his Amex Platinum card and told me to book it. All he wanted in return were some photos."

She looked at Giles and smiled.

"I kept it from you because I wasn't sure I'd have the courage to go when the time came."

"And will you?"

"I think so. But we'll have to wait and see."

Chapter Eleven

When Fiona entered the lobby at the end of a day that she knew she would remember for the rest of her life, Giles was snoozing in one of the many rattan chairs, an empty wine glass lying precariously on his lap. His feet were resting on a white polystyrene box, the lid of which, secured by brown plastic adhesive tape, bore a label with something written on it in Arabic. A nervous black, brown, and white Jack Russell terrier eyed her threateningly from the umbrella stand, to which it was tethered by a long plaited leather leash.

Dropping her handbag to the floor at a measured distance from the dog, now trembling and emitting a continuous low-pitched growl, Fiona made herself comfortable on a sofa while keeping an eye on the hound. She looked around, hoping to spot its owner. But there was nobody. The reception desk was unattended.

"Giles," she whispered, prompting the dog to leap onto the box and spread itself so that its paws reached the four corners. As Giles didn't stir, she glanced at the pineapple-shaped clock on the wall and saw it was 7.30 pm . Assuming Mouktar must have been and gone, she guessed the box contained the blood samples packed with pellets of solid carbon dioxide to keep them frozen. But what was the dog all about?

Afraid to approach should she alarm it again, she was screwing up a piece of paper to toss at Giles when she sensed the arrival of someone at her shoulder.

"Excuse me," a soft male voice with an unfamiliar accent enquired, "are you Dr Fiona Cameron?"

A tall, dark-skinned, bearded young man of about twenty-five, wearing a floral T-shirt, denim shorts and flip-flops, offered his hand.

"Yes, I am actually. Hello!" said Fiona.

"I'm Mouktar. Pleased to meet you. I've only been gone for a few minutes to collect this from the car."

He placed a plastic supermarket bag on the sofa.

"The professor was awake when I left. He must have gone out like a light. That's *Sindibādu*, my dog, by the way, or 'Sinbad the Sailor' to you. He always protects that sort of box as if his life depends on it, grasping the corners if he can reach them. Another thing about him you need to know is he doesn't like women. In fact, he *hates* them. He was found on a beach, wandering around, very thin and hungry, and was taken to an animal refuge. He was there for two weeks before I adopted him. My theory is he was pushed off a boat at sea by a woman, and survived by climbing into an empty box like that one, until the two of them were washed ashore. He's never forgotten what happened, or the sort of person who did it. You should see what he did to the dress of my boss's favourite lab tech when I let him get too close the other day. Not *deliberately*, of course!"

"Was that the girl who took over from you in the lab?"

Mouktar nodded with a barely concealed smirk.

"Was she the one who gave the presentation in Mexico City?" asked Fiona.

"Yes. She was lucky she wasn't bitten. But, don't worry. *Sindibādu* won't attack you, as long as you use this whenever he's around."

He opened the plastic bag to reveal several green plastic bottles with tall necks.

"*Brut* aftershave?" Fiona gasped.

"That's right."

"Four bottles! What's…?"

"It fools him into thinking you're a man," said Mouktar with a wink. "I discovered it a few weeks ago, when I put some on a cut on my sister's ankle in the hope it would prevent any infection. After being really aggressive towards her for days, he suddenly calmed down, even to the point of licking her toes and wagging his tail. My theory… sorry, hypothesis, strictly speaking… is that his master used to use it, and so he associates the smell with 'maleness', if there is such a word."

"That's very interesting. I suppose it's a conditioned reflex of the type Pavlov discovered. But I'm getting confused. Why do I need four bottles of *Brut* to protect me from *your* dog? As long as you keep him on a lead, hopefully a much shorter one than that, I'll just keep my distance. No problem."

Mouktar glanced nervously at Giles, still asleep.

"You mean you don't know?"

"I don't know what?"

"I assumed he'd told you."

Fiona shook her head vigorously.

"Whatever it is… he didn't."

"Oh dear!" said Mouktar. "Well, last night I learnt that, before going to INDOMED, I will have to go to Amman to give my side of the story about what happened in the lab. I couldn't possibly take *Sindibādu* along with me – not from here to Jordan and then from there to Indonesia. And I can't leave him here alone. My sister's gone back to Qatar, where she lives. So… the professor suggested you could take him with you."

"Oh, did the professor? How clever of him. Why not kennels?"

"He'd think he'd been abandoned again."

"What about vaccinations, permits, and so on? You'll need those."

"They're already done. He'd had all his immunisations and so on before I adopted him. "

"Pity!"

"Pardon?"

"Nothing! So Professor Butterfield said we would take him to Nusa Ceningan, and I would look after him until you arrive?"

"He said you love dogs. So I've been to the drugstore and bought every bottle of *Brut* they had on the shelf so that you'd be safe."

"Thank you," said Fiona coldly. "So all I have to do to avoid being eaten alive between now and your arrival is to smell like Henry Cooper?"

"Like *who*?"

"A famous Cockney boxer who used to do *Brut* commercials on TV. Anything else I should do for good measure? Smoke a pipe… chew tobacco… wear a false beard? I know, even better… how about taking steroids? A shot of testosterone in my bum every morning should do the trick."

"Ha! No, of course not."

Fiona stared maliciously at Giles before her face lit up.

"I know! Mouktar, tell me something. Does this *Brut* trick work the other way round? I mean, if a man were to put on ladies' perfume, would Sinbad think he was a woman… and attack?"

"Absolutely. I had the same thought once and did an experiment. My brother acted as the guinea pig. And it worked. He needed six stitches, poor boy."

"*How very interesting!*"

Mouktar nodded sheepishly, prompting Fiona to rub her hands in anticipation of her next move.

"Mouktar, as a fellow scientist, I'm sure you appreciate that all experimental observations need to be independently confirmed before being accepted as fact… yes?"

Mouktar nodded.

"Could you please take Sinbad to the reception desk… on his lead, of course?"

Struggling to maintain her composure, Fiona took a bottle of *Estée Lauder* from her handbag, crept across the floor to Giles's side, and started spraying it liberally onto his socks before working her way up. Only when she had reached his shirt collar did he awaken.

"Good God! What's going on?" he exclaimed. "What the hell are you…?"

"Hello, Giles, wakey-wakey!" said Fiona. "I'm back from my trip. Don't get up, whatever you do. I'm just doing a little experiment. You're quite safe. But it's essential you stay exactly where you are."

Fiona retreated to the far side of the room.

"Okay Mouktar, bring Sinbad towards the professor… slowly… gently does it… and hold on to that lead *very* tightly."

Reluctantly, Mouktar did as instructed until the dog, now only two feet from Giles, began yapping aggressively in his direction, his paws slipping on the tiles as he pulled against the leash.

"Okay, stop there!" said Fiona. "I think we've confirmed your hypothesis, Mouktar. Sorry, Giles… sort of! I must admit to being tempted to go one step further. But I'll be merciful. After all, I'm not sure who'll be suffering more with Sinbad around. Can you imagine, Giles, what it'll be like living with a woman who smells of *Brut* day and night?"

"What *are* you talking about?" asked Giles.

"Mouktar says we're taking Sinbad with us while he goes off to Amman, but there's a bit of a problem because he hates women. However, as Mouktar has discovered, *Brut* aftershave is the perfect antidote, and he's bought some supplies. We were just testing the reverse hypothesis, so to speak."

Not sure how to cope with the situation, Mouktar decided it was time to leave. Taking Sinbad with him, he bade them both goodnight and wished them a safe journey.

"And *bon voyage* to you too, Mouktar," Giles called before turning to Fiona. "Jesus! You gave me such a fright. I smell like a bunch of roses. I hope this stuff washes off."

"Don't worry. It does."

"Sorry about Sinbad," Giles added. "I really am. But Mouktar dropped him on me. I imagine we'll survive until he returns from Jordan."

"He seems quite nice."

"Yes, he is. And bright, too. I think we'll get on well together. So, anyhow, tell me about your trip to Ni'ihau. That's much more interesting. I'm longing to hear."

"Actually, you jumped to the wrong conclusion there," said Fiona. "Although it's true I did take a peek at Ni'ihau, the real purpose was to look at another island, about a hundred and fifty miles farther out to the north-west, a *very* special one that

I dreamt of visiting as a teenager when doing a school project on natural selection. It's tiny. Ni'ihau, almost a hundred and fifty miles long, is huge by comparison. This one is less than a mile. But it has sheer cliffs soaring two hundred feet straight out of the ocean. And much, much more. I'll come back to that in a minute. First, let me get Ni'ihau out of the way."

Taking a seat next to Giles, she made herself comfortable.

"It took us about half an hour to get there. I asked the pilot to encircle it a couple of times... some pretty scary banking! I took some photos that I'll show you later. It doesn't look much from the air, I must say. Pretty flat and dry. There are some cliffs and a few nice beaches on which some seals were basking. Quite a few trees here and there, which the pilot said had been planted by the owners over the years. Apparently, when Captain Cook's crew were in these waters, it had no trees at all. I also saw some dried-up lakes, and a few wild animals – a group of sheep and what the pilot said were boars. He said the owners had introduced them, and also some oryx and elandwhich, to my disappointment, I didn't catch sight of. They were all introduced for the convenience of game-hunting day trippers, apparently one of the island's sources of income."

"Horses?"

"Several, corralled in a sort of paddock."

"So, if they got bitten, which is likely given most mosquitoes go for horses, the virus was obviously not lethal to them. Interesting."

"The pilot said the residents use only horses and bikes to get around."

"Did you see any horses?"

"No."

"What sort of trees were they?"

"Difficult to tell. Perhaps acacias, which I gather grow elsewhere in Hawaii. If you're wondering whether they'd conceal a germ warfare establishment, I very much doubt it, to be honest. But you could probably hide the entrance to an underground one."

"That would do. Did the pilot mention the epidemic? Had he heard about it?"

"He said he'd heard rumours, but that's all."

"Well, it certainly doesn't sound like mosquito country."

"Definitely not… unlike the other islands. So that's Ni'ihau."

Fiona rubbed her hands at the prospect of moving to other things.

"Okay, now for the really interesting part, she said. "The island I was talking about is called Nihoa, which in the local language means tooth, which is what it's like… at least, a badly decayed one. It's surrounded by a huge coral reef. I told you it was small. Well, its surface area is about a quarter of a square mile. That's less than half the size of London's Hyde Park, and less than a fifth of the size of Central Park in New York. It's not very interesting for your average tourist with its almost non-existent beach, but for nature lovers like me it's mind-boggling. Because, believe it or not, this little pebble of an island has been completely isolated for millions of years, for so long that it's even evolved its own fauna and flora. Imagine! It's a little world of its own, in the middle of the Pacific, and has been for eons. There are *totally unique* species on it – animals, insects, and plants that occur nowhere else on the face of the earth, and have never existed anywhere else. There's a *huge* cricket that can't fly. It doesn't need to. It's got nowhere to go, and there's nothing to run away from. There's also a spider and two species of bird that are unique, and at least three species of plant, including a gorgeous palm tree and a weird carnation with flowers that don't have any petals."

"Are you having me on?"

"Of course not! You can look it up, if you wish. It's protected, by the way. Nobody's allowed to go there in case they tread on insects, frighten the birds, leave germs behind, and so on."

Fiona looked at her watch to give the message she was ready to retire.

"It's been a long day, and we have to be up early," she said. "So, how about we hit the hay?"

"Agreed."

Just as they were about to enter the elevator, the manageress, a middle-aged lady whom Fiona thought was half Hawaiian and half Japanese, appeared in the hallway.

"Oh, hello!" she said cheerfully. "I've some news for you. I bumped into your friend in the drugstore earlier today. He told me about the problem with his dog. You can leave it here if you like, and then when your friend gets to Indonesia I can arrange for a courier to take it to him. It'll cost something, of course, but if you'd like to consider it, I don't mind. I love Jack Russells. And don't worry, I know all about the *Brut* business! You could leave me a bottle or two."

Giles propped the doors open with a leg, and took a couple of bottles from the bag.

"Thank you so much!" he said. "You're an angel. Here, take these. I'll call the people there to check they'll cover the cost. I imagine they will. Assuming I'm right, I'll ask them to get in touch with you about the arrangements."

Chapter Twelve

As Teuku had promised, one of his new assistants was waiting in Jakarta's Soekarno-Hatta airport in readiness to collect the box of samples and take them to INDOMED. And, just as Teuku had assured, Giles and Fiona had no problem spotting her in the crowd.

"Just look out for a Chinese girl in her twenties with blonde hair and green eyes," he had said. "Yeah, that's right: *a Chinese blonde with green eyes.* There won't be many of those around!"

A Hui Chinese from the city of Ürümqi in Xinjiang, the region of north-west China notable for its large population of Muslims, Mingzhu had inherited her unusual features from grandparents in Gansu, the small province on the edge of the Gobi desert thought to have been settled in ancient times by a lost legion of Roman soldiers. A graduate in genetics at Wuhan's Huazhong University, she'd been unsure about what to do with her life and opted for twelve months of overland adventure travel while she thought about it. After making her way by train through Vietnam, Thailand and Malaysia, she'd spent a week with an aunt in the Woodlands area of Singapore before boarding a cargo ship bound for Australia. During the passage, she'd fallen for a merchant sailor from Brunei, and the two of them had disembarked in Jakarta before the vessel had left for Fremantle. Paid for by Mingzhu's father, a wealthy silk manufacturer in Jiangsu, the couple had rented an apartment in Pondok Indah, one of the capital's more affluent suburbs.

It had been in the local Golf and Country Club that Mingzhu had seen INDOMED's call for applications in a copy of the *Medical Journal of Indonesia* that someone had left on a coffee table. She'd applied for the job the same evening, and travelled to Nusa Ceningan for an interview three days later. Impressed by her sharp intellect and irrepressible enthusiasm, Teuku had snapped her up and given her one of INDOMED's apartments overlooking Blue Lagoon.

Fiona took to her instantly. By the time they had chatted over a pot of green tea and deposited the precious polystyrene box with Garouda airlines for the flight to Bali, it felt as if they'd known each other for years. A written message brought from Teuku confirmed that he'd collect Giles and Fiona from the Bandara International, at eight o'clock the next morning.

***

Upon entering their new laboratory the following afternoon, while Fiona was busy unpacking and getting to know the villa, Giles was more than pleased with the preparations Teuku had made. While it didn't have the ageless ambience of their usual workplace, what it lacked in character it made up for in other ways. Compared with the cramped laboratory they'd occupied in the New Building, it was nothing less than palatial. Gone were the corners occupied by cardboard boxes of disposable glassware, the stained bench tops and wobbly stools, the photocopies of articles stacked in sinks, the overgrown plants in cracked pots. All was bright, spacious, spotlessly clean, and air-conditioned, with panoramic views of the island replacing the glimpses of grey sky through grimy windows.

Moving into the adjacent office, Giles wondered how such luxury might affect their work. In Britain, university researchers were accustomed to working in cramped, dusty, and untidy laboratories. It was part of the culture. Many even welcomed it, believing it focused the mind on the job in hand. As long as you had the essentials, that's all that mattered, they reckoned. The rest was down to brain work. Anyone who had seen a photograph of Francis Crick standing next to his model of the DNA molecule, fashioned out of bits and pieces of wire and hexagonal and pentagonal cut-outs of aluminium sheet, held together by an old pipette stand, knew that. But was that story really true? Giles had no way of knowing.

For Fiona, of course, there would be the bonus of having Mingzhu around. What a breath of fresh air she would be after suffering Aram for so long. According to Teuku, she was a treasure, always busy, cheerful, and full of ideas. Her approach to everything, he'd said, was positive. Although her appointment had put an early end to her treasured globetrotting, Mingzhu was comfortable with her decision, looking forward to learning from Fiona, and excited at the prospect of playing her part in unravelling the mystery of the Ni'ihau virus.

***

Contrary to expectations, Sinbad arrived on INDOMED's doorstep several days ahead of his owner. The hotel's manageress had called to announce she'd cured him of his aversion by applying increasing dilutions of *Brut* to her legs on a daily basis, until, after six days, she hadn't needed to put any on at all. True enough, when Mingzhu opened the box that had been his home throughout the journey, he did little more than glance at her before wagging his tail vigorously and running to the bowl of water Fiona had prepared. Mingzhu took to him on the spot, volunteering there and then to look after him until Mouktar arrived, relieving Giles and Fiona of the unwanted responsibility.

Conscious that even a small leak to the media about their work could have serious repercussions, Teuku had already decided to limit the Ni'ihau team to the absolute minimum. Announcing to the other staff that only Giles, Fiona, Mingzhu, and Mouktar would be allowed in the laboratory, he explained merely that the project was to do with a new disease, and that its outcome could be as important for INDOMED as the discovery of *Achilles* had been for MECCAR. In fact, the truth was it might be even more important. There had been some devastating outbreaks of infectious diseases down the ages. For example, the Spanish Flu after the Great War had affected half a billion people, of whom a fifth had died, and the Black Death of mediaeval times had probably killed half the population of Europe. However, the uncontrolled spread of a mosquito-borne virus that was invariably lethal would be in a class of its own.

While waiting for Mouktar to arrive, the others got on with the task of organising the laboratory to suit their needs. With that part of the operation entrusted to Fiona, Giles spent his time in the villa finalising his plan of action. As there were only a few drops of serum available from each of the Hawaiians, they would need to make the very best use of them. Once the last tube was dry, there would be no going back. By then, they would need to know precisely what sort of virus they were dealing with and have a good idea where it had come from. When millions of lives could be at stake, half answers would not be enough.

The prospect was as daunting as it was exciting. Putting aside the occasional breakthrough, of which the discovery of *Achilles* had been a stunning example, Giles knew that medical research normally progresses in small stages, achieved by different teams, often in different parts of the world, carrying on from where others have left off.

"It's like a relay hurdle race in athletics," he used to tell his students. "Each runner passing the baton to the next one after clearing the latest set of obstacles until the finishing line is reached."

But solving the riddle of Ni'ihau would be more like a one hundred-metre sprint. They were going to be on their own, completely, and there could be no break until the job was done.

As Mouktar's involvement was going to be critical, a message received from Rashid Yamani, just a couple of days after Sinbad's arrival, stating that Mouktar's departure from Jordan had been delayed, was worrying. With no reason having been given, Fiona dared not imagine how they would cope if the Directorate of the Alhazen organisation had decided to post Mouktar somewhere else at the last minute. Having always been fearful that Rashid might one day regard INDOMED as a threat to his institute's pre-eminence, Teuku was inclined to believe the worse. But there was a simple and happy ending to the drama. Arriving the following week with an unexpected companion, Mouktar introduced everyone to his childhood sweetheart, Kamilah, who had decided to leave her job in Qatar's Weill Cornell Medical College and join him. Teuku responded with his usual generosity by offering her a training scholarship in his own unit.

The development was as good news for Sinbad as it was for everyone else. From that day on, Kamilah took all responsibility for his morning walks, usually to the promontory of Tanjung Batumelawang to watch the waves crashing against the rocks and feel the wind in his face, or to Secret Beach where he would scamper on the sand before chasing the ever present shoals of tiny fish in the shallow water.

As soon as Giles was clear about what they should do, he mustered the others to the villa. Over a pot of tea and a plate of apple butterscotch pie, Fiona's favourite Scottish pastry, baked the previous evening, he described the task ahead. The first job would be to identify which of Mouktar's samples contained viable viruses. While it was a safe assumption many would contain virus particles, that on its own would not be enough. To determine their precise nature, they would need many more than a few drops of serum could contain. They would need millions. And the only way of obtaining that sort of number would be to grow them in cultures of living cells. Fortunately, several lines of cultured mosquito cells had already been offered to INDOMED by the Eijkman Institute in Jakarta in preparation for their work on malaria. The starting point would be to screen each sample of serum for the presence of West Nile viruses, whether dead or alive, using a so-called nucleic acid amplification test. As this was a technique that Mingzhu had used for her studies in China, she volunteered to get the ball rolling.

By the time Mouktar had returned from the Eijkman Institute with the cultures of *vero* cells, Mingzhu had already completed the RNA amplification tests, and was ready to help Fiona with the challenge of growing viruses from the samples of serum that had given a positive result. Although virology had not been a major part of her university course, Mingzhu knew that viruses are not considered to be alive or dead in the same way bacteria are. Whereas bacteria can multiply anywhere as long as they have the right conditions, viruses can do so only inside living cells. Even then, they do so only by hijacking a cell's metabolic machinery to force it to make endless copies of themselves, using the code inscribed in their genes as the recipe. The hapless cell becomes enslaved as a virus-producing factory until, engorged with new viruses, it ruptures to release them, infecting more cells in the vicinity in the process. The cycle of infection, multiplication, rupture, and infection of other cells continues until either the entire organism dies, or its immune system produces enough antibodies to halt the process.

Mingzhu knew also that, structurally, most viruses can be likened to microscopic golf balls in which the long strand of rubber coiled in the centre is the nucleic acid molecule containing the genes, and the capsule on the outside is composed of proteins, some of which enable the virus to attach to cells and enter them. In contrast to all animals and plants, whose genes are invariably made of DNA, in viruses it can be either DNA or the closely related, but very different, chemical called RNA, short for ribonucleic acid.

Though she had known all of this and more about viruses in general, Mingzhu hadn't known anything about the West Nile virus in particular, until she'd picked up the courage to knock on the door of Giles's office.

"It's what's called an arbovirus, Mingzhu," he'd explained over a pot of green tea prepared by Fiona. "In other words, a virus that's carried by insects, in this case certain species of mosquitoes. And, like all arboviruses, it's an RNA virus. Its genes are made of RNA, not DNA like the viruses that give us cold sores, for example smallpox and the common cold."

"Is that likely to be important?"

"I suspect it might be, Mingzhu. But time will tell."

After Mingzhu had infected the *vero* cells and incubated them for long enough for the viruses to multiply, she extracted and purified their RNA molecules, working through the night and the next day to get it done as quickly as possible. The end product, a small volume of clear liquid – which, to an outsider, could be merely tap water – was, to her, like liquid gold.

As she held the glass tube to the window and swirled it to catch reflections of the warm evening sunlight, jumping excitedly in her juvenile manner, Mouktar crossed the floor to share the moment in his own quieter way. Little had he realised, when secretly placing the extra samples in liquid nitrogen in Honolulu, how important they would become in the course of time. As he smiled at Mingzhu and patted her lightly on the back, he knew that his own big moment, the one he had been contemplating during the long journey with Kamilah, had arrived: that of determining the precise order of the series of more than ten thousand letters that make up the West Nile virus' genetic code. It was time for Mingzhu to have a well-earned rest.

The good news for Mouktar upon arriving at INDOMED had been that Teuku had purchased the latest model of the best type of automatic sequencer on the market. Having had the time to familiarise himself with it while Mingzhu had been busy, he was confident he would have the information in little more than a few days' time. It would then be up to Fiona to enter the data into a computer program that would compare the code with the known genetic code in the RNA of normal West Nile viruses. Any differences between the two, even of only a few letters, would be instantly identified, and hopefully provide the answer to why the mutated Ni'ihau virus was so lethal, when normal West Nile viruses usually produce at most only a minor flu-like illness. At least, that was the assumption.

"You'll soon experience the emotional high that real research can give you," he said to Mingzhu. "It beats everything else on earth. Learning about the natural world from books, lectures, videos and so on is wonderful, of course, but discovering something entirely new gives you an incredible lift. Once you're into it, you'll be hooked. It's like a drug. Because you never know what's round the next corner; what the next experiment will reveal; what new questions it will raise. Every minute is an adventure. But, before I start, let's go for a walk. It's something I always do before embarking on a big job like this. It clears my mind, steadies my nerves."

As they arrived at the edge of the Blue Lagoon, Mingzhu looked up at the stars as if searching for the answer to the mysteries of the universe.

"I'm sure you're right, Mouktar, what you were saying before. It *is* exciting, incredibly so. But, at the moment, it's also a little scary, quite honestly. I feel a bit like those two over there. We're both taking a big leap, and have no idea what we're jumping into."

She nodded towards a couple of excited girls picking up the courage to jump off the lagoon's forty-foot cliff into the sea below.

"They're techs from one of the other labs – sisters, from Kalimantan," said Mingzhu.

"Where's that?"

"Borneo."

"Borneo?" replied Mouktar. "Isn't it remarkable? All of us from different parts of the world – me from a tiny country in the Middle East, you from China, two places thousands of miles apart that couldn't be more different. And yet, here we are, on a tiny Indonesian island few people have heard of, helping two scientists from Britain solve the mystery of something that happened in Hawaii. Hardly anyone apart from a few people in Jordan and Oxford knows what we're up to. And yet, what we're doing could save the world from an unimaginable disaster."

Mingzhu held her hands to her ears as a splash announced the arrival of the two girls in the water.

"I hope they're okay!"

"They will be. I've been told many do it. It's famous. Let's go."

As Mouktar and Mingzhu were making their way through the long grass to the accommodation centre to collect Sinbad for his evening runaround, Giles and Fiona had just finished clearing the dining table.

"Mingy and Mucky are a nice pair, aren't they?" Fiona remarked as she closed the dishwasher with a sigh.

"Very, yes."

"He was an Alhazen Fellow, wasn't he?"

Giles nodded.

"So, does that mean he was acting as a spy in Honolulu on top of his lab work?"

"Too soon for that, I imagine," said Giles. "After all, presumably any confidential information he collected would be on infectious diseases for INDOMED's benefit, not MECCAR's."

"Yes, but that's not what's on my mind," said Fiona. "What I'm thinking about is the fact that he's just been to see the top brass in Jordan, hasn't he? What if we were right about Aram's sudden departure – that, when Jane opened her big mouth about Brigitte Dubois Yusuf's identity card, he suspected we'd cottoned on to what happened to Ahmad in Sorrento, and rushed to give them the news? Perhaps Mucky's recall to Jordan was to do with that, not to give his side of the story about what happened in Honolulu. What if he was given instructions while he was there to keep an eye on us… or, worse? It's not impossible. I think we should watch our backs, Giles."

"Mouktar, an assassin? Another Brigitte? He's the last person I'd entrust that job to!"

"Me too. And that's what worries me."

Chapter Thirteen

As each day passed while Mouktar was working, the clock on the wall of Giles's office had seemed to tick louder and louder. Rarely had he felt under such pressure to get a project on the road. His days in Oxford, browsing journals in the library, helping Fiona at the bench, writing in his office while listening to Jane's radio through the half-open door, were beginning to seem like a stroll in the park – a protected world where deadlines were self-imposed, targets optional, and timetables of his own making. He was one of the fortunate few in academia, he reckoned, who did not see themselves as being in competition with others, but rather as members of a worldwide team, a virtual clan as Fiona would say, with a common purpose. The responsibility of fathoming the answer to the Ni'ihau mystery against the clock was already weighing heavily on his shoulders. If they did not find the answer within a few weeks, someone else would surely get in on the act. How would Teuku react to that? And what about Sir Quentin?

While waiting for the big day to arrive, much of Giles's time was spent reading about the life cycles of the different species of mosquitoes, three and a half thousand of them, in the hope he could come up with a plausible explanation of what had happened to Ni'ihau's invaders. Teuku had reaffirmed that the entomologists who had visited Ni'ihau with traps soon after the epidemic had failed to catch a single infected specimen. Nor had they found any on the neighbouring island of Kauai, thirty miles to the east. Giles's greatest concern was that some might be lying low in the forest. Although most species lived for just a few days or weeks, he'd learnt that, under the right conditions, some could survive for much longer, even several months.

And there was worse. As the mosquitoes had clearly included females that had recently mated, within a few days each could have deposited one or two hundred eggs in water somewhere. Although, in contrast to the other islands of the chain, Ni'ihau is an arid place, tiny pools in potholes, gutters, tin cans, discarded tyres and the like, even dew on leaves, are known to be sufficient for some species. Was it possible that thousands of young mosquitoes would one day, without warning, blacken the island's skies?

Although Giles had known mosquito eggs normally take just a few days or weeks to develop into larvae, then pupae, then adults, he'd learnt to his alarm that eggs can sometimes enter a state of suspended animation called diapause, and remain like that for months, even years, until a change in temperature or humidity wakes them up. Given also that some species' females are known to transfer the West Nile virus to their eggs, many of the new generation could be carrying it from birth. What if they headed towards the moisture-laden forests of Kauai, Oahu, and the other islands?

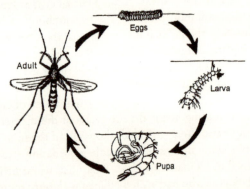

Giles knew the answer to that question. It was the nightmare scenario. Thousands of the islands' residents, perhaps hundreds of thousands, would be bitten and infected. And what if some of the insects got onto a ship or into an aircraft and laid infected eggs in other countries? But if that was on the cards, he asked, why hadn't anyone sprayed the island with insecticide? Surely they could have found some way of concealing the truth behind what they were doing? It was a puzzle, and a worrying one at that.

To his great relief, Giles did not have to wait very long for Mouktar to finish the job. With typical irrepressible enthusiasm, Mingzhu had insisted on helping him to very good effect. As she was later to reveal, the long hours with Mouktar had been among the most rewarding of her life. The late nights and long weekends of her student days, poring over books and lecture notes at a time of such uncertain consequence for her future, given her father's insistence she should take over his business, had been more than worthwhile. Equally important, she had experienced how demanding and challenging research can be. New equipment can be a huge advantage, but it can also be frustrating when it comes with a heavy instruction manual or develops a fault and there's nobody around who knows how to fix it.

Mingzhu had also learnt that, no matter how much care is taken, problems occur. Research is a world apart from laboratory exercises as an undergraduate. Samples get accidentally destroyed or contaminated; cells die for no apparent reason; expensive reagents sometimes let you down. She and Mouktar had suffered all of this and more. There had been times when her frustrations and disappointments had almost got the better of her. During those moments, Mouktar's placid manner had saved the day. His unruffled approach to tackling problems was exactly what she needed, and another lesson learnt. He'd had enough experience to know that the popular image of laboratory life as easygoing is a myth. While it might not seem so to outsiders, medical researchers are as conscious of the responsibilities on their shoulders as those at the sharp end of medicine. Success is justly treasured when it arrives. And, when it did so on this occasion, Mingzhu could not resist taking the printout from Mouktar's hand and bursting into Giles's office.

"*Eureka!*" she screamed. "We've done it! And it's astonishing."

Having witnessed the pain of more than one 'false breakthrough' during his time, Mouktar followed at a more leisurely pace, appearing at the doorway with a guarded smile.

"I've learnt to be a bit cautious, Professor, but I think on this occasion she may be right. I hope so."

"This looks wonderful," Giles enthused after studying the roll of paper for a few minutes. "It looks like you've done a magnificent job. Why don't the two of you go and have a well-earned cup of something, while Fiona and I go through it with a fine-tooth comb. We'll join you when we're done."

Giles had already spotted that the summary statement on the report's first page said that the genetic code carried by the RNA of the virus differed from that of the common form of West Nile virus. And, what was especially intriguing was that it did so in more ways than one. When the nucleic acid of a virus mutates spontaneously in nature, usually only one part of the genetic code becomes altered at any one time. Often, just a single letter out of a series of thousands will be missing or replaced by a different one. Nevertheless, such tiny changes can have dramatic effects on the virus's behaviour by altering the structure of one of its proteins.

Never one to rush into a hasty assessment, Giles took his time scanning the rest of the document while Fiona watched in silence. Only when he had checked that the text described the data accurately did he take his eyes off it.

"Have you seen what I've seen?" he said.

Fiona nodded thoughtfully as she lifted the roll from the desk and took it to the window.

"Well, it's certainly a West Nile virus," she observed. "That's for sure. But it's equally certain it's not the strain that originally turned up in New York all those years ago. There are some very interesting differences between the two lots of RNA. And, what's more, there's also what looks like an insertion in the Ni'ihau virus, a piece of extra RNA that's not present in the normal strain."

She turned to sit on Giles's desk as she tossed the report onto his lap.

"Our two young helpers did a very good job there, Professor Butterfield. This is getting very interesting, very interesting indeed."

Fiona turned to gaze through the tall Moorish window behind her, so different from the Romanesque arches of the College's New Building. A gleaming white catamaran in full sail, its two crew members at full stretch over the water, was passing through the Toyapakeh Strait that separates the island from Nusa Penida. From the fifth floor of INDOMED's laboratory block, the vessel's regular motion with the turquoise-blue water foaming against its bows seemed almost surreal, yet strangely calming in a way that helped her to focus on the questions running through her mind.

Although virology had never had been her forte, she knew that not all viruses of the same species are identical. Most species include several different strains that differ slightly in their genetic codes, a consequence of the slow accumulation of spontaneous mutations that had occurred over thousands of years. She also knew such natural mutations occur more frequently in viruses whose nucleic acid is RNA, like the West Nile, than in those in which it is DNA, like smallpox and herpes. This is partly because RNA is inherently less stable, but also because, when an infected cell manufactures copies of a DNA virus, but not of an RNA virus, it checks every one for spelling errors and corrects any it finds.

After waiting for the catamaran to reappear from behind a group of giant tree ferns, she turned to Giles, still deep in thought.

"I think this can mean any one of three things, Giles. The first is that one of those small mutations makes the virus a killer, and it just happens that the Pentagon's scientists put it into a strain of West Nile that already contains several harmless ones, perhaps in the hope it would be overlooked. Alternatively, it could be the insertion that's the killer. Or, thirdly, it's the combination of the two that makes it so lethal, for example if one increases its infectivity and the other its virulence."

Giles nodded as he chewed on his pencil, pausing to spit a splinter into the trash can.

"Sorry about that!"

"It reminds me of the flu virus that acquired several mutations before spreading around the world to cause the Spanish Flu epidemic after the First World War."

"Agreed. So what do we do next?"

"I think the first thing is to compare the genetic code of the Ni'ihau virus with the codes of every natural strain of West Nile that have ever been described. There must be online databases for that. It might enable us to identify the strain they used as the starting point, which in turn might tell us where it came from, if each strain has a particular geographic distribution"

"Good thinking," said Giles. "So, now we know what we'll be doing tomorrow?"

"Did you say tomorrow? I'm starting *now.*"

Chapter Fourteen

True to her word, while Giles was dining with Teuku and his wife in their penthouse that evening, Fiona was scouring the internet for descriptions of the RNA in different strains of West Nile viruses isolated from birds, horses, and people in different parts of the world. When she'd set off for the villa after sharing a bowl of ice cold *es campur* with Mouktar and Mingzhu in the cafeteria, she'd been expecting a long night wasahead of her. But the prospect had not been burdensome. On the contrary, it was something she'd relished. Although the lab work had been exciting, it had been tinged with concerns that an unexpected problem might arise. The release from that burden had been exhilarating.

After completing her literature search in the early hours, and checking everything over a late breakfast in the kitchen, she was keen to show the results to the others. She looked at her watch.

"Ten-fifteen," she said to herself. "By now, they'll be in the Japanese garden preparing for the weekly barbecue. Off we go."

As she emerged from the thicket of cherry trees that bordered the patio, disturbing a family of myna birds feeding on the fruit, Giles broke off his conversation with Teuku's new secretary.

"Hello, dear! Had an accident?"

"Ah! All this mud on my knees?" said Fiona, looking down at her jeans. "Yes, I tripped over by the pond in the rush to get here. But forget about that. It's not important."

Recovering her composure, she introduced herself to the gathering. After accepting a glass of orange juice from the bar, she beckoned Giles, Mouktar and Mingzhu to join her at a distance from the rest.

"You won't believe this," she whispered. "I've got the answer, or at least part of it. I've discovered where the strain of West Nile virus that was engineered to produce the Ni'ihau killer originally came from. And I think you're going to be surprised. Have a guess."

"Timbuktu," Mingzhu offered mischievously, giggling behind her hand.

"Wrong! Try again."

"Iceland," said Mouktar.

"Sorry, Mucky, that was a complete non-starter. Iceland has no mosquitoes."

"None at all?"

"That's right. Any more ideas?"

"Come on, Fiona, get on with it!" Giles urged.

"Okay, then, the answer is... Mexico."

"*Mexico*?" they gasped in unison.

"That's right, Mexico," said Fiona. "But that's only part of the story. It turns out that the original virus was actually a hybrid. In other words, its RNA originally came from two different strains of West Nile virus, not one."

Seeing the confused look on Mingzhu's face, she knew she needed to explain.

"Hybrid viruses, Mingy, can be produced in nature when an animal, in this case almost certainly a bird, gets infected with two different strains of the same species of virus at the same time. In this case, it could have happened only if a bird was bitten by two mosquitoes, each carrying a different strain of West Nile virus, at about the same time. Any of the bird's cells that became infected with both strains would then have manufactured both at the same time. As a consequence, bits of the RNA of one strain got attached to bits of the RNA of the other strain, resulting in new viruses, whose RNA was a mixture of both. This sort of thing happens with flu viruses, a cause of concern in case one day a hybrid is formed between a nasty strain that normally infects only pigs or birds and one of the strains that infects humans. But, as far as I can tell, a hybrid West Nile virus has never been described."

"Do you know anything about the two strains that got combined in this case?" Mouktar asked.

"Indeed I do, Mucky. They're both well established in Mexico. One's called the Tabasco strain, and the other the Tecate strain. The former was first discovered in a dead raven in Tabasco county, in the south-east of the country, near the Yucatan peninsula. That was about ten years ago. Since then, it's spread among the local bird population. The other strain is one that crossed the border from California or Texas at some time in the past, either in birds again or in mosquitoes. It's common in Baja California, the part of Mexico in the north-west of the country with a long peninsula, where it gives horse breeders a problem."

"But those counties are on the opposite sides and opposite ends of Mexico," Giles remarked, his brow furrowed. "They must be two thousand miles apart. And they're very different places. Baja California is mostly desert, while the Yucatan is tropical rainforest country. On top of which, there's a range of mountains between them, the *Sierra Madre*. How on earth could…?"

"I know what you're about to say," Fiona interrupted. "How could a bird or any other animal have been bitten by two mosquitoes, one carrying the Tabasco strain and one the Tecate strain, when their habitats are so far apart and so different? That's exactly the point I was coming to. How could it have happened? It seems impossible. But clearly it did… somehow, somewhere. And it must mean something."

Having overheard everything while sitting in the shade behind a wattle bush, Teuku's head was buzzing.

"Hi there!" he said. "I've been listening to you guys. Congrats!"

"Ah, there you are, Teuku," Fiona responded, a little embarrassed. "We weren't leaving you out. Don't worry!"

"Sounds fascinating," he said. "Can I ask something? Is either of those two strains you mentioned particularly nasty on its own?"

"No, they're not. There's nothing special about the Tecate one, and if anything the Tabasco strain seems very mild. It's not clear why, but studies in mice have shown it's much less likely than other strains to invade the nervous system."

Teuku raised himself from his bench and moved to the buffet to help himself to a bowl of fruit salad.

"My, the fruit round here is so yummy!" he said. "So, presumably, the nastiness of the Ni'ihau virus is down to the extra piece of RNA that Giles told me about last night… the insertion? What have you learnt about that, Fiona? Anything special? Has it been found in a West Nile virus before?"

Fiona shook her head vigorously.

"No, it hasn't, Teuku. It's definitely not a piece of RNA that's ever been described in any natural strain of West Nile virus anywhere in the world. In fact, I'm pretty sure it hasn't been seen in any virus at all… although, I do need to finish checking that one out."

Fiona pulled a folded sheet of notepaper bearing a sketch of the virus's RNA from the back pocket of her jeans, and handed it to him.

"Very interesting, very interesting indeed," said Teuku. "Well, I must say, the four of you have done brilliantly. So what's next on the menu?"

"How about some of that Indonesian sausage that smells so good?"

"*Dutch* sausage, actually, Fiona. It's called *rookworst*, a leftover from the old colonial days in these parts, thanks to the Dutch East India Company – like that dollop of mashed spuds, onions, and carrots in the copper pot, which is called *hutspot*."

"With all the wonderful flavours in this part of the world, what made you put that on the menu…?" asked Fiona in surprise.

Teuku responded with a smile that smacked more of resentment than of pleasure.

"The rest of us voted for *ayam bakar* with some *sambal belacam*. But Giles here reckoned that was too 'fancy and spicy' for his down-to-earth taste buds. He'd rather have some 'good old-fashioned nosh', as he put it."

"Thank you, Professor Butterfield, for that contribution," said Fiona. "At least I had the pleasure of looking forward to today's barbecue! And now I can look forward to next week's even more."

Chapter Fifteen

After they had finished the barbecue and made their way back to the villa, Fiona reminded Giles that, during their first spell at INDOMED, he'd promised to take her to the neighbouring island of Nusa Penida to the east, should the opportunity arise. As things had turned out, it hadn't been possible. However, as they had made such great progress, she suggested now would be a good time to have a break and make the trip.

"It would be nice to reward Mucky and Mingy, too," she pointed out. "And, what's more, it'll give us time to think about what the lab results might mean and what we should do next. Yes?"

"Good idea."

During her childhood in the west of Scotland, Fiona had developed a heartfelt love of islands that had never left her. To her, the islands of Skye, Rum, Eigg and the rest were not the misty, wind-swept, craggy outcrops they were to Giles, but jewels where nature, tranquility, and kindly people blended harmoniously. They were quiet paradises, remote from the troubles and turmoil of so many parts of the world. Her father had a pet description for the isles of his birth, "wild yet mild", which he would often repeat in his soft brogue during their tramps through the heather or while salmon fishing on the banks of the River Sligachan.

To Fiona, there was also an endearing paradox about them. For, while their physical isolation provoked a happy sense of self-sufficiency and security, whenever she scanned the sea's horizon from a rocky outcrop or cliff edge it would provoke a yearning to explore what lay beyond. There was something about an island – almost any island, anywhere – that drew her like a magnet and yet, at the same time, felt liberating.

If she was honest with herself, it was partly for this reason that, within an hour of Giles's receiving INDOMED's first invitation, she'd been at the kitchen table with her old school atlas, studying the multitude of green and brown patches scattered across the Java and Banda Seas. After finding Nusa Ceningan, she'd scanned left and right for others of interest. She'd known about the natural beauty and wonderful artwork of Bali to the west, but also its far less appealing popularity as a tourist hotspot. Far more interesting had been the smaller island of Nusa Penida to the east. Perhaps it was the rough similarity of its shape and topography to those of Rum in the Inner Hebrides that appealed to her, or the mere fact she'd never heard of it despite the proximity to its famous big sister. When they seemed to be so similar… the same sort of features, rain forests, cliffs, and beaches… why should one island have attracted so many tourists and the other hardly any ? Whatever the reason, she suspected there wasn't much difference between them, and that Nusa Penida would have the benefit of being unspoilt, more the real Indonesia, more her sort of place. This was the case she had presented to Giles, and he'd agreed wholeheartedly.

And so, forty-eight hours after the barbecue, the time it had taken Teuku's personal assistant, Indah, to make the arrangements for a private boat at INDOMED's expense, the four of them set off together. It was an opportunity to bond in a way that had not yet been possible with so much on their plates. The only cloud was the recent departure of Mingzhu's partner, having decided that a life on *terra firma* with a girl buried in books and test tubes was not compatible with his seafaring character. They had parted amicably and promised to keep in touch.

The arrived at the yellow suspension bridge at sunrise, where the boat was already waiting – a red and white double-outrigger *jukung* with four benches, each wide enough for two passengers. A young Malay in white shorts and shirt and a broad-brimmed green hat was seated at the stern splicing a short length of sisal. Upon seeing his passengers, he tossed the rope and his marlinspike to one side to greet them with a friendly smile.

The first part of the journey through the strait soon brought them to the mangroves of Nusa Lembongan on the port side, prompting Giles to tell the others about the near encounter he had had with the cobra near the temple. While the incident horrified Mingzhu, in his characteristic way Mouktar took it all in quietly, seemingly more interested in the snake than the incident itself.

"If it had bitten you, would that have been fatal?" he asked earnestly.

"You could bet your bottom dollar on that one, Mucky!" Fiona answered. "He was very lucky."

Ever since that episode, Giles had been on the lookout for the girl who had probably saved his life. Knowing he wouldn't recognise her by now, so similar to his eyes were the faces of most of the local girls of her age, he had got into the habit of scanning crowds for the watch he'd given her. But, to his great disappointment, they had never crossed paths again.

Upon reaching the northern head of Nusa Ceningan, the boat turned to starboard and headed across the open sea, the water getting noticeably choppier as it headed into a fresh breeze. Waiting for them in Toyapakeh harbour on Nusa Penida's coast was an elderly islander wearing only sandals and baggy, tattered shorts of faded denim supported by plaited leather suspenders. Raising himself from a piece of sun-drenched driftwood, he eyed the visitors quizzically; they were so different from the young Australian snorkelers and surfers he was accustomed to meeting.

After spitting out a plug of tobacco, he smiled to himself and wiped a hand on his shorts before offering it to Giles. As he accepted his firm handshake, Giles perceived a reluctant acceptance on the old man's part that the rumours about Nusa Ceningan having changed must be true.

After leading them to the 1960s Morris Minor Traveller that Indah had also organized, he tossed their knapsacks into the rear of the vehicle.

"*Selamat datang di pulau saya*," he said softly. "*Saya harap Anda menikmati kunjungan Anda.*"

Not understanding a word, Giles pressed a crumpled banknote into the man's hand. Clearly as surprised as he was delighted, he proceeded to help the girls into the rear seat, before slamming the door and tugging on its rusting chrome handle to be sure it was securely closed. After polishing the windscreen with a rag from his pocket, he stood aside to wave them off with a toothy grin.

"What did he say? Does anyone know?" Fiona asked without any expectation of an answer. "How much did you give him, Giles?"

"One hundred thousand rupiah."

"About ten dollars?"

"Give or take a few dimes," said Giles. "Okay, let's drive along the coast to the hotel. What's it called?"

"The Kubu Ganesh Guesthouse, Prof," Mingzhu answered chirpily, her face buried in a map. "It's at a spot called Sampalan Point. It shouldn't take more than ten minutes or so."

Situated in its own leafy gardens, just five minutes' stroll from a sandy beach, all agreed as Giles was applying the handbrake that Indah had chosen a wonderful spot for their first night. The only downside was that Giles and Mouktar were obliged to share one room and the girls another, the only two available. As far as Fiona was concerned, it was a small price to pay for the experience of a lifetime. She and Mingzhu were now like old pals, anyhow. But Giles was not so enthusiastic. Mouktar was not the tidiest of colleagues. On top of that, he was in the habit of rising each morning at around five for a jog, after which he would return to puff on a cigarette over a cup of coffee, his only breakfast.

They'd agreed that after such an early start they should spend the rest of the day at leisure. While the girls went swimming and Mouktar cycled to the local market on one of the hotel's bikes, Giles put his feet up with *The Straits Times* and his first glass of Dark 'n' Stormy for far too long. Come the evening, everyone enjoyed a spread of traditional Indonesian food on the terrace overlooking the garden.

Fiona in particular relished the local scents and sounds: the rush of the cool breeze off the sea through the swaying palm trees, the distant surge of foam on the shore, the owner's pet cockatoo squawking on its perch. The only blemish was the intermittent buzz of a hungry mosquito. Although they knew the risk of malaria or any other serious illness was low on the island, its presence prompted Fiona to offer everyone her bottle of repellent.

"Got it!" Mouktar shouted triumphantly after swatting his forearm with a placemat. "No need for the bottle, thanks. I'll have to go and wash this mess off now. Excuse me while I go to the bathroom. I wonder whose blood it is?"

"Probably mine," Giles answered. "It got me a few minutes ago. Obviously, it needed a second helping."

As Mouktar stood up, Fiona caught sight of a basket he'd collected from under the table.

"Nice basket, Mucky. Beautiful pattern. Where did you get it?"

"The market. It's from Lombok… handmade, rattan."

"I might get one for myself. Can I peep inside?"

Mouktar pointed to the tightly knotted leather strap that secured its lid.

"Later. I'd like to wash this off as soon as I can."

"Is there something inside?"

"No. Why do you ask?"

"It looks heavy. I'm sure there must be many things in the market. I wondered if…"

"There were, yes, but I didn't get any. It's empty. Look."

Mouktar dangled the basket over the table and swung it to and fro.

"Must go now."

After he had left the terrace, Fiona supported her chin in her hands, her elbows on the table.

"Not like him to be so uncooperative. Would have only taken him a second. I might buy one, anyhow… if I get the chance."

She paused for a moment. "Anyhow, sorry to return to the subject when we're having such a nice time, but at the risk of spoiling these lovely desserts, what do you think will be the next stage, Giles?"

"You mean in the lab?"

"Mmm."

"Well, as we were discussing the other day, there are some big questions, aren't there? One is, why did the perpetrators use a hybrid of two different strains of the natural virus? Was it done deliberately for some reason, for example to amplify the rate at which it multiplies, or make it more lethal? Or is it of no consequence? Did it happen by chance? Does such a hybrid exist in nature, and it just fell into their hands? The fact it has never been described in the literature doesn't necessarily mean it doesn't exist, does it?"

Happy that there'd been no resistance to discussing a question that had been bugging her for much of the day, Fiona encouraged him to keep going.

"Absolutely…" she said. "But, if it *does* exist in nature, Giles, how on earth did it happen? How could a bird have been infected with those two strains at more or less the same time, if they only exist in different parts of the country?"

"How about bird migration?" Mingzhu spluttered eagerly, her mouth occupied by a coconut rice ball.

"I don't think so, Mingy," said Fiona. "There's no flyway, to use the technical term, between those two parts of Mexico. Remember, Baja is in the north-west and Tabasco the south-east. Migrating birds don't cross Mexico. I've checked it out."

"What if a bird got bitten by a single mosquito that happened to be carrying both strains of the virus? Is that possible?" asked Mingzhu.

"Good question! But also a non-starter, I'm afraid. Simultaneous infections of mosquitoes with different strains of the same virus have been described. There've been a few papers on that. Mosquitoes catch it from birds, remember, never from us humans. So, for one to have got infected with two strains, it would have to have bitten a bird in the north or south before flying the full length of Mexico over a range of mountains, and then bitten another one. There's no way a mosquito could make that journey. Typically, they don't fly more than a few miles from where they hatched."

"What about being carried in someone's car?"

"Once again, I doubt it, Mingy. I imagine the driving time between Baja California and Tabasco must be at least four or five days with overnight stops. While mosquitoes usually live for much longer than, generally, several weeks… it varies between species… I can't imagine one that's stuck inside a car for a few days not getting swatted by the driver or a passenger during that time, can you?"

"Probably. What about an aircraft?"

"Not impossible, I guess, if there are flights between say Tijuana and the south-east, which I suppose there must be. Perhaps that is how it happened. It's difficult to think of anything else right now, isn't it?"

Fiona paused, sighing in frustration.

"But, whatever the explanation," she continued, "looking at the big picture, what's inescapable is that, in one way or another, Mexico was connected with that epidemic. The RNA that you and Mucky sequenced is giving us that message loud and clear. By some means, West Nile viruses that originated in Mexico, or modified versions of them, got into those mosquitoes in Ni'ihau, thousands of miles away across the Pacific Ocean. How did that happen?"

Mingzhu shook her head.

"If you or Mucky have any ideas, don't hesitate to tell us," continued Fiona. "Don't worry about making a fool of yourself. You won't. What we need are ideas, any ideas. Over the years, Giles and I have tossed lots around, and trashed most of them before coming up with the answer. In retrospect, some of them were bonkers. But we always got there in the end. It's a wee bit like trying to find your way out of a maze. But it's part of the fun, even if at times frustrating."

"Fiona's right," Giles added enthusiastically, nodding while still wiping a dollop of cream off the corner of his mouth. "And don't feel intimidated by her encyclopaedic knowledge of mosquitoes and the rest. She's an expert on umpteen things these days, thanks to the hours she spends on her laptop. Sometimes – in fact, very often – she ties me in knots."

"And he's not talking about you know what!" Fiona laughed with a wink. "Only joking! Sorry, Giles, carry on!"

Giles leant forward to lift a tall bottle of straw-coloured liquid from the centre of the table.

"Thank you, Dr Cameron. Too much of this *tuak*, I think. Now, where was I? Oh, yes. I was about to say that, although the origin of that virus is a mustery, there must be an answer. And, if we stick together, we'll find it."

"Which takes me to the other big question…" said Fiona. "The extra piece of RNA that's there, the part that probably makes it a killer. As I've said, I've searched the journals and databases and seen nothing like it in any other virus. Any ideas, either of you… Mingy?"

While Giles poured himself another cup of tea, Mingzhu doodled a sketch of the virus's RNA on a linen napkin.

"As you say, Fiona," Mingzhu replied, "that extra piece of RNA must have been put there specifically to make the virus the killer that it is. It's the bullet in the gun. We need to know why. What exactly does it do? Was it synthesised in a lab? If so, how did whoever it was know it would have such a terrible effect? Or was it taken from a natural source? Excised from the RNA of a totally unrelated virus, for example?"

"All very good questions, Mingy. Giles, how do you think it was done?"

"Step by step, I imagine, working backwards," Giles replied. "Wouldn't you? First, they decided which biochemical process in which cell type they wanted to knock out or exploit. Then, they asked themselves: 'What are the key enzymes, receptors, or other proteins that influence that process?' After choosing their target, they thought about what controls it. They looked at genes, gene enhancers, promoters, and so on. And, finally, they decided on the most effective way of making a hit. So… one step at a time."

Fiona laughed.

"Crivens! Yer seem t'noo an awful loot! Are you sure you havna been in the boggin business yersel?"

"Don't be alarmed, Mingy!" said Giles. "It's that *toak* again. Booze always brings out the frustrated actress in her. Believe it or not, she used to go to a drama school in Scotland. To her Gaelic ears, what she just said sounded like something from Shakespeare."

"If yer nae careful, I'll gie ye a skelpit lug!" Fiona followed up with a wink in Mingy's direction.

"I'm not sure I like Gaelic!" Mingzhu laughed, receding into her chair.

"Nor does anyone, Mingy, except a handful of people north of the border," Giles retorted. "But, to be truthful, I misled you. That wasn't Gaelic. Believe it or not, it was English. Hard to believe, I know. But that's how they talk in places like Glasgow."

"Not true, Mingy," said Fiona. "A few perhaps, in the poorest areas. And anyhow, you should hear how English villagers used to talk in places like Somerset and Yorkshire around the time Giles was born. If you could call it talking… more like animal noises."

"Perhaps we should change the subject!" Mingzhu suggested, a little flushed. "I was thinking earlier what a shame it is how some scientists get drawn into such horrible work, like germ warfare and nuclear bombs. Imagine being employed by a company that develops germs and deadly chemicals, knowing that their only function will be to kill people. Why do you think they do it, Prof… lots of money?"

"Not if the military's behind it, Mingy, as it must be in this case," Giles opined. "I can't imagine they get paid any more than the rest of us. Maybe it's the intellectual challenge of creating a designer genetic code or a complicated molecule, that grabs them, like solving the ultimate crossword puzzle."

"What about patriotism? I imagine some could do it for that reason, couldn't they? They might not like the idea, but feel they should do it for their country. Americans, in particular, can be pretty patriotic, can't they?"

"You're so right," Fiona groaned. "But is that a strength or a weakness? That's the issue. I think it's the latter. Personally, I have no time for patriotism. I might be a Scottish nationalist at heart, but that's to do with health services, the economy, education, that sort of thing. I'll never be patriotic. To me, it makes no sense. A nation should have to earn your loyalty, respect, and love, not get it as an inalienable right merely because you were born on its soil. That's the kind of stupid mentality that causes wars."

Before either Giles or Mingzhu could respond, a familiar voice from the entrance to the terrace asked a question nobody was in the mood for.

"What does everyone think about religion?" said Mouktar. "That causes wars, too."

"Well, that's quite a question to ask a Chinese muslim, a Scottish protestant, and… well, you know what I am!" said Giles in surprise.

During the uncomfortable silence that followed, Mouktar finished drying his hands on a hand towel he had brought with him, dropping it to the floor as he returned to the table.

"Isn't the restaurant's washroom available, Mucky?" Giles enquired, trying not to show his discomfort at Mouktar's display of untidiness.

"Pardon, Prof?"

"I recognised the hand towel as one from our room. They're green in the communal washrooms, red in the bedrooms. So, I asked if the restaurant's WC is out of action."

"Er... not that I know of," replied Mouktar hesitantly. "I didn't look. I just prefer to use ours. That's all."

"Why's that? It's ten times the distance."

"I just do, that's all. Never have liked public ones."

"I see," said Giles. "Okay then, everyone, I'm off to relieve myself. While I'm away, could someone order another pot of tea, please? Some more of that *oolong* would do nicely."

Keen to escape from any possibility of a theological discussion, Mingzhu went to look for the waiter.

"I heard what you were saying about patriotism, Fiona," Mouktar continued. "But what do you think about loyalty to your religion? That's rather different, isn't it?"

"Different?" replied Fiona. "Well, I would call it adherence, not loyalty. And the real difference, I'd say, is that you can *choose* your religion, can't you? You can also choose *not* to have one, or to keep an open mind. You can also choose where you live. But you can't choose where you're born. That's done for you. Right?"

"Yes."

"What are your feelings about MECCAR's mission, and INDOMED's, Mucky? They're tied up with religion in a way, aren't they?"

"It's more complicated than that, Fiona. Religion comes into it, for sure. But what it's really all about is regaining the glory of a past civilisation, in fact two civilisations – one in Baghdad, the other in Spain. They were times when Islamic scholars were the greatest in the world. And I don't mean just scholars of theology, but of every conceivable subject, especially medicine and the sciences. It was a culture in which knowledge, teaching, and the discovery of new things transcended almost everything else. It really was a Golden Age. Those Islamic scholars changed the world, not only theirs, but everyone's... then and now. That's what it's all about. But I thought you knew that... no?"

"Yes, I did," said Fiona. "I just wanted to hear it from you, that's all. It's a great aspiration. And, thanks to MECCAR, it's off to a flying start. Let's hope we can make our small contribution."

"I have a feeling we will."

"I'm sure you know MECCAR has been criticised for its methods: specifically its secrecy, and the way it announces its discoveries on websites instead of in journals. Are you comfortable with that?"

"Absolutely, for the simple reason it works," said Mouktar. "I don't think it matters what others say. The goal is too important. We're all committed to achieving it at any cost."

"At *any* cost?"

"Yes."

"By any methods?"

"Pretty well. What matters is the end result. If it saves lives, reduces suffering, it must be the right thing to do."

Fiona frowned.

"What if, for example…hypothetically… oh… never mind."

Sensing the alcohol was leading her in a direction she would regret, Fiona took advantage of Mingzhu's return to change the subject.

"Hi, Mingy. Welcome back. Mucky and I were just talking about MECCAR's somewhat controversial methods, which I assume INDOMED will also be using. I was about to mention that Giles has been an ardent admirer from the outset. I don't think either of you know he's an expert on Islamic and Arab history, do you? He got hooked when living in the Middle East. His parents were diplomats there. Anyhow, now's not the time to go into that. Better get it from the horse's mouth."

Mingzhu stared at Fiona blankly.

"Sorry, Mingy! You look confused. The bit about a horse means it would be better if you heard it from Giles than from me. And, speak of the Devil… there I go again! Here he comes."

Fiona waited until Giles had returned to his chair.

"Giles, I was just telling our two young colleagues how you spent your youth in the Middle East."

"Ah, yes," replied Giles enthusiastically. "Never got to your neck of the woods though, Mucky. Nearest was Aden. I'll tell you all about it one day. But not now. Here comes the tea. As soon as we've emptied the pot, I'm off to bed. And I suggest you all do the same. We've got an early morning ahead of us if we're going to get to Puncak Mundi in good time."

Chapter Sixteen

After a bone-shaking drive along the road that led from the north coast through the island's forests and farms to its highest point, Giles parked the car on the roadside to view the panorama and to stroll around the temple of Puncak Mundi.

"Come on, everyone, time to get out," he urged. "We don't have too long."

"Of course," replied Fiona, as if her thoughts were in another world.

As exhilarating as the scenery was, she had been unable to rid her mind of the previous evening's conversation. By her own admission, the extra piece of RNA in the virus had become an obsession. Her breakfast, delicious though it was, had been consumed in a haze. Giles's oft repeated advice to take a rest whenever the solution to a problem seemed out of reach had never taken root in her case, at least not sufficiently to put a question of this importance to one side. She'd remained the same throughout the morning, saying little while going through the motions of admiring the countryside. Giles's attempts to snap her out of it by singing English folk songs, joking about the bumps and potholes, and swearing at each passing motorcycle that threw stones at the windscreen, had been to no avail.

And yet, now, at the very moment he was applying the handbrake, for no apparent reason, she suddenly came alive.

"You go ahead and leave me here for a while," she said, as Giles stood on the side of the road with the others, waiting to close the door.

"Er… okay… as you wish," he said. "We'll make sure we stay in sight."

Having seen the same look on her face many times in the past, Giles knew that whatever was on her mind was too important to interrupt. Closing the door gently, he beckoned the others with a finger to follow him to a roadside trader.

Upon returning to the car, no more than ten minutes later, they found it empty. Alarmed, given the number of young men who had been around but were now nowhere to be seen, Giles peered inside and saw that Fiona's handbag was also missing.

"Chances are she's gone to the washroom," Giles offered, attempting to calm the others. "Mingy, could you go and have a look? Meanwhile, Mouktar, you explore the bushes and trees in case she heard a bird or something. You know what she's like. I'll go and look around the temple."

Before Giles had reached the buildings, Fiona appeared from behind one of the ornamental columns, bare-footed and with her hair in disarray.

"Giles! You won't believe this!" she cried, running towards him. "Where are the others?"

"Looking for you."

"Oh, sorry! It was so hot and humid in the car, I went to get some fresh air. Ouch! Hold on. I need to put my sandals back on. The earth is scorching."

By the time she had fastened the buckles, Mingzhu and Mouktar were approaching in haste.

"I've made a huge discovery," she announced before they could say a word. "Something's been bugging me all morning, but I just couldn't put my finger on it. Remember this moment, because I'm sure it's a breakthrough. I can feel it in my bones. But first, let's go into the shade of that banyan tree."

As the others propped themselves against the tree's roots, each with a topped green coconut from the trader, Fiona collected a stick from the grass. Giles could feel his pulse racing, so reminiscent was the atmosphere of when she had cracked the puzzle of Ahmad Sharif's writing on the *Achilles* website report. He recalled how, on that wet night in Oxford, she had made meticulous preparations for her presentation and dressed for the occasion. The present circumstances could hardly have been more different. But her mood was tangibly the same. He knew she was onto something.

"Right," she started, "about sixty years ago, two scientists, one English, the other American, entered a pub in Cambridge to announce they'd discovered what they called 'the secret of life'. What they were talking about, of course, was the structure of DNA, the molecule that explains so much in the living world around us: how a tiny seed that settled in the bark of a tree grew into this amazing banyan; why every single one of the seeds in its fruits contains a similar coded message; and how, millions of years ago, honeybees gave rise to the ancestors of the wasps that have made their nest in its branches. It's all down to DNA. What I have to announce is also to do with DNA, but more to do with death than life. It's the explanation of why a single bite from one of those mosquitoes on Ni'ihau was invariably fatal."

She paused to write a series of eighteen letters in the soil with the stick.

CTGCGTGCTGTCTCGTGC

"Come round this side, all of you."

Giles encouraged the others to follow her instruction.

"This series of letters is the only part of the genetic code of the *Achilles* gene's DNA that ever stuck in my mind," Fiona continued. "Why? Well, as you know, like every other gene in our bodies, the genetic code contained in *Achilles'* DNA is a long series of the four chemicals, namely cytosine, thymine, adenine, and guanine, which we abbreviate to C, T, A and G. The precise order of thousands of those four letters in our genes determines everything about us. Tiny differences can have huge effects on the proteins that our cells manufacture, which, in turn, determine how we look, how we think, our health, and so on.

"On average, the total genetic code in any two of us differs by only one in a thousand letters. And yet, Giles has the misfortune to look like Giles, and Mouktar is a good-looking hunk. Even the DNA of chimpanzees differs from ours by only about four per cent. It was the colossal impact of such small differences that fascinated me about genetics as a student. I sometimes get mesmerised by those four letters. And so, it was one evening when I was studying a picture of the *Achilles* gene, that I noticed something unusual about part of it. And that's the part that you now see in front of you."

Fiona paused, waiting for the others to say something.

"Do you notice anything?" she pressed.

"Well," said Giles in an instant, "I can see something pretty obvious. There isn't a letter A, only the other three."

"Which is exactly why it caught my eye in the first place. But there's more to it than that."

After they'd been staring at the line of letters for another minute or so, she gave them a clue.

"In a way, it's something to do with maths."

"Ugh! Another one of those?" Giles groaned, scratching his head. "I might have guessed."

Mingzhu was the first to pick up the courage.

"I'm quite good at patterns," she said hesitantly. "In fact, I think most Chinese must be, because our writing has about ten thousand characters in common use. We have to remember them all. I'm wondering… but I'm not yet sure… if what you've written is every possible combination of the three letters."

"Well done, Mingy!" said Fiona. "It's not obvious when they're all together like that, but if you put a space between every three, it looks like this."

Fiona wrote the letters again, this time as six sets of triplets.

CTG CGT GCT GTC TCG TGC

"There we are," she said. "Why didn't you spot that, Professor Giles Butterfield FRS?"

"If you'd given me more time…"

"Never mind," Fiona interjected. "Now, whenever a gene in one of our cells is activated, it causes the cell's enzymes to synthesise a specific protein, doesn't it? The series of letters in the gene's DNA tells the enzymes the order in which different amino acids should be strung together to create a particular protein. It's a set of instructions, a recipe. But the enzymes don't read the code letter by letter, they read them in groups of three at a time. Each *triplet* represents one word that translates into a specific amino acid. Okay?"

Mingzhu nodded and smiled in her usual polite way, Mouktar remaining expressionless.

"Now, in truth, it's not quite so straightforward, because the gene doesn't transmit those instructions to the enzymes directly, does it? It can't, because genes… almost all of them, anyhow… are in the cell's nucleus, and the enzymes are outside it. There's a wall separating them, the nucleus' membrane. So, nature has got round this by using messenger molecules that act as go-betweens. And these messenger molecules in you and me are RNA molecules. The genetic code in DNA, the series of word-triplets, is first copied into an RNA molecule, and it's that which leaves the nucleus to give the message to the enzymes. The enzymes then obediently string a series of amino acids together in the order instructed to create the desired protein.

"There's something else important too, isn't there? When the code is transcribed from the DNA molecule to the RNA molecule, it isn't copied precisely letter for letter. The Cs, Gs, and As are all copied as such, but T becomes U. In other words, wherever there is the chemical thymine in the DNA, the corresponding RNA contains the chemical uridine. So… returning to the series of triplets that I wrote down, when copied from the *Achilles* gene's DNA to make the corresponding messenger RNA, it would look like this."

Fiona wrote a second series of letters under the first.

DNA = CTG CGT GCT GTC TCG TGC
RNA = CUG CGU GCU GUC UCG UGC

As she did so, a group of curious children from a nearby village gathered around to see what was going on. After shrugging their shoulders at the sight of the letters in the soil, two giggling boys climbed the banyan tree's roots and reached for the fruits to throw at each other. Meanwhile, the girls collected as many leaves as they could reach and placed them into a basket.

"Never mind our little friends," said Fiona. "They're okay."

Standing up straight, she looked round at the others.

"Now, a bit more about the *Achilles* gene, something you may not know much about. But first, any questions?"

They stared at her blankly.

"No? Okay. The *Achilles* gene that sits inside every one of our cells has the potential to kill the cell should it ever turn into a cancer cell, doesn't it? Whenever a cell becomes cancerous, the gene should become active. Its genetic code would then be copied into a messenger RNA molecule in the way I've described, and that would give the cell's enzymes the recipe to make the killer protein. End of cancer cell, end of problem, back to normal. Unfortunately, none of that happens. Why? Because the *Achilles* gene has never acquired a switch to turn it on. Evolution hasn't finished the job. At the moment, it's a suicide bomb without a fuse. Fortunately, thanks to MECCAR and the chance discovery of *Deidamia,* medicine is on the verge of gene therapy to give the *Achilles* genes of cancer cells a switch. But, until then, we will remain vulnerable.

"Next stop, viruses. There are two basic types, aren't there? In one type, such as the ones that cause cold sores and chickenpox, the genes are made of DNA, just like ours. In the other type, to which the West Nile virus belongs, the genes are made of RNA. Now… hold on a second…"

Fiona opened her bag to take out the lab report on the Ni'ihau virus, and found the section that showed the genetic code of its extra piece of RNA.

"Have a look at this everyone. Notice anything?"

Not surprisingly, Giles was the first to respond.

"Good God!" he uttered. "The genetic code of the virus's RNA insertion is identical to part of the RNA that an activated

Achilles gene would produce. Not all of it. It would be too big to fit into a virus. But probably enough to kill any cell the virus infected."

"Exactly," said Fiona. "As a consequence, any cell that the Ni'ihau virus infected… whether in the skin, liver, kidneys, heart, brain, wherever… would be killed. Which is exactly what seems to have happened."

Mingzhu walked up to the tree, now abandoned by the children, and flopped to the ground.

"That's amazing!" she said. "Engineering a DNA virus to contain the *Achilles* gene, or part of it, wouldn't have worked, because the DNA would have remained inactive in whatever type of cell the virus infected. But putting *Achilles* RNA into a virus ensured that every cell infected would promptly be forced to produce the killer protein and die."

Having been quiet up to this point, Mouktar was keen to make a contribution. He raised his hand as if in a classroom.

"Yes, Mucky?"

"Has the genetic code of *Achilles* been published?"

"Yes."

"So, anyone could have come up with this idea?"

"Yes. It doesn't take us any closer to who did it…only what they did and why."

Mouktar thought for a moment.

"It would certainly explain those ulcers, instead of the familiar itchy lumps, where the mosquitoes bit."

"Absolutely."

"Presumably, at least some of the cells in the Hawaiians must have survived long enough to produce new viruses before they died? Otherwise, they wouldn't have spread around the body, would they?"

Fiona nodded enthusiastically.

"Good thinking, Mucky. Do you agree, Giles?"

By now, Giles had joined Mingzhu at the tree, and was fanning himself with his Panama. He was gobsmacked. If Fiona's theory was correct… and he was sure it must be… it was a very smart piece of work. A lot of knowledge, experience, and planning must have gone into it. That's for sure. On top of which, it would have needed a first-class laboratory, in fact more than one.

"Giles, are you in a dream?" Fiona called. "I asked if you agreed, not how many blades of grass are at your feet."

"Pardon?"

"Never mind."

Meanwhile, another question had occurred to Mouktar.

"Can I mention another point, Fiona?" he asked without waiting for the answer. "If you're right, it would also mean the killer protein is lethal only to human cells and not to insect cells, wouldn't it? Otherwise, the virus would also kill the mosquitoes, which obviously it doesn't."

"Quite. But that wouldn't be surprising, Mucky," Giles intervened. "There are big differences between our biochemistry and that of insects."

He looked at Fiona.

"Fiona, my old girl, it really looks as if you've cracked a big nut here. I'm wondering why whoever created the virus decided to exploit *Achilles* to make it so deadly. There must be many genes in nature that contain the genetic code for a lethal protein, which they could have used instead."

"Interesting point, Giles," said Fiona. "There are all sorts of toxic proteins and peptides out there, aren't there? Some bacteria produce them, so do snakes, some toads, mushrooms, even some ants. Yes, why did they choose *Achilles*? I wonder."

After erasing the letters with the fallen frond of a palm tree, the four set off towards the temple to complete the original purpose of their journey. The beautiful, if neglected, ornate red-roofed buildings that had been a source of such fascination when Fiona was reading her Lonely Planet travel guide were now of less interest to her. The urge to return to Nusa Ceningan and get back to work was irrepressible. But would the idea be rejected by Giles, such a firm believer in the value of taking breaks every now and then? And how would Mingzhu and

Mouktar feel about it? They deserved a say in the matter, too.

Trying to take her mind off it, Fiona wandered from the others to chat to an Australian cyclist who had just climbed the steep road from the Pegyuyangan waterfall in the south-west. No sooner had she introduced herself, however, than he explained he needed to fix a punctured tyre urgently, as his girlfriend was waiting for him at Pura Ibu a few miles away. As Giles was now nowhere to be seen, she wished him a safe journey and rejoined Mouktar and Mingzhu, now inside the car.

"You know, you two," she began hesitantly, "I've been thinking. I know I was the one who suggested we should come on this trip – in fact, more than suggested. I absolutely pleaded, didn't I? And also that we should stay here for at least three nights. But now I'm not so sure. The question is whether we'd really enjoy it now we've made this breakthrough. To be honest, I'm itching to get back and get on with it. So, I'm wondering if that's what we should do?"

"You mean go back to Nusa this evening?" Mingzhu asked. "Yes."

"Oh, no!" Mouktar whined. "I think we should forget about work for once and make the most of the trip. After all, we many never get the chance again."

Fiona glanced at Minhzhu, looking for support, but Mouktar made sure she didn't have the opportunity.

"It shouldn't be up to *her*. She's the junior one. And there's the professor to think of. Ask him when he's back."

"Age isn't relevant, Mucky," said Fiona. "We all have equal rights. And anyhow, Mingy has worked as hard as you in the lab. In fact, probably more so, considering she's always at the bench an hour before you. Mingy, how do you feel about it?"

"I'm easy," she sighed, shrugging her shoulders diplomatically. "I don't mind either way. Perhaps the professor should decide. Look, he's coming now."

When Giles arrived, he jumped into the car without a word and started the engine.

"Hold on, Giles, not so fast," Fiona urged. "Where have you been?"

"Why do men of my age sometimes run off into the bushes?"

"To pick berries?"

"That's right."

"Tell me," said Fiona. "What do you think about returning to Nusa tonight, now we've made this great leap forward? It changes things, doesn't it?"

Pausing to lower the window, Giles wafted some fresh air into the car with his Panama.

"Funny you should say that," he said. "I was only just…"

"I disagree," Mouktar interrupted, making no effort to hide his disapproval. "I think we've earned this break."

"You're right about having earned it, Mouktar," replied Giles. "There's no doubt about that one. And I'm sure Fiona agrees. But I have to admit, her brainwave does change things a bit. Think about it. When we decided to come on this little trip, we thought it would prepare us for the next stage, didn't we? We had no idea what the extra piece of RNA was all about. We were hoping a break would clear our heads, and we'd come up with some big ideas. Perhaps that's what happened, at least in Fiona's case, and it did so far more quickly than we imagined. Now we've got to this point, it could be argued we have a moral responsibility not to waste any time. What if another epidemic breaks out somewhere? How would we feel?"

"Yes, that's a good point, Giles," Fiona added with enthusiasm. "We shouldn't lose sight of the fact we're not in this just out of intellectual curiosity, meeting a challenge, helping Teuku, and so on. It's a job… a hugely important one that has the potential to affect many peoples' lives. Sometimes, one can forget that in medical research, especially when sitting in a lab looking down a microscope, or waiting for a chemical analyser to finish. We have a big responsibility on our shoulders. Unlike a paramedic, a surgeon or a nurse, laboratory types like us never meet the people whose lives we save. But they're out there, somewhere, and in vastly greater numbers than any doctor could ever treat in his or her lifetime. And, on this occasion, it's especially true. A few days could make a big difference."

Sensing that Mouktar was not convinced, she decided to illustrate the point.

"Just imagine what might have happened, Mucky – or rather, might not have happened – if Florey and Chain had decided to take a holiday instead of growing those smelly *Penicillium* fungi in their collection of bath tubs and bed pans, or if Banting and Best…"

Fiona stopped in her tracks as Mouktar got out of the car and strutted off to the far roadside, where he remained with his hands buried in his pockets, staring at the distant farm fields.

"My! Does he ever behave like that in the lab, Mingy?"

"Although normally he's easygoing, he is inclined to sulk at times…" replied Mingzhu, "but not to this extent. Perhaps he's not feeling well."

"Okay, why don't we meet him halfway?" Giles suggested, tossing the map in Fiona's direction. "But instead of returning to Nusa tonight, we do so in the morning, and between now and then take the long route back to the hotel to make the most of what's left of the day. If you look at the map, you'll see that if we go south from here, we'll meet a road that leads to the east coast. It should be a pleasant run. And then, this evening, we can have another spread on the terrace."

"Good idea, Giles!" said Fiona. "And if we set off at sunrise, we might even make it to Crystal Bay before boarding the boat. Teuku said it's well worth a visit."

"Okay, that's it then," replied Giles. "So… why don't you jump out and use your Scottish charm on our friend over there?"

Never having seen Mouktar in such a mood, Fiona cautiously made her way across the gravel, trying not to make too much noise lest he took it as a signal to run off. As she arrived at his shoulder, he removed his hands from his pockets to cross his arms defiantly.

"It's you, isn't it, Fiona?" he snarled.

"Yes."

"I could smell your perfume."

After placing a hand gently on his arm, she put Giles's proposition to him. He listened, but said nothing, keeping his eyes on the horizon. Only after several silent minutes, broken by the occasional deep sigh, did he turn to lead the way back to the car.

"Mucky's agreed," Fiona announced softly upon their arrival, giving him a peck on the cheek. "Isn't he a good sport?"

To everyone's surprise, for the rest of the day Mouktar was back to his usual positive amiable self. After all, he pointed out, what more could they want? They were in a beautiful part of the world, a tropical island unspoilt by tourism, and about to tell their boss about something that could put his name on the front pages. He even offered to pay for lunch and to accompany Fiona to the bank of a nearby river to collect some flowers.

Upon reaching Suana, Giles took his foot off the pedal to take in the picturesque scenes of fishing boats, broad yellow beaches, and seaweed farms, before pulling onto the grass verge to visit the limestone cavern of Goa Karang Sari. Although the long climb up steep steps was almost too much for him, with a few breaks on the way and much frivolous pushing and shoving by Fiona and Mingzhu, he was soon squeezing through the narrow entrance to get his first sight of the spectacular Hindu temple that had been created inside the cave so many years ago.

From then on, it was a non-stop drive to the hotel, with Mingzhu and Mouktar asleep on the back seat and Fiona photographing every bird she set eyes on. Apart from the now familiar rattles and one or two backfires, the car performed adequately until they were entering the hotel grounds, at which point a cloud of steam appeared from under the bonnet.

"Damn!" Giles shouted. "Obviously a leak has sprung in the cooling system. And, as I can't imagine we'll get it fixed tonight, it will mean a taxi in the morning… assuming they exist. Do they? Does anyone know?"

"They do," Mouktar groaned, rubbing his eyes, "although you might not recognise them. They're those small blue vehicles you see around. There was one parked near the temple. They're called *bemos*. The woman who sold me the basket told me about them. She'd brought her wares in one. I had a look inside. They're not very comfortable, no proper seats, just a wooden bench on each side. But it would get us there."

During a repeat of the previous evening's dinner on the terrace, this time with the extra excitement of a tropical downpour, Mouktar announced that, as soon as they'd finished, he was going to walk the full length of the beach to enjoy the view of Bali across the moonlit sea.

Fiona glanced at Giles, eyebrows raised.

"Are you sure, Mucky?"

"Why do you ask?"

"Well, it'll be around midnight. Will you be safe? The locals are pretty poor. They probably think we're super-rich."

"Doesn't mean they're criminals though, does it?" replied Mouktar. "And anyhow, I can look after myself."

He flexed his muscles in a gesture of bravado.

"Very impressive, Mucky," said Fiona. "But they wouldn't be much good against a knife. And what about the weather?"

Looking slightly irritated, he said no more.

"As you wish," Giles added. "But when you get back, please try not to wake me up. I'll be having a shower soon and hitting the hay. We didn't cover many miles today, but every one was hard work. While you lot were enjoying the view… or snoozing… all I could see were potholes, stray dogs, and chickens."

"I'll be quiet, I promise."

"Before you go," Fiona asked, "could you do me a favour and bring that basket you bought? I'd like to have a look at it."

"Why?" asked Mouktar.

"I noticed when we arrived there was a stall in the harbour selling baskets, along with pots and wooden bowls. I might get one in the morning if she's still there."

"She might not be, though."

"True, but just in case."

"And, even if she is, she mightn't have any like mine."

"If it's a local style, there must be a good chance it will be similar. It doesn't have to be identical."

"Anyhow, couldn't it wait until breakfast?" said Mouktar. "It's in the bedroom, you see. I'd have to go and get it."

"Perhaps Giles could show it to me while you're out?"

"He said he wants to go to bed… didn't you, Professor?"

"Never mind," said Fiona. "Tomorrow will do."

"Are you alright, Mucky?" Mingzhu asked.

"Yes, of course."

"Nothing's the matter?"

"No. I'm fine thanks, absolutely fine."

Mouktar hesitated before continuing, as if not sure what to say next.

"But I'm worried about Sinbad… you know, leaving him alone in the flat. I wouldn't like him to think he's been abandoned again. It's well known that Jack Russells suffer from separation anxiety. How he survived at sea I cannot imagine."

"You never know," said Mingzhu. "He may be enjoying having the place to himself."

"I hope so. Anyhow, I don't think I'll wait for dessert, as delicious as I'm sure it will be. It's beautifully fresh out there. I love this sort of weather. We hardly ever get it where I come from. So I don't even mind if I get soaked to my skin. See you later."

"Okay," Giles called, as Mouktar leapt onto the grass. "But please remember to be careful when you get back. I'm sure I'll be out like a light."

"I hope so," Mouktar replied.

It was not until well after midnight that Mouktar returned to the hotel. As there was no sign of the others, he walked to his room on the far side, passing the girls' room on the way. Finding his door ajar, he tiptoed inside and closed it quietly behind him. As Giles's bed was empty and he could hear the shower running, he took off his shoes and dropped into the chair by the dressing table.

After a few minutes' flicking through a copy of *Kartini* magazine from the drawer, he saw there was no light visible under the bathroom door. Venturing inside the bathroom, he found it empty, the walls and mirrors dripping in condensation. The basket from the market, which he had placed behind the door, was now on its side under the sink, its lid detached and lying a few feet away. Giles's bath towel, which had been on one of the brass hooks when they'd left for dinner, was nowhere to be seen.

Still in his socks, Mouktar ran to the girls' room and hammered on the door. Fiona answered in her dressing gown, looking distressed.

"Fiona, where's the professor? He's not in his room."

"Yes, I know, Mucky. Come inside."

Mouktar entered to find Mingzhu lying on the bed, her face buried in a pillow.

"What's happened?"

"He's in hospital, Mucky. He was bitten by a snake getting into the shower."

"What! Another cobra?"

"No, a blue krait, the hotel owner said."

"That's even worse! They're terrible. A bite can kill you in hours."

"Yes, he said that too," replied Fiona. "Giles has no idea where it came from. He didn't see it until it bit his foot. After hitting it with the toilet brush, he took the leather thong from your basket and used it as a tourniquet round his ankle. Then he ran to Reception. By a huge stroke of good fortune, there's a medical centre nearby. It's just ten minutes by foot. You go along the coast with the sea on your right, turn left, second right, and in a few yards you're there."

"A medical centre *here*? I never imagined…"

"Yes, fortunately. The owner rushed him in his car, and a nurse gave him an antidote. We wanted to stay, but they wouldn't let us. He was on a trolley when we left."

"Will he be okay?" asked Mouktar.

"It's too soon to know. The antivenin arrived only last week from Thailand. Otherwise, they wouldn't have had any. The doctor said without it Giles would have had no chance."

"Did he say what his chances are?"

"About fifty-fifty."

"Incredible, isn't it?" said Mouktar. "He escapes from a cobra near that temple and then gets bitten by something even worse."

"If you'd like to see it, it's under a bush outside his door… or, at least what's left of it. The hotel owner's son chopped it up with a spade. It's got black stripes on its back."

"Yes, I know," said Mouktar.

"Oh! You saw it?"

"No."

"So how did you know about the stripes? Do you have kraits in Djibouti?"

"Er… no. We have other snakes, though."

"But not kraits?"

"No."

"I see."

"I know what they look like, because I've been interested in snakes ever since medical school. There used to be a rod of *Asclepius* over the gate… you know, the stick with a snake coiled round it."

"I can see you're quite an impressionable laddie, then?" said Fiona. "Much more so than me. I was at St Andrews, but didn't get hooked on lions."

She raised her necklace to show him the university's crest engraved on its silver charm.

"Ha! But you do like cats, don't you?" said Mouktar. "The professor told me."

"That's true. Anyhow, the nurse said she'd call if there was any news. Otherwise, if all goes well, they'll probably discharge him in about forty-eight hours."

"Should we let Teuku know?"

"We have done. He said he'd have INDOMED's helicopter ready to take him to a hospital in Bali, if necessary. It seems it would only take ten minutes to get here, and then another twenty to Denpasar."

"What could they do there that they can't do here?" Mingzhu asked from under a blanket.

"Artificial respiration, I imagine," Mouktar answered grimly. "The krait's poison paralyses your muscles, so you can't breathe."

As Mingzhu started sobbing again, Fiona placed a hand on her shoulder and sat on the bed beside her.

"Don't worry, Mingy. I've got a feeling he'll be okay. He may not look it, but he's a tough nut. When he was young he survived a dose of cholera in Iraq, and a few years later a sting from a scorpion in Yemen. And he put on a tourniquet. That will have helped, won't it, Mucky?"

"I'm not sure, actually," replied Mouktar. "Let's hope so."

Chapter Seventeen

Convalescing in the villa, Giles was beginning to feel restless. The dose of antivenin from Bangkok had done its job well and he'd been spared the complication of a wound infection. Rather than the ordeal he'd been expecting, his time in the medical centre had been little more than an inconvenience. Never one to waste time, he'd taken the opportunity to write his monthly letter to Conrad in Cape Town and to draft a report to Sir Quentin, in each case carefully avoiding any mention of the incident. Though he had urged the others to return to Nusa ahead of him, they'd refused to do so, Fiona spending her time sketching plants in the hotel garden and Mingzhu lazing on the beach, while Mouktar went off for scuba diving lessons with a group of vacationing New Zealanders.

But now they were back, Giles was itching to make progress.

"Fiona!" he called through the bedroom door. "I can't take much more of this. I don't need to be in bed. As it's past eleven, why don't I get up for some brunch? Mucky and Mingy must have finished by now. They're bound to be here soon with something to get our teeth into."

"Okay, if you insist," said Fiona. "By the time you're dressed, I'll have prepared something more solid to get them into."

"Thanks, but nothing too Indonesian, please," said Giles. "I'm not in the mood. Some good old-fashioned scrambled eggs on buttered toast would do nicely, and a pot of that Yorkshire tea we brought along."

"Aye aye, sir! Three scrambled *Ayam Cemanis* coming up."

"On, no thank you! The last time I suffered black eggs was in Hong Kong many years ago. They left a wound that still hasn't healed."

"They were Chinese preserved eggs, I imagine," replied Fiona, laughing. "These look like normal fresh eggs. So you can relax."

By the time Giles was on his last piece of toast, Mouktar and Mingzhu were on the doorstep. Having looked up the genetic code of *Achilles*, they were able confirm that Fiona had been right – the code of the extra piece of RNA in the Ni'ihau virus was, indeed, identical to part of the RNA molecule that an activated *Achilles* gene would produce in an infected human cell.

"So, where should we go next?" Giles asked, his eyes flicking between the two young assistants as if they were students in one of his college tutorials.

As usual, Mingzhu was the first to make a suggestion.

"As the insertion corresponds to only part of an *Achilles* RNA molecule, we should probably check whether the virus is, in fact, lethal to human cells, shouldn't we?"

"And how should we do that?"

"Get some cultures of human cells, infect them with the virus, and see what happens. We've got good stocks of cultured human fibroblast cells. So we could use those."

"Perfect!" exclaimed Giles. "Off you go, then. But Fiona had better keep an eye on you. So keep her up to date. We don't want this little blighter escaping into the lab."

***

It was while Fiona was having a break in Giles's office, at the same time keeping one eye on Mingzhu through the glass wall, that she raised an issue that had been troubling her since they'd left Nusa Penida.

Raising her feet onto the desk and pulling her white coat tightly around her waist in a way Giles knew always meant serious business, she waited for him to finish typing his sentence.

"Giles, sorry to interrupt, but can you stop there? There's somethingworrying me about Mucky."

Giles turned in his chair to look at her over his glasses.

"I know what you're going to say," he said. "He can be moody, I agree. I thought the incident at the temple might have been a special case, but he reacted badly when I insisted you supervise him, didn't he? We'll just have to cope with it, I'm afraid."

"It's not that."

"No?"

"No. It's more important, much more important."

Giles closed the lid of his laptop and placed his glasses to one side.

"You know that basket he bought in the market, Giles, the one I took a liking to? Do you remember how I asked if he could let me have a look inside? I wanted to be sure they were clean enough for food before getting one for myself. It would only have taken a second or two. But he wouldn't. I thought that was unhelpful, but, rather than make an issue of it, I let it drop."

She paused while waiting for Mouktar to move away from the refrigerator outside the office door.

"Now…" she continued, lowering her voice, "I don't know if you noticed at the time, but the leather strap attached to the lid of the basket was tied in a double knot. That was what you used for a tourniquet, wasn't it?"

Giles nodded.

"Where did you find it? On the basket?"

"No," replied Giles. "The basket was behind the door, and the strap was on the floor beside it. If it had been knotted, I certainly wouldn't have wasted precious time undoing it. I would have used something else, like the chord of my dressing gown."

"That's what I assumed," said Fiona pensively. "How long were you in the shower?"

"The usual time, ten minutes or so."

"And you were bitten as you were getting out?"

"Yes. As I've said before, I'd put my leg between the two

plastic curtains and it got me on the foot. God, it was painful! Far worse than that scorpion years ago."

"I wonder why Mucky put the basket there, and didn't leave it in the bedroom? It was an odd place, wasn't it?"

Giles stared at her.

"What are you thinking?"

"I'm wondering if the snake had been inside it all along, and Mucky put it there for a purpose…"

Fiona paused, checking to make sure no one was listening outside the room.

"Think about it. He wouldn't let me look inside, and the lid was secured tightly with that strap. He took it straight to your room and, while there, must have untied the knot and left the basket in the bathroom. Why?"

"I don't know," said Giles. "He also bought a batik beach towel at the market. It was hanging by the sink. Perhaps that had been in the basket? He took it out, hung it up, and left the basket on the floor?"

"Possible, of course. But he took his small canvas bag with him to the market, didn't he? He might have brought the towel back in that, and the basket contained you know what. After all, if all it contained was the towel, why was the knot tied so tightly?"

"It was pretty windy."

"But why a *double* knot?"

"Good point. I'd been assuming the snake had been under the bed or somewhere, and entered the bathroom while I was in the shower."

"Perhaps that's what happened," said Fiona. "I hope so. But how did it get into the bedroom? Was the window open?"

"No. The air conditioning was on. But I've noticed the maid leaves the bedroom doors open when she's cleaning."

Giles eyed Mouktar as he took a bottle from one of the incubators, and proceeded to pipette the rose-coloured cell culture medium into a series of small plastic dishes.

"You're suggesting he did it deliberately? That he wanted to…?"

"It's pretty suspicious, isn't it?"

"But why?"

"What about this scenario?" said Fiona. "We can't be sure why Mouktar went to Jordan before coming here, can we? He said it was to give his side of the story of what happened in Honolulu. Quite plausible. But we don't know if it's true. What if he'd been summoned for another reason? What if Aram's sudden disappearance after Sir Q's sherry party was not because he was upset by the idea of you and me having an affair, but to tell Rashid Yamani what Jane had said during the sherry party… about sending Brigitte Dubois-Yusuf's ID card to Rome? Rashid would surely have put two and two together and concluded we knew the truth behind Ahmad Sharif's death, but for some reason had been keeping quiet about it. 'But why? And for how long?' he would have asked himself. 'Is their silence going to last forever? Or have they been gathering more evidence before going to the police or blackmailing me?' There would be only one way of eliminating the threat. And you know as much about Rashid's methods as I do."

"So, you're suggesting Mucky was instructed to finish me off? That he'd bought the snake in the market, hidden it in the basket, placed that in the bathroom, and loosened the leather strap, knowing I would take a shower while he was out walking?"

"It's not impossible, is it?" said Fiona. "After all, a blue krait would have been a very good choice. Apparently, it's the most poisonous snake around here. Without a shot of antivenin, the chances of surviving a bite were very small. Mouktar seems to know a lot about snakes. And he seemed genuinely surprised when I told him there was a medical centre on our doorstep."

"When you put it like that, it does sound suspicious, I must say. But can you buy kraits?" "I don't know. You can buy cobras, can't you?"

Fiona stared ahead for a moment. "Do you think I'm crazy, Giles?"

"I learnt a long time ago never to let that thought cross my mind, Fiona. But would Rashid give such an important job to a complete amateur?"

Fiona shrugged her shoulders.

"He might think Mucky wouldn't attract suspicion. And it would be rather difficult to send a hitman here, wouldn't it?"

"But if I'm in the firing line, it means you must be, too," said Giles. "So, if he'd succeeded, you'd be the next in line. And that would look pretty suspicious, wouldn't it... both of us being killed in accidents?"

"Not if they were very different," replied Fiona, "yours a snake bite and mine falling off a cliff, for example."

"But why would Rashid have donated so much money to the College if he wanted to get rid of us? It wouldn't make sense, would it?"

"I don't know," said Fiona. "He might do so to deflect any suspicion away from himself. Or perhaps there's something we haven't thought of."

Chapter Eighteen

It was during one of their lunchtime meetings that Giles got Teuku up to date with their progress since returning from Nusa Penida. He'd begun by taking out his fountain pen and sketching a simple representation of the Ni'ihau virus on his napkin.

"It looks a bit like this, Teuku. As you know, the little bugger is a relatively harmless West Nile that's been taken to pieces and reassembled with an extra piece of RNA in the middle. The big mystery was what this extra piece was all about. The breakthrough came when Fiona realised that its nucleotide base sequence, its genetic code, is identical to part of the RNA molecule that an *Achilles* gene would produce when activated, specifically the part that instructs cells to make the killer protein."

Giles flipped the napkin over and made another sketch on the other side.

"Since we got back from our trip, Mingzhu and Mouktar have confirmed that Fiona was absolutely right. So, what we think happens when the virus infects one of our cells, any cell anywhere in the body, is that it not only causes the cell to manufacture more viruses in the usual way, but it also causes it to make the killer protein. This starves the cell of energy and eventually it dies, in the process releasing the new viruses that infect more cells. This is why wherever the mosquito bites, an ulcer develops owing to tissue necrosis where normally there'd only be an itchy red bump. And, from there, it spreads throughout the body, killing every cell it infects."

Teuku put his chopsticks down to take the napkin from Giles's hand.

"Presumably the virus multiplies before the cell dies?"

"Yes, we did some experiments on that. Many cells are killed very quickly, but others survive long enough to release a host of new viruses when they die. We're still working on that."

"Sounds pretty sophisticated stuff, Giles. I can see I made a very good choice with you two Brits. But, of course, I knew that already."

Teuku twisted his trunk to give himself a pat on the back.

"So, to summarise, Giles, let me be one hundred per cent sure I've understood. It goes like this? If the *Achilles* genes that are in all our cells each had a DNA switch, they would immediately become active if a cell ever became malignant. This would lead to the production of RNA within the cell that, in turn, would cause it to manufacture the killer protein. It would be a four-stage process: one, the switch detects the cell is multiplying out of control and turns on *Achilles*; two, the gene produces the RNA; three, the RNA directs the cell to manufacture the protein; four, the protein kills the cell."

"Yes, that's right," said Giles.

"Now…" continued Teuku, "effectively, what the Ni'ihau virus does is to give every cell a dose of the same type of RNA. The viruses do to *normal* cells what activated *Achilles* genes should do to *cancer* cells."

"Precisely!"

"Gee, that's real smart."

Giles nodded enthusiastically. "It's not just smart," he replied. "It's *bloody* smart! What really impresses me is its simplicity. If it hadn't been devised for something as ugly as germ warfare, it would be a thing of beauty."

"So, what's next maestro?"

"You'll recall that the strain of West Nile virus that was used as the starting point was a hybrid of two Mexican strains, which, as far as we can tell, has never been described before. Part of the virus came originally from the Mercate strain, and the rest from the Tabasco strain. You also know that hybrids formed from two strains of viruses are known to occur in nature. They can be formed when two different strains infect the same cell at the same time. The cell starts manufacturing both strains at once, and bits of one virus get joined up to bits of the other. It's as if two car mechanics start stripping down the engines of a VW and a BMW at the same time, and then when they're reassembling them, they mix up the parts. When they've finished, both engines work, but each is now a mixture of the two – in other words, a hybrid."

"And so, the big question is, how and where the West Nile hybrid was formed?" asked Teuku.

"That's right," replied Giles. "And why hasn't it been described before? Did it occur naturally, or was it created artificially? The former doesn't seem likely, as the two strains are normally found at opposite ends of Mexico. Birds don't migrate between the two regions, and it's an impossible journey for a mosquito. So, our guess is it was probably created in a lab. But, if so… why? What was the purpose of going to all that trouble?"

"And why Mexican strains?"

"Absolutely."

"Perhaps it was to point the finger of suspicion at the Mexican government should the programme ever go public?"

"But why a hybrid, not just a single Mexican strain?"

"Good point," said Teuku. "Well, to look on the bright side, Giles, the bigger the puzzle, the bigger the publicity we get when you sort it out, which I'm sure you'll do. And the bigger the publicity, the better it'll be for INDOMED."

Teuku reached for the bottle of red wine that had been waiting in the centre of the table.

"Let's drink to that," he said. "I wonder what your British palate will think of this. You probably didn't know Bali has a wine industry. You've heard of New World wines and Old World wines. Well, these days there's also what they call New Latitude wines, from places like Indonesia, Brazil, India, and Thailand. The winery in Bali is called *Sababay*, and this is my favourite. Cheers!"

"Cheers."

"What do you think?"

Giles sniffed the glass and took a mouthful.

"Pretty good, I must say."

"Quite a coincidence, isn't it?" said Teuku. "After all your involvement with that *Achilles* gene, it seems to have gone full circle and come back to haunt you… or, perhaps, I should say to *taunt* you. Ha!"

Teuku broke off to take a long sip of his wine.

"A man called Alan Moore once said there's no such thing as a coincidence, Teuku, only the illusion of one."

"Oh yeahs? Who was he, Giles?"

"An English writer."

"Do you believe him?"

"Ask me again, when it's all over."

Chapter Nineteen

It had been more than an hour since Fiona had disappeared into the villa's bedroom, her hair wrapped in a towel, to organise the many photos she'd taken since their arrival from Oxford. After procrastinating for several days, a message from Ros, her legal secretary friend in Oxford, requesting a selection had given her a push. Meanwhile, Giles had been getting up to date with his backlog of emails, the villa's wi-fi having been down after a contractor had sliced through a cable while working on INDOMED's latest addition, an auditorium overlooking Secret Bay.

"Giles, Giles!" Fiona called excitedly, the towel falling to the floor as she ran across the living room towards the study. "Are you there? I've got something to show you."

Giles appeared at the doorway in his dressing gown and slippers.

"I've come across something quite extraordinary," said Fiona. "But first, let's sit down."

She pushed him into the armchair, and held her mobile phone in front of his eyes.

"Too close?"

Giles lifted his glasses onto his forehead.

"Not now."

"Okay. I've been sorting through my photo collection, putting them in different folders and choosing the best ones for Ros. And I was going through the shots of Mexico City when I spotted something. Do you remember when we were in that restaurant and I ran outside to follow a guy who had a passing resemblance to Steve? He was with a rough-looking friend, who had had an altercation with the barman."

"How could I forget?"

"Then you'll also remember I took a photo of them getting into their cars. I'm not sure now why I took it. It was a kind of reflex. But this is it here. They'd parked at an angle to the kerb between two vans. The guy I thought might have been Steve had already got into the one on the left. Forget about the cars, though. The interesting things are their number plates. As you can see, the plate on one of the cars was yellow, and the other one was orange. This sparked my curiosity. I wondered if they were from different countries. However, when I zoomed in, I saw this wasn't so. They were registered in different parts of Mexico. Here's the one on the left. You'll see above the registration number it says 'Baja California' in a sort of longhand script. And, if you look at the plate of the other car in the next screenshot… you'll see it says 'Tabasco' in white capitals at the bottom."

Giles took the phone from her hand.

"Indeed I do."

"So, the left-hand car was registered in Baja California, and the other one in Tabasco. Ring any bells?"

"Do you think I've been asleep the past few days?" said Giles.

"So, what d'you think?" pressed Fiona. "Could it be just a coincidence that the cars came from the same two parts of the country, thousands of miles apart, as the strains of virus that had got combined to form the Ni'ihau hybrid?"

"Could be, I suppose. Why not?"

"*And also* that Steve, a world expert on *Achilles*, could have been driving one of them?"

Giles looked at her.

"*And* that he was in Mexico City during a congress on virus genetics?" said Fiona. "Could it be all too much of a coincidence?"

"I don't know what to say, quite frankly, Fiona. If we assume it was Steve, why would he be in that sort of company? After what happened to him, I could understand if he'd slipped down the social ladder, but not to the bottom of the cess pit in the cellar."

"I'm going to bite the bullet, Giles. What if he's involved in the Ni'ihau virus programme, employed by the Pentagon? It could explain a lot. After all, nobody seems to know where he is or what he's doing these days. It wouldn't be the first time a lawbreaker with precious knowledge and rare skills had been taken on by a US government agency. If the CIA and FBI can employ some of the world's best computer hackers, why wouldn't the Pentagon put Steve on their payroll to help create a killer virus?"

"Since when have you been able to read my mind?" said Giles.

"I'll tell you another time. It might embarrass you."

"Ha! It's certainly true that it would fit. And it's quite possible he'd go for it. In his situation, the challenge and the money might be too much too resist. This is getting interesting."

Giles took his glasses off and gave them a polish. "And one thing's for sure. That's the last time I'll complain about you and your photos. Why don't we sleep on it and resume in the morning?"

"More likely toss and turn on it," said Fiona. "It's time for one of my herbal teas. Fancy one?"

"No thanks, but a large D 'n' S would do nicely. There are some fresh limes in the fridge. And I've just of thought of something else to keep you awake."

"What's that?" said Fiona, winking. "A nice cup of cocoa?"

"Not likely! Not the right time. Do you remember, during the congress in Mexico City, a local professor told us about a lady who died on a Hawaiian cruise? She developed an ulcer on her foot, and then went downhill rapidly. The ship's doctor diagnosed septic shock. It had been reported in one of their newspapers."

"Yes."

"And he wondered if a mosquito could have got on board in Hawaii?"

"I remember, yes."

"Well, they took her body off when the ship called into Ensenada."

"Where's that?"
"Pacific coast of Baja California."
"*Baja California*? Are you sure?"
"Yes."
"Presumably, that *has* to be a coincidence?"

Chapter Twenty

"The bits and pieces of the jigsaw puzzle are shown here," Giles explained, pointing to the graphic that was projected onto the large screen overhead. "The beautiful handwriting is Mingzhu's, by the way. I wish I could write Chinese that well!"

INDOMED's new auditorium with its idyllic view across the bay, far removed from unwanted ears and eyes, had been chosen by Teuku as the best place for Giles and Fiona to give a behind doors summary of their progress to his staff. Although neither of them had been too enthusiastic about the idea, fearing it was a security risk, Teuku had thought it essential.

"I agree about the danger, Giles," he'd said as they walked to the building after meeting in his office. "A leak would be disastrous. But it's critical we say something at this stage as a public relations exercise. There's a lot of gossip and speculation going on about what the four of you have been up to. People don't like being kept in the dark. I wouldn't either, if I were in their shoes. And anyhow, I don't think the risk is as great as you imagine. Every one of them has been hand-picked and vetted. I trust them implicitly. They're as committed to INDOMED's mission as I am.

"You don't have to say anything about the Ni'ihau epidemic, by the way. They already know what happened. You can go straight to the virus."

"Fair enough," Giles had sighed, "as long as everyone has signed a non-disclosure agreement and their mobile phones are collected."

"Already done, Giles. Not only that but they've had strict instructions to leave their laptops in the lab or office, on top of which they're not even allowed to take notes. If you spot anybody writing, stop talking and once and let me know. I'll be at the back with the slide projector."

Upon entering the auditorium, Giles had been surprised by the attendance. Just about every scientist and laboratory technologist in the centre seemed to be there, the faculty members in crisp white lab coats, the technologists in light green. With the most senior faculty seated on the front row, it was clear the event was being taken very seriously. The chatter of excited conversation that had been audible from outside the entrance had ceased the moment Teuku had opened the door. No introductions had been necessary. Teuku had merely led Giles to the rostrum, showed Fiona to her seat at the end of the front row, and then climbed the central stairs to take his place in the projection room.

After greeting the audience and giving a brief summary of the background of the project, Giles had indicated to Teuku that it was time to project the first slide. Taking a laser pointer from the linen jacket he'd carefully folded on the table behind him, he circled the first item on the list with the bright spot of red light.

"Thanks to the hard work of Fiona and our two young colleagues here," he said, nodding in the direction of Mouktar and Mingzhu, "we already know what the Ni'ihau virus looks like. It's unique, a genetically engineered RNA virus designed with the singular purpose of killing as many people as possible, as quickly as possible. Whoever created it used the West Nile virus as the starting point, a mosquito-borne species that in its natural state usually causes no ill effects or only a mild flu-like illness in humans. One of the interesting things about it is that it wasn't an ordinary strain of West Nile virus. For some intriguing reason, they'd used a hybrid, a virus that's a mixture of two different strains. One of them was a strain normally found in Tabasco, the tropical region in the south-east of Mexico, while the other one is common in the region of Baja California in the north of the country, bordering on the United States.

"As many of you will know, hybrid viruses can be produced when two different strains of the same species of virus happen to infect the same animal at the same time. The animal's cells start producing both strains at once. In the process, parts of one get attached to parts of the other, producing a virus that's a mixture of the two. On rare occasions, that sort of thing happens naturally in the wild. If that's how this one originated, it would probably have happened in a bird, as birds are the chief reservoirs for West Nile viruses. It would then have been picked up by any mosquito that bit the bird at a later date. Alternatively, it could have been created deliberately, for some reason, in a laboratory. At present, we have no idea which is correct. Given the extreme unlikelihood of two mosquitoes from opposite ends of Mexico, thousands of miles apart, with a mountain range between them, biting the same bird at about the same time, it doesn't seem possible it occurred naturally. But we cannot be sure. The truth is, we don't know.

"Viruses are, of course, composed of proteins and genes. In some species, the genes are made of DNA, like ours are, but in others they're made of RNA. The West Nile virus is an RNA virus, and another thing we discovered about the Ni'ihau version is that it has an extra piece of RNA that is not normally present. Not only that, but this extra piece is identical to part of the RNA molecule that is synthesised by a cell when its *Achilles* gene has been activated. Consequently, when the Ni'ihau virus infects any cell anywhere in the human body, this extra piece of RNA causes the cell to manufacture the *Achilles* protein, which kills the cell. The addition of this extra piece of RNA to the virus could not have happened naturally. It could only have done so in a laboratory.

"So clearly, people who knew a lot about genes and insect-borne viruses were behind its development. That much is inescapable. Which takes us to the next big question on my slide up there."

Giles paused for a moment as he directed the laser pointer at the image again.

"Who were they? Given the resources needed, obviously it must have been state sponsored. And that, of course, points the finger at the Pentagon. It's on record that the US military is very aware of the advantages of using insects to deliver biological weapons. As the American lawyer William Schaap once pointed when considering a mysterious outbreak of dengue fever in Cuba in 1981, 'Dengue and other arboviruses are ideal as biological weapons…' one reason being that they can be 'transmitted easily through the introduction of infected mosquitoes'. As many of you will know, dengue viruses and West Nile viruses are closely related.

"So, either the Pentagon has a secret biological warfare facility hidden on the island, perhaps underground, from which the insects accidentally escaped, or the military developed the weapon somewhere else and used the Ni'ihau islanders as human guinea pigs. Either is possible. The island is the perfect place for a secret laboratory – isolated in the middle of the Pacific, forbidden to tourists, privately owned, just a small group of residents. But, equally, it could have been a test run in which the islanders were used as human guinea-pigs. What better for that purpose than to release the insects with their lethal cargo on a remote island, where its few inhabitants and their ancestors had never been exposed to anything resembling the West Nile virus? It wouldn't be the first time in the history of biological warfare that that sort of atrocity had been perpetrated. I could give you several examples of such crimes committed by the USA, UK, and Soviet Union."

Giles paused and looked around at everyone.

"Any questions… no? In that case, I'll now ask Fiona here to describe an experience we had in Mexico City. It may not be relevant. But it's certainly intriguing. Fiona?"

"Thank you, Professor Butterfield," Fiona began as she walked to replace him on the rostrum.

"Hello everyone, or I should say *Selamat pagi semuanya*?"

There was an amiable nodding of heads and polite greetings in return from those present.

"On the way here from England," she continued , "we called into Mexico City to attend this year's gathering of the International Society for Infectious Diseases. We did so expressly to listen to a presentation on the Ni'ihau epidemic. As it turned out, it didn't tell us much we didn't know already. However, an interesting thing happened during question time. A local professor said he recalled reading a newspaper article about a female passenger on a Hawaiian cruise who had died from an illness that sounded very similar to the one that had just been described. He said the ship's doctor thought it was septicaemia. He didn't mention the name of the ship or the ship's company; nor could he remember the dates. So…"

"Which way was the ship going? To or from Hawaii?" a bespectacled man interrupted from the front row.

Fiona turned to Giles "I don't think the doctor said, did he Giles?"

"No," replied Giles.

"Is there any way of knowing if the doctor's diagnosis was correct, Professor?" asked the man from the audience.

"Not at present," said Giles.

"If it *was* the same illness," Fiona resumed, "it raises the question of how the passenger caught it."

"Had she disembarked in Hawaii for a tourist trip?" the man's neighbour enquired.

"We don't know, sir," Fiona answered.

"I see. Did she tell the ship's doctor she'd been bitten by a mosquito?"

"Again, we don't know," Fiona answered. "There are also plenty of other questions to which we don't have answers. For example, how is it that the mosquitoes seem to have completely disappeared? Are they hibernating somewhere? Did they fly off into the blue yonder? If so, did any make it to the neighbouring island of Kauai? Given the distance, we think it unlikely, but perhaps not impossible. Also, the fact they were biting means they must have been females developing eggs. Where did they lay them? Did they hatch? If not, are they still alive somewhere?

That's very important, because there's a good chance they were infected with the virus."

Her brief contribution thus completed, Fiona remained by the table to await the comments and questions she was sure would begin to flow. But there were none. Were the attendees confused, stunned, disappointed, or simply disinterested? From the rows of blank faces, there was no way of knowing. She was about to return to her seat, when a tall man, who she thought might be an Egyptian, waved his hand.

"Yes?"

"Is it necessary to do any further research?" he asked brusquely. "After all, we've already gathered enough information to make headlines. Although they are of interest, the questions you raised are not really pertinent to INDOMED's mission, are they? Perhaps we should leave things as they stand."

The man glanced around, looking for gestures of support. As there were none, he continued.

"As I'm sure President Crabb would not be pleased to see the Pentagon's dirty washing hanging out to dry, no doubt you'll want your findings to be reported by INDOMED rather than you personally. After all, why take the risk of Crabb knowing it was you who exposed the story? So, why don't we just write up what we've got, and post it on our website? If you give me the data, I'd be happy to relieve you of the burden of the first draft. You must have a lot on your plate."

The man smiled slightly.

"The name's Abboud, by the way. Tadeas Abboud."

Giles's expression gave nothing away. But he knew exactly what was going on. He'd been around long enough to recognise an attempt to hijack credit for the research achievements of others. He'd seen it many times during his career. In some cases, co-authorship of a research paper had been the price for accepting the offer of a special chemical, such as an antibody, some bench space, or a piece of equipment; in others, merely because he or she had been the head of the department in which the work had been carried out. It was an insipid but widely accepted practice that diluted the value of the authorship of publications. But the tactic of proposing collective ownership of a study in an institute's name to avoid revealing the identity of the owners of the work was a new one.

"I'm sorry, I didn't catch your name," Giles responded tersely, making no effort to hide his feelings as he fixed his gaze on the batik of elephants that hung on the far wall behind the speaker. "But never mind. We will write it up eventually, of course, and I will be happy to give you a signed copy of the paper once it's been published."

He looked around at all those present.

"So, does anyone else have any questions? No? In that case, we should adjourn. Thank you for attending."

On their way back to the villa, having left Teuku in the auditorium chatting to one of his staff, Giles and Fiona kept their distance behind the Egyptian as he walked ahead of them, one hand deep in his pocket, the other holding a smartphone to his ear.

"I don't trust that man," Fiona whispered. "Did you notice how he deliberately avoided eye contact on the way out? I saw him chatting to Mucky through the bedroom window this morning, just the two of them. I think we need to watch him."

Chapter Twenty-One

Fanning himself with a banana leaf from the verandah, Giles was stretched on the sofa wearing only the tartan Bermuda shorts he'd bought during their first visit, when Fiona kicked open the front door, her arms overloaded with brown paper bags. The linen suit, cotton shirt, and cravat Giles had chosen for the morning's presentation had been tossed on to one of the dining chairs, his socks and shoes scattered beneath the table.

"Don't tell me they haven't fixed the air conditioning yet!" Fiona exclaimed, dropping the bags to the floor. "It's like a Turkish bath in here. I was fearing the worst when I saw the engineers outside, but never imagined it would be this bad."

She took the leaf from Giles's hand and continued to waft it over his head.

"I'm trying to think of an apt description of you," she giggled, covering her mouth. "I know… an overcooked Burns' night haggis, almost bursting out of its sac."

Giles struggled to rest his back against a cushion, wiping his brow with the back of his hand.

"Thanks for that. It made me feel young again. After all, you could have likened me to a stale haggis, lying on a shelf in the larder."

"Only joking. Don't take offence."

"Too late! "

"To make amends," continued Fiona, "why don't I make a salad with all this stuff from the market? We could take it to Secret Beach. There'll be a breeze down there by now. There always is at this time."

"Good idea. But first, I'm off for my third shower, as cold I can stand, assuming the water hasn't been turned off by our friends out there."

As Giles plodded across the room holding up his shorts, Fiona taunted him in her best Ayrshire accent.

> "Fair fa' your honest, sonsie face,
> Great chieftain o the puddin'-race!
> Aboon them a' ye tak your place…"

"I thought you said you were joking!" said Giles. "Obviously not. And sorry to tell you this, dear, but I've never taken to Burns since being forced at school to decipher something he'd scratched on a pub window. It was a punishment for being late. I couldn't undertstand a word of it, and still can't. Actually, I don't believe any of you lot understand him, either. It's not possible. It's all pretence. He's a kind of national obsession, the only poet you Scots seem to have heard of."

"Not true in my case…" replied Fiona. "And you know it. And the fact you don't understand him means nothing."

"Ha! Do you?"

"Yes, of course!"

"Okay then, what does… er… *sonsie* mean?"

"It's changed over the years," said Fiona. "These days it means plump."

"Oh, does it now? Well, I'll have you know, I'm not plump, just…"

"I said that's what it means *today*. In his day, it was generally used to describe someone whom others admired for his or her qualities. So…?"

"Ha!" said Giles. "Even if that's true, I'm still not sure I like being compared to a pudding… even if it is one of supposedly admirable qualities."

"You're losing your sense of humour, Giles," said Fiona. "I can see I'll have to be more careful. Now, I'll go and get the meal prepared. While you're in the shower, try that Indonesian safflower soap while you're at it. It's nice."

"I'll stick with the usual, thanks."

"As you wish… *fatso*."

***

Secret Beach, barely a thirty-minute amble from the villa, had become one of Fiona's favourite spots on the island. A smooth stretch of fine sand at the foot of a deep bay, protected on either side by tree-covered cliffs, its name had been well chosen. It was one of the few places outside the Scottish isles where she felt completely at one with herself. Lying on her back watching the birds overhead, the turquoise water stretching to Nusa Penida and the waves thundering against the eroded rock face, it was the perfect place to cool down in the heat of the day.

Seeing Giles had woken up and was adjusting himself in the lounger provided by the nearby Villa Trevally, she hastily finished her coconut juice and crawled towards him.

"Giles," she whispered.

"Yes?"

"I've been thinking."

"Always useful."

"Pleased you agree. We've got to return to Mexico, haven't we?"

Giles opened his eyes and pulled down the brim of his Panama.

"I've thought about it a lot," continued Fiona. "And the prospect of leaving this place, not to mention Mingy, who's really grown on me, is painful. But, as I see it, there's no choice. Do you agree?"

"Can we talk about this morning's meeting first?"

"Okay."

"It was strange," said Giles. "I was expecting at least some discussion, given the assembled brainpower. But they seemed lost for words. Rather odd."

"Yes, I agree. The atmosphere wasn't what I'd expected at all."

Fiona reached for the jug of *liang teh* they'd collected in the bar and sucked on one of its pink bendy straws.

"Oops, sorry, what a slurp! Want some?"

"Not just now, thanks."

"Do you know who the guy was who tried to persuade us to call it a day?" asked Fiona.

"Arrived from Cairo quite recently," replied Giles. "That's all I know."

"From his reaction, I suspect your snub upset him. What if he retaliates in some way?"

"What can he do?"

"Leak something."

"To whom?"

"How about the university where Mucky used to be? It would only take a telephone call."

"All calls to and from INDOMED are recorded," said Giles. "Same as MECCAR."

"What if he used his mobile or called from his flat?"

"Same."

"A public telephone, local restaurant?"

"Pass."

Fiona frowned.

"I didn't like the look on his face. And talking of Mucky, I'm still stressing about the reason for his trip to Jordan. About whether it was connected with Aram's sudden departure, whether that snake was planted, and whether…"

"Your imagination's connecting too many dots, Fiona. We've been over all that. But I'll watch him, don't worry. And I doubt if our Egyptian friend would do anything, no matter how he feels. Don't forget, we're here at Teuku's invitation… *and* with the blessing of Rashid. We're important people."

"Suppose so," replied Fiona with a sigh. "So, back to where I was. Was I right? About Mexico?"

"Carry on."

Fiona turned over to lie on her back once more, and covered her face with a towel. "Ah, that's better. This is bliss. It reminds me of…"

"Can you get on with it?"

"Why are you so grumpy today?"

"I'm not. I'm just keen to know what's on your mind."

"Well, it's like this, Giles. As I said, while you were snoozing, I was thinking. We need to know exactly what happened to the passenger on that cruise. It's really important to know if it was anything to do with Ni'ihau. Was the ship's doctor right about the woman having septicaemia? Or had she been bitten by one of the mosquitoes when the ship called into the Hawaiian islands? For me, that's the number one question. And to get the answer, we need to go to Mexico."

"And when we're there, what would we do?"

"Find out which newspaper reported the story, get access to the archives, and take it from there."

"It was *La Jornada*," said Giles. "I heard him telling someone on the way out."

"That's a good start. Presumably it's in Spanish?"

"Yes. But before we jump on a plane, why don't we see if the archives are online? Who knows? There might even be an English version."

"Good point," said Fiona. "As soon as we're back in the villa, that's what I'll do."

"Can I have another forty winks now?"

Fiona handed him a tube of sunscreen from her washbag.

"Only when you've spread this on me."

***

By the time Fiona had finished searching for the article, the moonlight was casting long shadows across the bedroom. Memories of her toils in The Jefferson hotel with Giles's laptop, now collecting dust on the top shelf of his rosewood bookcase in Oxford, had come flooding back. It was promising to be another long night; but, as before, she was determined not to give up until the job was done.

Having found to her relief that www.jornada.unam.mx did, indeed, have an accessible archive, with the help of an online dictionary she had tried several search terms before finding a successful combination. The article's title "Vice-cónsul de San Francisco muere en crucero a Hawái" had answered the question of why the death of a single passenger on a cruise was deemed important enough to be reported in one of the country's national newspapers. The fact that the woman in question had been a high-ranking Mexican diplomat also explained why her body had been taken off the ship at Ensenada, the first and only port the *ss Oosterdam* had been scheduled to call into during its return to San Diego.

Although diagnosed with diabetes many years ago, the column reported, Margarita Díaz had appeared in good health from the first day of the cruise, by night socialising in the Pinnacle Bar and by day swimming in the Sea View Pool, before developing a fever after the ship had left the last port of call in the islands. She had then deteriorated rapidly and died. The ship's surgeon, a Dr Chandra Bandaranaike from Sri Lanka, had diagnosed a bacterial infection of the blood, septicaemia, caused by the spread of infection from a diabetic ulcer on the woman's foot.

"The organisms were probably *Staphylococci*," he had asserted during an interview, "a common cause of skin infections. Although I could not confirm this by culturing a blood sample, my small laboratory not having the equipment, the clinical picture was sufficient. Diabetes is known to lower the body's resistance to infection. Although I gave her large doses of three antibiotics, regrettably it was not possible to save her."

To Fiona, the account sounded reasonable enough. She could imagine that an ulcer infected by a particularly virulent organism might rapidly get out of control in someone with weakened defences. But could he have got it wrong? Over the years, she'd learnt that whenever doctors are trying to pinpoint the cause of an illness, they start with a list of the most likely ones, the differential diagnosis, before doing blood tests, X-rays, and other investigations to narrow the field. However, if Dr Bandaranaike had not been able to do a blood culture, how could he have been so confident? And, if it had *not* been septicaemia, but a virus infection, Fiona knew enough about antibiotics to know they would have had no effect whatsoever.

Clearly, there was enough uncertainty to keep open the possibility that Margarita Diaz had been bitten by one of Ni'ihau's mosquitoes. But two pieces of information were missing, both of which were critical: the exact dates of the cruise and the boat's itinerary. It was certainly clear from the article's publication date that the tragedy had occurred around the time of the epidemic, but no more than that. The dates of arrival at the different ports of call as the ship cruised among the islands, and the date of its departure for Ensenada, were not available.

Switching to the website of the *Oosterdam*'s owners, Holland America Line, Fiona searched for information on previous cruises in the hope that might help. However, there was nothing. The only details were about current and future cruises.

"Damn!" she uttered uncharacteristically, stamping her foot. "I'll have to call them. No doubt there'll be umpteen recorded messages before…"

"You have to endure some ghastly canned music interrupted by comforting reassurances about how much they value your custom," Giles chuckled from the bedroom door. "Sounds like you've caught my habit. First sign of madness, they say."

"Giles! You gave me such a shock. I thought you were next door listening to the radio. How was Berlioz?"

"Very 'suite' and simply *fantastique*!"

"Is that the best you can offer?"

"At this time, yes. It's almost midnight. Have you finished?"

"Yes and no. The good news is I've found the article we need. It took me an age, but here it is. Take a look. See what you think."

Giles took her place in front of the laptop and read the column carefully. By the time he'd finished, Fiona could see something was worrying him.

"Any thoughts, Mr Holmes?"

"Just one, Dr Watson. It says she'd been swimming in one of the ship's pools. That strikes me as odd. It doesn't fit."

"Why?"

"Diabetic ulcers are chronic things. If that's what her ulcer was, she would probably have already had it when they set sail. And yet, she'd been swimming. I can't imagine she'd have gone swimming with a diabetic ulcer. She'd have known how important it was to keep it dry. No, I think whatever she had on her foot was likely to have started *after* she'd boarded, and was nothing to do with her diabetes."

Fiona glanced at her watch. "Crikey, I didn't realise it was so late!" Collecting her phone, she checked what the current time was in Seattle.

"Perfect! It's morning there."

"Where?" said Giles.

"Seattle, where Holland America has its office. That's who I want to call. With any luck, it will have just opened. Hold tight."

After listening to recorded music for long enough to cause Giles to leave to prepare himself a pot of tea and several slices of *kaya* toast, Fiona eventually got through to the appropriate office. By the time Giles was on his way back, she was just about to finish.

"Thank you, Angela," she said, winking in his direction. "I look forward to receiving it from you."

"Success?" asked Giles after Fiona had ended the call.

"Sort of. Very nice lady that. After she'd complimented me on my 'cute Scotch accent' and told me how porridge topped with maple syrup… yuk!… is her favourite breakfast, I said that I was a novelist and needed the itinerary during the cruise in question for a book I'm writing. It turned out she remembered this particular cruise very well because of the publicity it had attracted. Apparently, the fact that a high-ranking Mexican diplomat had chosen one of their ships boosted their ticket sales in Mexico no end. The small detail that the poor lady hadn't got off alive hadn't seemed to matter! You should have heard her at the other end, when she was telling me. Talk about guffaws of laughter!"

Fiona laughed for a moment. "After she'd recovered, she

said she didn't know the exact itinerary, but was sure it would have been in December, because that cruise always departs during that month. She also thought it unlikely it would have gone anywhere near Ni'ihau. Being a small, dry, and relatively featureless private island, and the most northerly one at that, it's not a destination for any liners. The nearest the ship was likely to have got would be the east coast of the neighbouring, larger island of Kauai. So, while she was talking, I had a quick look on Google Maps and saw that Kauai's east coast is more than fifty miles from Ni'ihau. That's a huge distance for a mosquito, even for the strongest flying species, on top of which Kauai has mountains in the middle. So, even if the ship did call into Kauai around the time of the epidemic… and we don't know if it did… we can probably rule out the idea that one flew on board."

"Could one have been blown there?" asked Giles.

"Interesting thought. Let me have a look while you munch your toast."

After several minutes, a despondent look told Giles the answer.

"The Trade Winds are pretty constant, at around fifteen miles an hour or more… in exactly the *opposite* direction. So we can throw that one out of the window."

"So is that it?" asked Giles.

"No, Angela's going to send me the complete works, with dates, ports of call, and so on. She may not have time today, as she's got meetings, but will do as soon as she can."

"But what use will it be if the vessel didn't go anywhere near Ni'ihau?"

"Perhaps one of us will come up with a new idea," replied Fiona. "You never know. Do you mind if I have that last piece of toast before we nod off?"

"Be my guest."

"Am I'm putting weight on?"

"On what?"

"Never mind!"

***

199

It was a little past four-thirty in the morning when Fiona gave Giles's pyjama sleeve a gentle tug. For the past twenty minutes, while watching the shadows of the palm trees dancing across the mahogany chest at the foot of the bed, she'd been trying to come to terms with a dream. She'd never been convinced they could unlock the secrets of past events, but, perhaps on this occasion, she'd been wondering, she might be wrong.

"Giles," she whispered, giving him a light prod in the back. "Are you awake?"

"Ugh… yes, I am now! What is it?"

"I've had a thought. I imagine you'll say this is silly, but I'm going to say it anyway. I've had a dream."

"I hope it wasn't about…"

"No, it wasn't. It was about what happened in Mexico City, when I saw that guy who looked a bit like Steve. In the dream, it actually *was* Steve Salomon. And he was helping the Pentagon with germ warfare. But it wasn't for just a single virus. It was for a much bigger programme that included weaponised viruses, bacteria, and fungi. And what was really interesting was *why* he was there. It was because the Pentagon had subcontracted the work to an American biotech company with a research facility south of the border. Steve was being paid as a consultant. I couldn't tell exactly where the company was. It certainly wasn't Mexico City. It was a much smaller place, less affluent. But it was definitely Mexico, because there was a green, white and red flag with an eagle in the centre fluttering over a delapidated colonial building. Something else I remember is a high arch over a road, a bit like the one in St Louis."

"So…?"

"I'm wondering if I was getting a message? Steve would be perfect for that sort of job, and Mexico would be a good place for the US to hide its dirty work. It's not impossible, is it?"

Giles turned over to gaze at the Balinese copper lamp over his head, as it swung in the breeze from the half-open window.

"Yes, of course it is," he replied. "I mean, no, it isn't. But that could be precisely why your brain invented the story, couldn't it? One part of your brain recognises the possibility, another part makes a picture book story out of it, and then a third part believes it to be true. Sorry to be so unenthusiastic, but I'm not a great believer in the mystical powers of dreams."

Fiona thought for a moment.

"Not so long ago, you *were* a believer in the mystical powers of the moon. Remember those messages you thought you were getting about the Middle East when you saw the moon over Christ Church common, and then again through your window? And how you reacted when your eyes happened to land on Lawrence's *Seven Pillars of Wisdom* in Conrad's study? And how you thought it a huge coincidence that the date of *Al Hiraj…*?"

"Okay, okay, point made!" said Giles. "But they weren't dreams, were they? They were events, real happenings. And they turned out to be meaningful, didn't they?"

"Yes, as it happens. Which is exactly the point I'm making. I don't see any reason to distinguish between your experiences and my dream. Dreams are natural events, too."

"But is it likely the Pentagon would subcontract a project of such importance and secrecy to a commercial lab in another country?"

"They might do," said Fiona. "Especially if the lab belonged to an American company. Somebody once told me the US Department of Defense buys eighty per cent of its components from foreign companies, even China, something that keeps a lot of people awake at night."

"Me included, it seems."

"Sorry, but I had to get this out while it was on my mind. Some American pharma and biotech companies do have a presence in Mexico, you know. Pfizer and Merck, for example."

"Actually, I can think of a few others too, like Novartis."

"There you are! Companies like them might be more than happy to have the Pentagon's business. There'd be buckets of Federal dollars. And, as a bonus, they might discover something useful for their drug discovery programmes. And, keeping on the right side of Ted Crabb wouldn't do any harm, either. Who knows what influence he might have on drug prices and the policies of the Food and Drug Administration – things that affect the companies' very survival?"

"That's true."

"Steve could have been in Mexico City not just to attend the congress, but to meet executives, review the latest results, give advice, troubleshoot problems, and so on."

"Fair enough. But where does all this take us?" said Giles, yawning.

"That's what I'm coming to. As I was lying here and you were snoring... well, breathing heavily, to be fair... I envisioned an arrangement..."

"*Envisaged?* Please! I hate that word. Why can't the Americans...?"

"Giles! This is more important than your petty preferences. I was about to say, I can *imagine* a situation in which Steve would be employed to help such a company develop a lethal virus. And the idea of using *Achilles* RNA would be a no-brainer to him. It would probably be the first thing he'd think of. And then, once they'd got up to a certain point, the virus might be transferred to one of the Pentagon's own labs for the finishing touches. You know, purification, quality control, characterisation, and so on. A small lab hidden in a place like Ni'ihau would fit the bill perfectly."

"Carry on. I know my eyes are closed, but I *am* listening. That lamp was making me sea sick."

"Well, what I'm thinking is they might not use a US Navy vessel to transfer the viruses. They might just use a regular merchant one, like the *Oosterdam*."

"But it would be illegal to take that sort of stuff on a cruise liner."

"So what? The entire programme would be illegal."

Giles struggled up to close the window, then returned to lie on his back again.

"That's better. So, to get to the point, you're suggesting a batch of viruses might have been in the process of being transported to Ni'ihau on the *Oosterdam*, when some of them escaped and infected Margarita Diaz?"

Fiona nodded.

"But hold on, Fiona. Like all arboviruses, West Nile viruses have to be injected directly into the blood to infect someone, don't they? You know that. They're not like the common cold or the flu. So, if your theory is correct, either somebody crept up behind Margarita Diaz and jabbed a needle and syringe into her bum without her noticing… a rather unlikely scenario… or a mosquito did something similar. But, if it was the latter, you have to explain where the mosquito came from – how it got infected with the virus, in the first place, and a few other things. Right?"

"Yes."

"And…?"

"I've thought of that."

"And…?"

"Perhaps it wasn't a batch of viruses, but a batch of infected mosquitoes," said Fiona. "There might be a reason why they'd prefer that. As long as it was a species that transfers viruses to its eggs, and as long they took males along as well as females, they wouldn't need too many. Once they'd reached their destination, the boys and girls could be put together. In next to no time, they'd have hundreds of infected eggs; and, in a week or two, hundreds of infected mosquitoes."

"But that would be a bit complicated, wouldn't it… transporting live mosquitoes? What reason could there be for doing it that way?"

"What if there was something special about the mosquitoes, too?" said Fiona excitedly. "An uncommon species uniquely suited to the job, for example? Or a genetically engineered strain that had been modified in some way for the purpose?"

There was a pause before Giles answered.

"Genetically engineered mosquitoes armed with genetically engineered viruses, heh? What a thought! Goodbye helicopter gunships, here come the mini-helicopters from hell. Now that *would* need the input of someone like Steve."

"Exactly. So can I go on?"

"There's more? What did you put in your tea?"

"Honey. Pure wild honey from the forests of Sumbawa."

"I must try some. But how on earth would anyone go about transporting live mosquitoes, genetically modified or not?"

"Actually, it's not too difficult," answered Fiona. "This is something else I've learnt. It's simply a question of reducing the temperature to the right level and keeping it there. You can do it with ice, nothing more sophisticated than that. It slows down the mosquitoes' metabolism and they go to sleep, hibernate, or something like that. Then, when you warm them up again, they're back to normal in next to no time. It's used regularly for the so-called 'sterile insect technique' for depleting the population of disease-carrying bugs, when thousands of sterile males are released to compete with the normal ones for the females, thereby reducing the number that produce eggs."

Receiving no reply from Giles, she prodded him in the back.

"Are you still awake?"

"Of course. I'm fascinated."

"Thank you," said Fiona. "So, what I'm getting at is this. If someone was transporting mosquitoes on a ship, and accidentally spilled a few on the deck without noticing, as long as there was at least one male and one female, in a day or two there'd be a female looking for blood to feed its developing eggs. And, if it happened to be carrying the Ni'ihau virus, one of the passengers on that ship would soon be very ill. Margarita Diaz could have been bitten in her sleep and known nothing about it until she developed the ulcer on her foot."

Having heard enough to take the idea seriously, Giles raised himself to sit on the edge of the bed.

"Well, I must say, you've given me something to think about, Fiona. Do female mosquitoes lay just one or several batches of eggs?"

"Quite often, several."

"Do they suck blood between each batch?"

"I think so."

"So, how do we explain the fact nobody else got bitten?"

"What if it got blown overboard?" replied Fiona. "I imagine it would be very difficult for a mosquito to hang around on a ship for very long."

"Fair enough. But there's also the matter of the eggs, isn't there? Mosquitoes are not ducks. They lay hundreds, right?"

"Yes."

"And in the scenario you described, many of them could have been infected, ready to develop into new infected mosquitoes."

"Yes."

"So, why wasn't the ship swarming with them on the way back?"

"Perhaps they were blown overboard before they got the chance to lay any?"

Giles got up to stretch his legs in the half-darkness.

"Ouch! Why the hell did they have to carve tigers' paws on the legs of this chest of drawers, I wonder?"

"Probably because it was made in Sumatra. You should wear slippers."

"Can't argue with that," said Giles. "Anyhow, although it's certainly a very interesting idea, Fiona, you have to admit it's a pretty long shot. After all, we don't yet know what Mrs Diaz died of, do we? We don't even have a proper differential diagnosis. We're pretty sure she couldn't have died from a diabetic ulcer, but we're only guessing she caught the virus. We're bending over backwards to make it plausible, but the truth is we've not an ounce of evidence. Let's sleep on it, and see what the morning brings."

Chapter Twenty-Two

To her delight, the moment Fiona opened her inbox over breakfast, she could see that the much anticipated email from Holland America had arrived. It was exactly what they needed.

OOSTERDAM ITINERARY

Day 1	Depart San Diego, USA (5 pm)
Days 2-6	At sea
Day 7	Nawiliwili, Kauai, Hawaii (8 am-6 pm)
Day 8	Honolulu, Oahu, Hawaii (arrive 7 am)
Day 9	Honolulu, Oahu, Hawaii (depart 7 pm)
Day 10	Lahaina, Maui, Hawaii (8 am-10 pm)
Day 11	Kona, Island of Hawaii (7 am-6 pm)
Day 12	Hilo, Island of Hawaii (8 am-6 pm)
Days 13-17	At sea
Day 18	Ensenada, Mexico (2 pm-10 pm)
Day 19	Arrive San Diego, USA (7 am)

After printing a copy, she pushed her cup to one side and drew up an extra chair.

"Giles, put that newspaper down, and come over here," she called through the open window overlooking the terrace. "Angela was true to her word. We've got it. "

Hastily collecting a map of the Hawaiian islands from the magazine rack, she spread it out on the table and weighed it down with abalone shells and pieces of coral that Teuku's wife had given them as welcoming presents.

"Hasn't she done a nice job?" she said. "Very professional. You study the map, Giles, while I go through it.

"So, they sailed directly from San Diego across the Pacific to Hawaii," Fiona continued, "where the first port of call was Nawiliwili on the island of Kauwai. That was the seventh day of the cruise. Then, for the next five days, they island hopped, until they reached the last port of call, Hilo, on the island of Hawaii. Have you found those places?"

A grunt from Giles provided enough reassurance for her to continue.

"From there, they sailed back across the Pacific to Ensenada on Mexico's coast. What a wonderful trip!"

"Only up to a point, I'd say," said Giles. "The island hopping would have been interesting, but I'm not sure I'd have liked those long stretches across the Pacific. I had a dose of that sort of thing when I sailed to Sydney in my youth. Life at sea can get tedious. You can only play so many games of table tennis and Scrabble with old maids and retired generals."

"But that was a regular passenger route, not a luxury cruise," replied Fiona. "That's different. I'm sure there would have been plenty of entertainment on this trip."

"What? Like extra sets of tiddlywinks, snakes and ladders, Monopoly…?"

"No, they have lots of things: cabarets, dancing, magicians…"

"Still not my cup of tea. Sorry, go on."

"Thanks. So, let's think about these dates. According to Angela, the ship set off from San Diego on the first Saturday of December. I'd like to know what date that was. Where's my…?"

"I can do it on mine…" said Giles. "Hold on… it was the sixth."

"Thanks. So, the *Oosterdam* will have arrived at Nawiliwili on the morning of the twelfth. The passengers had a day on Kauai, and…"

"Hold it there!" Giles interrupted. "That means they toured the islands from north to south. Kauai is the nearest the ship got to Ni'ihau. If someone had been taking infected mosquitoes

208

to Ni'ihau for a trial run, as you suggested, surely that's where they would have disembarked? Why take the risk of staying on board longer than necessary with such a fragile, hazardous, and top secret cargo, only to make the journey to Ni'ihau longer and more difficult in the process? It wouldn't make sense. They would have got off in Nawiliwili on day seven. Yes?"

"Yes."

"Which means, the latest any mosquitoes could have escaped on board would also have been day seven."

"Yes."

"But according to *La Jornada*, Margarita Díaz became ill on the second day after the ship left the island of Hawaii, day fourteen of the cruise. Judging by what happened on Ni'ihau, if Margarita's illness was due to the same virus, she would most likely have been bitten the day before. That would make the time from the mosquitoes escaping on board to her being bitten six days at the very least. That seems far too long to me. They would have mated in twenty-four hours, wouldn't they, or at the most forty-eight?"

"Under normal circumstances, yes."

"And then the females would have bitten whoever was around more or less immediately?"

"Yes, you're right, Giles. Six days does seem rather a long time."

"So, highly inventive though your idea is, Fiona, I don't think it can be correct. Do you?"

"Probably not. You're right. She would have developed her ulcer several days sooner than she actually did. Can you remember the date on which the epidemic occurred?"

"Third of January, I think. I wrote it down after chatting to Teuku during one of our lunchtime chinwags. Let me check."

After flicking through his diary, Giles's nod provided the answer.

"That's more than two weeks after the *Oosterdam* left the islands," said Fiona, "and about three weeks since the courier would have disembarked on Kauai. So that raises another point. Is it likely they would have kept the mosquitoes chilled for that length of time before waking them up and releasing them on the island? Why? What would have been the point? I don't understand."

"No, nor do I," replied Giles. "Not for the first time, we need to think again, Fiona."

"I don't feel like breakfast now. This news has ruined my appetite. I'm off to the terrace. Enjoy your eggs."

"They're very big, aren't they?"

"They're duck eggs. The maid left a note saying they're perfect for a pancake called *kerak telor*."

"Did she leave the recipe?"

"No," said Fiona, picking up her shoulder bag and sun hat. "Okay, I'm off."

"Don't forget the mosquito repellent."

Chapter Twenty-Three

Having agreed they should spend a few hours apart in the hope that one or other would come up with a new idea, by mid-morning Fiona had made preparations to spend some time with the street food vendors on Nusa Lembongan. Giles, meanwhile, had pulled on a pair of cotton trousers and comfortable sandals and decided to go for a tramp around their own island, something he'd been promising himself for a while.

It was the sort of decision that, in the past, had often borne fruit when they'd been faced with an impasse of some sort. In the course of their research in Oxford, the greatest challenges had never been presented by the practical aspects of their work in the lab, the nuts and bolts of designing experiments and performing them, but the unseen process of coming up with new hypotheses to explain unexpected results they didn't understand. Though at times frustrating, in reality it was the process they enjoyed most, one in which patience and persistence had usually been the most important ingredients in the recipe for success. When combined with a brief period apart, safe from any external influence that could interrupt or deflect a nascent line of thought, it was "the two Ps", as Fiona called them, that would so often lead to the spark of much-needed inspiration. This wasn't always the end of the story, as even the best ideas usually needed refining. But it was a critical step.

And so it was with a sense of optimism that they wished each other good luck as they stepped from the villa's shade into the sunlight of the winding, gravel path that led through the garden.

Fiona's journey was to be much shorter than Giles's. More or less straight across the island to the west coast and then over the yellow suspension bridge, it would take scarcely half an hour, even at her customary slow pace to take in the scents of the flowers and the sounds of the birds and insects along the way.

Upon reaching the bridge, she saw that the daily gathering of vendors were already serving their wares to throngs of surfers, scuba divers, and local residents along the coastal road that leads to Nusa Lembongan's lush mangrove forest. As she crossed the strait, waving to a now familiar fisherman below, the heady mix of aromas carried by the breeze was intoxicating. The spices of the region had already grown on her so much that a day trip to the Asian market in London's Gerrard Street had been on her agenda since their first visit. But that would be just a shopping spree. This was the real thing.

Strolling among the tricycles and carts parked this way and that, Fiona negotiated the overflowing fruit baskets swinging from their poles, and marvelled at how her attitude had changed since their stopover in Mexico City, where she'd limited their eating to restaurants and cafés lauded in Nicholas Gilman's guidebook. Culinary hygiene in particular was no longer something that concerned her. Perhaps it was the character of the people that made a difference... generally polite, happy, and courteous... away from the pressures and bustle of a metropolis. She wished she could speak to them in their own language and feel part of their world.

As she'd learnt to expect from Teuku's descriptions over coffee in the common room, most of the mobile kitchens had been constructed with popular fried foods like *nasi, ayam*, and *bami goreng* in mind. Then there were those offering bowls of chicken noodle soup or *bakso* with beef meatballs, or steaming fish dumplings over pans of boiling water. A few had mini barbecues for chicken *satay* or *ikan bakar* prepared with carp or other freshwater fish. More than welcome in the heat of the late morning were those offering salad bowls of *rojak, asinan*, and *gado-gado*, or paper cups of cool mango juice and jelly-like desserts of flavoured coconut milk.

After sampling five or six dishes, each as delicious as the one before, Fiona left the crowd to drop into one of several bamboo chairs she'd spotted in the shade of the forest. Despite the presence of a family whose young children were playing hide and seek among the trees, it looked like a good spot to return to the real purpose of the trip.

As she made her way along the pavement, cautiously stepping between the weeds and overnight puddles, she saw that the last cart was attended by a young boy cooking chicken *satay* over glowing coals. Succumbing to the temptation to join the queue, she found herself standing next to an elderly artist from Amsterdam, who had settled on the island 'to get away from it all' and open a studio of her paintings. An ardent reader of Somerset Maugham, she'd been persuaded by his descriptions that the region would provide everything she needed in retirement. After a couple of weeks' bed and breakfast in Sedok Jineng Villa, she had rented a small house overlooking Dream Beach on the south side of the island with her German husband. It had been from there that she had made the journey by tricycle to stock up with food for his birthday party.

"This lad's *satay* is the best in the region", she confided. "His secret's in the sauce, made from freshly roasted Sumatran peanuts. It probably sounds a little silly, but one of the things we love around here is the popularity of peanuts in the cooking. And, of course, they're rich in vitamins B and E, so important as we get older. This boy's *satays* are my favourites."

When they reached the front of the queue, Fiona's new friend helped her to choose some of the best pieces of chicken, before accompanying her to the bamboo chairs.

"I'll leave you to your poultry now," the woman said with a wink. "Don't worry about the calories. You can live on salads tomorrow. Here's my business card, the one for the studio. I'd love to have you and your husband over for dinner one day. I love cooking. So don't hesitate to give me a call."

By the time Fiona had finished her snack, the children had departed with their mother. Alone at the edge of the clearing with only unseen birds and cicadas for company, she wondered how Giles was getting on. The sight of what she took to be a yellow-crested cockatoo cracking open a palm nut with its powerful beak prompted her to look at a couple of germinating peanuts the vendor had given to her. As she examined them, she realised there was something vaguely familiar about their shape – in fact, more than familiar. There was something strangely significant, as if it was the key to a door. But why?

And then it came to her.

It was time to return to the villa.

***

"Never mind, tell me later!" she insisted, as Giles tried to explain why he was sitting on the doorstep in nothing but his underpants.

"I'm sure there must be a good reason, assuming the maid's not hiding behind the jasmine bush over there," she continued. "But first I've something more important."

Giles swept the dust from the step with his hand and beckoned her to sit down.

"The thing is this. It worked. I mean, going for a walk. I've had an idea. Once again, getting away from each other did the trick."

"Well, that's good news," said Giles. "Because I didn't have a single brainwave, nothing approaching it… not even a ripple."

"It doesn't matter," replied Fiona. "Listen to this. After I'd stuffed myself with what must be the most scrumptious street food on the face of the earth, I thought I'd be a pig and have one more dish. Looking around, I spotted a young lad cooking chicken *satay* in one of those three-wheeled things. He must have arrived later than the rest, as he still had plenty of thighs and wings to cook, even though plenty of customers were queuing. I found myself standing next to a charming Dutch lady, who said the secret of the boy's success was his sauce. He makes it himself from fresh peanuts his uncle grows in Sumatra, she said. Apparently, he soaks them in water from a spring in the Barisan mountains, roasts them over a wood fire… he refused to say which type of wood, but she reckoned it was Sumatran pine… and then grinds them with a mortar and pestle.

"He was so proud of them that he even had some on display. Not in their shells, just the beans… which, botanically speaking, is what they are by the way, *not* nuts as most people think. They were lying on the soil around a lovely citronella with pink flowers that he was growing in a pot. As I'd never seen fresh peanuts before, I took a close look and saw they'd started to germinate. A single root was poking out of each one. As I was showing so much interest, he gave me a few as a keepsake. I dropped them into my pocket and thought no more about it.

"Then, later on, when I was sitting in the shade taking in the sounds and smells of the forest, I realised they reminded me of something. At first, I couldn't put my finger on it. And then… bang! It came to me. Can you guess?"

"No."

"*Pupae*! Mosquito pupae."

"But they're tiny, much smaller."

"That's right. Just a few millimetres. But magnified under a microscope, they look exactly like germinating peanuts. They have an oval brownish body and a curved tail that looks just like a developing root."

"Yes, I suppose you're…?"

"Well, as you know, the pupa is the stage in the life cycle that comes *after* the larva and *before* the adult. It's the same for all mosquitoes. It goes egg, larva, pupa, mature mosquito, mating, blood-sucking, more eggs, larvae, pupae… and so it goes on. It's been like that non-stop for a hundred million years or more. No break, just one generation after another. It's the same with butterflies. The egg becomes a caterpillar, that becomes a chrysalis, and out of that comes the adult butterfly, which mates and lays more eggs… if it's a female. The only difference is that butterflies don't bite, thank goodness. Imagine having to swat a Red Admiral or a big, yellow and black Swallowtail on your arm!

"Anyhow, the pupae usually take two or three days to mature into adults, although it depends on the conditions. Can be as many as five or six days. It's usually then another twenty-four or forty-eight hours before they're sexually mature. They mate and the females go looking for blood. Yes?"

His brow deeply furrowed, Giles nodded expectantly.

"So," continued Fiona, "it usually adds up to somewhere between four and seven or eight days from pupa to biting, which means if it was *pupae* that were being transported on the *Oosterdam*, and not adult mosquitoes as we assumed, the time from the ship calling into Kauai… the seventh day of the cruise… to Margarita Díaz being bitten… on the thirteenth… would be about right. So perhaps that's what happened? *Pupae* were being transported to Ni'ihau. A few were spilled on the deck, perhaps when the courier was disembarking. They matured, two adults mated, and she got bitten."

"Interesting," said Giles. "Are you sure pupae can be transported for days?"

"I'd be surprised if they can't given adult mosquitoes can, as long as you keep them cold. But let me go and check it out. I have a review article on this sort of thing. And there's no time like the present. Don't go away."

When Fiona returned from the study, the answer was written all over her face.

"Apparently, the ideal temperature to keep pupae dormant is between two and eight degrees Celsius. So, no problem. A box of ice cubes or crushed ice would have done the job."

Giles frowned.

"But we'd still have to account for the three weeks or so between the courier disembarking on Kauai and the onset of the epidemic, wouldn't we? Would that fit?"

"It could, as long as they had a lab hidden somewhere. And, actually, that would have made good sense. Instead of coping with lots of dangerous mosquitoes on the cruise, all they would have needed is a much smaller number of pupae. Each pupa develops into one adult, but once a female has mated it can produce hundreds of eggs. So, just a few pupae would have been enough to produce a large colony. You can tell which are male and female pupae, by the way, by their size. So they could have taken both sexes along."

Giles stretched to hand Fiona a piece of chalk and a slate the maid was in the habit of using for her shopping list.

"Why don't you work out how much time it would have taken to get from a few pupae to a few hundred blood-sucking females?" he suggested.

After a couple of minutes, a look of satisfaction lit up her face.

"Okay," she said. "Let's assume it would have taken a couple of days to get the pupae from the ship to a laboratory. To let those pupae develop into adults… all infected with the virus… allow them to mate and produce infected eggs, let those eggs develop into a second generation of hundreds of adults… again, all infected… and, finally, let them mate… It could have taken about three weeks, plus or minus a few days."

She passed Giles the article she'd brought from the study and propped the slate against his leg.

"The life cycle's there…" said Fiona, "and here are the sums. The article also describes the ways in which you can feed mosquitoes in a lab. You don't have to let them bite you. There's simple equipment for the job. Once they'd mated, they could have been released, and…"

"Bob's your uncle."

"Exactly," said Fiona. "So, that could have been it. Some pupae were accidentally spilled onto the deck before whoever it was disembarked with the rest. That's why Margarita Diaz got bitten so soon *after* the ship left Kauai, and…"

"Many days *before* the epidemic broke out on Ni'ihau."

"Precisely."

Rubbing his nose pensively, Giles stared at the slate.

"It certainly could fit," he said. "But, of course, that doesn't mean that's what happened. It's a nice story. But it's only speculation. We have no evidence. And there's something else… about those pupae. To develop into adults that could have bitten a passenger, they'd need to be around water, wouldn't they?"

"Yes. But there must have been pools of water on a ship's deck. "

"True. But that would be salt water, wouldn't it? Even if the pupae landed in a puddle of rainwater, decks would be covered in dry salt from sea spray, especiallywhen the crew hose them down. To my knowledge, mosquitoes need to lay their eggs in stagnant rainwater… ponds, puddles, water in cans and gutters, old tyres, and so on. Would pupae develop in salty water?"

"Hadn't thought of that one," said Fiona. "Good thinking! Stay where you are."

Throwing off her cotton jacket and kicking off her sandals, she ran into the villa again. Five minutes later, she re-emerged excitedly brandishing her laptop.

"Got the answers! First of all, this website here confirms that pupae can definitely be kept alive on ice for many days without maturing. It's a common practice used by entomologists. So there's no doubt about that one."

She then clicked on another website.

"And listen to this. Of the three and half thousand species of mosquitoes on the planet, there are a few that not only prefer, but actually *need*, salty water for their eggs to develop – not pure saltwater like sea water, but *salty*, brackish, sort of between the sea water and fresh. For the obvious reason, they're called Saltmarsh mosquitoes. So, the scenario does seem plausible. Agree?"

"In that case, I suppose so, yes," said Giles. "Obviously, your peanuts were much more stimulating than mine."

"You had peanuts too?"

"A chicken and peanut stew with spinach. I assumed it was Indonesian, but the owner of the restaurant, from Ghana, said it was a West African dish called chicken *palava*. Went down nicely with a bowl of rice. However, I ate too much and it put me to sleep. Then, while I was dozing at the table, the waiter knocked a pot of something called *dadih* over me, apparently fermented buffalo milk. By the time I got back here, sweating in the tropical sun, I stank like a ripe *gorgonzola*. Hence, the underpants."

"I believe you," said Fiona. "No sane man could invent a story that bizarre to conceal an infidelity."

"Perhaps I'm smarter than most?"

"Undoubtedly, but I don't think you're that crafty."

"So, let's get back to where we were," said Giles. "The problem with your idea, brilliant though it is, Fiona, is that it's guesswork, isn't it? There are so many questions to which we don't have answers, such as where the mosquitoes came from, and what species they were. Were they bred and infected with the virus outside the US and then taken to Ni'ihau, as we've been saying? Or engineered in a covert lab on the island? Did Margarita Diaz have the same illness, or was the ship's surgeon right about septicaemia? It's a great idea, no doubt about that. But I think we're going too fast again. We need to hold our horses."

"I suppose you're right," said Fiona with a sigh. "You know, Giles, I think the next step is for you to talk to that ship's doctor."

"Agreed. But first, we should have a chat with Teuku tomorrow. We need to keep him up to date, anyhow. And, who knows, he might think of something that hasn't occurred to either of us."

Chapter Twenty-Four

Teuku was pacing the length of the stainless steel terrace on the top floor of INDOMED's library by the time Fiona had finished getting him up to date with developments. As he passed the potted plant that stood on the glass table, he plucked a few of its red and green leaves and crushed them in his chubby fingers before holding them to his nose.

"Ah! Love that smell. Calms me down. Never fails. *Perilla frutescens*, from Korea, great for cooking. You should try it, Fiona."

After tossing what was left of the leaves over the balcony, he returned to the easy chair he'd brought from the reading room.

"I must admit, the idea of the military outsourcing a secret biological programme to Mexico, of all places, and then shipping the product across the Pacific to a private island to try it out on unsuspecting Hawaiians is like the stuff of James Bond movie. But it's undeniably plausible. More outrageous crimes than that have been committed by our politicians over the years. For example… oh, never mind!"

More agitated than Giles had ever seen him, Teuku jumped up from the chair to rest his hands on the railing and look down at the garden far below.

"Someone told me that that fountain down there," said Teuku, pointing to the ground, "was added by the architect to 'sooth the overactive minds of scientists', as he poetically put it, while at the same time representing the 'fountain of human knowledge'. Apparently, the rate of flow changes every day, sometimes more, sometimes less, and is controlled by a computer chip generating random numbers. Nevertheless, in spite of the ups and downs, the water level in the pool, supposedly representing the cumulative knowledge bank of mankind, increases by the same tiny percentage every day."

Giles leant forward to peer beneath the handrail.

"How come?"

"The rate at which water is allowed to flow out is controlled by another chip," replied Teuku," That is fed information on the flow rate of the fountain and calculates what the size of the outflow aperture, commonly known as the plug hole, needs to be to achieve the desired water level at the end of the day. Isn't that cute?"

"What happens when the water eventually reaches the top?"

"I asked that, too."

"And…?"

"It'll take a very long time for that to happen. But, when it's almost at the top, valves will open to allow the water to escape through multiple tubes at the side. In so doing, it'll wash concealed collections of dormant seeds into the surrounding soil… where they will germinate."

Fiona raised her eyes from her notes.

"That's interesting. And odd. If they're truly *dormant*, water alone isn't usually enough. There has to be something else."

"My! I see we have a plant expert in our midst," said Teuku. "You're absolutely right, Fiona. Before the water passes over the seeds, it'll pick up a chemical that does the trick. I forget its name. When the plants grow, they are supposed to represent the fruits of scientific endeavour. The problem is, the pond fills up so slowly that Giles and I will probably never see it happen."

Teuku laughed for a moment before continuing.

"Anyhow, to return to the matter in hand… if the action's been in Mexico, it has to have been with the Mexican government's complicity. And we can only guess what the *quid pro quo* might have been for that. This story could be massive, guys. If we expose it to the world, we'll *all* be off to Stockholm, the three of us. Move over Rashid Yamani! Move over MECCAR! Here come the INDOMED gang. Ha! Love it."

Giles leant forward to pluck one of the potted plant's leaves and gave it a sniff.

"The big issue, Teuku, is whether we should chew it over a little longer. We don't want to go rushing into something we might regret, do we?"

"True, very true," said Teuku. "Okay, guys, give yourselves another twenty-four hours. But I wouldn't drag it out too long. Time's precious. Agreed?"

"Agreed."

"Great! Now let's finish this Indonesian cheesecake. I love it with expresso. No resemblance to…"

"*Espresso,* Teuku."

"Huh?"

"It's *espresso,* not expresso," said Giles. "You see, it's nothing to do with being quick to prepare. It's from the Italian for… ouch! Sorry… Fiona's right."

"I'll apologise on his behalf, Teuku," Fiona intervened. "Giles has an unfortunate habit of being very picky over words. I've been trying to cure him of it for ages. He's improved, but we're not there yet."

"No problem, Fiona," said Teuku. "You can explain later, Giles. I was about to say it has no resemblance to our cheesecake. *Bolu penggang keju* they call it. Basically, just a sponge cake with butter cream and grated cheese on top. Nothing fancy, but very tasty. Enjoy!"

Before entering the library, Giles and Fiona had agreed that the big question was not what to do next, but how to go about it. The reason for getting Teuku updated was mostly to ensure he didn't feel left out. From the moment they'd arrived, he'd given them a *carte blanche* with no obligation other than to keep him informed of their progress every now and then. Although Giles was in the habit of doing so during their lunchtime meetings, he'd never been under any pressure. As far as Teuku was concerned, his visitor's record spoke for itself. He could leave them to it. Nevertheless, Fiona in particular felt it important to keep him happy. They were in uncharted waters. Who knew what storms might lie ahead? It was critical to keep him on their side should they ever need a lifebelt.

As they made their way from the building towards the yellow suspension bridge, now their favourite spot for taking stock, the big question on ther minds was how to get in touch with the ship's surgeon, who presumably spent most of his life on board. Was it possible to telephone a ship while at sea?

Upon reaching the bridge, Fiona sat down to dangle her legs over the edge, while Giles remained standing to admire the small fishing boats in the strait below.

"Isn't it amazing?" she sighed. "A few years ago, who would have imagined I could surf the internet on a telephone while sitting on a bridge between two tropical islands? Thank goodness INDOMED's planners had the forethought to equip the island with all the paraphernalia for mobile data."

She looked around her. "Where are the masts, by the way? Do you know?" "Disguised as trees, I've been told, Fiona."

"Clever! Perhaps those coconuts over there are actually satellite dishes in disguise. Now, pipe down please, while I call the shipping company."

It wasn't long before Fiona was through to Holland America's office in Seattle. Giles dropped onto his haunches to listen to her every word until she'd finished.

"Well, that was a bit of luck."

"Why?"

"Angela's working late yesterday."

"That's a peculiar way to talk."

"No, it isn't. They're fourteen hours behind us, and she's working as we speak. So…?"

"Jesus! Okay, carry on."

"Fortunately for us, their office is short-staffed and she won't be finished for another two hours. Otherwise, she'd be at home by now. She said Dr Bandaranaike is still on the *Oosterdam*, which at present is docked in Tampa, Florida, being kitted out for a seven-night cruise in the Gulf of Mexico. Normally, the

Rotterdam does that particular trip, but it has a problem with its engines. She gave me the itinerary, which I jotted down here, on the back of this letter from Ros."

"I wondered what the scribble was."

"It leaves Tampa nine days from now, a week on Sunday. It goes straight across the Gulf to Cozumel, a small island off the coast of Yucatan, not far from Belize, and then sails to Roatán, another island, this time belonging to Honduras. From there, it goes to a place in Guatemala, whose name was too long for me to take down; and finally to Costa Maya, on the east coast of the Yucatan. After that, it's straight back to Tampa. The round trip takes seven nights. The good news is there's no problem calling it, either in Tampa or after it's set sail. It seems these days you can call cruise liners via satellite wherever they are in the world. Wonderful isn't it?"

"Unless you're trying to get away from it all, and you have a secretary like my Jane. She can be a pest at times when I'm on holiday. Seems to make any excuse to call me."

"Perhaps I told her to keep an eye on you. You never know!"

"I wouldn't put it past you."

"Only joking."

Fiona paused to reflect before continuing.

"You know, when you think about it, although modern technology has made travelling so comfortable, it's also taken away the romance. It's made the world much smaller, less mysterious, almost too accessible. There's no real adventure travelling anymore, not *true* adventure. Smart phones are just part of it. We can't begin to imagine what it was like for the early explorers. If you and I had been sitting here two hundred years ago, it wouldn't have felt much different from being on the moon today. In fact, being on the moon today is probably *less* of an adventure than being around here was to Alfred Russel Wallace, or standing on the edge of Lake Tanganyika was to Richard Burton, or trudging along the bank of the Murrumbidgee River was to Sturt. Those people and others like them had no idea where they were going to end up. It took

Apollo 11 about four days to get to the moon, but it took James Cooke almost a year to get to Tahiti."

She paused to raise her feet onto the edge of the bridge and rest her chin on her knees.

"Oops! I hope that fisherman down there didn't see my bum. Hold on. There, that's better. These 1950s retro skirts defintely have their advantages."

Fiona paused a moment to pull the folds of her skirt around her legs.

"And," she continued, "unlike astronauts, all those explorers were completely cut off from the world they knew. For much of the time, the USA was still in view for the astronauts. Picture what it was like before phones could tell us exactly where we are on the face of the earth, show us a satellite image of the area, and zoom into the exact spot. Or before TVs were telling us of events on the other side of the earth within minutes, or before recordings familiarised us with the sounds of tropical insects, arctic birds, the steam from a geyser, and the creaks and groans of an iceberg long before we experienced the real thing."

"In case you've forgotten," Giles chuckled, "I don't have to picture it. I'm old enough to remember some of it… very clearly, too. And I have to admit, only fifty years ago travelling was much more exciting than today. What it was like for our forefathers, I can't imagine."

He changed position to sit down next to her.

"Actually, your mentioning astronauts reminds me of how the discovery of *Achilles* and all it's led to has parallels with the space race of the sixties. It's a sort of re-run in biology and medicine instead of engineering and astronomy. Now the USA is racing with MECCAR for a cure for cancer, whereas in those days it was racing with the USSR for the conquest of space. *Sputnik* lit the fuse then. *Achilles* has now. Rashid Yamani and Ahmad Sharif did to Ted Crabb what Yuri Gagarin and a dog called *Laika* did to JFK."

"But, whereas JFK eventually won that race," said Fiona, "it doesn't look as if Ted Crabb's going win his, unless the NIH achieves something quite spectacular. I wouldn't put it past

Crabb to do anything to make up the lost ground… and, if he fails, to take some sort of revenge. He can be pretty ruthless. Remember how he treated Steve?"

"What sort of revenge?"

"Who knows? I just think we should keep it in mind. You and I can't be the most popular people in the White House these days. After all, effectively we denied the USA another Nobel. And we certainly have to be on Steve's hit list."

Giles pictured the scene outside the bookstore in Bethesda, when Hank Weinberg had made his sinister warnings and glib references to the Wild West.

"Alas, what you've said is undeniable, Fiona. But at least we should be okay with MECCAR. We did them a huge favour by exposing Steve."

"But I'm not sure that means we're okay, Giles. I can't get out of my mind how Aram left in such a hurry after Jane had told everyone about sending the identity card to Rome. If he'd been in the know about Ahmad's death, as he might have been as an insider, we could be in Rashid's crosshairs. He didn't waste time getting rid of Ahmad, did he? I still have my suspicions about Mouktar and that snake. Don't think I'm getting neurotic. I just think we should watch our backs, that's all."

Standing up and crossing to the other side of the road, Giles watched as a flock of sparrows sped under the bridge before circling to perch on one of the cables overhead.

"I suppose I have to agree with you," he said. "But there's a danger of getting paranoid, you know, and seeing danger and conspiracies everywhere. It may sound boringly repetitive, but don't forget we're scientists. We do need to stay objective. That's the bottom line."

"Talking of which," said Fiona, "I'm sure that fisherman's been under the bridge longer than necessary. What's he waiting for… a gust of wind?"

"Forget about him! How do we call the *Oosterdam*?"

"It turns out to be very simple. From outside the USA, Angela said we call 1-321-837-6106. We listen to the menu, select the number of the ship we want, and take it from there. It's all here on the back of Ros's letter."

She stretched to hand the letter to Giles.

"If you can read my writing. Over to you, and over and out. But don't let it blow away, please. It's got her new address in Godstow on it."

"What's the time in Tampa?"

"I asked her that, too. About eleven-thirty pm yesterday."

"Is that too late to call, do you think?"

"I don't think so. I doubt the doctor has much to do in port. He's probably sitting in his cabin, feet up, knocking back his daily ration of rum."

"That was the Royal Navy. And they don't do it anymore."

As Angela had assured, the call went directly to Dr Bandaranaike's cabin. Relaxing with the *Journal of Occupational and Environmental Medicine* after a day of routine health checks on the officers, his instinctive reaction to Giles's laboured introduction was one of suspicion.

"You say you're a don at Magdalen College in England?"

"That's right, doctor."

"Beautiful place! I had a friend there once. We used to meet in the St James's Quad."

"Where?"

"The St James's Quad. You know, near the porter's lodge."

"St *James's*? I think you mean St *John's*?"

"Ah yes, of course! The old grey matter's not what it used to be. Then we'd walk to the Senior Common Room to have lunch together. I can picture the Cloister square now, so pretty with its manicured lawn and all the honeysuckle hanging from the old stones."

"Yes, it's very attractive, isn't it? But it's Wisteria actually, not honeysuckle."

"Really? I'll take your word for it. My friend eventually joined the editorial staff of the *British Medical Journal*, in my view the best monthly in the business."

"Actually," said Giles, "the *BMJ*'s a weekly, like the *Lancet* and *New England Medical Journal*. Perhaps you're confusing it with…"

"Congratulations, Professor!" said Dr Bandaranaike. "Full marks. Three out of three. You passed my authenticity test with flying colours. Sorry to do that to you. But I had to check. A few weeks ago I had what I thought was an innocent enquiry about an accident on board, and it turned out to be a New York attorney fishing for business… rather successfully, I'm afraid! Since when, I've had strict instructions from head office."

"Poor you!" said Giles. "Lawyers can be a devious lot, I know. I've had a couple of close scrapes myself over the years. Anyhow, my reason for calling is that I'm studying the epidemiology of medical emergencies at sea. It's a neglected subject, as I'm sure you know. There's virtually no information relating the onset of different illnesses to things like the weather, days at sea, and so on."

"Yes, I'm sure that's true. I've never seen anything on it. What's the hypothesis you're testing?"

"Oh…" said Giles, thinking quickly. "Well… it's based on the premise, or hypothesis as you correctly say… that's exactly the right word… most people, of course, would quite incorrectly use the word theory… but yes, I'm testing the hypothesis that… er… our body's defence mechanisms – antibodies, white blood cells, and so on – are affected by the sort of things I mentioned. It's all based on experimental work a colleague of mine did on… er… mice."

"He studied *mice* on ships?"

"Er… no, in a laboratory."

"I was going to say, between you and me, there's no shortage of those, I can tell you," said Bandaranaike. "Has the work been published? I'd be very interested…"

"No, not yet. He hasn't got round to it, which is why I can't give you any details."

"Pity," said the doctor. "Anyhow, it sounds interesting, and I'd be happy to help. What can I do for you?"

"I'm collecting most of the data I need from shipping companies' records," explained Giles. "But there are a few cases of special interest about which I need information from the physician involved. In some cases, it's to check that the diagnosis in the records is correct, in others to see if there could have been a factor that was overlooked, various clinical details, and so on."

"Fascinating. So how can I help?"

Long before Giles had finished relating all he knew about Margarita Diaz, Dr Bandaranaike was fishing in his filing cabinet for her records, his telephone handset tucked under his chin.

"I remember the poor lady very well," he said. "I've still got her records somewhere, but just can't put my hand on them at the moment. I think my nurse must have put them in our archives."

The line went quiet for a moment while Dr Bandaranaike searched through some cabinet drawers.

"Yes," he continued, "I was astounded by how quickly she went downhill. It's very challenging, you know, when a medical emergency is dropped on you at sea. It can be very stressful. I don't think hospital doctors can imagine what it's like. Each case remains with you for ever."

"I'm sure it must have been a nightmare," Giles sympathised. "I gather your diagnosis was that an infection of a diabetic ulcer got out of control and spread to her blood."

"Yes, I was convinced of that. Nevertheless, I do worry I may have overlooked something or made an error – not the best choice of antibiotic perhaps, insufficient intravenous fluid."

"Yes, I can imagine. But from what I've read, I'm sure nobody could have done more."

"Thank you."

"I'd like to ask you a few questions about her diabetes, if I may," said Giles. "It's an aspect I'm particularly interested in."

"Please go ahead."

"Thank you. Was she on insulin?"

"No," said Bandaranaike. "That was something of a relief, actually, knowing how the dose needed can increase dramatically during infections."

"Can you recall what sort of tablets she was taking?"

"None. Her physician had been treating her with a diet only."

"She'd lost a lot of weight then?"

"No, none at all. She'd never been overweight. Her mother was the same apparently."

"You mean diabetic?"

"Yes, but also very mild and not overweight."

"I see," said Giles. "I gather the ulcer was on her foot?"

"Yes, where they often are in diabetics, of course," replied the doctor. "The left. If it hadn't got infected, she would have had a wonderful holiday and still been alive today. It's very sad."

"It is indeed. She was quite well when she got onto the ship?"

"Perfectly well. I remember how she said she'd been having a marvellous time – bridge, table tennis, swimming, dancing into the early hours."

"I see. One final question, if you don't mind. Did you do any blood tests?"

"We did some tests," said Bandaranaike, "the usual routine ones in urgent cases: blood glucose, serum potassium, sodium, white cell count, and so on. We don't have much in the way of clinical pathology facilities, of course. The small laboratory my nurse looks after has a analyser for clinical chemistry and another one for basic haematology. But we can't do blood cultures or any fancy things."

"Of course," replied Giles. "Well, thank you for that information, doctor. You've been very helpful. If it's okay with you, I'd now like to go through your records to get a complete picture of her signs and symptoms, temperature chart, blood pressure, blood tests, etc. Would that be possible?"

"I appreciate how important it is for your research, Professor," said Bandaranaike, "but I'm afraid I could not send you a copy. I would need to get it authorised by the company and approved by the lady's physician, possibly also by her nearest relative. That would take a while. And there's always the possibility permission would be withheld."

"Yes, yes, I understand," said Giles. "I imagined that might be the case. What if I were to visit you before you set sail again?

Do you think I could have a quick look at her records in your office in your presence? That would be enough. There'd be no question of my wanting to take a copy away with me."

"I imagine that might be permissible. But I would need your assurance that your notes would not refer to her by name, and even then I might still have to get clearance before you publish your paper or present your study in a congress."

"Of course. I gather you're in Tampa at present, getting ready to sail across the Gulf?"

"That's correct," said the doctor. "It's the Seven-night Western Caribbean Cruise. It's one of my favourites, partly because we're never more than twenty-four hours away from land should anyone get seriously ill. It helps me sleep."

"I can imagine. And you pull up the anchor a week on Sunday?"

"That's right. I can see you're very well informed. Always on a Sunday at four o'clock in the afternoon."

"Sounds perfect," said Giles. "I'm doing a lecture tour at the moment. I'm calling from… er… Los Angeles, having just given a talk to the UCLA medical faculty. Over the weekend, I go to Dallas to give an evening seminar to… family physicians in the… er… Ritz-Carlton on Monday. After that, it's Tulane University in New Orleans to give a seminar to medical students. And the final stint will be in Miami during the Friday, when I'll be lecturing on… recent progress in endocrinology to a group of physicians over a buffet lunch. Would it be possible to visit you on the Sunday, the day you set sail? Perhaps late morning or early afternoon?"

"I should think so," said Dr Bandaranaike. "If we have the time, I could show you round the ship, too. Between now and then, I'll get security clearance for your visit from the company and let Captain Morgan know about it. But that shouldn't be a problem."

"No relation to Sir Henry, I suppose?"

"Pardon?"

"No relation to Sir Henry Morgan, I suppose? You know, the notorious privateer who set himself up in Jamaica in the seventeenth century?"

"Ah, yes… I mean, no, not that I know of. I think he would have told me if he was a descendant."

"Oh, you never know. The family might still have some pieces of eight stacked away!"

"Ha! I'll tell him that."

"Well, thank you very much, doctor," said Giles. "I'll look forward to meeting you. Tell me, if I were to rent a car in Miami, how long would it take me to drive across the state to Tampa, do you think?"

"I've done it a few times," the doctor replied . "The quickest route is the I-75 through the Everglades, then north roughly following the coast through Fort Myers, Port Charlotte, and Sarasota. It would take about four hours. You'll enjoy it. Quite scenic in parts, even if rather flat."

"So, let me think," said Giles. "If I set off after an early breakfast, I could be with you around eleven o'clock. How does that sound?"

"It sounds very good," replied Dr Bandaranaike. "I'll meet you on the gangway. Be sure to have your passport with you, as we'll need to check it and log you into the visitors' book."

"I should let you know, by the way, that I'll have my wife with me," said Giles. "She couldn't resist the opportunity to accompany me from Oxford. It's the old story. While I work, she plays! I hope that's in order?"

"Of course."

"Thank you. Goodbye."

As Giles returned the phone to his pocket, Fiona was on her feet rubbing her dress with her handkerchief.

"Did you see that idiot of a cyclist?" she said angrily. "Straight through a puddle! I'll have to go back to the villa now, and drop this into cold water straight away. But never mind, your call was much more important. Talk about a master of improvisation! Or would it be better if I were to call a spade a spade, and simply call you a master of dishonesty, duplicity, and deception… in other words, a liar? How did you manage to think that lot up?"

"It just flowed," said Giles. "I hardly had to think about it. I can't say I'm proud of the fact. Not so long ago, I would have had to think it through hours in advance. And even then it would have sounded as wooden as these boards."

Giles stamped on the slats beneath his feet, causing a blue and white kingfisher to take flight from one of the suspension cables.

"It was so convincing, I'm not sure I'll believe anything you say again!" laughed Fiona. "You're definitely not the man I used to know, Giles Butterfield. But, to change the subject, is it really necessary to visit him? It will be such a big journey. Why didn't you suggest a video conference call? It would be much quicker and simpler, and cheaper."

"Because I have something else in mind that he doesn't know about."

"What?"

"We're not just going to meet him on the ship. We're going to *stay* on it."

"You mean hide, become stowaways?"

"Of course not!" replied Giles. "I might have become a liar, a fraudster, and a burglar, but I haven't stooped that low yet. We're going to join the cruise as legitimate fare-paying passengers, assuming it's not already fully booked."

"It isn't, actually," said Fiona. "Angela commented it's half empty. So, we're going to have a holiday? How wonderful! I've never been on a big ship before. But it's still a long way to go to join a cruise. Why don't I ask Angela if they have one nearer to here? They must have some Pacific or Asian ones."

"Sorry, it needs to be the same ship."

"Why?"

"Because I want enough time to go through the doctor's records carefully, talk to his nurse and other staff, perhaps even borrow some frozen blood samples that were left over."

Giles gave Fiona a wink.

"*Borrow* frozen samples!" she said. "You mean *steal* them?"

"Strictly speaking, I suppose that is nearer the truth."

"To do some blood tests of our own? But that would be illegal… *and* very naughty!"

"That's me."

"Very clever, too! What sort of blood tests?"

"DNA."

"Why?"

"You remember after reading the newspaper article," said Giles, "I said I thought it unlikely Margarita Diaz's ulcer could have been diabetic, otherwise it would almost certainly have already been there when she boarded? They don't suddenly develop out of the blue, you see. They're chronic lesions. And there's no way she would have gone swimming with one."

"Yes, I remember."

"Well, it seems she did definitely have diabetes. On the other hand, she doesn't seem to have had either of the two common types. She wasn't on insulin or medicines, just some sort of diet. But she'd never been overweight. Apparently, her mother was the same."

"So?"

"I'm wondering if she had one of the rare types of diabetes due to mutations affecting one or other of the genes that control the blood sugar level," said Giles. "It's a long shot, but if that was the case, then it's important. Very important."

"Why?"

"Because they *never* cause skin ulcers."

"Oh! And he hadn't thought of that?"

"Apparently not. So, my reason for wanting a leftover blood sample is so our two young friends could test Margarita's DNA for mutations that are known to cause these types of diabetes. It might take a while, because there are quite a few. But it would be worth the effort."

"I can see it would… definitely. This is exciting," said Fiona. "Okay, why don't we go back to the villa now, so I can wash this mud out of my dress? And, while we're on our way, I'll call Angela to book us a cabin."

"Good idea," said Giles. "Here, you can use my credit card. I'm sure Teuku will eventually pay the bill."

Chapter Twenty-Five

After the American Airlines flight from Dallas-Fort Worth had dropped out of a blanket of heavy clouds to reveal only rain, swaying palm trees, and white horses across Tampa Bay, the final leg of the long journey from Jakarta almost at an end, the prospect of sailing across the Gulf of Mexico had been far less attractive to Fiona than when she'd been chatting to Angela. However, after a couple of nights in the Marriott Waterside, making good use of the sauna and gym between breakfast in bed and dinner by the marina, she'd recovered her appetite for the task ahead, even if she wasn't optimistic about the outcome. The idea behind the trip had been brilliant, one of Giles's best. And she knew they could rely on Mucky and Mingy to play their part should they be needed during the coming days. But would they be needed?

As the taxi now made its way past the Amalie Stadium towards Tampa's passenger terminal, Fiona strained her neck in the hope of catching a glimpse of their home for the next few days. Giles, meanwhile, sitting in the seat next to her, was engrossed in a newspaper.

"Almost there," the driver announced in an accent she imagined was a mixture of Turkish and Texan. "The liner is at Cruise Terminal 3. I brought the captain here a few days ago. Morgan's his name. Nice guy. Looked the part, that's for sure – tall, tanned, bushy white beard and moustache, patch on his eye. The only thing missing was a parrot on his shoulder! Actually, I shouldn't joke. He said he had a nasty eye infection."

When the cab stopped alongside the terminal building, just ahead of the ss *American Victory* in Ybor Channel, Fiona's first view of the *Oosterdam*, suddenly just a few yards away, took her breath away. The company's website had prepared her for the gracefulness if its lines, but not for its size. She had never been so close to a liner before. In fact, she'd never been anywhere near one. As a teenager, she'd often watched vessels coming and going during weekends in Oban and Mallaig on Scotland's west coast, but they'd been little more than fishing boats and car ferries. The edifice that now towered overhead brought to mind her first face-to-face encounter as a toddler with the soaring walls of Inveraray Castle by the waters of Loch Fyne.

As she waited for Giles to collect their bags from the driver, Fiona propped herself against a nearby capstan, comfortingly warm in the late morning sun, and scanned the decks for signs of life. Not seeing anyone to wave to, she turned her mind to Giles's experiences during his passage to Australia as a young man, recounted over *sushi* and *sake* during their stopover in Tokyo. She remembered his excitement on seeing West Africa for the first time, when the *Arcadia* dropped anchor off the coast of Senegal, albeit dampened by his awareness of the part the *Ile de Gorée* had played in Britain's ascendency as a trading nation; the perfect reflection of the full moon on the South Atlantic's glassy surface as the ship eased its way through the doldrums with uncanny smoothness; the heady mix of sea spray, oil, and turpentine as the Goanese crew, precariously suspended from ropes and pulleys, painted the hull; the flying fish and dolphins in the Indian Ocean that had seemed so intent on guiding the monster in their midst all the way from Durban to Perth.

"Wakey, wakey!" Giles called as he approached. "It's almost time to splice the mainbrace and dance the hornpipe."

"Not in that order, I hope," she replied. "Unless you want to fall overboard!"

Giles dropped the bags to wipe his brow with the sleeve of his linen jacket.

"And I thought Nusa was sticky!"

"You should have taken your jacket off."

"One more thing to carry."

"Sorry, I should have offered to help," said Fiona. "I was in another world, thinking of your trip to Australia."

"Ah, that explains why you looked as if you were in a dream."

"I was," said Fiona. "And I still am. I'm in a constant dream these days. Life has become a fantastic dream. I'm supposed to be a medical scientist locked up in a dusty laboratory to be let out only every now and then to lecture to rowdy students. But here I am in Florida, waiting to join a luxury cruise liner to take us to the Yucatan. And then there's the excitement of our work, whether it's our research in Oxford or this sort of thing, knowing how worthwhile it all is, the challenge, the stimulation. And, to top it all, I'm doing it with the most wonderful man in the world. I'd be happy doing anything anywhere with you, Giles."

"It's a dream we're sharing, Fiona. 'Hold fast to your dreams, for if dreams die, life is a broken-winged bird that cannot fly!'"

"Did you make that up? I'll ask you to say it again when we get on board so I can write it down."

"Sorry to disappoint you," said Giles. "But alas, such word magic is beyond my capabilities. Those lines were penned almost a century ago by an African American, James Mercer Langston Hughes, who wrote what is regarded as his greatest poem at the tender age of eighteen. As it happens, like us, he was on his way to Mexico at the time. But he took the train. He was a leading light in the 'Harlem Renaissance', the flowering of culture in New York in the twenties and thirties, when black artists, writers, and musicians moved north from the Deep South in search of work."

"Was the one he wrote on the train the one you just quoted from?"

"No, it was called 'The Negro Speaks of Rivers,' which he was prompted to write as the train was crossing the Mississippi."

"Do you know it?"

Giles nodded thoughtfully as he settled on one of the suitcases.

Her interest heightened by a unexpected solemnity in his manner, Fiona asked him to recite a few lines.

"Do we have time?" he said. "We're running a little late."

"That's okay."

"If you insist. But I'm not sure I can do it justice. Remember, this was written at a time when the life of a black American writer was one of great struggle and frustration – although, in Langston Hughes's case, to his great credit, not one of despair or anger."

Fiona smiled, listening intently.

"So, let's try to put ourselves in his position," continued Giles. "A highly creative young man, travelling alone through a country in which he, his friends and relatives were segregated and treated as inferior beings, merely because of the colour of their skin."

After pausing to undo a button of his shirt, he waited for the horn of a departing vessel to finish. Then, looking up and down the length of the quay before resting his chin on his knuckles and clearing his throat, Giles began to recite the poem.

"'I've known rivers:

'I've known rivers: ancient as the world and older than the flow of human blood in human veins.

'My soul has grown deep like the rivers.

'I bathed in the Euphrates when dawns were young.

'I built my hut near the Congo and it lulled me to sleep.

'I looked upon the Nile and raised the pyramids above it.

'I heard the singing of the Mississippi when Abe Lincoln went down to New Orleans, and I've seen its muddy bosom turn all golden in the sunset.

'I've known rivers:

'Ancient dusky rivers.

'My soul has grown deep like the rivers.'"

After opening his eyes, it seemed like an age before Fiona spoke.

"Yes, I can believe he didn't go one better than that," she whispered, wiping an eye. "Look at me! Silly, aren't I?"

"Not unless I am too," said Giles. "Shall we go?"

Straightening her back and raising her chin, Fiona attempted a smile.

"Aye aye, captain."

As they walked up the gangplank, Giles guessed that the short, portly man dressed in a spotless white open-necked shirt with blue epaulettes, blue trousers, and black shoes would be Dr Bandaranaike. And there was no doubt who was by his side. Dropping their bags, Giles shook their hands warmly.

"Good morning, doctor, and to you also, Captain Morgan. Giles Butterfield. My apologies for being a little late. Let me introduce you to my wife."

"Hello, Fiona's the name," she said, offering her hand. "If you're wondering about the bags, we've decided to do more than just visit Dr Bandaranaike. When we saw your itinerary and the pictures of the ship, it looked too good to miss. So, at the last minute, we decided to sign up for the cruise. I've never been on one, and it's been many years since Giles was on a ship, too."

Clearly pleased with the news, Captain Morgan asked a passing steward to pick up their bags.

"What's the number of your cabin, Mrs Butterfield?"

Giles withdrew their ticket from his inside pocket.

"Thank you, Professor," said the captain. "A Verandah Stateroom on the Navigation Deck! Not your honeymoon, by any chance?"

Both Fiona and Giles laughed while searching for an explanation they could offer for such apparent extravagance. Giles was the first to speak.

"I can understand your surprise, Captain. Not what you'd expect for a couple of academics, is it? Our honeymoon, several years ago, was a much more modest event, nothing more indulgent than a few days in Palma Mallorca. Last year, I inherited a cottage in Kent, when a much loved aunt of mine passed away, God bless her. As I've just found a buyer, we decided to splash out."

"Good decision," replied Captain Morgan. "After all, you can't take it with you, when you go, can you? Sorry, that wasn't very appropriate, was it? Anyhow, you'll certainly be very comfortable in this cabin. And, as you'll be on the starboard side, you'll get a very nice view of the Yucatan in a couple of days."

He smiled politely at them both and gave a salute. "Now, I must go, I'm sorry. I'm needed on the bridge. The steward here will show Mrs Butterfield to your cabin, while Dr Bandaranaike takes you, Professor, to our little medical centre. It's been lovely meeting you. I hope you enjoy your time with us."

After being shown the medical facility and introduced to a young Indian doctor and a nurse making their final preparations for their departure, Giles was led into a smart, oak-panelled consulting room and offered a chair.

"Make yourself comfortable, Professor, while I call for some tea and find the lady's records on my computer," said Dr Bandaranaike. "I couldn't access them when you called, as my PC had crashed. By the way, I hope it didn't seem rude, leaving your wife with the steward. It's just that…"

"Of course not," said Giles. "I understand entirely. I'm sure Fiona does, too. We know there's an important issue of confidentiality."

"Thank you."

While Dr Bandaranaike searched through his computer's folders and files, Giles watched the nurse through the open door, and tried to imagine what life would be like working on a ship. He recalled how, as a medical student, he and his friends had considered being a ship's surgeon as one of the "soft" options, a career one could slide into for an easy life and a good time in sunny climes, in contrast to the serious business of specialties like orthopaedics and cardiology. But now he'd seen the size of the *Oosterdam*, so much bigger than the *Arcadia*, he wasn't sure the job would be the "pushover" they'd joked about so disparagingly in the Students' Union.

Curious to know what the chances were of a passenger becoming seriously ill during a cruise, he tried to estimate the number of heart attacks and strokes that might occur.

"Let me see," he thought, "it said in Angela's email that this ship can hold close to nineteen hundred passengers. Let's assume it's full, and half are men and half are women. And I read somewhere that about forty per cent of cruise passengers are over the age of sixty-five. Okay…

A quick calculation on his mobile phone told him that that would come to 380 older and 570 younger men, and the same for women. Switching to the browser, he looked up the yearly rates of heart attacks and strokes in people of different ages reported from the Framingham Heart Study, the famous long-term follow-up study of residents in the small town of that name in Massachusetts.

"Right, so… it says the annual rate of cardiovascular events in healthy men over sixty-five was a little more than two cases per hundred. In older women and younger men, it was about half that, and in younger women it was half that again. And let's imagine we're talking about a cruise of thirty-six days, one tenth of a year."

Having jotted the numbers down with his ballpoint on his sleeve, he returned to the calculator.

"So," he continued to ponder, "during such a cruise lasting a little more than a month, you might expect two passengers to have either a heart attack or a stroke, if to begin with everyone is healthy, is a non-smoker, has normal blood pressure, and has a normal cholesterol level. That's the average. Sometimes, it would be less, sometimes more. Of course, in the real world, many passengers, especially the older ones, would have risk factors. So, the overall rate is more likely to be four cases per cruise. And, for each one, the doctor would have to look after the patient, perhaps in heavy seas, until he or she could be put on *terra firma*. On top of which, there'd be occasional cases of appendicitis, dental abscess, migraine, skin rashes, gastroenteritis, back strain, you name it. And then there's a few hundred so crewmembers to think about. That's a serious workload. So much for the 'soft option' we used to…"

"Found it!" the doctor exclaimed. "Sorry, Professor, I hope I didn't interrupt anything important. I saw you were…"

"No, nothing important, thank you," said Giles. "Please continue."

"You may be wondering why it took so long," said Dr Bandaranaike. "I had spelt her name incorrectly on her folder."

At that moment, a steward arrived at the door holding a silver tray.

"Ah, here comes the tea, Professor. I hope you don't mind green? I forgot to ask. Sorry."

"Suits me to a T, as you might say!" quipped Giles. "It's supposed to be healthier, anyway."

"I'm sure it is," replied the doctor. "Antioxidants. So, let me pour you a cup. Then I'll print out the lady's records. There are nine pages in all. The first seven are my clinical notes, and the last a scan of the letter she brought from her physician. You can take as long as you want, Professor. As you can see, I have a long-overdue job in front of me. If I don't sort through all these documents very soon, I won't be able to see who's on the other side of my desk. Computers were supposed to get rid of all this paper, weren't they? Do you remember? I tried to get started yesterday, but one of the Petty Officers slipped on the Sky Deck while it was being swabbed and fractured his left radius. Fortunately, I didn't have to put his arm in plaster. An ambulance took him to Tampa General. Nevertheless, it kept me busy for most of the day."

"That's quite a stack of journals that you have," said Giles. "You obviously keep right up to date."

"It's essential in our business, isn't it?" replied the doctor. "Especially when you're working on a ship. There are so few colleagues to call on. And, as I can't get to many congresses, the only way to keep abreast of the latest progress is to read the journals."

"The titles look interesting, very different from the ones I usually read," said Giles. "If you could ask your nurse to drop a few outside my cabin, I'd enjoy browsing through them."

"Yes, of course. No problem. So, here's the printout. If you have any questions, just ask."

Nothing had happened during the few days since their departure from Nusa Ceningan to change Giles's view on the questions that needed answering, the most urgent of which was encapsulated by the two words the nurse had written in the box in the top right-hand corner of the first page. Given the circumstances under which Dr Bandaranaike had been working, "Acute septicaemia" remained a defensible diagnosis. But would it stand up to scrutiny?

Although bacteriology was far removed from his own specialty, Giles had learnt enough when perusing journals in the College library of a Saturday morning to know that several unrelated illnesses could produce the same clinical picture. He also knew that the time-honoured way of confirming or refuting the presence of septicaemia was to add a few drops of the patient's blood to a nutrient broth, incubate the mixture for a few days at body temperature, and then look for bacteria under a microscope. Alternatively, for a much quicker answer, one of the new breed of high-tech commercial kits could be used to see if a blood sample contained bacterial DNA. But, as neither test had been available to Dr Bandaranaike, the details of Margarita Diaz's clinical history were going to be critical. Would the records contain sufficient detail?

By the time he had finished reading the print-out and making notes, nothing had altered Giles's assessment of the tragedy. On the evidence of Maragarita Diaz's clinical signs and symptoms, her temperature record and other vital signs, and her blood tests, the diagnosis of septicaemia remained viable, but no more than that.

Seeing that his host was now engrossed in sorting through journals and papers strewn across his desk, Giles hesitated before clearing his throat.

"Would now be a convenient time to ask a few questions, Doctor?"

"Of course, Professor."

"Thank you. The records are very clear. It's been most valuable, and I've made a few notes as I've gone along. I assume that's in order?"

"Of course. As long as any eventual publication acknowledges Holland America's contribution."

"Naturally. My first question is whether Margarita Diaz had a local problem in her leg, like varicose veins or skin diseases, that could have caused an ulcer, instead of it being due to diabetes?"

"No, she didn't. Definitely not."

"Is it possible she'd injured herself then? If she'd been on the deck in bare feet, she might…"

"No, that wasn't the case either. I'm sure."

"What about a bite from a bug or a venomous spider the ship might have picked up on a previous cruise?"

"That did occur to me, actually," said Dr Bandaranaike. "When I first saw the ulcer, I thought it might have been a recluse spider, which I know from experience can produce ghastly ulcers remarkably quickly. Mexico has the brown recluse, you know, and Hawaii the Mediterranean type. I was wondering if one had crawled on board during a previous cruise. But the lady said she hadn't seen any spiders."

"Or strange insects?"

"No."

"She hadn't been bitten by anything?"

"Not that she knew of, although that doesn't completely exclude it, of course."

"Quite," replied Giles. "Another point concerns the various blood measurements you made: white cells, sodium, haemoglobin, and so on. You certainly kept a close eye on them. Very commendable. As I didn't see any results for bacterial DNA, I assume the ship doesn't carry any of the new kits for that purpose?"

"No, it doesn't. But that's an excellent thought. It would have made a huge difference. I'll suggest it to the company."

He looked at Giles for a moment. "You're not thinking it was an act of negligence on the company's part, I hope… that the ship was not adequately equipped?"

"No, no, of course not! The ship can't carry everything," said Giles. "I imagine, like most of us, you took rather more blood than was necessary as an insurance against accidents, the need to do re-runs, and so on? And that you placed what you didn't use in a freezer… yes?"

"No, we didn't," said the doctor. "We incinerated it, because of the potential danger. As we hadn't been able to identify the organism, we didn't know what we were dealing with. It was a health and safety issue."

"Yes, of course."

"Why did you ask?"

"Oh… nothing of great importance."

"So is that it? Do you have any more questions?"

"No," replied Giles. "I mean, yes, I've finished. It's been very informative, thank you. I'm enormously indebted."

"Not at all. It's been a pleasure to help. Would you like another cup of tea before you go?"

Giles looked at his watch.

"Thank you, but I must get back to Fiona. We spotted the Florida Aquarium from the taxi on the way here, and I promised we'd make a quick visit before the ship sets off. I see we've got about four hours. Do you think we'll be able to get a snack there?"

"Yes, look for the Caribbean Cantina. I often go there."

"Thank you."

"No doubt I'll see you around… hopefully not as a patient!"

Chapter Twenty-Six

While Giles had been in the medical centre, Fiona had been busy unpacking and organising their clothes in the cabin. She had seen from the company's brochure how well furnished the cabins were, but not until now had she appreciated the luxury that a modern cruise liner can offer. Captain Morgan had been right. Teuku had certainly done them proud.

Having heard so often from Mingy about her privations on the Java Sea, Fiona emailed her a few photos before settling into an easy chair with a peach from the fruit bowl and switched on the television. She was halfway through a video about the *Oosterdam* when she heard Giles's long-awaited knock.

"You don't look very happy!" she sighed, closing the door behind him. "Don't tell me we've wasted our time."

Giles walked the length of the cabin before turning to face her.

"Let's go outside."

"First, let me pour you a drink," offered Fiona. "We've got a complimentary bottle of mineral water and another of Californian white. That's it, I'm afraid. No chance of a D 'n' S. How about *San Pellegrino* with a slice of one of those Florida lemons over there? The fruit bowl is gorgeous, isn't it? There's something about *Lalique* I find calming yet sensuous at the same time."

Running her fingers along the bowl's glossy rim, she selected an apple and polished it affectionately with a linen napkin.

"It has the same effect on me as Henry Moore," she said.

"Not that fifth-year medical student with the overgrown biceps, I hope?" scoffed Giles.

"No, you can relax. The English sculptor, *Sir* Henry."

"I'll take your word for it."

"Here you are, Giles. One juicy apple, all shiny and ready to crunch. Now, while you're enjoying it and the view of the harbour, you can get me up to date."

"Thanks," replied Giles. "He was very helpful. Couldn't have done more. Poured me a cup of tea, printed out a copy of Margarita Diaz's medical record, and gave me as much time as I wanted to go through it. No pressure at all. I made some notes, which are in my jacket if you want to take a look later."

"Okay. And…?"

"There was one thing. You remember I was speculating if she had one of the rare very mild forms of diabetes, which are inherited and never produce skin ulcers?"

Fiona nodded.

"Well, I still feel that way. The blood sugar levels in the ship's records were certainly consistent with that possibility."

"Did you mention this to the doctor?"

"No."

"Okay, let's move onto the septicaemia? Was he right about that?"

Giles put his feet up as he sank his teeth into the apple.

"Not impossible. The clinical history and blood tests were compatible. But equally, it could have been a few other things. Not surprisingly, the ship's medical centre isn't set up to do blood tests for bacteria."

"And the ulcer?"

"He'd taken a photograph. It was horrendous. As if it was eating her flesh away."

"Is it not at all possible it was diabetic?" asked Fiona. "Not even a wee chance? Even if she did have one of those types of diabetes, perhaps in rare instances they can develop a very small ulcer? Not everything is necessarily in the books. If it was tiny, so small that she hadn't noticed, it could have got infected when she went swimming, couldn't it? Public pools can be a a cesspit. Did you know that?"

"Carry on."

"The list of microbes that can exist in a public pool is as long as your arm. When I was doing my PhD, a friend in the same digs was studying microbiology. One evening, when we were cleaning the bathroom, she told me that, according to our old friend the Centres for Disease Control, for every hundred people who go for a swim, on average they leave behind half an ounce of poop. That's fourteen grams. If you can't picture how much that is, one Oreo, America's favourite cookie, weighs about eleven grams. She knew that because she'd worked in a cafeteria in Houston during the summer. Now, according to UNICEF, just one gram of human poop can contain... wait for it... ten million viruses, a million bacteria, a thousand parasite cysts, and a hundred parasite eggs. So, if you take a pool of one hundred cubic metres, for example, that adds up to about one thousand five hundred of those little treats in every litre. While you're splasing around having a good time, all that's going in your mouth, your eyes, your nose. All from just one hundred people. Imagine five hundred, six hundred... yuck! And we're talking about healthy swimmers. Unlike some countries, in the good old UK you can go swimming in a public pool, if you so choose, with a suppurating carbuncle on your bum. Nobody checks, do they? One reason why I never use a swimming pool, only the sea."

"Horrible thought!" said Giles. "So you're suggesting that, even if she had a very small ulcer, she hadn't noticed it could have got infected if the pool contained something nasty?"

"Yes. It's a remote possibility, I suppose, but..."

"Did your friend say what sort of bugs could be there?"

"From memory, the most common were *Pseudomonas, E coli...*"

"*Pseudomonas* can certainly cause wound infections and septicaemia... especially in people with low resistance. And they can be drug resistant."

"Why don't you call her specialist?"

"Too risky. He's bound to wonder what's going on. I doubt if my story about doing research on sickness at sea would pull the wool over his eyes. He'd start asking questions. We don't know where it would lead."

"True, I suppose," said Fiona. "Did you learn anything else?"

"Yes. Apparently, when asked if she'd been bitten by anything, she said she hadn't. But... wait for it... there had been a mosquito in her cabin."

"What! So she *could* have been bitten in her sleep?"

"Theoretically, yes."

"So what next? Does he have any frozen blood left over?"

"No. Unfortunately, my expectation that there would be some sitting in their freezer was wrong. To avoid any risk of infection, they incinerated everything as a safety measure."

"Ugh!" said Fiona, showing her frustration. "So no DNA tests? The main reason for coming here?"

"Yes...or no, whichever way you look at it."

"So, what do we do? Teuku paid a fortune for our tickets. Do we call him and tell him it's been a waste of time and money, and fly back? God, what a thought! I'm so in need of a holiday, Giles."

"And a holiday you shall have, my dear. As you say, you need it. I'm sure Teuku would want you to have it. And he probably wouldn't get the money back, anyhow. So let's make the most of it. Take it easy for a change, and enjoy the cruise like everyone else. And who knows? This salty air may give us some inspiration."

"Let's hope so. If not, at least the inspiration will give us some salty air."

"Clever!"

Chapter Twenty-Seven

Giles was soon to find that life at sea had changed a lot since he had made the journey from Southampton to Sydney in his youth. In the waning years of ocean-going travel, when P&O liners and the rest had regularly taken immigrants, national sports teams, civil servants, businessmen, and wealthy tourists between Britain and its colonial and post-colonial outposts, it had been a means of transport, nothing more than that. You could travel First or Tourist Class, and it would take four weeks to reach Australia via Cape Town, about the same time to return via the Pacific and Panama Canal. The journeys were leisurely affairs, during which time seemed to stand still while you were detached from the real world, reconnecting every now and then to take a quick look at the prettiest and most interesting parts. There was some entertainment on board, but, compared with the cabarets, opera singers, ice-skaters, and circus acts of modern cruise packages, it was very low key. There might be a baroque ensemble of flute, oboe, violin, and cello in the lounge during afternoon tea; a pianist playing Chopin or Debussy in the bar; ballroom dancing of an evening; table tennis when the swell permitted; poker and bridge if you were that type; chess, draughts, or dominoes if you were not. There was something for everyone. But not a lot. The emphasis was on quiet relaxation, dining, socialising, reading, writing letters, reminiscing about the last port of call, and looking forward to the next one.

As passengers were relatively few in number, faces soon became familiar. Lasting friendships were forged during long, sunny, breezy days with little else to do but chat over the muffled rumble of the turbines and the gentle slosh-slosh of the waves against the bow. The ship became a home from home, one whose lights were a welcoming sight whenever your coach returned from a day in the hinterland, or your taxi escaped from the bustle of the city traffic onto the quayside.

On the evening of the *Oosterdam's* departure, Giles was contemplating all of this on the veranda as Fiona placed their complimentary bottle of wine in the ice bucket.

"Cheers, Giles, and *bon voyage!*"

"*Bon voyage!*" Giles replied. "You know, Fiona, from what we saw during our after-dinner stroll, this is going to be about as different from my one and only previous sea trip as you can imagine. It will be a holiday experience, a good one I expect, and educational to a degree... but not an adventure. When we return to Tampa, it'll feel like we're checking out of a five-star hotel, nothing more. But, in the old oceangoing steamers, when a one-way passage came to an end, you found yourself in a strange land you'd only marvelled at in atlases and read about in books. You felt a very, very long way from home, disconnected from all that was familiar and dear to you in a way that you never experience these days. The Earth seemed so vast. If you've never experienced what maritime travel was like in those days, I don't think you can imagine it."

He paused to take a sip of his wine and gazed out at sea.

"When the moment came to leave the cabin, to say your goodbyes, and disembark, you were excited, fascinated, grateful to have reached your destination safely, and looking forward to a new life. But it was all tempered by a painful anticipation of the nostalgia you knew must lie ahead. You descended the gangplank with a beat in your chest and an ache in your stomach, knowing that this time it wasn't to be *au revoir*, but *adieu*. As you stepped onto the dockside, you turned to look at her for the last time, like a dear old friend, and gave her a wave with a tear in your eye. And when, many years later, you learnt she'd been scrapped, it felt like a real bereavement."

"Your ship was the *Arcadia*, right?"

"That's right. A lovely lady."

"And when was she… you know?"

"1979… in Taiwan… a long way from the place of her birth, John Brown's shipyard in Clydebank. I suppose she was recycled into nails, screws, nuts, and bolts… lavatory chains and kitchen knives. And, like an old fool, I've just made myself feel really sad."

He paused to look at Fiona with heavy eyes, and wiped his check with his sleeve.

"Am I going mad?"

"Definitely not!" said Fiona. "I've been on this one for only a few hours, and I'm already sensing a strange sort of bond, like it's becoming part of me. Obviously, ships can have a strange effect on you."

"I can't imagine what it's like to be an old sea dog. How must they feel when they have to change ship after many years – or, even worse, retire?"

"What is it, do you think, that draws people to a life at sea?" Fiona asked as she also scanned the vast expanse before her.

"Years ago," replied Giles, "I suppose for most it was either adventure or poverty, unless you'd been press ganged in the docks after too much grog. But today it could be other things, I imagine: escape from the pressures and stresses of life on shore; the feeling of freedom and space that's so difficult to find in other walks of life? Perhaps, in some cases, even a masochistic attraction to unpredictability or danger. I don't know. It's an interesting question, isn't it?"

Fiona rasied her glass.

"Well, whatever it is, let's drink to the *Arcadia*."

"To the *Arcadia*. May she rest in pieces," laughed Giles.

Fiona reached to hold his hand.

"That's the spirit! To change the subject, have you had any thoughts about where to go next?"

Giles merely shrugged his shoulders as if his mind was elsewhere.

"I'm wondering if it would be worth asking one of the nurses about those blood samples?" said Fiona. "Perhaps they'd popped some in the freezer without the doctor knowing?"

"Unlikely, I think. But worth doing, I agree. You never know."

"Okay, so that's one thing I can do to make myself useful," said Fiona. "I'll nip down to the medical centre in the morning and have a quiet word. How many does he have?"

"Nurses?"

"Yes."

"I only met one, but the place was empty. Now we've set sail, they may be busy. First day is probably the worst one for sea sickness… as you may be about to discover."

"Fortunately, we're near the centre of the ship, Giles, which I gather is the best place. That was a tip I got from Angela. She said that, if I could afford to, I should choose cabin VA8071, because it's almost dead centre."

"Where was Margarita Diaz's cabin, by the way?" asked Giles.

"Can't recall. But I did jot it down. It's in my notes." "I'll go and fetch them. In the meantime, perhaps you can give me a re-fill."

When Fiona returned, she pushed the glasses to one side and placed a deck plan framed in brass in their place.

"Sorry it took so long," she said. "I also made a trip to the loo. And while I was there, lo and behold, I saw this on the back of the door. Isn't that convenient? I had to unscrew it, but my nail file did that job. So, never complain about me and the ladies' room again!"

Fiona looked at Giles's notes in the centre of the table. "Now, I've seen at the top of your notes you wrote down 'SB8140'. Was that the number of her cabin?"

"Yes."

"Okay, let me see… here it is. She had a Neptune Suite. Even bigger than ours. Mind you, she did come from a wealthy family. I looked her up. Her mother was descended from Mexican nobility. And look, it's on the same floor… sorry, deck… as us, right at the back… sorry, stern… on the port side."

"How many decks are there?" asked Giles.

"Eleven in all, seven with cabins, of which there are more

than nine hundred. It says so here, at the bottom. I wonder how many maids they need to look after that lot?"

"I think they only have cabin stewards, not maids," said Giles.

"*Men?*"

Giles nodded.

"That's interesting!"

"Why?"

"Er… nothing, really. It's just that… oh, never mind."

"Mmm… this sounds worrying!" said Giles.

"Don't be silly! It's just that it's given me an idea. That's all."

"An idea?"

"Yes."

"Can you let me in on the secret?"

"Eventually," said Fiona. "But not just now. I need to work on it. You'll have to be patient. Sorry!"

Squeezing his hand, Fiona got up to lean over the railing and inhale the sea breeze.

"I think I'm beginning to understand why people get addicted to cruises," she said. "You feel so detached from the world, when all you can see around you is water and the sky. It's so quiet. And the sky's so clear. Just look at those stars… and the moon. You get the feeling you could reach out and touch it. It has such a calming effect. Perhaps that's the attraction for Captain Morgan and Dr Bandaranaike? In one fell swoop, as soon as the ship sets sail, you leave so many problems behind… the traffic, the crowds, the pollution, wars, economic crises, politics, earthquakes, the kitchen sink. I think that's it. A kind of escapism."

"And who can blame them?" replied Giles. "It must hit them though, when they drop anchor for the last time, and have to return to the real world on dry land – to a home instead of a cabin, a garden instead of a deck, a kitchen instead of a galley, an unchanging motionless landscape instead of an ever-changing seascape, to a sweater and jeans instead of a uniform, to hordes of strangers' faces instead of the reassuringly familiar ones of crew members."

Giles moved to join her as he searched his head for a few fitting lines. As usual, it didn't take him very long.

"'Like a battered hulk seems he,

'Cast high on a foreign strand,

'Though he feels in port, as needs must be,

'And the stay of a daughter's hand.

'Yet ever the round of the listless hours,

'His pipe, in the languid air.

'The grass, the trees, and the garden flowers,

'And the strange earth everywhere!'"

"The *strange* earth," sighed Fiona. "That's how it must feel, I suppose. It puts it in a nutshell... or, should I say, a seashell? I suppose now you're going to tell me who wrote it, and his or her life story?"

"Correct," said Giles. "I always think one owes it to the writer. In this case, another American, James Whitcomb Riley, born in the mid-eighteen hundreds in Indiana. One of the very few people to become rich in his lifetime from writing poetry."

"What was his secret?"

"Mostly children's poetry. He used to go around the country reading his poems at public meetings and special events for a fee."

"Clever!" said Fiona, standing up. "I suppose poetry can be a type of escapism too. But that's one for another day. I'm off for a bit of escapism of my own now... to soak in a bubble bath. Thought it would be an unusual experience afloat. But also, there's something I need to think about... and it's not about cabin stewards... or even poetry."

"Anything I can help with?"

"Apart from scrubbing my back, not just now, thanks. I really have had an idea. A big one. Possibly my best yet, dare I say. But I need to work on it."

Chapter Twenty-Eight

After completing her exercises on the veranda, leaving Giles to sleep off his previous night's excesses, Fiona had called cabin service for porridge, kippers, oat cakes, chunky marmalade, and a pot of tea.

"Wakey-wakey! It's eight-fifteen," she whispered in his ear. "I'm popping down to the medical centre to ask the nurse if she has any blood that Dr B doesn't know about. They should be open for business by now. You'd better get up. I expect the steward will be knocking on the door soon. I heard the clatter of his cleaning trolley go past."

Giles opened one eye as he sniffed the air a few times.

"Why so much perfume? And the dress?"

Opening the other eye, he studied Fiona up and down.

"Not to mention the high heels, net stockings… and is that mascara? What's going on? Am I missing out on a party?"

"Nothing's going on. We're on holiday, aren't we? We're on our way to Mexico on a luxury liner, and the sun's shining. So, I've dressed accordingly. You'll be seeing more of this. No point leaving my gorgeous new dress in the wardrobe. I want to show it off."

"From where I am, you're showing off more than your dress."

"It is a wee bit short, I have to admit. But don't worry. You can trust me. I'll be back soon. *Ciao*!"

On her way to the cabin door, she turned around. "Oh, and by the way… I've ordered a nice Scottish breakfast for us."

***

When Giles was disturbed from his sleep again by a knock on the door, he withdrew his arm from under the pillow and looked at his watch.

"Past nine-thirty! Must be the steward. Jesus, Fiona, are you here?"

Hearing no answer, he pulled on his dressing gown and opened the door to find it was not who he expected.

"Still snoozing?" Fiona asked cheerily before skipping past him and flicking off her red stilettos.

"Why so long? Weren't they open?"

"You'll find out soon. I've something *very* interesting to show you. But as I ordered breakfast for nine forty-five, let's wait. It could be one you'll remember for quite a while."

"I doubt it, quite frankly, if it's what you ticked on the menu that was lying on the bed. If it had been hot English muffins dripping in Cornish butter and a plate of Cotswold eggs and Cumberland sausage, it would be different."

"Ha! Here we go again. English Pub Grub's Man of the Year."

Grasping her shoulders, Giles kissed her on the forehead.

"You've got a sample, haven't you?" he said. "I can tell. The nurse had some? Brilliant! Blood, blood, glorious blood! Where is it? In there?"

Fiona held her handbag to her chest as if it contained the crown jewels.

"There is something in here, yes. But it's even better than a blood sample.."

"*Two* blood samples?"

"Even better," said Fiona. "But I'm not letting you in on the secret until you've started your breakfast. It should be here any minute. So go and get yourself spruced up. You look as if you've been sleeping under a bush."

"I feel it too. But why the secrecy?"

"You'll see. Hurry up! I don't want the steward to see you looking like that. It's more than my reputation's worth."

Giles looked at himself in the full-length mirror and rubbed his eyes.

"Ugh! I knew I shouldn't have mixed my drinks last night."

It was not long before Fiona's treat arrived on a silver trolley complete with tartan napkins and a cut glass vase containing a single flower of Scotland's national plant. After declining the steward's offer of help, she wheeled it onto the veranda, transferred everything to the table, and placed her handbag between the two chairs. As this was going to be an experience to remember, she wanted to make the most of it.

She was pouring herself a cup of tea, when Giles reappeared looking his usual self once again in light blue cotton trousers, a dark blue woven belt, white canvas deck shoes, and a pink and white striped cotton shirt, a birthday gift his niece had brought back from one of her business trips to Shanghai.

"My, that looks better!" Fiona rejoiced, clapping her hands. "Welcome back, the real Giles Butterfield. Come and sit down. As you can see, everything's ready. And note there's a not a drop of honey or Tate and Lyle syrup anywhere near your porridge. As you Sassenachs don't know how to eat the stuff, I'm going to teach you. For once, you're going to have it the way it was meant to be."

Giles eyed the crystal glass salt cellar next to his bowl.

"Is it obligatory?"

"Definitely!" said Fiona laughing. "If I can get up in the early hours to achieve a minor miracle while you're sleeping off a hangover, you can learn to eat porridge the proper way. Covering it in syrup is akin to burying chicken *cordon bleu* in tomato ketchup."

"Which, in my opinion, is all chicken *cordon bleu* deserves…" quipped Giles, "before it's pushed aside to make way for some down-to-earth traditional English fare. If you'd said it was like pouring ketchup on a roast of Lakeland Herdwick lamb, or an Aberdeen Angus steak, I would have taken you seriously. But you win. Anything for a quiet life. Meanwhile, you can get on with your minor miracle."

Fiona glanced in his direction with a self-satisfied smirk before picking up her handbag and placing it gently on his lap.

"Take a look in there. But be careful."

"I hope it isn't some jewellery from one of those fancy boutiques we passed yesterday."

"It's *much* more precious than mere trinkets," said Fiona. "So much so I couldn't put a price on it. And yet it didn't cost me a dime."

"What *are* you talking about?"

"What are *you* waiting for? It won't bite… not now, anyhow!"

As she was layering marmalade onto an oatcake, Giles withdrew a clear polythene bag and placed it on the table. He removed his glasses to take a closer look.

"Good heavens! Where on earth…?"

"Cabin SB8140."

"The one Margarita Diaz…?"

Fiona nodded.

"How?"

"I'll tell you soon."

"But it's a…"

"That's right."

"And you're thinking it may…?"

"That's right."

"But this is incredible! How on earth?"

"Are you sitting comfortably?"

"I suppose so."

"Then let me pour you a cup of tea. It's from Scotland, by the way."

"Good one! Everyone's heard of Scottish tea, of course. They even sell it in China, don't they?"

"It *is* Scottish! Look at the label… Dalreoch. It's the real thing, grown in the Highlands. And it's delicious. You'll eat your words, when you get round to it."

"If I do, I hope they taste better than what's in front of me. They should make putting salt on porridge illegal. My blood pressure's high enough as it is, thank you very much."

"Well, you could lose some of that paunch for a start!"

She gave Giles a playful prod on this midrift.

"To continue…" she said, "last night, when you weren't looking, I emailed Angela in Seattle. I told her we were so impressed with the *Oosterdam* that we're already thinking of booking another cruise next summer in one of the plush Neptune Suites. But as they're so expensive, did she think we could look at one before committing ourselves. Fortunately, she was working late again. She replied to say we'd have to ask the ship's Chief Steward. But as he's normally very busy, and would need to stay with us for security reasons, it's unlikely he'd have the time. So instead, I developed a little plan."

"Since when have we been planning to go on another cruise?" asked Giles.

"We haven't," replied Fiona. "I've been learning from the master. All will be clear very soon. Now… you know how every nice girl loves a sailor? Well, on the assumption it's also the case that every sailor… at least, every straight one… loves a nice girl, as soon as I was out of here, I caught the steward's eye. He'd just appeared from the cabin two doors down, and by good fortune was the one who'd carried our bags. After a wave, a cheery 'good morning' and a sweet smile, I gave him the same line I'd given Angela and asked if he could show me cabin SB8140. And guess what? He couldn't have been more obliging."

Fiona broke off to take a spoonful of porridge.

"Mmmm! You *are* eating yours, aren't you, Giles?"

Picking up the salt cellar, she shook it over his bowl.

"There."

"Hold on!"

"It's part of your education."

"A part I could do without, thank you."

"Where was I?" continued Fiona. "Ah, yes. So, with a big grin on his face, the steward downed tools, took me to the suite, accompanied me inside… and in next to no time, I was on the bed."

"What! You and he, you…?"

"Giles! How *could* you? Go and wash your mouth out."

"I plan to as soon as I've finished this spoonful!"

"I didn't say *we* were on the bed, did I?" said Fiona. "By then, he'd left, and I was *standing* on it."

"Why?"

Fiona pointed towards the plastic bag on the table.

"My real reason for going there was on the off chance of finding *that* somewhere. And as you can see, I did! Near the ceiling, directly over the bedhead, was a tiny black smudge with two wings and a red blotch. I could hardly believe my eyes. Using a fruit knife from the coffee table, I scraped the whole lot into that bag, which I found in one of the drawers."

Giles could hardly contain himself. Dropping his spoon, he held the bag up to the light.

"This is brilliant, Fiona! Absolutely brilliant. So if we're lucky, that red stain could very well be Margarita Diaz's blood?"

"Exactly," replied Fiona. "After all, there can't have been many passengers who swatted a mosquito just after being bitten in that particular cabin."

"Thank goodness the steward hadn't spotted it and cleaned it off."

"As I said, Giles, it was near the ceiling."

"You didn't touch it, I hope?"

"Of course not! I didn't want to leave a trace of my DNA on it, did I? That's elementary."

Giles leant forward to have another look at the contents of the bag.

"But can we be sure her DNA would still be there?"

"DNA has survived for thousands of years in Egyptian mummies, hasn't it?"

"Yes, but in an insect's stomach there are enzymes. It might have been digested."

"Some, inevitably, I suppose. But hopefully not all," said Fiona. "Obviously, it was swatted very soon after biting someone. This wouldn't be the first time a swatted mosquito's been used for this sort of thing. There was a murder case in Sicily that was solved, when the forensic lab found blood from the deceased in a mosquito in the accused's car."

"Well, that's certainly encouraging," Giles enthused, rubbing his hands together. "So if that tiny spot of blood is human and contains one of those rare mutations that's known to cause mild diabetes, it *has* to be hers. Could we look also at the mosquito's DNA to confirm the species?"

"No doubt about it," replied Fiona. "The gene for mitochondrial cytochrome C oxidase is the one to look at. It differs between *every* single species of mosquito. In fact, some people think it can probably be used to identify every living species on the planet, believe it or not, not just mosquitoes. It's like a DNA bar code in the supermarket of earthly life."

"Brilliant! And then presumably we can see if the mosquito was carrying West Nile virus. Oh… no we can't. Damn!"

Giles slapped his head in frustration.

"I'm still half asleep. *Her* DNA might be intact, and the mosquitoe's DNA too, but the West Nile virus doesn't have DNA, does it? Its genes are made of RNA, and that degrades very rapidly. There's no chance of there being any left. Shit!"

As Giles raised his eyes, he saw that Fiona was now reclining in her chair, legs crossed, arms folded, smiling confidently.

"Professor Butterfield! I'm surprised at your language. Really!"

"What are you looking so smug about? Do you know something I don't know?"

"Probably quite a lot," said Fiona. "There's no problem. Although all the virus' RNA will have gone, any viral *protein* is likely to have survived. And, believe it or not, there's a test for West Nile virus protein that's been shown to work really well on dead mosquitoes."

"How do you know that?"

"You should read the journals more often, Professor. Get your nose out of the newspapers."

"Come on, get on with it!" urged Giles.

"I've seen a paper on it from our old friend," replied Fiona. "Teuku's one-time employer?"

"The CDC?"

"Yes. Specificity and sensitivity were excellent. So, if that poor wee insect happens to have been carrying a West Nile virus of any type, we can be pretty confident Mucky and Mingy will be able to detect it. All they have to do is get the antibodies."

Giles planted a kiss on her forehead. "Fiona, I know I've said it before, but you're more than a treasure. To think this tiny creature may be such a storehouse of information, information that could hold the keys to saving millions of lives."

He raised the bag to the light once again.

"It makes me think of something an Lebanese-American writer called Khalil Gibran once said. 'In one drop of water are found all the secrets of all the oceans.' In the same way that the history of the oceans must be written in the countless atoms and molecules in sea water, so this insect might encapsulate all the secrets of Ni'ihau."

Giles had been so enthralled that he'd already finished his porridge.

"Thought it would grow on you!" said Fiona.

"What?"

"Porridge, done the proper way."

"Ha! I only suffered in silence to keep you talking."

"Really! Well, stay where you are. I'm going to record this for posterity."

When Fiona had taken her photographs, she moved to the railing to take some of the hungry gulls that were circling overhead, occasionally swooping in search of fragments of food from the decks and balconies.

"Someone else, whose name escapes me… perhaps you know who it was, Giles… once said that, whenever we look out to sea, it's never with 'tired eyes', but with 'hope and expectation'. I used to think only mountains had that effect on me, especially Scottish ones. But I'm beginning to understand what she meant. It's not the sea itself that gives you hope and expectation. That can be rather foreboding. It's the *horizon*. A mountain can inspire because it presents a challenge, one that is touchable, accessible. And as you climb, you can sense the progress. You can see the summit getting closer and closer, the valley more distant, with every step. At sea, the horizon pulls you just as strongly, but it's unattainable. Unlike granite or conglomerate or gabbro, it's always out of reach. It's like a mirage."

Fiona paused and took a deep breath.

"Scientific research is often likened to conquering mountains," she continued. "But I think it's more like being at sea, forever looking ahead. There's never a moment for tired eyes. And you never reach the end. Whatever you discover, there's always more to come. And you don't know really where it's leading."

"You're so right," said Giles. "And on the way, if you're not careful, you can drown and never be heard of again, like my poor old friend John Bates!"

"The guy in Cambridge who published that paper with a big statistics blunder, sent everyone in the wrong direction for a few years, and hasn't been heard of since?"

"Yes, that's the one. You could also say... SHIT!"

Fiona spun round to see Giles dropping onto his hands and knees to peer under the partition separating their veranda from their neighbour's.

"Damn wind!" he screamed. "It swept the bag... the mosquito... under there."

"Oh my God!" shouted Fiona. "Can you see it?"

"Yes, and it's creeping towards the edge! I can see someone in the cabin. Can you..."

Fiona grabbed a kipper from her plate and tossed it over the partition to thud against the neighbour's glass door.

"Damn!" she said. "He didn't hear it. And now here come the gulls for the kipper. What a din! With any luck that should get him out. Yes, here he comes."

The cabin door opened and the occupant stepped out onto the veranda.

"Hello!" called Fiona. "I'm awfully sorry, sir. Can you see that plastic bag on the floor? It's ours. It's very important. Could you catch it?"

Unshaven and dressed only in pyjamas and rubber flip-flops, the old man looked furious as he tried to scatter the gulls.

"Forget about *them*!" shouted Fiona. "The *bag*, please! Quickly, before it's gone!"

"*Jeg beklager, jeg forstår deg ikke,*" the man bellowed above the cacophony. "*Jeg snakker ikke engelsk.*"

"Bloody…! Just our luck!" Giles gasped. "What was that, Swedish?"

"I'm not waiting to find out."

With that, Fiona disappeared, leaving Giles struggling to communicate, first in French, then Italian.

"*Jeg skal rapportere deg til kapteinen!*" the man screamed seconds before Fiona appeared behind him. After charging at two gulls having a tug of war with the bag, she picked it up and retreated into the cabin.

Giles waited several anxious minutes before she returned.

"Oh dear! I had a chat with his wife," she giggled, throwing herself onto the sofa as she waived the bag triumphantly. "She speaks some English. They're Norwegian. She said her husband used to work in the oil industry. And guess what? Like you, he speaks fluent Arabic! So when you catch up with him, you can have a good chinwag together."

"I was terrified when you set about those gulls," said Giles. "They can be very aggressive. They kill pigeons, you know – dogs, even."

"Dogs? I'm glad I didn't know. They look so small… well, medium-sized at least… when they're in the sky. But when they're on top of you, they're *huge*. And their beaks… ugh! And these are only herring gulls. Can't imagine what a greater black-backed is like close up."

"How did you get into their cabin?"

"I was lucky," smiled Fiona. "The door had been propped open by one of the stewards collecting their linen."

"When you've recovered, we'll nip off to the restaurant and celebrate your achievements with a *real* breakfast: streaky bacon, fried bread, kidneys, black pudding…"

"No, thank you! I'll stay with what we aleady have."

"I doubt it."

Giles moved to one side to reveal a group of voracious gulls on the table, now bereft of crockery, fighting over the last few remnants of a kipper.

"I see what you mean," said Fiona. "Okay, you can have your 'traditional English', while I have a cup of coffee and a slice of toast. Then we'll stretch our legs for an hour and agree on a plan of action. And as soon as that's done, I'll give Mingy a call. What time will it be in Nusa?"

Giles looked at his watch.

"By then, I suppose about two o'clock here… so the middle of the night there."

"That's okay. This is too important."

Chapter Twenty-Nine

"It's me, Mingy… Fiona. Sorry it's so late. Don't worry, there's no problem. Giles has seen the ship's doctor. It was very useful, but he had no blood samples, none at all. They'd destroyed them as a precaution. But we've got something just as good, in fact potentially even better. There's not much time, and there's going to be a lot to do at your end. So grab a pen and paper and make some notes."

Upon returning from the Pinnacle Grill, where he'd eaten rather more than he should, Giles had gone onto the veranda to recover, leaving Fiona with the job of getting Mingy up to date. During their walk around the deck, they'd agreed they should waste no time getting the insect to INDOMED. And the only way of doing that would be to disembark the next day at the *Oosterdam*'s first port of call, Cozumel, the small island about ten miles to the east of the Yucatan peninsula. Being one of the best places in the Caribbean Sea for scuba diving and snorkelling, and with a wealth of exotic wildlife, Fiona would have loved to remain there for a few days. But it was not to be.

After updating Mingy with all that had happened since boarding the ship, Fiona moved onto the challenging logistics that lay ahead.

"We'll pack our bags tonight, Mingy, and leave the ship tomorrow morning when it docks at San Miguel de Cozumel on the island. Then, we'll get the specimen to you as quickly as possible. Sending it from the island will be out of the question. We might never see it again. We'll need to get to a city on the Yucatan peninsula, one with good services and international connections. But at present we're lost on that one. Could you ask Teuku's PA to make the arrangements? Air tickets, hotel, whatever – and, most importantly, to find a courier service that can transfer biological material between continents. There are companies that specialise. It would be a bonus if the city could be within reach of one of the archaeological sites in the region, as I'd love to make a day trip when this is off our backs. But, of course, it's not essential. Tell her to email the details to me. And it's critical we have them *before* we get off the ship. So ask her to drop everything as soon as she's in the office…with Teuku's permission, of course."

Mingy informed her that Teuku was not there, that he was at a congress.

"Oh! Well, if there's a problem, let me know and I'll talk to her."Have you got all this down, Mingy? Good! So now we can talk about what preps you and Mucky need to make. But hold on a second…"

Fiona returned to the phone a few minutes later.

"Sorry about that, Mingy. Desperate for the loo. Too much coffee while waiting for Giles to finish his huge English breakfast. Right… the second thing on the menu is the lab work. There are a few assays you and Mucky need to do. So, listen carefully.

"When the mosquito was swatted, its last blood meal ended up on the wall, of course. Fortunately, it looked as if it had been rather greedy. Apparently, they can drink two to three times their own weight of blood. I scraped the blood stain and the mosquito into the same plastic bag.

"We want you to treat the blood in exactly the same way you would a normal blood sample, namely extract and amplify the DNA until you've got enough to work with. Then we want you to see if it contains one of the mutations that cause a goup of uncommon types of diabetes known collectively as 'maturity-onset diabetes of the young'… something of a contradiction of terms… generally abbreviated to MODY. There are several types, each due to a different mutation. Giles thinks the first gene to look at should be the one for GCK, which stands for glucokinase, an enzyme in the pancreas that acts as a sensor of the level of glucose in the blood. A mutation of this gene is one of the most common causes of MODY, and it would fit with the clinical history and glucose levels in the lady's records. If that gene turns out to be normal, you should then sequence the HNF1A and HNF4A genes. That'll do for a start.

"You'll need to burn the midnight oil, I'm afraid, and mug up on the subject. I knew nothing about it until Giles educated me over breakfast, and I don't have time to go into the details right now… Did you get all that down too…? Good! Do you know how to use the high-throughput DNA sequencer in the central lab?

"You say you don't need to because a new girl's arrived who's an expert? Oh, brilliant! Leave it to her then, but remember not to reveal too much. Tell her the DNA is from a diabetic patient or something. I'm afraid Giles and I have learnt that lying is an essential tool of the trade in this business.

"And while you're at it, see if it was a man or a woman. Do you know how? You do… that's right, the amelogenin gene.

"Okay, so now let's move onto the wee beastie itself. We want you to have a go at confirming the species. There's a published method for distinguishing between different ones based on variations in the gene for mitochondrial cytochrome C oxidase. I have a paper on it I will send you. One of the best places from which to extract the DNA from dead mosquitoes is the legs, by the way. Don't use the thorax or abdomen, because you're going to need that for what comes next. But before you do anything, have a careful look at its physical features. You may need a stereoscopic microscope. We don't have one, but I'm sure the malaria people next door will, probably several. See if you can identify the genus it belongs to, if not the species. Teuku may have some contacts in the CDC who could help you with that. Are you happy with all that…? Just about…? Good!

"Now for the last thing. It's critical for us to know whether this little fellow was carrying West Nile virus. We won't be able to look specifically for the Ni'ihau version, as by now the virus'

RNA will have been destroyed. So the best we can do is test for its protein. Fortunately, there are published methods for doing that. Over breakfast, Giles called an entomologist friend who's an expert on this sort of thing to see if there's a commercially available test kit specifically for West Nile virus protein in mosquitoes. And there is. It's called the RAMP WNV test. And it's made by a company called Response Biomedical Corporation in Canada.

"And that's it... a lot to do, I'm afraid. Order all the reagents you're going to need as soon as you get into work. Any questions? Where's the mosquito now? Still in the bag in our cabin's refrigerator.

"Am I sure the DNA will be in good condition? To be honest, we can't guarantee it. But we're hopeful. After all, some German scientists have been analysing DNA collected from the dirt on the floor of caves that's thousands of years old. And I've seen a study that found that human DNA in a blood meal in a mosquito's stomach is okay for a few days. We're hoping that if one is swatted and dries out within that time, the DNA will then remain intact for a long time. In fact, there's a paper describing forensic DNA profiling of human blood from a single dead mosquito. If you want to check it out, it's... wait a tick... it's here somewhere... yes, it's by Curic and coworkers, published in the journal *Forensic Science International: Genetics*. So let's hope for the best.

"How will we ship it? We've thought about that. In case there are delays in transit, we'll put the bag into a polystyrene box with pellets of dry ice. If we can't get dry ice, we'll use normal wet ice. I don't want to revisit past horrors when I've had precious samples ruined after being left under a tropical sun between flights.

"Anything else? No? Good. Okay then, bye for now. And good luck! Give my regards to Mucky."

Fiona ended the call and turned towards Giles, now stretched on the teak sun-lounger holding an open journal above his head.

"Mingy sounds happy," she said. "Very excited, in fact. She'll order everything, and hopefully between now and the morning we'll receive the travel details."

Giles dropped the journal to his chest and removed his sunglasses.

"Well done! I suppose now we'd better ask Dr B to tell Captain Morgan we're about to abandon ship. Otherwise, they might think we've fallen overboard!"

Fiona stooped to take the journal from his hand.

"Good article?"

"Not bad. It's from the *Journal of Maritime Research*. I found it in the pile Dr B sent over."

"What's it about?"

"How the movements of a ship's hull induces seasickness. I never knew you could describe them in so many ways. There are six types of movement: surge, sway, heave, yaw, pitch, and roll, depending… wait for it… on whether you're talking about rotational or translational motion and the vertical, horizontal or transverse axis of the hull."

"Wow! I'm impressed!"

"It seems that sea sickness is produced when pitch, roll and heave occur together, even though on their own they have little or no effect at all."

"I see. What exactly are those three movements?"

"If you have a look, there's a diagram in the article. Pitch is rotation up and down around the hull's transverse axis. Roll is the tilting rotation around its longitudinal axis. And heave is the linear vertical up and down motion."

Fiona watched pensively as, with each description, Giles moved his torso in the corresponding manner.

"And it takes all three of those at once to make you feel seasick?" she asked. "One or two are not enough?"

"That's right."

"That's *very* interesting, actually. Long before I moved to Oxford, I had an affair with a sailor, who used to stay with me for weekends whenever he returned from a voyage."

"And…?"

"Well, now you've told me all about that, it explains something I never understood."

"What exactly?"

"None of your business!"

***

It was twelve hours later when Fiona was awakened by the familiar sound of her smartphone announcing the arrival of an email.

"Giles, wake up! It's arrived," she cried, kicking his foot. "What we've been waiting for. Let me see…"

She picked up her mobile from her bedside table and read the message.

"Teuku's PA has arranged for a vehicle and driver to meet us at the cruise terminal. We need to look out for an orange and white minibus. The driver will have a bag of ice cubes with him from a local gas station. We'll join the eleven o'clock car ferry to Punta Venado, which will take about an hour. From there, we'll take the road up the east coast of the Yucatan peninsula to Cancun airport… about sixty kilometres. That's where he'll drop us off. We don't have to pay him anything. It's already been taken care of. But she advises us to give him a big tip in advance.

"From there, we take the only daily non-stop flight to Villahermosa, on the other side of the peninsula. The ticket will be ready for collection at the VivaAerobus counter. The flight leaves at ten past six this evening, and we should arrive at Villahermosa at twenty to eight. We'll stay the night at the Fairfield Inn, another Marriott, which is about fifteen minutes by cab from the main FedEx depot. She's given us the address. Alternatively, if we want them to collect it from the hotel, she's given us the local telephone number. Either way, FedEx can provide a suitable box and tape, she says. Finally, she reminds us to send her the air waybill number as soon as we've got it, so she can track its progress."

"Sounds like she's done a good job," said Giles, giving a confident thumbs-up.

"Doesn't it? And we're staying in Villahermosa of all places. That's a bit of good luck."

"Why?"

"She says it's within a few hours of some fantastic Mayan temples. Interested?"

"Try and stop me!"

Chapter Thirty

Although the prospect of missing out on Cozumel's seductive turquoise sea and exotic fauna had been unwelcome when Fiona had been packing her suitcase the previous evening, by the time she had seen the panorama from the *Oosterdam*'s observation deck the following morning her attitude had changed. The flat and featureless terrain stretching out to a hazy horizon, with seemingly no vegetation other than mangroves broken by the occasional sinkhole in the soft limestone, it no longer held any appeal.

"You and I are so fortunate, Giles," she sighed, picking up her suitcase in preparation for their departure. "I'm so glad INDOMED's not in a place like this. I don't think I could survive here, no matter how interesting or important our work."

As they turned to go, Captain Morgan appeared from a door with his arms outstretched to greet them.

"Wondered if I might catch the two of you here," he croaked, raising a hand to his mouth. "Don't get too close! Picked up a virus in Florida. I've just seen Dr Bandaranaike. He gave me the sad news you're leaving today. Said you have to return urgently to Oxford. What a pity! So I came looking for you to say goodbye."

"Er… yes, that's right, Captain," said Fiona. "Very disappointing, but that's life, isn't it?"

"Nothing terrible, I hope?"

"No… just unexpected developments at work. That's all."

"Well, you are obviously taking it very well," said the captain. "I'll give the company a call and see if they can reimburse you. Wait a few days, and then email the head office in Seattle. I'm sure they'll look after it. And have a safe journey home."

"Thank you," said Fiona. "You've been most kind."

After disembarking, Giles led the way down the long wooden pier towards the car park. The promised orange minibus was already there with the driver sitting on the rear fender puffing a cigar. Upon arriving and shaking his moist chubby hand, Fiona could see he was everything she had feared.

"I suppose some people would describe him as archetypically Mexican, if you know what I mean," she would later relate to Mouktar and Mingzhu over tea and biscuits on the terrace of INDOMED's cafeteria. "Although, I hasten to add I regard such generalisations as bigoted. He was in his late twenties or early thirties, short and fat with shiny black hair, moustache, and a seven o'clock shadow… in fact, more like ten o'clock! All that was missing was the sombrero and a serape. Nothing wrong with any of that, of course, but what alarmed me was the vehicle – a 1950s Volkswagen microbus that had recently been given a paint job – as much to hold it together as anything else, I imagine. And the tyres! I doubted they would last the day. And I was right. Less than two hours later, as we were leaving the *Transcaribe* ferry on the other side of the water, the rear left tyre went completely flat. The next twenty minutes were a nightmare. Can you believe he changed it in front of the ferry's exit, completely blocking the way of other vehicles? Cars, buses, trucks, vans, you name it. There was pandemonium, horns honking, people shouting and shaking their fists. But he didn't care a bit. He just quietly got on with the job, even grinning and blowing a kiss to the irate lady driver behind us, and then lighting another cigar while sitting on the spare. I didn't know whether to cry or to laugh. Giles knew what to do, though. He said it reminded him of some bygone television commercials for Hamlet cigars… long before my time… in which a young man in a world of his own, oblivious to shouting, gun fire, explosions, and chaos all around him, contentedly puffs away and blows smoke rings. Giles even started playing Bach's 'Air on a G String' on his phone, as it was the commercial's regular background music. With one leg over the front seat, he tucked into a banana he'd lifted from the ship's breakfast bar, and flicked through an old magazine he'd found on the vehicle's floor.

"Once we'd got going again, now with the old wheel, complete with mud and oil, dumped on our nice new bags, he darted off at speed. The old banger sped along the pot-holed highway that follows the coast, and didn't stop until we'd reached Cancun's airport, gratefully about ten miles short of the city. What it would have been like with him negotiating the congested streets in that crate and the stifling heat I can't imagine. Anyhow, once he'd found the car park, he dropped us off, dropped our bags onto the sticky bitumen, and set off again with nothing more than a wave.

"Quite extraordinary. But, to be fair, at least he got us there in time to collect the tickets. So I suppose we can't complain. After that, apart from a few storm clouds, the flight to Villahermosa was mercifully smooth. The hotel was very nice, and we downed some scrumptious *enchiladas* and a bottle of local red wine before retiring. The next morning, we battled through the rush-hour crowds to the FedEx office, packed the specimen with dry ice, and sent it off with our fingers crossed. Thank goodness it arrived safely!

"Released from that heavy responsibility, we went for a stroll across the city to the *Palacio de Gobierno*, and then to a pretty nearby park with a lake, whose name I've forgotten. We sat on the grass with a gorgeous fresh breeze in our faces, and enjoyed a take-away of fish *tacos* and red rice. At least, I enjoyed it. I'm not so sure about you-know-who. I suspect he would have preferred a hot Cornish pasty or a Melton Mowbray pork pie with pickled onions, if that means anything to you. Anyhow, coming after the previous day's journey, it was all very restful. In fact, we enjoyed it so much we decided, there and then, to remain in Mexico for a while to have a well-earned break. And, as you know by now, that's what gave us our really big break!"

Fiona paused while she stretched towards the tea pot.

"More green tea?"

As Fiona refilled their cups and offered Mingzhu one of the *kue nastar* pineapple cookies the maid had prepared as a homecoming gift, she would begin to describe the remarkable journey that had started as a simple day trip from Villahermosa, but ended more than two thousand miles away after the journey of a lifetime. Fearful that their two young colleagues might accidentally leak details of their movements, Giles had insisted on keeping them in the dark until the adventure was over, keeping only Teuku informed of their progress.

And what an adventure it had been!

Chapter Thirty-One

It all began with a trip to the colourful town of Palenque, to the south-east of Villahermosa and a little more than a two-hour drive from the coast. Departing from the hotel after an early breakfast in the mid-sized Chevrolet Giles had rented, they aimed to arrive in time for lunch before making their way on foot through the Lacandon rainforest to the nearby Mayan temples. As Fiona had left her driving licence in Nusa Ceningan, Giles took the wheel while she acted as the navigator. Not that one was really necessary, for, apart from a gentle change in direction every now and then, Federal Highway 186 was tediously straight – so much so that, after little more than twenty minutes, Giles had become so quiet that Fiona feared he was succumbing to the after effects of their late night.

After putting on a CD of lively Mexican music she'd found in the glovebox, Fiona chatted about anything that came into her head. But she needn't have worried. Far from being drowsy, Giles's brain had been in overdrive from the moment they'd joined the highway. Despite his enthusiasm for their destination, his thoughts had wandered back to Oxford. Perhaps it was the green fields and trees on either side, or the mere fact of driving a car again after so many weeks. But, whatever the reason, the huge donation sitting in the College's bank account thanks to Rashid Yamani's unexplained generosity had made an unwelcome return to his consciousness.

"What *on earth* was that all about?" he agonised inwardly. "If it had been for all I'd done for him, as he'd said to Sir Q, what had he been referring to? My efforts to get him a Nobel? For lifting the lid on Steve? Or was he looking to the future, hoping it would guarantee more nominations until we are home and dry? Or, as Fiona had suggested, coming so soon after Jane's gaffe about Brigitte Yusuf in Aram's presence, could it have been a reward for keeping quiet? Or as Fiona said, was it to *keep* our mouths shut until he finds a permanent solution? But if Mouktar was trying to kill me with that snake, why hasn't he tried again one way or another? And Mouktar wouldn't be a very good choice for a hitman, would he? Why risk an amateur messing it up, panicking, or spilling the beans, when Rashid can afford the best, like he did in Sorrento?"

He reached for the strip of chewing gum Fiona had slipped into his top shirt pocket when boarding the flight in Cancun. Watching him struggle to unwrap it with one hand, she took over and popped it into his mouth. Without acknowledging the gesture, he continued to brood, his eyes fixed on the road.

"And while we're at it," he thought, "there's also the small matter of the Steve lookalike in Mexico City, isn't there? Could it really have been him? In a metropolis of eight or nine million, there must be many with a passing resemblance to Steve. Although I don't suppose many can have a mole like that peculiar one of his. Fiona was right about that. And nobody seems to know where he ended up, do they? He could be anywhere. Why not Mexico?"

Although these questions had been troubling Giles for a while, only lately had they been getting on top of him. It wasn't that he was averse to having conundrums on his mind. On the contrary, normally he enjoyed it. Back in Oxford he loved the fact that, whenever they found the answer to one question, it invariably presented them with a new problem. And, when that had been solved, it would create another. And so it went on. That's how humans, he would tell his students, got from rubbing two stones together to computers and gene therapy. But he *did* get exasperated whenever a pressing question couldn't be addressed through lack of time, resources, or opportunity.

Already tired of the first piece of gum he'd chewed in many years, he offered it to Fiona for disposal, his eyes still fixed ahead.

"Charming! Thank you, Professor Butterfield," said quipped. "I was really hoping you'd share it with me."

"Sorry, dear! I wasn't…"

"Are you all right?" asked Fiona. "You've been so quiet, at first I thought you might be nodding off. But then I could see you were just thinking. Of course, I've been wondering what's going on in there."

She raised her hand to tap him lightly on the temple. "A penny for your thoughts?"

"They're not worth that much, I'm afraid," said Giles. "Not even a farthing, if you know what that is… or was."

"I do," replied Fiona. "It was worth a quarter of a penny in the old pounds-shillings-and-pence days. It had a picture of a little wren on it. I remember my aunt showing me one, and one of those lovely twelve-sided threepenny bits with a Tudor portcullis on one side. Coins are so boring these days compared with them."

"Actually, I was thinking about a rather larger stack of cash, namely the mysterious donation Rashid gave to the College. Then I drifted onto your suspicions about Mucky and that snake, even if I still think they're a bit far-fetched. Finally, I ended up with the time you thought you might have seen Steve. Those things are like three spiders dangling over me by threads of gossamer. Wherever I go, they're always there, teasing me and tickling my nut with their legs. I want to catch them and follow each thread to its source. But I can't. So they just keep tickling."

"Ha! I like that. Very picturesque! Twenty-four little legs teasing you. I can see the mischievous grins on their sinister arachnoid faces. Of course, you *could* simply swat them and have done with."

"I wish it were that easy. How far to go?"

"Let me see…"

Fiona opened up the map on her lap and studied it for a few seconds.

"Judging by the lake on the left, we're about fifteen miles from the border with Chiapas. After another twenty or so, we turn right. Then it's another ten miles or thereabouts."

Having agreed during the previous evening's stroll around Villahermosa that the only meal they were ever likely to have in the heart of Maya country should be according to local traditions untarnished by Spanish influence, Giles brought the car to a standstill outside a *taberna* near Palenque's *Plaza de las Artesanias*. Twenty minutes later, sitting on a veranda of cobwebbed timber, festooned with flowering climbers from which Fiona had sneaked a couple of cuttings, they were dining on *tamales* and grilled *pejelagarto*, the local freshwater fish, seasoned in lime juice and *chile amashito*. In place of dessert, Fiona indulged in a mug of *chorote,* the corn and cacao drink that has been a staple with the Maya people for centuries. Less adventurously, Giles opted for a fruit salad of bananas, *saramuyo*, and *guanábana*. With the veranda to themselves apart from the owners' noisy parrot and occasional visits from a curious oriole, it was an occasion they would remember as one of the high notes of their trip.

Though the walk to the archaeological site through the forest was, for the most part, flat, in the heat and humidity of early afternoon it proved to be more challenging than Giles had bargained for. Seeing how he was suffering, Fiona waved down a Jeep carrying two young Americans and asked if they could hitch a lift as far as the *Motiepa* waterfall, ten minutes by foot from the ruins. Upon arriving at the footpath that followed the fast-flowing river through the trees, she presented the couple with a bottle of *Xtabentún*, the local liqueur made from anise and fermented honey, which she'd bought when leaving the restaurant. It was a gesture that, by the end of the day, would bring its rewards.

As Fiona led the way towards the sound of rushing water, the vegetation became denser and taller, the air cooler, the footpath darker. The atmosphere reminded her of the pictures of luxuriant forests in her books of Scottish fairy tales she had loved so much as a child in Sligachan. Though in many ways very different, the almost impenetrable walls of branches and leaves on either side evoked the same thrill of mystery and adventure.

"You know, Giles," she called wistfully above the cacophony of a troop of howler monkeys, "being in a place like this makes you realise that, even if we were to spend a thousand years exploring the four corners of the earth, we'd still see only a fraction of the life forms that occupy it. Most are hidden in forests like this, in the oceans, in rivers, in the soil even. It's awesome. We live our lives on the planet and feel at home here. But it's a home we hardly know. It's like living in a Scottish manse of a thousand rooms, but only ever entering a handful and having no inkling of who's in all the others. It's our abode and yet it isn't. Most of it is inhabited by thousands of distant relatives we'll never meet."

"Relatives?"

"Yes. Perhaps that sounds odd. But to me, all living things are our relatives. Living creatures are just one big complex family."

"Including plants?"

"Why not? Somewhere, billions of years ago, we all had a common ancestor. I've always felt that very deeply, ever since my childhood."

The monkeys now having moved on, Fiona held her breath as she listened to the music of the forest, cupping her ears to encourage Giles to do likewise.

"Shush!" she said. "Listen to that! Isn't it incredible? So many sounds. There's an unimaginable host of creatures in there. Hundreds of eyes could be watching us. And we know nothing of them. It makes me feel so ignorant. It's staggering to contemplate the teaming variety that surrounds us at this moment."

Fiona clasped her head in her hands and turned full circle as she scanned the scene.

"First Indonesia, now this! I don't think I'll ever recover from this trip, Giles. It's going to change me forever. In fact, it has done already. I can feel it."

She approached a flowering bromeliad at the river's edge and peeked inside its clusters of glossy leaves, each holding a small pool of rainwater alive with insects and their larvae.

"And here's some of them swimming around in their own little world, their own ocean. I once read that the water held by these plants is home to hundreds of species of insects, even salamanders too, and tree frogs."

Fiona separated a few clusters of leaves and peered inside.

"No frogs in this one, though. Isn't this thing beautiful? As you know, I've always had a love affair with plants. In fact, sometimes I think I should have been a botanist. They're taken for granted by most people, as if they're mere statues, ornaments, or pictures on a wall. Admiring the prettiness of flowers or their aroma is usually about as far as it goes. But let them spot a squirrel or a lizard on the same branch and they get all excited. And yet, in some ways, plants are more interesting. The problem is that most people know nothing about them… their structure, their chemistry, their place in the natural world, their importance in evolution and by guaranteeing the survival of the rest of us. Ralph Waldo Emerson once said 'The wonder is that we can see trees and not wonder more' – or something like that, anyway. And he was right."

Equally moved by the sudden immersion in nature, Giles had been listening from the roadside. As Fiona approached, he turned towards a soaring kapok, perhaps two hundred feet tall, and placed a hand on one of the massive buttresses that supported its trunk in the soft organic earth.

"Couldn't agree more, Fiona. Just look at this specimen… a veritable lord of the forest… at a wild guess, perhaps a hundred tons or more. And to think it was once nothing more than one of these."

He stamped on one of the tree's fruits lying between his feet to release its dark brown seeds.

"And somehow, with nothing more than sunlight, the air we breathe, and the water and minerals in the soil, its tiny speck of DNA, invisible to our eyes, in the course of time created this giant. You mentioned Emerson. He also said 'The creation of a thousand forests is in one acorn'. Even after a lifetime in biological research, I find it all quite staggering. Working within four walls all day, focusing on the minutiae of what's going on inside our own cells, you can lose sight of the big picture. On the one hand there is the enormity of life and its complexity. On the other, how in so many ways we're all so similar... all of us, plants, animals, even bacteria... just as you said."

Giles paused as he raised his eyes to the canopy of leaves above them.

"To think that those branches overhead, the bark under my hand, and that huge clump of moss on the riverbank, are made of the same types of molecules as you and me. And those molecules can be so similar. Who would imagine that the chlorophyll in these leaves around us, the extraordinary green pigment that soaks up the sun's energy and makes it available for the synthesis of glucose, is almost identical to the red pigment that carries oxygen around in our blood, hemoglobin? The only difference is that where a chlorophyll molecule has an atom of magnesium in its centre, the heme part of hemoglobin has an atom of iron in exactly the same place. And yet, their functions are so completely different."

Fiona had never seen Giles in a mood quite like this before. Sure, he had always been in love with nature. They couldn't be so in tune with each other if that were not the case. But rarely did he speak of it with such passion. More often than not, when away from work, he would talk about history or poetry or art. This was a very different Giles.

"Yes, it's so amazing," she sighed, more than happy to continue on the same theme. "You know, I read that chloroplasts, those microscopic bodies in leaves that contain the chlorophyll, originated from chlorophyll-containing *bacteria* that infected a single organism many millions of years ago, and that organism became the ancestor of all today's plants. Mind-boggling! Botanists know this because they've found that chloroplasts have many features that are unique to cyanobacteria, even down to having a special type of DNA that's very similar to bacterial DNA and differs from the rest of the DNA in plants... in the nuclei of their cells. Apparently, if you remove all the chloroplasts from the cell of a plant, it can't make any new ones. New chloroplasts can be created only by the duplication of existing ones. It's as if they were still the bacteria that had infected the leaf, living and multiplying under their own steam."

"Pity our ancestors didn't also develop chloroplasts out of invading bacteria," Giles quipped. "Just think – we wouldn't have to eat, just lie in the sun all day and photosynthesise! Mind you, there would be one big problem."

"What's that? Go on, blind me with science."

"Nothing to do with science. Imagine trying to find naughty green children in this lot!"

Giles scampered into the undergrowth before retreating in haste.

"Jesus! You should see the size of some of the beetles in there. And I'm sure I heard a snake in the undergrowth. From now on I stay on the paths... You probably know," he added, "that mitochondria, the microscopic batteries in our own cells that release energy from glucose, are also the decendents of bacteria. That's why they look so similar."

"Yes, extraordinary, isn't it?" said Fiona. "To think we're partly made up of the leftovers of microbes that infected our ancestors millions of years ago. And this includes our genes. Apparently, the DNA in every one of our cells, yours and mine, contains about a hundred thousand bits and pieces of DNA from viruses that infected our distant ancestors."

At that moment, an orange beetle emerged from under a twig and made its way across Fiona's foot, before opening its wing cases and taking to the air.

"I'll tell you something else amazing, Giles. Even the transfer of genes from plants to insects has happened during evolution. You know we humans and other animals can't manufacture carotenoids, the chemicals from which vitamin A is derived? They're synthesised only by plants. Well, in fact there's one exception. It's a type of aphid. Millions of years ago, an aphid got infected with a fungus, and some of the fungus's DNA got into the genes of the aphid's cells and was passed on to the next generation. As a result, instead of being green like most aphids, this species became the colour of carrots. And it's still that way."

By now, the two of them were sitting at the base of the tree, Fiona having placed her knapsack under her skirt. She reached towards a seedling with the intention of pulling it out for close examination before deciding to leave it alone.

"Plants are so precious," she sighed caressing its young leaves. "Without them, there'd be virtually no life on earth. They create both the fuel and the oxygen we and millions of other species need to survive. We should have more of them in the lab, you know, not to make the place look nicer, but for their significance, what they mean to the world. Without them, the earth would still be the same vast barren emptiness it was for millions of years, the only sounds those of water and the wind. I can't imagine it."

"I can," Giles replied emphatically, tossing a stone into the river. "When I went to central Australia as a young lad, I got up early one morning to climb Ayers Rock. In those days, it wasn't discouraged like it is today. Sadly, nobody cared about the fact it's a sacred place for the Aborigenes. When I got to the top... and it was pretty hairy climb, I can tell you, nothing to hang on to in those days, no ropes like now... the sky was every shade of orange, red, and purple you could imagine. It was glorious. I've never seen sunsets like those in the Red Centre before or since. I could see the horizon for 360 degrees, and was completely alone. There was absolute silence up there, and not a sign of life – not a bird, a spider, a lizard, an insect... nothing. The air was cool and still. It was surreal. Between me and the horizon was nothing but flat, red desert. Although it had some sparse vegetation, you couldn't make it out from where I was, more than a thousand feet up. It was as if I'd been transported back in time.

"I took off my shoes and socks to feel the rock against the soles of my feet. And then, in a sudden strange impulse, everything else, the lot... jeans, T-shirt, even my watch...

until I was standing there stark naked. As I didn't even want to see my clothes, I bundled them up and hid them behind a rock. And then I stood there, mesmerised, looking around, raising my eyes to the sky and gazing at the desert as if I were a prehistoric man."

"I'm trying to imagine it," said Fiona.

"You can't, unless you've been there," replied Giles. "I've often thought about that moment and what drove me to it. I suppose it was a sort of primitive urge to return to our roots, to recreate the experience of our distant forefathers, the challenges they faced in that condition in that sort of environment, not just to survive but to make progress. My guess is they might have been as intelligent as us, with the same emotions, the same aspirations, the same curiosity, the same ingenuity, the same ambitions. And yet, all they had to work with was what lay around me as I stood there.

"We tend to think we're at the end of that evolutionary road, don't we? The end product, the finished article of a production line. But we're not. We're no more the finished article than they were. I wonder what *Homo sapiens* will be like in another million years? Will our species exist? And what will the earth be like?"

"I think I'd rather not know, Giles," Fiona replied gloomily, as she gave the seedling a final caress. "Let's go and see the waterfall."

After their musings in the forest, the visit to the temples was something of an anti-climax. Climbing the tall limestone steps of the Temple of the Cross required more effort than either was ready for in the hot, heavy air. But Fiona was determined to get to the summit. Upon doing so, she lowered her eyes from the forest's canopy and, in her mind's eye, replaced the tourists mingling below with images of Mayan men, women, and children gathering for a ceremony. She wondered what they would have achieved. What inventions, what discoveries? In the course of time, would they have had their own industrial revolution? After all, their civilisation disappeared almost nine hundred years before Hargreaves, Arkwright and the rest revolutionised Britain's textile industry. Clearly, they were very clever people. After all, they'd invented their own systems of numbers and mathematics, hadn't they? They'd studied astronomy, devised their own calendar and writing, built cities without the advantages of iron or the wheel.

She had been brooding on all this when she caught sight of Giles frantically waving from below. Interpreting the gestures that followed to mean that the two new friends they had recently made had offered them a lift back to Palenque, she dusted the seat of her skirt and began the long descent. By the time she had reached the base of the temple, the other three had left for the car park, where she found them sharing a bottle of water inside the couple's vehicle.

"My, that was an experience!" she gasped jumping inside. "Pleased to see you're only drinking water. I have to admit, I was a wee bit worried when I saw Giles with a bottle to his mouth."

The driver offered it to her.

"Thanks. Where do you two hail from?"

"Pardon?"

"She asked where you've come from," Giles explained from the back seat, Fiona having raised the bottle to her mouth.

"Seattle," replied the driver, a quiet red-bearded young man of about twenty-five. "Drove down, all the way. Four thousand miles, including the detours. Wanted to for years, hadn't we Claire? Pissed off with city life, we packed a tent and the rest, set off, and here we are. The name's Jim, by the way."

His blonde, chubby companion in denim dungarees and a loose green T-shirt nodded.

"I'm an ecologist," she said with a tired smile. "He's into geomorphology, if you know what that is. Met in Johns Hopkins. They have a programme on environmental health and engineering there. After graduating, we set off for Washington State hoping we could find jobs in the great outdoors. But instead we ended up behind desks under fluorescent lighting.

Two years later, we decided to start living. And now here we are. Broke, but happy, and actually seeing what interests us, not filling in bloody forms all day. And you?"

"Fiona's the same as me," Giles answered from the back seat. "Geneticist. We work together."

"It's hardly work," Fiona chipped in. "I love it. We both do. We're here on a holiday, a vacation. Giles has a passion for history and archaeology, I for for plants. I've always had a longing to visit a tropical rainforest like this."

"Well, you certainly chose the real thing with this one, didn't they, Jim?" said Claire. "Apparently, there are about two thousand types of plants around here."

"It's a paradise. Where are you heading?" Fiona asked.

"From here it's Guatemala, and then on to Belize, if we survive," said Claire. "After that, it's anyone's guess. Perhaps we'll stay there a while and become a couple of beach bums. Could be worse."

Claire smiled ambivalently before tapping the face of her wristwatch.

"Message received!" said Jim. "Claire keeps me on the straight and narrow. We're camping in the *Pantanos de Centla* biosphere reserve tonight. If you two are returning to Villahermosa from here, you'll be going the same way for part of the route."

Jim pulled a soiled and tattered map from under his seat and tossed it over his shoulder.

"If you follow us in your car for a while after we leave Route 186 at Bajades Grandes, you'll at least get a taste of it before the sun sets. It's a huge area of wetland, moist forests, and mangroves fed by two rivers, the Usumacinta and Grijalva, as they meander towards the Gulf. There's a big mix of fresh and salty water, creating a totally different ecosystem from around here. And millions of birds."

Fiona glanced in Giles's direction, who gave a nod of approval.

"Sounds wonderful."

Chapter Thirty-Two

Having collected their Chevrolet at Palenque, Fiona and Giles set off after Jim, who sped off into the distance. Struggling to keep up with him during the winding downhill run, Giles was relieved to see the Jeep come into view once again, waiting at the junction with the highway. After Fiona had jumped out to ask Jim to slow down from now on, they continued at a more leisurely pace until reaching the small town of Jonuta. From there, in the company of a multitude of birds gathering in the setting sun, among which Fiona was thrilled to identify herons, egrets, ibis, spoonbills, bitterns, and storks through her binoculars, they followed the tortuous course of the Usumacinta on its reluctant journey towards the coast.

By the time they had reached Rivera Alta, an isolated community in a deep bend of the river in the heart of the reserve, the sun had disappeared below the flat horizon. The air was still and the birds' calls were replaced by an eerie silence, interrupted every now and then by the sound of an unseen insect. Jim stopped the Jeep in front of the church and jumped out.

"That's about it, folks," he said through the Chevrolet window. "Hope you enjoyed all the sights and sounds. We'll be pitching our tent near the river… if we're not eaten by mosquitoes before we get under cover! The quickest way back to Villahermosa is not to retrace your steps and rejoin the 186 where we turned off, but to carry on down the road for about twenty miles to Frontera on the coast, where you can join the 180. Turn left, and it'll take you all the way there, about another fifty miles. If you're feeling peckish, you should be able to get a bite at the *La Cabaña del Pescador*. According to our travel guide, the fried fish gets rave reviews. It's on the left-hand side. If you need any gas, I imagine you could get some in Frontera, or later on at El Espino, just after the restaurant. Claire's jotted all this down, with a little sketch, so you don't get lost on the way."

He handed Giles a scrap of paper through the open window.

"We'd better get on with our tent now," he added. "Thought we might get here a little sooner. So, if you'll excuse, we'll say goodbye. It's been nice meeting you. Good luck!"

"Yes, bye, Jim, Claire," Fiona returned. "And thanks again. Enjoy the rest of your trip. Send us a card from Belize. 'Butterfield, Magdalen College, Oxford, England' will reach us."

As the Jeep sped away from the church and disappeared down the small road that leads to the edge of the river, Fiona was left feeling isolated and strangely vulnerable. She took Giles's hand and leant forward to look at the dashboard.

"It's so quiet here now and lonely," said Fiona. "I hope it's safe. Do we have enough petrol? I'd hate to run dry. It looks a bit low to me."

"From what Jim said, I'm sure we've got enough," replied Giles.

"Sure you're sure?"

"Yes. It looks as if it's close to empty, I know, but these gauges always underestimate what's actually in the tank. Don't worry!"

Giles was soon to learn that his confidence was sorely misplaced, for, by the time they'd reached the restaurant, having opted to forego two petrol stations in Frontera, the needle that had become Fiona's obsession had long touched zero. As they walked back to the car an hour later, she could well believe the fried fish, caught in the local rivers, was the best in Tabasco. In fact, it could very well have been the best fish she'd ever eaten. But Giles's promise that they would go straight from there to El Espino, spread along the slow-moving Rio Gónzalez, had done nothing to quell her fear of being stranded for the night.

The moment she had been dreading came soon after they had left the main road to enter the town, the engine spluttering several times before dying. On top of which, it had started raining.

"Okay," Giles sighed, pulling on the handbrake, "I guess my apologies are due. Sorry! So there, I've said it. My old Austin-Healey sitting in Oxford has never let me down like this. I'm afraid they don't make cars like they used to."

"Giles! The reason why your old banger has never let you down, as you say, is probably because its petrol gauge is faulty, and is telling you there's less petrol in the tank than is actually the case. Presumably, this one is doing what it's supposed to do. It's what we scientists call 'accurate'. In other words, when it says it's empty, it's because that's what it actually is… empty! So what do we do now? I'm terrified."

"Message received! It looks like there's no option, I'm afraid, but to get out and push until we find a petrol station. There must be one around here. Pray hard it's not too far. It could be worse. At least we're on level ground."

"Yes, aren't we lucky! And look, it's only raining too, when it could have been a hurricane! Indeed, we are truly blessed."

After accepting an offer from two teenagers kicking a ball under a neon billboard, Fiona took the wheel while the three males pushed. To her great relief, it was less than five minutes before an illuminated green and white 'Pemex' sign came into view. From then on, Giles left it to the boys, trotting ahead of the car in case it was about to close. After Fiona had stopped alongside two battered pumps, Giles gave the boys a generous tip and began to fill the tank, while she remained inside and took some photographs for the record.

After disappearing into the darkness for a few minutes, Giles reappeared to enter the kiosk before returning with a couple of very wet magazines over his head.

"Poor you!" Fiona gasped. "You look as if you've been for a swim with your clothes on."

"You noticed?" said Giles. "The worst part was when I saw a sign on the pump saying they don't take credit cards. At least, that's how I translated it. Which is when I disappeared.

As I didn't have quite enough cash, I went to look for the two lads to beg the tip back. Not easy when you're reduced to sign language and a mishmash of English and Italian. They weren't very cooperative. So I gave them my Swiss army knife and Montblanc fountain pen in exchange. Never mind. Villahermosa, here we come… assuming we don't get washed off the road. Have you ever seen such lightning?"

Fiona picked up her phone and placed it in the glovebox.

"Been looking at your photos?" asked Giles.

"No," said Fiona. "Took some snaps to remember the occasion."

"You won't need them. You'll have the medical records from my impending bout of double pneumonia to remember me by."

By the time they were back in their hotel, it was well after midnight. As the rain continued to beat against the window, Fiona prepared Giles a D 'n' S from the mini-bar.

"Just look at that!" she said. "Will it never stop? I don't know how you managed to see the road, quite honestly. We might complain about the rain in Oxford, but at least it's never like this. Any emails?"

Giles was lying on the bed in his paisley dressing gown, scrolling through the messages that had arrived during the day.

"Funny you should say that," he replied. "There's one here from Mingy I was just about to read. The good news is the specimen arrived safely, and they took it to the malaria lab to see if they could identify the species."

Fiona placed his drink on the bedside table before making herself comfortable at his side.

"Thanks, I need that," Giles continued. "She attached their report, which I'll now read to you. Here we go. 'Insect type: mosquito.' That's a good start! 'Size: medium. Sex: female. Distinguishing anatomical features. Thorax: upper surface gold in colour. Abdomen: longitudinal stripe of white scales. Proboscis and tarsi: wide pale bands. Maxillary palps: less than half the length of both the antennae and the proboscis.

Conclusion: Features are uniquely those of *Aedes sollicitans*. Comments: If you would like it confirmed genetically, we can do so by determining the insect's cytochrome C oxidase 1 DNA barcode.' And that's it."

Giles paused to take a sip of his drink.

"Returning to Mingy, she says she and Mucky can do the genetic test themselves."

"Should we ask them to do it?"

"Why not? We need to be sure, don't we?"

"Yes, we do," said Fiona, "so I'll give her the go-ahead. Then, after room service has been, I'll look into *Aedes sollicitans* on the internet. Despite all my reading, I've never heard of that particular species. Mind you, it's not surprising, given there are more than three thousand."

Giles moved closer to put a hand on her thigh.

"You don't want to leave it until the morning, do you?"

"No! I couldn't sleep wondering where it might have come from, what viruses it can carry, and so on. I'm a wee bit weary, but this can be my best time of the day."

Fiona removed his hand and placed it in the pocket of his dressing gown.

"And not in the way you seem to be thinking! No nice cups of cocoa tonight, I'm sorry… not even here in the heart of Maya country."

It was a little after three o'clock in the morning when Fiona decided she'd learnt all she needed to know about *Aedes sollicitans* mosquitoes. Seated at the mahogany desk with her laptop and a half-eaten sandwich, she turned to check that Giles was still asleep. As she did so, memories of their night in The Jefferson returned, when she'd burnt the midnight oil to discover how Steve Salomon could have fabricated evidence to conceal his crime; and then in Rome, after Giles had translated the speech Ahmad Sharif would have given had he reached the safety of London after Sorrento.

The circumstances were so similar. Giles asleep, breathing heavily after their busy day; papers covered in notes, and pencil shavings scattered beside her laptop; her suitcase open on the patterned *Zapotec* rug by the open bathroom door. Her eyes followed the shadow of the tall Foxtail fern in its *Talavera* planter, and then settled on the curtains. She moved to draw them back and scanned the sky from left to right. But there was no waning moon on this occasion. In fact, there was no moon at all, just a flash of lightning dispersing among the heavy clouds.

Seeing that the distant rumble of thunder had caused Giles to move, she placed a hand upon his arm.

"Giles, wake up!" she whispered.

After a second attempt and a gentle nudge, his left eye opened slightly.

"What is it?"

"Sorry, Sleeping Beauty, I know you're worn out. But it's happened again."

"Hell! I was snoring? Sorry!"

"No, you weren't. And it's much more important than that. Once again, my time was well spent."

"Why? What have you found?"

As Giles half propped himself up against the headboard, Fiona collected her list and raised a pencil in readiness to tick the items off.

"I've learnt a lot about *Aedes sollicitans*," she began. "Are you ready? First, although they're more important as carriers of other viruses and even a worm that infects the hearts of dogs, they *can* carry West Nile viruses. Second, unlike some species, they can transmit the virus to their eggs. Three, their ability to infect us with the virus is well documented. Fourth, they tend to bite during the afternoon and twilight hours. Five, as they usually fly low above the ground, they don't get to bite birds as much as most species. Their usual victims are mammals."

Giles rubbed his eyes as he started to show real interest.

"Stop there! That last one's interesting because, as you may recall, they found no infected birds on Ni'ihau after the outbreak."

"Yes. The only…"

"Where are they found?"

"That's what I was coming to," Fiona sighed. "They're very common in the Eastern United States, including… wait for it… Florida."

"Ugh! So, it could have flown on board there, while the ship was tied up?"

"Precisely."

"But, at the time there were no passengers in that cabin to swat it, were there?"

"No, but how about one of the crew?"

Giles thought for a moment.

"Would a maid or a steward go to the effort of climbing onto the bed just to swat a mosquito? I doubt it personally. Why bother? And if they went to all that trouble, they'd also clear up the mess afterwards, wouldn't they?"

Fiona shrugged her shoulders.

"So, is that it?" said Giles.

"Nope! Take a look at this, buddy."

Fiona held her phone aloft with the familiar photograph of the two cars in Mexico City on display.

"Remember this?"

"Of course."

Fiona swiped the screen a few times.

"Now look at this pic. What do you see?"

Giles peered at it.

"It's the petrol station we were at earlier."

"Well done. Now describe it… in detail, everything."

"It's difficult, as there was such poor lighting," said Giles. "Apart from the dilapidated kiosk, I can see two petrol pumps, a pile of rubbish in a plastic bin, a tree bending in the wind, and a car with a flat tyre parked on the grass by the drive."

"That's right. Now zoom onto the car. What type is it?"

"A Merc saloon."

"That's right. And, like the two Mercs in the other pic that I took in Mexico City, it's silver. Now compare the number plates."

Giles removed his glasses to get a closer look, and swiped the two photos back and forth several times.

"Good heavens! The plate on the car with the flat tyre has the same number as one of the others."

He zoomed in with two fingers.

"That's…"

"Incredible… isn't it?" said Fiona. "Except for that fact it's true. The only reason I took tonight's pic was for the record. I hadn't spotted the car had the same number plate as the one in Mexico. How could I? Unfortunately, my memory isn't that sharp! The car just happened to be there."

"And when did you realise…?"

"While you were asleep. When I was having a break from the computer and browsing through tonight's photos, I noticed the car's aerial had a red and white flag attached to it. See?"

"Yes, so it has."

"That struck me, because I remembered that one of the cars in Mexico City had a flag like that one, too. You can't see it in the photo, because it was hidden behind a lamp post from where I was standing when I took it. But it stuck in my mind, because I have an uncle who's a member of the SNP and always has a Scottish flag on his aerial."

"At the risk of stating the bloody obvious," said Giles, "presumably it's the same car?"

"Unless the plates were switched for some reason," said Fiona, staring at the images.

"True… but what about the flag?"

"Quite."

"Was the car in question in Mexico City the one the Steve lookalike was driving?"

Fiona nodded. "That's the point."

"My! So, where does that leave us?"

"Presumably, he's down here for some reason. And as it's a very long way from Mexico City, there must be a very good reason. Is Steve interested in archaeology?"

"Not that I know of. His wife, yes, but not him."

"A keen bird watcher?"

"Definitely! But not the type of bird you're thinking of!"

"Yes, I remember once he…" said Fiona. "But never mind! Did he like fishing?"

"Only for opportunities to get credit for other people's ideas."

"He could just be on holiday, of course."

"Yes, why not? It's an interesting country."

"True, but how about this?" said Fiona. "It's a very long shot… but I can't help wondering if it could be something to do with Ni'ihau."

"Why should you imagine that?" asked Giles.

"Because there's something I haven't mentioned yet. I told you *Aedes sollicitans* are common in the Eastern United States. But what I didn't say, because it didn't seem relevant at the time, is that they're not only found there. They're also found along the entire coast of the Gulf of Mexico. Why? Because they're one of the very few species that need brackish water to reproduce. Unlike other mosquitoes, they can't use fresh water in lakes, ponds, puddles, and so on for their eggs. They need slightly salty water that rises and falls, typically where slow-moving rivers meet the sea, exactly the conditions in the reserve we've just visited. For that reason, their common name is the Eastern Saltmarsh. That reserve, a vast expanse of salt marshes and mangroves, must be perfect for them."

"Go on," said Giles.

"Well… if that guy in Mexico City *was* Steve, perhaps he's here for the mosquitoes. And *that's* why the mosquito in the *Oosterdam* was a Saltmarsh. It wasn't a local one that flew on board in Tampa. It came from *right here*. Either that, or its parents did. If you have any shady business to do with mosquitoes, where could be a better place to do it than down there? You can't get much more remote than this."

"Do you know for sure Saltmarsh mosquitoes live there?" asked Giles.

"Definitely. Not only that, but many are infected with West Nile virus. And guess what?"

"Tell me."

"Not surprisingly, the common strain of West Nile in these parts is the Tabasco strain – which, as you know, is one of the two strains that make up the Ni'ihau hybrid, the other strain being from Baja California. Now, you may recall that one of the cars in Mexico City was registered in Tabasco, and the other one in Baja. Look at the photos again."

Giles took her phone and looked at the images.

"Yes, I remember. And I see that the car in the gas station is the one from Baja."

"Yes."

"Tell me, is the Eastern Saltmarsh normally found in Hawaii?"

"No. I looked that up, too. They've never been seen there. The bigger islands have a few mosquito species, but not this one. Even if Saltmarsh ones did exist on the other islands, they couldn't survive on Ni'ihau for long. It's far too dry."

"So, if those mosquitoes on Ni'ihau were Eastern Saltmarsh, presumably any infected eggs they laid after biting people would not have hatched?"

"Yes. Once they'd died or flown away, that would have been it. There would have been no offspring. They would have disappeared without a trace."

"And from what you said before, the chance of any birds getting infected would also have been very small."

"Virtually non-existent, as far as I can tell."

Giles sat up and scratched his head as he struggled to take it all in. The scenario had a familiar feel about it. Were they on the edge of another breakthrough, or simply racing ahead too fast?

"Although it all fits, dear," he said, "and makes a nice story, we don't have any evidence, not a scrap, that the epidemic was caused by Eastern Saltmarsh mosquitoes, do we? It could have been any one of more than three thousand other species. Nor can we be sure that that chap is Steve."

"Unfortunately, that's undeniable," agreed Fiona. "And, quite frankly, right now I don't know where to go from here. I think it's time for a cup of tea."

By the time Fiona had returned with the teapot, two cups, and a basket of drop biscuits, Giles was on his back again gazing at the ceiling. She placed the tray on the bed, and stretched to switch off the bedside lamp before lying beside him.

"What's going on?" asked Giles.

"Don't get alarmed," replied Fiona. "I'm not getting friendly. It's just that I don't like looking at those fan blades overhead. They give me vertigo."

"You could have switched the fan off instead."

"Yes, but I haven't the energy to get up. And anyhow, it's nice to watch the flashes of lightning illuminating the curtains. The pattern with all those dragons and serpents looks so dramatic. Their eyes seem to shine momentarily."

"Well, let's see if you've got the energy to tell me something I don't understand."

"What's that?"

"There's a plausible explanation why none of the horses on Ni'ihau seem to have got ill, namely because, like most horses in the USA, they'd probably been immunised.. But why were no mosquitoes caught in the traps?"

"Remind me when they were set up, Giles."

"A few days after, they'd found increasing levels of West Nile virus antibodies in the blood samples."

"How long would that have taken?"

"About ten days after being bitten. The blood RNA level peaks about five days after infection. The antibodies kick off about ten days later. Busch and coworkers, *Journal of Infectious Diseases*, a few years ago."

"My! You're on the ball today. How come?"

"Bored with the papers Dr B sent me on the ship, I pulled out some I'd brought with me from the villa. This one stuck in my mind."

He sat up as Fiona passed him his cup of tea and a biscuit.

"Well," she replied, "although it can be as long as four, many females only live for two weeks or so after biting. Or perhaps they flew off in search of the right sort of water?"

"If they do that sort of thing," said Giles. "But why don't we give our brains a rest, stop all this guesswork, and wait until all the lab results are in?"

Giles quickly finished his tea and placed the cup back on the tray. He then made himself comfortable, pulled a pillow under his head, and closed his eyes.

"Not just yet, sorry!" said Fiona.

"What now?"

"It's to do with the *Aedes sollicitans* lifecycle. The eggs take one to five days to become larvae, and it takes them another eight to ten to turn into pupae. Then it's another two or three days before the adult emerges. It's the same sort of thing that happens with butterflies. Their eggs become caterpillars, each caterpillar becomes a chrysalis, and out of each one, as if by a miracle, emerges a gorgeous butterfly. After two or three days they mate... the mosquitoes, that is... and the females go in search of the blood they need. So, the time between the first lot of eggs being deposited and the next generation of females emerging biting is two to four weeks, let's say about three on average. Got it?"

Giles wriggled his feet, which Fiona took to mean 'yes'.

"Good," she said. "Now, let's consider the *Oosterdam*. After setting off from San Diego, we know it took six days to reach its first port of call on Kauai. Then, it cruised around the islands, until five days later it ended up at Hilo on the Island of Hawaii. The next day, it set off for the return journey to Mexico. And the day after that, Margarita became ill. So..."

She broke off at the sound of snoring.

"Giles! Are you still awake?"

Chapter Thirty-Three

It was little more than five hours later when Fiona decided she could not tolerate lying there any longer.

"Giles, Giles! Let's get up."

"Already?"

"You weren't asleep?"

"Too much on my mind."

"Me too. I'd started talking about the *Oosterdam*'s itinerary before you nodded off, but we can return to that. I'm more concerned about the fact we need to do something about that Mercedes. We can't just leave it sitting there, waiting to be fixed and then disappear. We *have* to see who gets into it. It's too big an opportunity to miss."

Giles appeared from under the sheet and rested his head on his hands.

"As it happens, that's exactly what I was thinking," he said. "But how? For one thing, we don't know how long it will take them to change the wheel. At the speed they seem to operate around here, it could be a week, even a month. On top of which, once it gets going, it could be difficult to follow without being spotted. It could be risky, very risky. Did you know that this place has about thirty thousand homicides a year?"

"But that's the drug cartels."

"And? Perhaps that's what this is. Nothing to do with mosquitoes?"

"I still think we have no choice."

Fiona put on her dressing gown and drew back the curtains before moving to the dressing table.

"I know!" she cried, brushing her hair. "How about this for a big idea? Why not call Conrad in Cape Town? Perhaps there's a way he could track the car over the internet? Not long ago, some academics showed it's possible to hack into a modern car's computer if it's got a wi-fi system. That expensive Merc must surely have all the latest gadgets."

"What a bloody good idea!" said Giles. "You're getting so good at this, Fiona, you won't need me soon. What's the time?"

"Eight-twenty, according to your watch," said Fiona. "Which means in Cape Town it's... where's your phone?"

"Catch!"

"Thanks. Let me see... three-twenty in the afternoon."

"Might be a little early," said Giles. "Usually, he doesn't get home till around six. Nevertheless, it's worth a try. You go and have a shower and all that stuff, and leave me to it."

When Fiona returned, wearing little more than a white cotton towel around her head, Giles had just replaced the hotel's telephone.

"Sorry about my appearance!" said Fiona. "Dropped my dressing gown onto the wet bathroom floor."

She walked to the wardrobe to slip on one of the beach dresses she'd bought in Nusa Ceningan's market.

"There, now you won't be distracted from more important things."

"Most thoughtful!" said Giles. "Which takes me back to Conrad. The good news is that he doesn't need to do anything fancy like hacking, which he said would be impossible anyway in the time available. All we need is a gadget called a GPRS tracker. His company has one fixed to every car in case they get stolen... or, being in South Africa, where he said more than fifty thousand get nicked every year, I should say for *when* they get stolen. They're also useful for keeping an eye on where their salesmen are in real time.

"Anyhow, we're in luck, because he says they have a few new ones still in their boxes. And, what's more, he'll send us one straight away. It's called a TK-104. When it arrives, we'll need to give him a call and he'll tell us what to do. He said they're magnetic, so with any luck we'll be able to stick it under the car.

Then we'd be able to follow it on a map over the internet. And there's a bonus. We can even send it an instruction, a simple text message, to switch on a microphone that will let us listen to any conversation within range. Incredible, but true. On top of which, we'll be able to activate a motion sensor that will send us an alert whenever the car starts moving."

"Perfect! But how long will it take to get here?"

"He called a courier service on his mobile while we were talking. They told him they *might* be able get it here in thirty-six hours… as long as he can get it to them within the hour. Knowing Conrad, we can probably count on that."

"Thirty-six hours…" said Fiona. "That's tomorrow evening. That would be good going! But what if it takes longer? We can't afford to wait too long. By the time we get back to the petrol station, the car might have gone. Somehow, we need to make sure it stays put until we're there. We need to do something, and quick!"

"Any ideas?"

"How about going back now and…. er… let me think… smash the windscreen? Or puncture another tyre? Anything to keep it hostage. You didn't happen to pack a brick in that suitcase?"

"Alas, that's one thing I didn't think of! But there were plenty of rocks lying around. I stubbed my toe on one."

Giles raised his foot to reveal a blue toenail.

"But hold on," said Fiona. "Today's Saturday, isn't it? I don't suppose there's much chance of that wheel being changed before Monday. That's a bit of luck. So, in fact we can relax and take it easy. As long as the tracker arrives by tomorrow night… or even early Monday morning, we're all set. Phew!"

Giles shook his head.

"Except, on Monday, we'd have wait all day for the sun to set. You couldn't stick it underneath in broad daylight, could you?"

"Oh, I see!" said Fiona. "It's going to be me who sticks it underneath, is it? I can see the days of chivalry have gone. No more the alpha male. More a beta or gamma one these days. I bet you wouldn't have said that when you were quietly fancying me a few years ago. You would have fallen over yourself to show how macho you are."

"I can assure you," replied Giles, "I'm the same knight in shining armour I always was. It's just you're so much slimmer than me. I doubt if I could get under that vehicle. If I could…"

"Stop!" said Fiona. "It's too painful to hear your lame excuses. Let's just say I believe you. So let's hope they don't fix it before I get the chance. Make sure you keep those stubby fingers crossed, Sir Galahad."

Chapter Thirty-Four

Parked a little more than two hundred yards from the gas station, Giles and Fiona were huddled in their car in pitch darkness, when the satellite phone on Giles's lap sprang into life. "This must be Conrad!" he spluttered through one of the cheese and tomato sandwiches provided by the hotel. "How do you work this thing? Oh, there we are. Hello… Conrad? Wonderful to hear your voice! Hold on while I take a slurp of lukewarm instant coffee…and another…that's better! Sorry, but I'd just opened the flask the hotel provided.

"As always, you did a great job, brother dear. The package arrived just before midnight, and we got to the gas station, which is where we are now, at around three in the morning. Fiona has attached the tracker to what she reckons was the chassis… What…? No, she wouldn't let me… ow! Pardon…? She just pinched me for some reason… can't imagine why. She's sitting next to me, smeared in a mixture of engine oil, grit and mud. Anway, we set it up according to your instructions on her laptop, in preparation for which we had the forethought yesterday to buy a pay-as-you-go Internet dongle in Villahermosa.

"We're waiting at the roadside, lights off, trying to keep awake, looking at yet more rain, with the car buffeted by the wind. Never again will I complain about Oxford's drizzle. According to a note on the kiosk door, they should open in a couple of hours. Apart from two very sore bums, our only problem is there's no 3G signal around here. It's very patchy in Mexico, despite there being four providers. Around Villahermosa it's pretty good, but not where we are now. So when the Merc moves off, we'll have to keep it in sight, which will be more than a little hairy if this downpour doesn't stop.

"What did you say? You knew there'd be no signal here…? That's why you put this satellite phone in the box? You're a genius, Conrad. Don't know what we'd do without you. Hold on! What's that, Fiona?"

Giles looked over at Fiona who was gesticulating silently.

"Fiona says she owes you a big kiss. And Giles says that's one debt she's never going to settle… What did you say? Is there any CCTV in the gas station? Very good question. There's a camera fixed to a telegraph pole, which I'm embarrassed to say we didn't spot until we'd finished… What…? Have we covered our number plates? No, I didn't think of that, either… Well, it may be 'bloody obvious' to you, dear brother, sitting in your plush office with nothing to do but play with your Newton's Cradle, or whatever else comes to hand. But here in the real world we're operating in wind, rain, darkness, discomfort, and something called fear. So we're not at our best. In fact, it's bloody terrifying. As you may know, we're deep in the heart of *Los Zetas* territory, and don't yet know for sure who the Merc belongs to. So, if you don't hear from us again, ask the local police to dredge the marshes. We've been up to some antics before, but nothing like this.

"So, if you don't mind, I'll finish my sandwich and try to get some more kip. We've had precious little, and it could be a busy day when the sun rises. We'll keep you up to date. What…? Not that again, please! How many times? Nothing has changed. Talk again later. Bye for now."

As Giles dropped the phone onto his lap, Fiona eyed him inquisitively.

"Everything okay? You seem a little…"

"Just Conrad's usual 'if you two don't tie the knot soon…' etc. I wonder why he's so obsessed with the idea. What's it got to do with him?"

Fiona touched his plastic cup with hers before kissing him on the cheek.

"Here's to us!" she said. "It is rather annoying, I agree. But he's such a nice man. And he's not the only one, you know. Sir Q was dropping hints before we left. And you know what Jane thinks about 'intra-collegiate affairs', as she calls them. Apparently, she thinks either we should get married, or I should move to another college. She reckons relationships like ours are bad for staff morale. Even Ros raised the subject recently. But for different reasons, of course. She's a big romantic. Thinks we were made for each other."

"What did you say?"

"No need to rush. We're not twenty-somethings. It's different when you're older, more experienced with people and life. She'll learn in time, I told her… and hopefully not after too many divorces. We love being together, doing things together, I said. We're a real team in every sense of the word. We bring out the best in each other. It couldn't be better than it is. So why change?"

"I'll slurp to that," said Giles. "How's Ros enjoying her classes at Ruskin College, by the way?"

"Loves them. She's into John Ruskin in a really big way: his essays, his poetry, watercolours, travel, politics, the lot. She's even read his autobiography. Did you know he once had a passion for the daughter of Pedro Domecq, who was in the wine business with his father? Her name was Adele. But it came to nothing. She wasn't interested in him. Ended up marrying a French aristocrat, which sent poor John into a depression so deep that he suspended his studies in Christ Church for a year."

"Very interesting. Presumably, it was the Frenchman who invented the expression '*Je t'aime ma* sherry'… Ouch!"

Giles rubbed his arm where Fiona had pinched him.

"Sorry, but you deserved that," she said. "Unrequited love is nothing to joke about, Giles. It must be so painful. Imagine how you'd feel if I ran off with a Mexican? I'm going back to sleep now, otherwise I'll be completely plonked out by the time we have to move. It'll be your turn in fifteen minutes."

***

After taking turns sleeping on the back seat, it wasn't until a little before midday that there were signs of serious activity around the Mercedes. Giles opened the glove box to take out Fiona's binoculars..

"Just as well you brought these along," he said. "Here, take a closer look."

Lowering her window, Fiona peered between the branches of a nearby manioc tree.

"There's a man in a red T-shirt and black shorts on his knees by the wheel. Now he's got up and opened the boot, trunk, or whatever they call it here. Let's hope he's getting the spare wheel out. Someone else has arrived now, a fat guy in a similar T-shirt and jeans, and yippee... he's pushing a jack! It looks as if we're in business. He's putting the jack in place… obviously knew exactly where to go. And now he's pumping it up."

Fiona broke off to polish the lenses with her handkerchief and get into a better position.

"My, they're quick!" she said. "The car's already up, and he's using a power tool to remove the nuts from the wheel. Meanwhile, the other one's dropped the spare to the ground... Now someone else has turned up on the other side. Must have come from behind the kiosk."

"The Steve lookalike?"

"Can't tell. He's got his back to us at present, leaning on the car door. Now he's walking towards the kiosk, taking something out of his back pocket. Now he's gone into the kiosk."

Giles collected the flask of coffee he'd been holding between his feet.

"Another cup?"

"No thanks. Not the right time."

By the time Giles had poured himself a drink and tossed the flask onto the back seat, the two mechanics were finishing the job.

"You should take back what you said about Mexicans, Giles. Those guys would get a job with any Formula One team. Here comes the other one again. He must be the driver. I think we'll be on the move any time soon. Still can't see him properly through the branches... But it *could* be the one I saw. Certainly about the right height and build. And he has a beard. But so many do around here, don't they? Hold on... He's lighting a pipe. Did Steve smoke a pipe?"

"He did in his twenties," said Giles. "But as soon as he got married, his wife stamped it out. Is he getting in?"

"He must be," replied Fiona. "One of the others is holding the door open while he takes a few puffs. Yes, he's getting in now."

She looked across to Giles.

"Oh dear! I'm getting really nervous, Giles. Soon we'll be on our way. God knows where to! This is a huge country. And that Merc's from Baja California, remember. I hope that's not where they're going. There's rainforests, plains, mountains, deserts, you name it, between here and there."

Giles put on his sunglasses, started the engine, and took a deep breath. Having packed their bags and checked out of the hotel, they were physically prepared for more or less anything... but not mentally. Wherever it would take them, following another car was going to be a hair-raising experience. What if it wasn't Steve? Even worse, what if it was, and they were spotted?

On the way from the hotel, Giles had thought long and hard about what he would do if the Mercedes were to suddenly block the road. The last time he'd tried to reverse a car at speed was in Woodstock, after spotting a policeman when going down a one-way street in the wrong direction The experience of mounting the pavement and striking a garden gate had been bad enough, but veering into a swamp or a river populated by crocodiles would be a different matter. And what if another car appeared from somewhere and got on *their* tail?

There were only two directions the Mercedes could take, both along highway 180. A left would go in the direction of Frontera, which they'd passed through after leaving their American friends in the reserve. A right would take them towards Villahermosa, increasing the chances of a long journey towards Mexico City or deep into the Yucatan peninsula.

Giles's hand was clammy as it rested on the gear stick and he watched the Mercedes pause on the gas station's driveway for what seemed like an age. Had the driver noticed them?

"There he goes, to the left!" he yelped. "Frontera, here we come. Hold onto your hat, Fiona. Wish us good luck."

"I think we're going to need it. He's certainly in a hurry."

After little more than five miles, to their surprise the Mercedes braked heavily and turned right at a junction into a minor road, kicking up mud as it accelerated away.

"Jesus! What the...?" Giles gasped. "So he's not going to Frontera after all. This must take us into the reserve. Check it out, Fiona."

When Fiona looked at her map, she saw he was correct. The road went straight as an arrow into the heart of the reserve. After passing through the small town of Tabasquillo, the road continued as far as a small tributary of the Grijalva River.

"This is starting to look interesting, Giles. Basically, it goes nowhere, with apologies to the residents of a place called Nueva Créacion. That's about eight miles. The road comes to a dead end at the bank of a river, where there's a restaurant. The surrounding area looks to be nothing but marshes, mangroves, and trees."

Giles followed at a safe distance, relieved that the Mercedes was kicking up so much dust that the driver probably couldn't see them. After what he judged to be about six miles, the Mercedes turned left into a narrow winding track that entered an area of dense, moist forest. Giles followed for a hundred yards at a snail's pace, before pulling over and bringing the car to a rest.

"Jesus! I'm sweating like a pig. I know we've lost sight of him, sorry. But I couldn't risk getting closer. I hope our wheels don't sink into this earth. It's pretty soft around here. Then we would have a problem!"

After getting out of the car and cautiously following the track through the trees, occasionally stumbling in deep muddy ruts and causing birds to take flight noisily, they spotted the Mercedes behind a large white motorhome at the edge of a black mangrove swamp. As they crouched behind a convenient buttonwood, the humid air was still and heavy with the smell of decaying vegetation. Fiona wiped her eyes and raised her binoculars to peer between the branches.

"Giles, this is weird!" she whispered. "The tops of the mangroves over there look as if they've been chopped off, and a net has been draped over them into the water, supported in places by bamboo poles. There's no way bamboos could grow naturally around here. Somebody must have stuck them in. And I can see a few birds fluttering around inside."

She paused for a moment.

"And how peculiar! There are what look like paper *espresso* cups hanging from the poles. One or two are floating in the water, too. Here, take the binocs and look for yourself. And look at the driver. Quickly! He's just got out. Is it Steve?"

Giles refocused and stood up to get a better view.

"I see what you mean," he said. "I suppose it could be Steve. He's about the right height and build. He's talking to someone now, who appeared at the door of the motorhome. He's also got the same sort of body language as Steve, the way he's waving his hands around while talking. But take a look at the other guy, Fiona."

Fiona wiped the condensation from the lenses with a sleeve of her cotton blouse.

"Good heavens! He's covered from head to toe. There's not an inch if him exposed. He must be as cooked as a kipper in there. Even his face is covered by a net. This is fascinating.

"Now I'm looking at those birds, Giles. Some are on the ground foraging. And I can see a dead one by the edge of the water. They're all the same type. Black with long legs and very long tails. Let me take a photo."

"Don't forget to switch off the flash," urged Giles. "It's pretty dark here."

"Good thinking."

Once she had taken a few shots, Fiona took the binoculars again and slowly moved forward, holding Giles's hand to be sure he was doing likewise.

"Keep your head down, Giles. This is a bit risky, I know, but I want to get a closer look."

She raised the glasses again.

"I'm focusing on one of those paper cups that's lying on its side. It has something in it. Looks like sugar lumps of all things. And I think there are insects on them. In fact, there are lots of insects. And not just there. They are flying around."

"Sugar lumps are used in labs", Giles interrupted, "to feed mosquitoes as a substitute for nectar and plant juices except, of course, when they need blood. That's what they must be. Let me see..."

Fiona passed the glasses to him.

"It's not possible to tell," she said. "They're too small. But I think… Oops!"

Without warning, Fiona jumped behind a *Laguncularia* bush, pulling Giles with her.

"Sorry, I thought he was about to look this way," she said in a hushed voice. "The guy in protective gear is now giving the Steve lookalike two large plastic boxes… and he's putting them into the car, on the back seat.

"These binoculars are marvellous, aren't they? They're the most powerful I could find. One hundred-and-sixty times magnification. I'm looking at the surface of the water now, and can see some small fish. And there's a huge red dragonfly. Question: what do dragonflies enjoy snacking on more than anything? Answer: mosquito larvae. This must be some sort of mosquito farm, mustn't it? The birds will be there for the females to feed on after mating. Poor creatures! Imagine being trapped under a net with a host of hungry mosquitoes and nothing to swat them with."

"If so," said Giles, "they could be Saltmarsh, couldn't they? Our friend *Aedes sollicitans*?"

"Must be a pretty good chance," replied Fiona. "Here, it's your turn again. No, it isn't. Wait a sec. The other guy's pulling off his garb. He's got jeans and a T-shirt underneath, and he's putting the other stuff in the motorhome. Meanwhile, the Steve lookalike has got into the car… and now his friend's joining him. They'll be coming back in this direction in a tick, I bet. What if they see our car…?"

"Yes, they are! Come on!"

Fiona gave Giles a hard push to get him moving. As fast as they could manage, every few strides slipping or sticking in the mud, they hurried back the way they'd come, keeping to the side of the track in the hope of not being seen.

Reaching the car ahead of Giles, Fiona waved to get him to move into the bushes as she could hear the Mercedes approaching. Jumping inside their car, she opened the sun-roof and, with one foot on each front seat, stood with her head and shoulders through the opening. Raising the binoculars, she pretended to be one of the many birdwatchers they'd seen on the way there. As luck would have it, the moment the Mercedes appeared, a flock of parakeets flew overhead.

"Phew! That was close," she gasped. "Come on, Giles! We can't afford to lose sight of them. There's no 3G coverage in the reserve for the tracker."

As Giles struggled to cover the last few yards, Fiona started the engine.

"I'll drive," she insisted, pushing the door open. "The chances of being stopped and asked for my licence are a million to one. So why don't you get Conrad up to date on the satellite phone?"

"Okay. But don't forget, they drive on the wrong side of the road round here… in more ways than one."

Chapter Thirty-Five

If Fiona had had any inkling of the gruelling day that lay ahead, she might not have made such a generous offer. The Mercedes travelled at speed the same way they had come, and was no longer in sight by the time they had reached the T-junction with highway 180.

"Which way should we go, Giles? Right towards Frontera, or left towards Villahermosa?"

"I think left makes more sense."

"Why?"

"They're obviously taking those boxes somewhere. And they're in a hurry. I'm afraid the chances are they're setting off on a long journey. If so, that means Route 186, either in the direction of Cancun or towards Mexico City... heaven forbid."

"Oh my God!" said Fiona. "What have we got ourselves into? Let me grab my laptop to see if we're getting a signal."

She lifted the computer off the back seat and looked for the red spot that would indicate the position of the Mercedes on the road map. While she was doing so, Giles did his best to lower the tension in his all too familiar way, whispering softly as he looked repeatedly from left and right.

> "'Two roads diverged in a yellow wood,
> 'And sorry I could not travel both
> 'And be one traveller, long I stood
> 'And looked down one as far I could
> 'To where it bent in undergrowth;
> 'Then took the other, as just as fair...'"

"Giles, sorry to interrupt, but shush, please!" said Fiona. "Very appropriate though it is, I'm trying to think. Did you make it up?"

"If only! An American, Robert Frost."

"The bad news is there's no sign of the Merc on the map. The signal's still too weak. So let's go left and hope for the best. The 3G should get stronger soon, according to the 'nPerf' website. In fact, with any luck, before long it will be 4G."

She looked up and sighed.

"But you know, Giles, I'm sorry but I think you'd better take over. I don't like this car. I feel uncomfortable."

After changing places, Giles took the opportunity to join the highway between two articulated trucks.

"Hold onto your hat, Fiona! And, for the umpteenth time today, fasten your *bloody* seat belt!"

***

During the rest of the afternoon and into the evening, the wetlands and coastal plains of Tabasco and the flat farmlands of neighbouring Veracruz were a wearisome ordeal. The incessant hum of the Chevrolet's tyres on the uneven road was broken only by the warning horns and deafening rattle of the occasional impatient truck.

To their delight, the website's depiction of the 3G and 4G cover was spot-on. As soon as they reached the town of Macultepec after a drive of about thirty minutes, the signal was strong enough for the longed-for red symbol to appear on the screen. The fact that the Mercedes was only a few minutes ahead was a bonus, but not big enough to rid them of their anxieties. For, as Giles had been pulling out of the reserve to rejoin route 180, Fiona had noticed a column of dense black smoke on the horizon, rising into the sky seemingly from where they had come. After agreeing there hadn't been any sign of a fire when they'd set off, Giles suggested it could have been one of the local garages burning old tyres. But Fiona was not convinced. She thought there was too much smoke for that. It was an image that was to trouble her for the rest of the day.

As they continued to tail the Mercedes, skirting Villahermosa and then heading towards the port of Coatzacoalcos, they passed the time in quiet conversation – about the scenery, the work Mouktar and Mingzhu were doing, the perpetual puzzle of MECCAR's donation to the College, the news that Sir Quentin was to become the University's new Vice Chancellor – anything to keep their minds off the brutal truth that they were not certain whom they were following, where they were going, or for how long. Would the journey end in a few hours, tomorrow, the day after, in a week? They didn't know. And what would happen at the end of it all? Would a great anti-climax be waiting for them, an embarrassment even? Or would they have made a great leap forward?

Every now and then, the sight of a flowering tree in a field or a colourful bird in front of the car would prompt a diversion into natural history, always a source of fascination for both. Despite the circumstances, Mexico was proving to be a fascinating country – its people, the culture, everything. Whatever the eventual outcome of the trip, the experience was enriching their lives in a way they'd never expected. And who could know what might lay ahead?

Their hope that the Mercedes might be heading for Coatzacoalcos to deliver the boxes to a laboratory were dashed when the red spot on Fiona's screen was seen to be joining route 1450, the highway that leaves the coast in the direction of Córdoba, the Spanish colonial city among the hills of the *Sierra Madre de Oaxaca* in the centre of the country.

By the time they were through the city, the sun was setting behind the snow-capped peak of Mexico's highest mountain. At almost a thousand metres above sea level, the clear air was such a welcome relief from the oppressive humidity of the plains below, and the view so beautiful that they decided to stop to finish the hotel's lunchbox and stretch their legs before continuing into the *Parque Nacional del Rio Blanco* a few miles ahead. It was the sort of place in which Fiona could happily have spent a week, a month even. But twenty minutes was the most they could afford, by which time the Mercedes appeared to have left the main road and stopped at a point between Puebla and Amozoc de Mota, about eighty miles short of Mexico City.

"Thank goodness for that!" Fiona sighed as Giles returned to the driving seat. "Let's pray it's their resting place. I was fearful we'd be driving throughout the night."

Closer examination of the screen showed that the vehicle was parked outside a small budget motel. As they were both in need of greater comfort after a such a long day and with the possibility of more to follow, they decided to continue for a few miles and stop at the Staybridge Suites, where they would be able to prepare a meal for themselves and wash the dirt and oil from Fiona's clothing in the launderette.

It was while she was waiting for her jeans to tumble dry, perusing a dog-eared first edition of Ernest Edwards' guidebook on Mexican birds that she'd spotted in the residents' lounge, that a ping from her phone announced the arrival of an email. It was from Mingzhu, with the good news that they'd burnt the midnight oil to complete the first round of laboratory tests. A glance at the message was enough for Fiona to abandon her washing and run up the stairs.

She found Giles busy cracking eggs into a frying pan in the suite's small kitchen. After dropping the book on the worktop, she slipped between him and the cooker to hold the phone in front of his eyes in her usual manner.

"Too close!" he complained.

"There, is that better?" replied Fiona, moving the phone farther away. "It's a text from Mingy. They've been working really hard. Thanks to that and INDOMED's fantastic equipment, they've made amazing progress. Are you ready?"

Giles nodded as he pulled her away from the frying pan.

"The DNA barcode of the mosquito's cytochrome oxidase gene confirmed it was an *Aedes sollicitans*," continued Fiona. "But there's another result that's even more interesting. Whoever that mosquito bit before it got swatted definitely had MODY diabetes, because she had one of the glucokinase mutations that causes it."

Giles looked at her inquisitively.

"And did I hear you say *she*?"

"You did indeed. The blood came from a female. And there's more. They also looked at the ABO gene to determine her blood group. Did you notice if Margarita's was recorded in her notes?"

"As you'd expect, it was, yes. Hold on."

When Giles returned, Fiona was shaking with excitement.

"Come on! Don't keep me in suspense."

"She was blood group AB, based on the usual red cell agglutination test."

"Yesss!" said Fiona. "That's exactly what Mingy found in the genes. As a matter of interest, how common is AB compared with the A, B, and O groups? Do you know?"

"Only about five per cent of us are AB."

"Then that settles it, Giles, doesn't it, without a shadow of doubt? To say the least, there can't be many blood group AB women with MODY diabetes who've been on the *Oosterdam*. We don't' need statistical calculations and probability theory for that one! It *was* her. Oh God, Giles, we're really in business now. That mosquito bit Margarita Díaz. That's certain."

While Fiona was twirling with exhilaration, Giles's telephone rang.

"Teuku!" he gasped. "You must have extra-sensory perception. We've just received some results from Mingy, Teuku… You already know…? She's in the room next door? I see. But not knowing anything about MODY diabetes, you wanted to know more…? Okay, but first let me deal with a few other things."

Giles stepped away from the hob so that he could hear Teuku better.

"Did you get my latest email…? Excellent. That'll save me a lot of time. And as agreed, you haven't told our two young friends what Fiona and I are up to, or what we're really doing…? Perfect! Can't take any chances. If we're right about what's going on, and the news of our shenanigans got into the wrong hands, we'd be up a gum tree – either that, or six feet under one.

"Hold on a sec… I was frying some eggs when you called. Fiona, could you take the pan off the hob? I've made the toast. It's under that green plate. The wine's in the fridge. Should be interesting.

"Sorry about that Teuku. Bet you didn't know Guatemala has a wine industry? We bought a white merlot from the local supermarket called *Château Defay*. Tickled my fancy, so I thought we'd give it a try.

"Anyway, back to where we were. We're in a sort of high-class motel with suites, not far from Mexico City. All day, we've been on the tail of the Merc I told you about in the email. After the garage got it going, we followed it to a nature reserve, where some rivers from the hills empty into the Bay of Campeche. It's a vast area of salt marshes and mangroves, teeming with birds, not to mention crocs. Fiona was in her element. Anyhow, to cut a long story short, the car stopped beside what looked like a mosquito farm… yes, that's what I said, a *mosquito farm*. They'd cut down most of the plants standing in the water, thrown a net over the stumps supported by a few bamboo poles, and left paper cups containing what looked like sugar lumps here and there. You could see insects flying around them. And there were birds inside the netting, presumably for females to feed on.

"We can't be certain, but we still think the guy driving the car could be Steve Salomon. When he got to the farm, another chap was waiting for him in one of those big mobile homes that are popular in the States. He was dressed as if he was about to blast off for the moon, apart from having a net over his face. What was also interesting was he put a couple of plastic boxes in the back of the Merc before they drove off. We've been following them ever since in the hope it would lead us to their lab. But no luck yet on that score. That tracker from Conrad, by the way, has been a godsend. Couldn't have managed without it.

"We don't know what's in the boxes, but we're guessing it could be mosquitoes. Either that, or their eggs. Both can be transported for long periods, if kept cold. It slows down their metabolism so they go into what amounts to a state of hibernation. Some types of mosquito do it naturally over the winter. Then, when the weather is warmer, they wake up to continue the never-ending cycle of eggs, larvae, pupae, adults… more eggs, larvae, pupae, adults… more eggs, *ad infinitum*. It's been the same ever since they were keeping *T. rex* awake at night."

"Giles, *your* eggs are also going cold," a voice called from the kitchen. "Time to eat."

"Yes, okay, Fiona," Giles replied. "Sorry, Teuku, I'll have to be quick. You've never seen her when she gets angry…

"It's possible the boxes have nothing to do with mosquitoes. They might contain food for a long journey, for example. We have no idea where they're going, or what they're up to. All we know is they're in one hell of a rush.

"So… to diabetes. Several things we'd learnt from the ship's doctor suggested to me that the ulcer on the lady's foot might not have been due to her diabetes. Having treated many diabetics during my Liverpool days, I thought the clinical history didn't seem to fit. Then, when I learnt that her mother had had a similar medical history, I wondered if she'd inherited one of the rare types of diabetes that are so mild they *never* produce ulcers. And that's why I asked Mingy and Mucky to check the DNA from the blood stain – which, of course, was from the insect's stomach. What they found was that the mosquito's victim, who must have been the last passenger to travel in that cabin, had a mutation of an enzyme, glucokinase, that causes one of those rare types of diabetes. So, clearly her ulcer must have been due to something else.

"What was that?… Did she have anything else that causes ulcers? Good question… no."

"GILES! EGGS!"

"Sorry, Fiona. Two minutes... I suppose Mingy's told you they've also confirmed it was an Eastern Saltmarsh? And that's a bit of a complication, because they're not just found in Tabasco. They're common throughout the Gulf of Mexico – which, of course, includes Florida. So it's easy to imagine how one could have nipped on board the ship when it was docked in Tampa, and have nothing to do with Ni'ihau.

"What was that...? Had the *Oosterdam* been to Tabasco at any time...? No. Anything else? You ask if Saltmarsh mosquitoes inhabit any part of the Hawaiian islands? The answer to that is no, they don't. And is there any way of knowing what? How long it had been on the cabin's ceiling? Not that we know of...

"Hold on a second, Teuku. Fiona's just plonked a fried egg and tomato sauce butty in front of me. Looks delicious! My sort of grub.

"Pardon? Was the *Oosterdam* near Ni'ihau when the epidemic broke out? The answer is 'yes and no'. It sailed non-stop from San Diego to the Hawaiian Islands, and then cruised around the islands for a few days before returning across the Pacific to Ensenada on the west coast of Mexico. But Ni'ihau was *not* one of the islands it called into. As you know, it's very small, very dry, and very private. It's also the most northerly. Tourists aren't allowed there apart from a few, mostly hunters who've paid for the privilege of shooting sheep, boar, and a few other animals the owners have introduced. The nearest the *Oosterdam* got to Ni'ihau was on its last day among the islands, when it called into Nawiliwili Harbor on the island of Kauai. If you look at a map, you'll see that's the nearest one to Ni'ihau. But before you jump to any conclusions, there are two things to consider. First, although Margarita Diaz became ill just after the ship left Kauai, this was about two weeks *before* the epidemic broke out. And second, Nawiliwili is fifty or sixty miles from the spot on the west coast of Ni'ihau where the Hawaiians lived. Saltmarsh mosquitoes are strong fliers, but to cover that sort of distance would be unusual, on top of which the prevailing wind around there is in the *opposite* direction at about ten miles an hour.

"It was Fiona who put all this together, by the way, not me. She's also confirmed that Eastern Saltmarshes can carry West Nile viruses and pass them on to their eggs. So, there we are. Got it…? Teuku, are you still there? Teuku! TEUKU!

"Thank God!" he gasped. "For a moment, I thought you'd dropped dead. You were what? Preparing to drop a bombshell? What sort of bombshell…? The fly in the ointment is the mosquito was *not* infected with West Nile virus? How do you know…? A few minutes ago, Mingy told you they'd tested it for the virus and she's just given you the result… And it was *negative*? Are you *sure*…?

"Yes…?"

Giles paused, while he scratched his head and looked towards Fiona.

"Well, I must say, Teuku, I'm gobsmacked. Not sure what to say. Can I speak to her? You'll need to go next door to fetch her…? Okay."

While waiting for Teuku to return, not a word passed between Giles and Fiona, now holding her head in her hands.

"Ah, hello again, Teuku," Giles resumed. "Mingy's disappeared? The lab tech said she'd got a text message and ran off somewhere. I see. Well, this is pretty shattering. But no doubt she'll send us the details pretty soon. Fiona's trying to call her now…hold on a tick."

Giles held the phone to chest while he waited for Fiona to speak.

"Doesn't look as if she's going to answer, Teuku. Pity! Well, on that very disappointing and confusing note, I'll say farewell for now. I'm not sure where we go from here quite honestly, except wherever that Merc goes tomorrow. We'll continue to keep you posted. And when you see Mingy, ask her to call either me or Fiona as soon as possible, any time of day or night."

After ending the call, and sharing a bewildered shrug of the shoulders with Fiona, Giles drifted in silence into the kitchen, leaving her on the sofa.

By the time Giles had returned, Fiona was standing motionless, her arms hanging limply by her side, staring at the almost perfect symmetry of *Popocatépetl* volcano barely thirty miles away, its slopes reflecting the moonlight onto Puebla's colourful rooftops.

"You know, Giles, I don't know why I was so worried about that other mountain. This one really looks as if it could be active. Is it? Do you know?"

"Yes, it is, actually, very," replied Giles. "It's been going through a period of activity on and off for a while. I didn't bother to tell you. No point. But if anything happened, we should be pretty safe here. Imagine how you'd feel if you were living in Pueblo."

He picked up the wine bottle and began pouring its contents into a glass.

"Wine?"

"Thanks," said Fiona. "I need it. I'll try not to think about that mountain exploding. There's enough on our minds after that call. We've had disappointments and setbacks before, but nothing to compare with this. No virus, he said? God! The miles we've covered, literally by air, sea, and land. And the risks we've taken. Not to mention the money, the energy, the emotions, the sore bums."

She rubbed her backside and grimaced as she turned to accept a glass from Giles and waited for him to fill it.

"Cheers! If that mosquito wasn't carrying the virus, Giles, what's the explanation of Margarita's illness then?"

"Goodness knows."

Trying not to look too disappointed, Giles set about arranging the plates on the table, added some sliced tomatoes and a few lettuce leaves to each, and opened a bag of *tortillas* they had bought from the same supermarket.

"There you are," he said. "All ready. Two lukewarm but perfectly fried eggs on crispy toast and butter waiting to be washed down with a bottle of local grog. A perfectly balanced meal. While the eggs and butter are pushing up your 'bad' cholesterol, the wine will be upping the 'good' one. Let the battle of the two cholesterols commence!"

"Why are you so light-hearted, Giles? That was such a blow."

"Well, as you know by now, Fiona, I'm not a great believer in letting setbacks get on top of me. If you think about it, nothing's changed, except we now know something we didn't know before. And that's progress. I'll admit that, when Teuku gave me the news, it did set me back a little. In fact, a little more than a little. I won't pretend otherwise. But I also know it's not the end of the story, unless we both want to pack it in, which is unthinkable."

Giles opened a napkin and tucked it into his shirt.

"It's no different from our research in Oxford," he continued. "We do an experiment to test an idea. If the result supports the idea, we know we've made progress. We feel good about it. And we move on. But if the result didn't support our hypothesis, and instead turns up something completely unexpected, something we can't explain on the spot, at first we might feel a tinge of disappointment. Life's so much easier if your predictions always turn out to be right. But, in truth, it's also less interesting, and potentially less rewarding. After a while, we start to feel a buzz of excitement again. Why? Because we know we could be on the verge of something we, or possibly anyone else, could have imagined. It's the same with this business. We know we must be onto something. That's beyond doubt. And we thought we knew what is was. Now we realise it may not be so simple. The answer is somewhere else. So we keep searching."

"You're right, of course… as usual," said Fiona. "It's just that it doesn't come so easily to me. I have to work at it. Let's eat."

"*Bon appetit!*"

After finishing their meal, each lost in their own thoughts, they took their glasses to the leather sofa. Giles glanced at the *Talavera* clock on the wall. Seeing it was midnight, he put a comforting arm around Fiona and offered one of the cubes of gold-wrapped *leche quemada* the maid had arranged on the pillowcases.

"Don't look so glum, dear. Remember what I said. There must be an explanation. Have you had any ideas?"

Fiona unwrapped her candy and nibbled at a corner.

"Nice… if a bit sweet," she responded pensively. "Sort of a cross between fudge and butterscotch."

She chewed a little more before continuing. "Well, assuming it *was* Margarita who got bitten, and there seems no doubt about that, either her illness was nothing to do with the mosquito – which would mean either Dr Bandaranaike was correct after all, or she had an illness modern medicine doesn't know about – or, alternatively, the mosquito *was* infected and passed the virus on to her. Yet, for some reason, Mingy and Mucky got a false negative result."

"Want to place any bets?"

"Not really. The assay we told them to use has been shown to be very reliable. And, knowing Mingy, she'll have repeated and checked everything umpteen times. She's very thorough. In fact, I'd say almost obsessively so."

"Something else occurs to me, you know," said Giles. "We shouldn't forget the assay was developed for detecting the *normal* West Nile virus, not a modified one like the Ni'ihau brute. What if the modification that was made to its RNA affected its proteins in some way? They might no longer interact with the antibodies in the test system. That would also produce a negative result even if the mosquito had been carrying it. When the medical centre in Honolulu concluded that those Hawaiians had been infected with West Nile virus, it was based on a very different type of test, one that detected the presence of *antibodies* against the virus in their blood, not the presence of the virus *itself*."

"That's true," said Fiona. "And it gives me a thought. If that were the case, it would mean the same test would also fail to detect the virus in what's left of the patients' blood samples. The same would apply. I'll send Mingy an email and ask her to check it out."

"And, on a different matter," said Giles, "I've had another thought. The tracker Conrad sent us is equipped with a small microphone. That's what the booklet says, anyhow. Which we can switch on with a text message from a mobile phone. Why don't we do that? We might hear them chatting when they're outside the car."

"Brilliant! This Guatamalan wine's obviously good stuff. I'll do it now. It'll only take a tick."

With renewed vigour, Fiona flipped open her handbag to find the instruction booklet Conrad had enclosed in the box, and grabbed her smartphone.

"There, that didn't take long, did it? Fingers crossed. Let me listen. Shush! Can't hear anything yet. Not a sound. Perhaps it didn't work. Oh yes, it did! I can hear a dog barking. Now two dogs… no, three! Now they've stopped for some reason, and I can hear a sort of rushing noise on and off, presumably the wind. We must make sure we're up in the morning before they are. Who knows what we might hear?"

"Excellent. So shall we…?"

"As soon as I've shown you something. One last thing."

Returning to the kitchen, Fiona collected the bird book she'd been reading.

"I found this on my way to the launderette, and was looking at it when Mingy's email arrived."

After placing the book on the dining table, she found the relevant page.

"Take a look at this bird, Giles. It's a painting, not a photograph. This book only has paintings, which I think is rather nice. Note the long graceful tail, long legs, bright yellow eyes, the glossy black iridescent feathers. It caught my eye and I compared it with the ones we saw this morning in the mosquito farm."

She flicked through the collection of photographs in her phone to find the ones she'd taken.

"Take a look. Very similar, isn't it?"

Giles adjusted his glasses.

"Looks identical to me."

"Which means they're male great-tailed grackles. According to the book, they're indigenous to the Tabasco region, as well as to a few other places, like parts of Colombia and Ecuador. They normally forage in pastures, wetlands, and mangroves."

"So?"

"I haven't finished. While I was listening to my jeans going around in the tumble dryer, I searched the PubMed literature database on my phone, using key words like 'birds', 'West Nile virus', 'strains' and so on. And I found some *really* interesting articles."

"Go on," urged Giles.

"Well, I learnt that, in the wild, many grackles are infected with West Nile virus. They're a major reservoir of it in these quarters. It's the familiar scenario. They get the virus when bitten by an infected mosquito. It multiplies inside them, and then they pass it on to any uninfected mosquito that happens to bite them. Not surprisingly, one of the strains of West Nile virus that's common in them is the Tabasco strain, the one that had combined with the Tecate strain to create the hybrid we all know about."

Fiona smiled. "Interesting, yes?"

"Very?"

"Ready for bed?"

"Very."

Chapter Thirty-Six

Only minutes after being awoken by two room maids arguing outside the door, the beep-beep-beep from Fiona's phone was the last sound she wanted to hear. Raising herself, she shuffled to the kitchen table to find the red spot on her laptop's screen moving in a way that could only mean the Mercedes was being turned in the car park. By the time it had come to a standstill again, she was listening intently on her phone.

"Giles! Pssst! Are you awake?" she hissed. "It's five past five, and it's moving. The Merc."

"What?"

"The car. It's moving."

"What! But I locked the door. I'm sure…"

"Not ours! Theirs! The Merc, on the screen."

"Oh! Why are we whispering?"

"I don't know. It's stopped now. But they might be getting ready to go."

"Jesus! At this time? But hold on. There's no rush, is there? We can give them an hour or so. As long as they're on your screen, we've got them hooked."

"Theoretically, yes. But I'd rather not be too far behind. We've no idea where they're going, have we? It might be just a few miles, or a thousand. Who knows?"

"Good point," said Giles, rubbing his eyes. "And if they're setting off at this hour, a thousand is more likely to be nearer the truth."

Shivering, Fiona wrapped her dressing gown tightly around her waist.

"Brrr! I think the thermostat on the air conditioning must be faulty."

"I'll switch it off."

"Thanks. You know, the more we get drawn into this, Giles, the scarier it gets. I'm starting to feel very much out of our depth. Despite our past experiences, we're real fish out of water this time."

"You can't have it both ways," Giles chuckled.

"What do you mean?"

"Being out of our depth because we're fish out of water!"?

"Clever! I wish I had some of those herbal teas left to calm me down. Anyhow, I'm off for my ablutions. At least that'll get me warm. When you've dragged yourself up, keep your ear to my phone in case they say something."

"Will do. Toss it over."

"No, I'll leave it here. Otherwise you might conk out again."

For the moment, Giles remained where he was while he reflected on the previous day's journey. How, during the long and tedious drive through Veracruz, they'd started to wonder if they were doing the right thing. After all, they could simply have watched the Mercedes' progress over the Internet, couldn't they, and then taken some sort of action once it had reached its destination? Were they putting themselves in unnecessary danger? If Steve had got involved in international crime out of desperation for money, his car might have an electronic gadget to detect if it's being followed, mightn't it? In which case, he could be leading them into a trap. Anything was possible.

Rolling over to ease an ache is his back from the bumpy roads, he recalled how, as they'd been crossing the Coatzacoalcos River on the approach to Minatitlán, Fiona had predicted they were heading for the mountains of the *Sierra Madre Orientale* in the centre of the country, raising the spectre of getting stranded in that remote region with an overheated engine or a punctured tyre, and becoming easy prey for bandits. And how a little later, when passing Juan Rodríguez Clara, she'd feared it might not be Steve in the car after all. As she'd pointed out, there was no shortage of dark-haired, bearded men in Mexico, was there? Some of them must have unusual moles like Steve's. And, even if it was him, he might be in Mexico for an entirely innocent reason. What if he was helping the country to fight local mosquito-borne diseases like dengue fever and malaria? What better way could there be of restoring his reputation?

After agonising over these and other concerns, she had eventually succumbed to the heat and the rhythmic rocking of the car and fallen asleep, her head propped against the door with her cardigan as a pillow, until the driver of a bus had blown his horn as they were exiting Fortin de las Flores. Her first sight through the grimy windscreen had been of the snow-capped peak of *Pico de Orizaba*, Mexico's highest mountain, soaring above tree-covered hills and colourful villages in the foreground. The contrast with the flat expanse of marshes and mangroves they'd driven through earlier had prompted her to lower the window and inhale the crisp clear air. It was a moment she would long remember. But, despite the mountain's iconic beauty, its sudden appearance against a blood-red sky, had somehow felt sinister and foreboding to her. Giles's reassurance that it had been dormant for two hundred years had failed to put her mind at rest. It was nothing to do with physical danger, she'd explained, but a strange irrational emotion, as if the volcano, waiting to explode, was an omen of an imminent disaster.

Giles was still thinking about the journey, now flat on his back with a cushion under his side, when Fiona reappeared from the bathroom.

"Giles! *The phone!* You're supposed to have it to your ear. Remember?"

"Err… yes, sorry, dear. I was resting my back. Yesterday's journey was definitely not what it needed!"

"Sorry! I keep telling you to join me in the gym, don't I? The best way of avoiding that sort of problem is to exercise. You know what they say? Strong backs feel no pain."

"You're right, of course. When we're back in Oxford, that's what I'll do. I promise."

Giles struggled to his feet, massaging his back with both hands as he did so.

"Anyhow, sorry about the phone. You'd better take it now. Where's my washbag?"

"Hanging on the door."

While pulling on her shirt and jeans, Fiona wedged the phone between her ear and shoulder.

"Hold on, Giles! I can hear someone talking… two men… in English. Could one be Steve, do you think?"

After tossing the phone to Giles, she moved to the dressing table to brush her hair. As she untangled and plaited her locks, she watched Giles's face for any clues as to what might be going on.

"Jesus!" he gasped, covering the microphone with his hand. "One of them just called the other one Steve."

"Does it sound like him?"

Putting a finger to his lips, Giles shrugged his shoulders and continued to listen.

"It's gone quiet now," he said. "They must have moved away. Didn't hear any doors slam. Perhaps they've returned to the hotel. They were talking about the route and mentioned a few places. I hadn't heard of any of them except what sounded like Guadalajara. He said he wanted to be there by lunchtime. How far's that? Any idea?"

"At a guess, four or five hundred miles, I'd say," Fiona answered. "Let me think. If they left now, they might be there by one or two o'clock this afternoon. Did the guy who spoke sound like a local?"

"Difficult to say. His English wasn't too good, I do know that."

"Pity they didn't say more," said Fiona. "Nevertheless, it's enough to go on. All those doubts I had yesterday are now out of the window. Let's go."

Giles moved to give her a kiss.

"Nice perfume," he said. "Haven't smelled that one before."

"First time on. It's a Scottish cologne called *Velvet Isle*. Quite special."

"Splash it on. It'll keep me awake during the long day ahead."

"You won't need to," said Fiona. "I've decided it's your turn to nod off. I'll do the driving. To hell with my rustiness, and the fact I've no licence with me. We haven't seen a single cop yet. So I doubt if we'll see one today. If we do, I'll simply use my feminine charms. And, in the unlikely event they don't work, let's buy a bottle of Tequila on the way as an emergency gift."

Once they'd checked out, Fiona took the driver's seat as promised, and drove like never before. If they had to follow the Mercedes to the end, she was going to throw herself into it. To hell with her sore backside; to hell with the police; and to hell with her doubts about the engine and tyres. There was no going back, and there could be no half measures.

Although the route proved to be more demanding than the previous day's, it was memorable for more than the heat, dust, and an annoying fly that refused to go away. After motoring through the hills and valleys of the central plateau, with a brief diversion to the Monarch Butterfly Reserve, the journey towards Guadalajara took them through lush forests and fields of maize, cotton, coffee, and sweet-smelling agave. But the highlights were the lakes, the pretty *Lago de Cuitzeo* and the larger *Lago de Chapala* with its elegant pelicans and blue-flowering water hyacinths, the latter providing the perfect spot to rest while they quenched their thirsts on *ataulfo* mangos and *cucamelons* bought from a roadside merchant.

By the time they were in touching distance of Jalisco's capital, they could see that the Mercedes had already skirted the *Bosque de la Primavera* on the other side of the city, and was heading in the direction of Tepic and Mazatlan on the west coast.

There being no time for lunch, Fiona continued to drive while Giles took her at her word. Upon awakening, it was to his great relief to see that the Mercedes was now stationary. Outside it was pitch black. He glanced at his watch. Ten-fifteen.

"I see they've stopped, dear," he announced, stretching his arms.

"Yes. It happened ten minutes ago. Let's hope it's for the night. I'm pooped."

"Looking at the map, they seem to be at another hotel," said Giles. "Pity! If it were a house or other building, there'd be a chance they'd reached their destination."

"Oh dear!" replied Fiona. "I couldn't see that detail from here. If they had to cover such a great distance, I wonder why they didn't fly?"

"Perhaps it's to do with those two plastic boxes... what's inside them."

"Or something simpler, like a fear of flying."

"Certainly couldn't be Steve, if that's the case."

"What sort of hotel is it? Can you tell?" asked Fiona.

"Quite small. On the coast road from Guaymas to the edge of the... let me read this... *Reserva Especial de la Biosfera del Diablo*. It's a State Park. Despite the ominous name, it looks like an attractive spot. Take a look."

Giles zoomed in and held the laptop to the side of Fiona's face.

"Careful, I do need to keep an eye on the road, you know!" she said. "Let me see. Looks quite promising. I could just do with a night within earshot of waves lapping on the beach from the warm waters of the Sea of Cortes on one side and a cool breeze from the Sonoran Desert on the other. That's bucked me up no end! Can't wait. Do you think we could risk staying at the same hotel? Or should we keep our distance?"

Giles adjusted his posture in an attempt to get more comfortable.

"That's better! It's tempting, I must admit. Last night's place was good, but the thought of a night under the desert stars has got me drooling too."

"Do you think Steve would recognise you? I don't. After all, he hasn't seen you in a while. And if you put on those awful sunglasses..."

"They're not awful," said Giles. "They're just unusual. It's very tempting. But I'm not sure. If he *did* recognise me, it would be a disaster, wouldn't it?"

"I think it's more likely he'd convince himself he must be mistaken," replied Fiona. "I mean, don't forget where we are, Giles. We're on the west coast of Sonora County in Mexico. Why on earth should you of all people be here? And if he spoke to you, you could shrug your shoulders, look confused, and mumble something vaguely Spanish."

"Even so, it might be a good idea to avoid being seen together," said Giles. "When I spoke to him on the phone way back… when I was trying to persuade him to lend you his supposed secret software… he said he recalled you very clearly."

"Doesn't mean much. Perhaps he was being polite?"

"He also said he liked your accent."

"Could have made that up too."

Fiona turned her head to give him a wink.

"On the other hand, perhaps he fancies me. After all, you do… or did, anyhow. And Sir Q does, too. So why not another brain box? He'd certainly remember me then. And, if so… wait for it… we might be able to take advantage of it. What do you think?"

Giles stared at her.

"Are you *serious*?"

Fiona unbuttoned the top of her blouse and pursed her lips.

"Well, it makes sense to use *all* our resources, doesn't it?" she said. "But don't worry. It would only be in an emergency."

She leant across to give him a peck on the cheek.

"Only kidding! But it's true, being in public together would be pushing our luck. So we should stay apart as much as possible."

She could see Giles still wasn't completely happy.

"But what if he saw my name somewhere?" said Giles. "Say, on some papers lying around in Reception? It's unlikely, I know, but…"

"We can book in my name," said Fiona. "Why not? And, to be on the safe side, I could use my middle name."

"Does that unpronounceable Gaelic abomination actually appear in your passport?"

"Of course it does. And it's only unpronounceable to Sassenachs, like you."

"That's an interesting word, by the way. Where does it come from?"

"Sassenachs? From the Scottish Gaelic word for Saxons."

"Really? I always imagined it was something offensive, likening us to eunuchs."

"Haha! Giles! What a ridiculous suggestion... although, on second thoughts, perhaps it's not so... Oops...! Sorry about that swerve. Probably a bobcat. Did you see our lights in its eyes?

"To change the subject, do you happen to know why cats' eyes shine like that?"

"Tell me."

"It's because they have a special layer of cells behind the retina that acts like a mirror. So the retina gets a double dose of light, which helps them see in the dark."

"Interesting. Anyhow, we've been digressing. What shall we do... same hotel or a different one?"

"Same."

"Sure?"

"Yes, because in my estimation the risk is tiny compared with the potential benefit. And anyway, by the time we get there, those two will probably be asleep. They must be worn out, too. Then, in the morning, we can lie low."

Fiona gave Giles a quick look.

"So, see if you can find the hotel number and give them a call. There's a good boy."

Quietly pleased she had called the tune, Giles found the number and did as instructed to book what proved to be the only room available.

Once they had left the small beachfront community of San Carlos Nuevo Guaymas behind, Fiona took her foot off the pedal while she treated her senses to the unfamiliar sounds, sights, and smells of the sea and desert. As they followed the gentle undulations and bends in the road, small beaches interspersed among rocky outcrops came into view, just discernible in the moonlight, while the Sonoran desert, with its silhouettes of countless saguaro cacti, stretched to a distant horizon. As she inhaled the earthy aroma of creosote bushes, their leaves dampened by a recent downpour, Fiona listened to the music of unseen birds: the whistle of a pygmy owl, the squeeking cry of a killdeer, the endless repertoire of a mockingbird.

Situated close to the southern limit of the *Cajon del Diablo* nature reserve, about a mile from the *La Manga Dos* peninsula in the Gulf of California, the colonial-style *Albergo Palazzo Ducale* was run by an Italian couple who had moved to Mexico after their village near Mantova had been damaged by an earthquake. Although outwardly authentic, it had been built by the owners with their own hands, he a former stonemason and she an architect and keen gardener, and skilfully finished to give the appearance of natural ageing. Plastered on the exterior and painted in Siena red with polished wooden window frames and yellow awnings, the building glowed with a welcoming warmth in the lighting from the garden.

After Fiona had parked at a measured distance from the doorway, she opened the sun roof and admired the starlit sky.

"Do you see what I see?" she whispered, squeezing Giles's hand. "You know what I'm thinking, don't you?"

"It's beautiful. But it could hardly mean anything this time round, could it? And in truth, I'm not sure those waning moons ever did."

"Perhaps not. Shall we go inside? I wouldn't want Steve to suddenly appear from behind one of those palm trees."

The only vacant room had been on the top floor, the fourth. After they'd climbed the broad staircase, Fiona kicked off her sandals and headed for the balcony to feel the *terra cotta* tiles under her feet. Flopping into one of the two pine chairs next to a potted *ocotillo*, she closed her eyes and enjoyed the breeze from the desert.

"Oh, this is wonderful!" she called as Giles was dropping the bags by the wardrobe. "Now the moon's come out of hiding, you can see the desert with all its cacti. And, to be able to enjoy it without my bum bouncing up and down, and cool dry air around my toes instead of hot sweaty leather is such a treat."

Fiona leant back in the chair and wiggled her toes.

"What a remarkable country this is! Pity there's so much crime. Of course, it's all down to poverty and drugs, isn't it? Never could understand why so many Americans, even successful ones, do drugs. What are they looking for? What's missing in their lives? I read a while ago that about ten per cent of Americans are thought to be current users of illicit drugs. At around the age of twenty, it's not much less than twenty-five per cent. Incredible, isn't it? And those numbers are not plucked out of the air. They're the official statistics. Thank God I was never tempted. And you?"

"Not likely!" said Giles. "The thought never crossed my mind…or anyone else's in those days."

"Shall we have a quick drink before we hit the hay?" Fiona suggested. "The owners have left a bottle of Chardonnay in an ice bucket here. And there are two glasses and a corkscrew on the table. Wasn't that nice of them? I'll let you open it. It's one of those old-style corkscrews and I don't have enough strength after struggling with that steering wheel all day. And when you've done that, I'll tell you something I discovered while you were snoozing."

After pouring them both a glass of wine, Giles made himself comfortable in an easy chair from the bedroom and readied himself.

"So, what was it you discovered?" he asked. "Cheers!"

"Cheers!" replied Fiona. "First, something you don't know. On the way, when you were in the Land of Nod, I pulled the car into a farmer's field to have a much needed pee. Those local melons and mangos might have been small, but they really packed a punch. The car was in the shade of an Indian bean tree. It was so peaceful, with just the birds singing and the buzz of the insects, that I left you alone and walked into the long grass. It was something of a surreal experience, I must say, crouched in the middle of a remote field in Mexico with nothing but an inquisitive field rat running around my legs. People eat them here, by the way."

"I'll pass on that."

"I almost did, actually. Twice."

"Pardon?"

"Never mind! I'd taken an article with me, the one I asked the concierge to print as we were leaving the hotel, and sat on a rock to read it. It was by a certain Guerrero-Sánchez in a journal called *Emerging Infectious Diseases*. They'd studied two different strains of West Nile virus, our two friends the Tabasco Tecate ones from the south and north of the country. They did some experiments to compare the rates at which these two strains multiply when given to different types of bird."

"Why?"

"They were interested in the fact that, although West Nile viruses are pretty common in Mexico, and blood tests have shown plenty of Mexicans get infected, in contrast to the situation in the USA hardly anybody ever gets ill. Furthermore, the few Mexicans who have got sick lived in the north of the country. So, they were wondering if it was something to do with the two strains of virus."

"Got it."

"Their idea was that the Tabasco strain might not multiply as rapidly as the Tecate strain. They tested it by injecting the two strains into pigeons, sparrows, thrushes, grackles, and chickens. They inoculated several of each type with the Tabasco strain, and several with the Tecate strain."

"And…?"

"They found both strains multiplied in grackles and sparrows, but hardly or not at all in the other birds."

"So…?" asked Giles.

"Of the two species, the grackles were the best hosts," explained Fiona. "Both strains of the virus multiplied rapidly in them."

"I think I'm getting the message," said Giles. "You're saying that, if someone wanted to grow large numbers of West Nile viruses in birds with the intention of using those birds to pass the virus on to mosquitoes, and they happened to be in Mexico, the best choice of bird would be grackles?"

Fiona nodded.

"And a wild grackle flying around in the south-east of Mexico is much more likely to be carrying the Tabasco strain than the Tecate strain?"

"Actually, I think nearer the truth is that the chances of a wild grackle in Tabasco carrying the Tecate strain is near to zero. If it's infected, it's the Tabasco strain.

"So, what d'you think?"

Expecting it might take a while for Giles to chew it over, Fiona turned to lean against the balustrade and await his response. But it wasn't necessary.

"What do I think?" said Giles. "I think you've done it again, haven't you?"

Throwing his arms around Fiona's waist, he lifted her off her feet.

"Careful!" she said. "We almost went over the edge then!"

"Sorry! Let's sit down again."

Fiona swivelled the chair to straddle it, while Giles rubbed his hands in anticipation of what he was about to say.

"So, to summarise, you're thinking it's like this. First, we know the virus that formed the backbone of the Ni'ihau killer was a hybrid of those two strains. Second, it's well known that hybrids can be produced when two different strains of the same type of virus infect an animal at the same time. The animal's tissues get confused, so to speak, and instead of producing two separate populations of the two strains, they produce viruses made up of bits and pieces of both. It's like they'd got infected with a red virus and a yellow one, and instead of producing a million red ones and a million yellow ones, they produce two million red-and-yellow ones. This is one of the big worries that we have with flu viruses, for example the possibility of it forming a hybrid with bird flu to produce one that we have little protection against.

"Now, keeping in mind where the two Mercs came from, if someone in the north of Mexico genetically engineered a West Nile virus to carry *Achilles* RNA, they would almost certainly have used the wild Tecate strain, simply because it's common up there. If the resulting Tecate-*Achilles RNA* combo, for want of a better word, was then taken to Tabasco and injected into grackles to get them to multiply and then infect hundreds of Eastern Saltmarsh mosquitoes…"

"And, by chance, one of those birdies had just got infected with the local Tabasco strain…" Fiona interjected.

"The viruses produced in the birds could be Tabasco-Tecate-*Achilles RNA* hybrids, so to speak," replied Giles. "In other words, exactly what we found in the Hawaiians' blood. And, any mosquitoes that fed off them would be infected with the same."

Giles slapped his head in excitement.

"That *must* be it, Fiona! It has to be. And those two bastards sleeping, or more likely boozing, somewhere in this building at this very minute are in the process of taking those very mosquitoes, or their eggs or pupae, back to Steve's lab somewhere in the north of the country."

"Presumably, yes," replied Fiona. "Let's hope so. What if it's somewhere else, though? What if they're up to some mischief and about to launch an attack in the USA? Perhaps Steve has a vendetta against the NIH or the White House? It wouldn't be surprising. Or maybe they're heading to a military facility to prepare for another test run? It could be anything."

She thought for a moment.

"By the way, Giles, do you have any ideas about why they've got two boxes with them, instead of just one?"

Giles shrugged his shoulders. "Could be just that one box was too small for the numbers, I suppose."

"True," said Fiona. "But why would they go to the trouble of using Saltmarsh mosquitoes, when it would have been so much easier to use a type that occurs in the north? I know I've suggested it could be because the biosphere reserve down there is so remote. But I'm no longer sure that makes sense. After all, there must be plenty of hideaways in Mexico where they could have bred mosquitoes. No, I think there must be another reason."

"Let's think about it tomorrow."

Giles got up to unpack, leaving Fiona on the balcony with her drink. However, it was not long before he reappeared, his hands buried in his pockets and looking much more sombre.

"Perhaps we're getting ahead of ourselves," he sighed, leaning against the door. "The truth is, we've no evidence the Pentagon's involved at all, have we? It's still pure conjecture on our part. Everything fits with what we know about past germ warfare programmes, whether American, British, or Soviet. But that's about it. On top of which, there's still a big fly in the ointment."

"You mean Mingy's negative lab result?"

"Absolutely. Right now, we don't have a shred of evidence to connect what's going on over here with what happened on Ni'ihau, do we?"

"No, we don't. You're right."

Chapter Thirty-Seven

With strong sunshine and the sound of distant conversation entering through the open window, Giles knew, even before his eyes were open, that it was much later than it should be.

"Fiona… where the hell are you?" he muttered groping under the sheets.

Discovering she wasn't in the bathroom, he ran to the balcony to find a peeled banana, a crust of bread, and a half-empty coffee cup on the table. A hand towel was lying on the floor. Stooping to collect it, he found it was damp, very damp, with a strong smell of coconut hair conditioner.

His watch, still on his wrist after dropping into bed in the early hours, told him it was 11.32 am.

"What the hell's going on?"

Like never before, Giles could feel all the signs of panic coming on – the pounding heart, the beads of sweat.

Unable to see her phone anywhere, even under the bed, he tried to call her. But there was no reply. In fact, it didn't even ring.

"That could only mean it's switched off," he muttered, "the battery's flat, or it's out of range."

Knowing how careful she was about keeping her phone functioning, he feared the worst.

"Has she been kidnapped! Could Steve have tempted her down and bundled her off?"

After pulling on some clothes, he checked Fiona's laptop to see if the Mercedes was still outside.

"Yes. Thank God for that!"

To make sure it was true, he leant out of the window as far as he could safely manage, holding onto a curtain. The distinctive radiator of a Mercedes Benz was just visible in the car park.

He moved to the dressing table to pick up the antique brass clock that Fiona had found so appealing.

"Pah! Stuck on four-twenty. Bloody hell!" he ranted, tossing it across the balcony. "So much for all her fanciful ideas about romantic awakenings!"

Giles sat on the bed as he tried to calm himself down. But it was to no avail. As he was reaching a point of rare despair, Fiona's voice was just audible from the direction of the balcony.

"Are you there, Giles?" she called.

Unable to see her from the balcony, he quickly put on his shoes and raced down the stairs and outside to find her standing between two saguaro cacti a hundred yards from where the gravel of the car park met the red earth of the desert.

"Ah, you're awake?" she said. "At last! These cacti are fascinating, Giles. I'd seen them in Western movies, of course, and so on, but I didn't know they had such pretty white flowers. Can you see them from where you are? Once I'd looked at them through the binoculars over breakfast, I couldn't resist coming down."

Taking off the straw sombrero she'd collected on her way through the lobby, Fiona waved a branch bearing clusters of bright yellow flowers.

"And look at this! You see those bushes on the hillside over there? It's from one of them. That's as far as I got. Anyhow, to change the subject, was it you who threw something from the balcony a few minutes ago?"

"Yes."

"What was it?"

"That old alarm clock. I told you we couldn't trust it."

Fiona lifted her cotton dress above her ankles and ran towards the building, beckoning Giles to follow.

On reaching the top of the staircase, she ushered Giles into a corner of the landing to explain how she had woken up at around eight, an hour after the alarm should have gone off.

Leaving him to rest, she'd asked room service to bring her some breakfast, but before she'd finished it, the shadows cast by the cacti in the early morning sun were creating such a stunning scene that she'd run outside to take some photographs.

"Sorry about that, Giles," she continued. "Hope it didn't scare you too much. But now I'll get to the important bit. On the way out, as I was going down these stairs, I spotted you-know-who chatting to the receptionist. So I reversed a few steps to hide behind one of those columns. By the way, did you know they're genuine eleventh-century Romanesque? Apparently, the owners recovered them from the ruins of their village church in Italy after the earthquake, and shipped them all the way here."

"Must take a closer look," said Giles. "But go on."

"Well, what snippets I heard left me in no doubt that 'Black Beard' is definitely Steve. Trying to impress the pretty girl behind the counter, he was boasting about having been 'the top man of America's top cancer centre' – his very words – until he had 'gotten bored and decided to look for a bigger challenge'. His short, fat friend said they wanted to stay an extra night to spend the day on the beach before taking the car ferry from Guaymas across the Gulf tomorrow evening. They would then drive up the Baja California peninsula. The receptionist said she would book them a ticket, and they gave her the car's registration number."

"Did they leave the hotel?"

"Yes. They went straight out. They certainly looked as if they were dressed for the beach. Steve has very skinny legs, by the way. I waited a few minutes before venturing down."

Fiona giggled briefly before continuing.

"And… oh yes, I nearly forgot! There was something else. Steve asked the girl if the hotel could give them some bags of ice cubes later on. When she asked if they'd also like some cans of beer, he said 'no thanks, just ice'."

"Interesting," said Giles. "Could be replenishments for those insulated boxes, I imagine. Any ice that was already in there must be pretty low by now."

"Actually, the fact they've gone off for the day might be a good thing. I've been worrying about the tracker's battery. It'll give me a chance to recharge it. In fact, I think I'll do it now. As soon as I've changed into a T-shirt and jeans, I'll nip to the car park and take it upstairs. Meanwhile, why don't you have a shave? You're starting to look like Desperate Dan."

Fiona rubbed his stubble with both hands.

"Actually, I'm thinking of letting it grow," said Giles.

"Growing a beard?"

"Just stubble… for a few days. We don't know what might be waiting for us in Tijuana. Perhaps a little disguise will come in handy."

Once Fiona had retrieved the tracker and plugged it into an outlet in the bedroom, she called room service and ordered a breakfast for Giles and a pot of coffee. Having already decided they should remain in the room all day, Giles opted to put his feet up with the only book he'd brought along, James Barr's *A Line in the Sand*, something he'd been intending to read for as long as he could remember.

Fiona had other plans.

"I know you've been talking about that book for ages, Giles, but could you do me a favour? You'll probably think I'm a bit barmy, but it's something I'd really love to do before the sun gets too high."

"What's on your mind?"

"Well, during the evening before we left Nusa, when I was on the veranda with just a big moth and a tiny gecko to keep me company, I downloaded a selection of Shostakovich, stuff he'd composed for movies. I'd been intending to ever since watching an old Russian film called *The First Echelon*, while you were showing that professor from St Petersburg around Oxford. There's a scene in which some old people in modest everyday clothes are dancing to his Second Waltz in the snow. The same music was used years later in the film *Anna Karenina*, but this time with lots of rich ladies wearing gorgeous dresses and handsome military officers prancing around an opulent ballroom. Most people know that one, but very few the first, which is actually the one it was written for.

"The point of all this is that, when I was sitting in that field I told you about, reading the article about the two strains of West Nile virus in different birds, I was listening to that music. And I was so taken by it that I actually got up and started dancing in the grass… until after a couple of minutes, a loud honking and cheering from a passing truck brought me to my senses. Very embarrassing!"

"They probably thought you'd had too much to drink," said Giles. "So, you're telling me that if I let you listen to it again while you dance around the room, you'll let me read my book? With that, I have no problem. It's a deal."

Giles offered her his hand.

"Sorry, but you've jumped to the wrong conclusion, Giles. You see, when I was in the desert before, I put on my earphones and listened to the Second Waltz again. In my mind's eye the desert was transformed into a ballroom, the sky into a pastel blue ceiling, the sun a chandelier, and those magnificent tall saguaro cacti the dancers, the ladies' dresses decorated in white flowers."

"Jesus! You've got an imagination! What about the officers? Were they dressed in white flowers too?"

"No. Not all the cacti have flowers. Some are just covered in spines. Think of them as rough, bristly beards!"

"I'd have to think very hard. But what's all this got…?"

"Hold on!"

Fiona walked past him, looking over her shoulder with a self-satisfied smirk before turning to stop with her arms crossed.

"You know how to waltz, don't you?" she said. "I remember seeing a black and white photo of you at a New Year's ball in a posh hotel in London. It was on a bookshelf in your living room. And there was another one of you as a dapper young man with your parents at what I presume was a diplomatic dance."

She approached him from behind to place her hands on his shoulders.

"Have you done much dancing since then?"

Giles shook his head.

"I haven't waltzed for years, either…" said Fiona. "Since I was student, in fact. You couldn't keep me off the ballroom floor in those days."

"In more ways than one, I imagine," Giles sniggered.

"I'll ignore that. So, I think it's about time we rectified the situation."

"What do you mean?"

Fiona smiled.

"In return for leaving you with your book for the rest of the day, my condition is that we go out into the desert before it gets too hot, walk well away from the hotel towards the rocky ridge, and… wait for it… waltz to the music. We can glide and swirl between the cacti, me in my long cotton dress, and you in… well… anything… your pyjamas, if you like. I'm sure you haven't forgotten how to do it. And even if you have, nobody will be watching. I can guide you. In fact, even better, we can practise in here first. It'll be such fun, and good exercise after all those hours on our bums."

Fiona moved around so that she was facing him.

"So, is it a deal?"

"Er… well… very interesting idea, I must say," said Giles. "I'm sure it'd be good fun, but alas there's a problem."

"Yes?"

"Yes. We can't both listen to the music at the same time, can we? Pity! Never mind."

Fiona wagged her finger. "Sorry, you can't get out of it that way! I've thought of that. My little travelling speaker doesn't have to be plugged in. It's got a battery. And it's Bluetooth. Which means we can leave it on a rock."

"It won't be loud enough."

"Yes, it will. It's pretty powerful for its size. You haven't heard it on full volume. So…?"

"There's something else," said Giles. "What about snakes? This is rattlesnake country."

"And sidewinder country, too, actually," replied Fiona. "I'm not afraid, if you're not. They probably won't have awoken yet. They'll be warming up. They're reptiles, remember. Cold blooded. Like you, it seems, at this moment. And anyhow, I've read they don't attack unless you disturb them. On top of which, rattlesnakes warn you with their rattle before they bite. So?"

"What if we tread on one?"

"We won't. We'll be careful. We'll keep a lookout, both of us."

"Okay… if you *insist*."

Fiona threw her arms in the air.

"Wonderful! This is going to be such fun. Let's get some practice now, a sort of rehearsal, so you don't tie your legs into knots outside. I wouldn't like you to end up with your bum on a prickly pear. So, let me find that Second Waltz. It's played by the Moscow Chamber Orchestra, by the way… Here it is."

Fiona held up her phone.

"Ready?"

"If you insist."

It was an hour or so later, when Fiona had realised her ambition. Their backs were drenched from the heat of the morning sun and their feet yellowed with desert dust. They were recovering in the shade of a rock-strewn hillock, when Giles swept back Fiona's hair to wipe her face with his handkerchief.

"That was wonderful," he panted. "What a marvellous idea. I must admit, I thought it was a little crazy when we were upstairs. But you were right."

After pausing to receive a peck on the cheek, he removed his arm from her waist to grasp her hand.

"D'you think anyone saw us?"

"Does it worry you?"

Giles gave a noncommittal shrug of the shoulders.

"I think those cute antelope squirrels saw us," Fiona giggled. "They must have had a good laugh. There's so much life around here. One tends to think of deserts as being dead. But they're not. At least, this one isn't."

She looked around at the wide expanse of desert and sighed.

"It's so beautiful. I never imagined one could feel like this. It's not the barren inhospitable place I expected. I don't feel I want to run away from it. It's strangely welcoming, atmospheric. Though you feel alone, it's not in a lonely way. It's a pleasant solitude. You feel detached from the rest of the world... your only company the cacti, each keeping its distance from its neighbours, as if they value their privacy. It's a bit like being at sea, when there's just you, the breakers, and the dolphins."

She thought for a moment.

"Paradoxically, even though there's less life around us at this moment, I feel even closer to nature than I did in the rainforest. Odd that. I wonder why?"

"Perhaps it's in our genes?" Giles offered. "A throwback to when our earliest ancestors roamed the African veld. Perhaps it was a bit like this?"

"Interesting thought," said Fiona. "Maybe you're right. There's also something strangely comforting about always being able to see a distant horizon, something you can never do in a forest. Could it be because you have a better sense of where you are, I wonder, than when surrounded by a wall of greenery?"

"Possibly," replied Giles. "Or maybe it's in our genes again, perhaps the ones handed down to us from Neanderthals. After all, as long as you have an uninterrupted view of the horizon, you can be pretty sure you're not about to be surprised by a hungry carnivore. So you feel better, not threatened. In a jungle, you don't know what the hell's going to happen from one minute to the next."

"Hadn't thought of that.

"You know," said Giles, "talking about Neanderthals, did you know geneticists have calculated that it's not necessary to invoke things like natural disasters, epidemics of infectious diseases, tribal wars, and so on to account for their disappearance. As there were never very many of them, it's possible to account for their disappearance merely on the basis of interbreeding with the far greater number of *Homo sapiens* who were around. Until geneticists found that a small percentage of our DNA came from Neanderthals, nobody had imagined that could be the case."

"So, you're saying it wasn't that *Homo sapiens* killed them? It was because they mated together?"

"Yes. Isn't that romantic?"

"One way of looking at it, I suppose."

"Care for another dance?"

"Not likely! I'm pooped."

"I have to admit, I'm quite exhausted too," said Giles. "Once we got started, I couldn't even stop to pick up my sandals. And now I've no idea where they are."

"If we can't find them, we can get you some flip-flops. I hope the saguaro that I bumped into survives. Why the hell didn't you warn me, by the way?"

Fiona grimaced as she examined the scratches on Giles's arms and hands.

"None on your bum, I hope?" she asked.

"A few, but now is definitely not the time to look. You didn't do it deliberately, by any chance?"

"Of course not! You know how much I love plants."

"Thank you! I think I'd better have a shower when we get back."

"I'll follow. Then I'll put that gadget back before our friends return."

***

No sooner had Fiona fixed the tracker to the underside of the Mercedes than she felt a buzz in the back pocket of her jeans. "Oh God! It's here at last," she gasped. "Where's Giles?"

The long delay in hearing from Mingzhu had been worrying. Although there was plenty of other work for her and Mouktar to get on with, it had seemed strangely out of character for

Mingzhu to have advised Teuku of the negative result before contacting Giles.

"There must have been a good reason," Giles had argued when Fiona had raised the issue over lunch. "She might have had concerns about the reliability of the result, for example, but wanted to show Teuku how busy they'd been. She gave him the information, not imagining he would pass it on to us."

Knowing too well how time consuming it could be to eliminate all possible causes of an erroneous test result, Fiona had been more inclined to focus on other possibilities. Apart from the need to repeat the assay at least a couple of times, there might be reagents to check, equipment to service, measurement methods to recalibrate. And, when all that was done, it might be necessary to buy new supplies of reagents, sometimes from the other side of the world. And there could have been other reasons. Perhaps they'd had an accident in the lab, or one of them had been unwell?

Whatever the explanation, knowing how irksome it could be to have others breathing down your neck when doing lab work, Giles had decided to sit it out.

When Fiona ran into the bedroom, Giles was sitting in the red velvet easy chair next to the window, a glass of Dark 'n' Stormy in one hand and his long-awaited book in the other.

"Giles! The nail-biting is over! It's arrived… from Mingy."

Giles dropped the book onto his lap as he looked over his glasses.

"I know. I've already read my copy. What do you think?"

"I don't know. I haven't had the courage to look. What did she say?"

"It's good news, very good. That mosquito *had* been infected with some sort of West Nile virus, after all."

Kicking off her sandals, Fiona dived onto the bed to make the most of it.

"So, the first test *was* faulty?"

"No, it wasn't."

"What do you mean?"

"That wasn't the problem," said Giles. "What Mingy had scribbled down for Teuku was not what we assumed. It wasn't the result for West Nile virus *proteins* at all. We jumped to the wrong conclusion. While they were waiting for the antibodies to arrive, Teuku had squeezed them into testing the insect for the presence of West Nile virus *genes*, knowing they could do that in a flash with his fancy new equipment. Of course, Mingy knew the nucleic acid in West Nile virus is not DNA, which can survive for many years, but RNA, any trace of which would have disappeared within a few days of the mosquito's death, as it gets destroyed by enzymes. But, instead of arguing the point, as she should have done, Mingy simply kept quiet and did as she was told. And, as expected, she got a negative result."

"Oh Mingy!" said Fiona. "She can be like that, even with you and me. Mucky told me it's a Chinese trait to be subservient to anyone of higher rank. And she's terrified of Teuku."

"Ah well, there you are! So when they got the negative result they knew they'd get all along, not wanting to embarrass Teuku by telling him it was predictable, she simply wrote it down and left it at that."

"What a relief! As they say, all's well that ends well. But what about my email? Why didn't she put me straight, when I told her to check whether the antibodies could detect the Ni'ihau virus' protein in the Hawaiians' blood samples?"

"Perhaps you didn't give the reason?"

"No, I didn't, actually."

"So, she didn't know it was to do with the result," said Giles. "She assumed you were just reminding her of good laboratory practice, the need to check the test was working properly."

"How stupid of me," replied Fiona. "But I must say, I'm a little surprised Teuku doesn't know that RNA gets broken down rapidly and disappears."

"I doubt he's ever worked on RNA. He's an antibiotics man, don't forget."

"Anyhow, you're *sure* about it? She definitely said the result for West Nile virus *protein* was positive?"

"Yes," said Giles. "In fact, it was more than positive. It was *strongly* positive. That insect was definitely infected with a West Nile virus."

Fiona propped herself up and looked into his eyes.

"For some reason, you don't look too excited. Any reason?"

"I'm relieved more than anything," said Giles. "It's a huge weight off my mind."

"You know," said Fiona, "when I spotted that black and red blotch in the cabin, I sensed it could be a turning point. But I didn't dare hope it would be this good. Just think, from that little splodge, we've learnt it was an Eastern Saltmarsh infected with a West Nile virus that had died after biting a female human of blood group AB who had MODY diabetes. Isn't science fantastic? Of course, it's still possible it was just a local mosquito that just happened to be carrying a normal West Nile virus and flew on board in Tampa, isn't it?"

"Afraid so. Unfortunately, without being able to look at the virus' RNA, there's no way of knowing if it was a natural one or the Ni'ihau version. So let's continue to keep an open mind."

"To change the subject, Giles, you know we've wondered why the Pentagon might have opted for *Aedes sollicitans* moquitoes out of all the other species? Well, I've been thinking about that."

"And?"

"The fact they need salty water to breed could make them very suitable for battlefield warfare. As foot soldiers and tanks don't operate in salt marshes or mangroves, the mosquitoes couldn't breed after doing their job. Their eggs would die. And, after a few days, there might not be a trace of them, just like on Ni'ihau."

"What about all the good guys, though?" asked Giles. "They'd be bitten too, wouldn't they?"

"Not if they had protective clothing or been immunised."

"Right."

"I'm still surprised, though, that not a single one was caught in the traps they set up on Ni'ihau," said Fiona. "If only a few had been released, I could understand it. But, from what Mucky told me, several of the islanders heard a buzzing noise in the sky before they were bitten. So obviously there was a lot of them."

As she struggled with the conundrum, Fiona gazed through the open window. As a solitary cloud sauntered across the sky, she imagined it was beckoning them to follow it north, the most likely direction the Mercedes would take after crossing to the peninsula.

"Too much to think about!" she said. "I think I'll call the receptionist to book us onto tomorrow evening's ferry. It would be a disaster if we couldn't get on."

"Good suggestion," said Giles. "The car's registration number is among the papers in my bag."

"I'll also call the rental company to let them know what's happening."

Chapter Thirty-Eight

After the ferry's departure from Guaymas across the Sea of Cortez had been delayed by the late return of several of the crew from a trip to Hermosillo, the overnight crossing was smooth and uneventful. Throughout the journey, Giles and Fiona remained in their cabin, reading and listening to music, for fear of showing their faces.

Upon arriving at Santa Rosalia, Giles drove the car onto the busy dockside. Concerned they hadn't seen the Mercedes, he parked at the kerbside as soon as the traffic permitted and looked around. As he admired the cloudless sunrise behind them, a lone osprey, alarmed by the revving and horn-blowing of so many impatient motorists, called to its mate in a high-pitched whistle. The air was heavy and humid, with no breeze to temper the rapidly rising temperature.

"I hope they didn't change their plans at the last minute," he sighed, opening his shirt collar. "We don't actually know for sure they got on board, do we?"

"No."

"Why don't you look at your laptop to see if… oh, hold on… there's no Internet round here, is there?"

"Nope, none at all," said Fiona. "And there won't be until we reach Ensenada."

"Yes, of course! That must be five hundred miles. And, as the road's straight as a die for long stretches, we'll have to keep our distanc; which means there'll be no way of knowing where they are until they reappear on your screen."

"Assuming they do! We've got a pretty nerve-wracking day ahead of us, Giles."

Giles looked at his watch.

"It'll be about seven this evening by the time we get to Ensenada, I imagine, allowing for two or three stops. By which time, it'll be getting dark."

Fiona was in the rear of the car preparing a makeshift breakfast from a few croissants, plastic packets of jam and butter, and a couple of bananas she'd collected from the ferry's buffet bar. Leaving her to get on with it, Giles got out to stretch his legs and do a few knees-bends. As his eyes cleared the roof of the car for the fifth time, he spotted Steve and his friend walking across the car park of a McDonald's restaurant on the other side of the road.

"There they are!" he gasped. "Over there, outside that McDonald's. Now they've gone behind that blue truck. Wait a tick. There they are again. See them?"

"Not from here, no, but I'll take your word for it," said Fiona. "Thank goodness for that! Anyway, your breakfast's ready."

After passing a croissant to him on a paper plate, Fiona unfolded the map the rental company had left in the glovebox to study the route up the long Baja California peninsula towards the border with the USA.

"Another very long hot day ahead of us, Giles. But at least there should be some interesting desert scenery on the way. So, let's make the most of it. It's certainly a journey we won't be doing again. When we've eaten, I suggest we fill up at the gas station over there."

By the time the Mercedes had started to move, visible from the gas station's parking lot, Giles had been drumming his fingers on the dashboard and steering wheel with the engine running for ten minutes or more.

"At long last, here we go," he rejoiced. "Steve always did overindulge for breakfast – pancakes, bacon, maple syrup, fried eggs sunny-side up, the complete American-style works. And, just as we guessed, he's joining Highway One."

While waiting, Fiona had been studying the map and noticed that the road immediately entered the *El Vizcaino* nature reserve, emerging just a few miles later to follow the park's perimeter as far as San Ignacio at about the peninsula's geographic centre. After re-entering the reserve, it continued north-westerly for a hundred miles or so, across what she assumed would be an extremely hot, cracked, and dusty surface, as far as the Pacific coast at Guerrero Negro.

"The first stage looks uncomplicated, thank goodness, Giles. We just go straight to the other side of the peninsula. Then the road turns north through a conservation area called the *Valle de los Cirios*. After leaving that, there's another thirty miles to a town called El Rosario. You can see it's going to be really parched, as the road takes every opportunity to touch the smallest rivers, lakes, and water holes. Good job we stocked up on mineral water."

It was an exciting but frightening prospect for a girl born and bred in Scotland, where water in all its forms seemed everywhere... rivers, streams, waterfalls, lochs, the sea... and a village or a town rarely more than fifteen minutes away. After raising her eyes towards the distant haze, she turned to mentally count the bottles of *Topo Chico* scattered over the rear seat. As Giles eased the car over the gas station's bumpy exit, she inhaled deeply and crossed her fingers.

"I suppose we should be through the two parks in six or seven hours, Giles. Then, if they're heading for the US, we'd have about another five to go, past Ensenada and through Tijuana. If that's the case, it would mean we've got about twelve hours on the road ahead of us, not counting any stops."

Fiona looked at the map again for a few moments before continuing.

"On the other hand, if they're not heading to the US, there are four forks in the road at different points. The first is twenty miles or so after San Ignacio, where a smaller road goes off to a place called Punta Abreojos on the west coast. But it's unlikely they'd be departing so early if they were planning to travel only that distance.

"The next fork is at El Marasal, where they could either continue straight ahead to Guerrero Negro or take a left into a sort of secondary peninsula that buds off the big one, at the head of which is a bay called Bahia Tortugas. But I can't imagine why they would want to end their journey in such a desolate place."

"Unless they wanted a remote place to transfer those boxes onto a boat, and take them to the USA by sea?" said Giles. "Might have advantages."

"But that would be risky. Presumably there are coast guards on the lookout for drug traffickers."

"That's true."

"Two down, two to go," continued Fiona. "The third fork is soon after Punta Prieta, where a right would take them to the *Bahia de Los Angeles* on the east coast. But if they wanted to transfer themselves or their cargo, or both, to a boat on the Sea of Cortez, they could have done so this morning from near the hotel. So, I think we can chuck that one out, too.

"And finally to number four, which is not so simple. It's near a lake called Laguna Chapala, where they could take a right onto Highway Five towards Mexicali, or continue along Highway One in the direction of El Rosario, Ensenada, and on to the border with California at Tijuana."

"And there would still be no signal from the tracker at that fork?" asked Giles.

"Not according to the maps of wi-fi cover I've seen. Only when we hit the outskirts of Ensenada."

"So, what will we do? Toss a coin?"

"No. Stay on Highway One, because the Merc's number plates are from Tijuana, aren't they?"

"But they could be false," suggested Giles.

"Yes, but there's no reason to think so. And who knows, he might be heading for San Diego, where his daughters live. Anyhow, as soon as the tracker starts helping us again around Ensenada, we'll be able to see if the Merc went off to Mexicali. By chance, the distance from the start of Highway 5 to Mexicali is almost the same as that to Ensenada. And, if that's where they are, there's a road that cuts across. It's Highway 3, which joins Highway 20."

Fiona looked ahead of them, then back at the map.

"I must say, this is a pretty good map, assuming it's accurate."

"Okay, I'm convinced."

Following the road for so many miles without the tracker's reassuring signal proved to be even more unnerving than had the risk of being spotted the previous day. As the car bumped and rattled on the baked surface, Fiona tried not to picture the Mercedes racing over the same potholes and cracks, anxious that the tracker's magnet might not be strong enough to hold it on.

As she tried to take her mind off the problem by keeping a record of the plants, she began to wonder why the deserts of Mexico had never been mentioned during the botany lectures of her student days, yet those of places like India and Australia had been, even if only as a source of natural oils and medicines. Giles suggested it was to do with Britain's history, a preoccupation with the Empire and the exploits of its explorers. Mexico had never been a part of Britain's past, and the colonising Spaniards only maritime enemies. But the deserts, mountains and forests of the Empire had been romanticised as places where 'the bold and the brave'… exploring, soldiering, governing, civilising, engineering, trading, or spreading the word of God… had faced danger and hardship for Queen and country.

"The Victorians were no more interested in that stuff," Giles finished, waving towards a spread of magenta and yellow flowers to his right, "than the Spaniards were in your heather or thistle, or whatever grows in an Irish bog."

"Like tormentil and cranberries, you mean?"

"If you say so."

After Giles had stopped the car so she could record the scene, Fiona scanned the landscape in the hope of seeing some of the animals for which she knew the *Vizcaino* reserve was famous. Though denied the pleasure on this occasion, she need not have fretted for, by the time the journey to Guerrero Negro was behind them, she was to have been thrilled by the sight of mule deer and bighorn sheep grazing in the shade of a rocky outcrop; and, best of all, a solitary pronghorn before it darted off at the sound of their approach, scattering stones and dust in the air as it went.

A panoramic photo of a sea of verbena and poppies scattered amongst tall organ pipe cacti was destined to become one of Fiona's all-time favourites. Framed and given pride of place on her desk in Oxford, the picture would catch the morning sun from the small window that overlooked the deer park. On damp winter days, after looking up from a grant application or manuscript and settling her eyes upon it, she would come to fondly reminisce about a journey that, though presently a cause of conflicting sensations… pleasure but also pain, stress and serenity in equal measure, anticipation, yet also reflection… will have been one of the most treasured experiences of her life.

***

By the time they'd reached the outskirts of Ensenada, the sun was setting and the timeless beauty of *Vizcaino* and the fascinating boojum trees of the later *Valle de los Cirios* seemed like other worlds. The moment that had been on their minds ever since leaving Santa Rosalia, five hundred miles ago, had arrived. For, at any second now, they would be within the range of a 3G network once again, and with it the knowledge of whether they had lost the Mercedes or were still on its track.

"Oh my God!" Fiona shrieked. "It's happened at last. We've got a pretty strong signal. But wait a minute… there's no sign of the tracker. There's absolutely nothing on the screen. You're sure this is Ensenada were coming into, Giles?"

"Of course. We've just passed a sign saying *El Bajio*. I've had my eyes skinned for it."

"So, what do we do?"

"Carry on, I suppose. Not much choice. I keep driving, and you keep your eyes on the screen. Nothing else we can do. What will the signal strength be like between here and Tijuana?"

Fiona hurriedly opened the maps of Mexico that she'd downloaded from the nperf.com website.

"Patchy. It's pretty good throughout Ensenada and once we get to Tijuana, but virtually non-existent between here and there."

"Perhaps that's the answer," said Giles. "Perhaps that's where they are, between the two."

"Good idea," replied Fiona. "Let's hope."

Apart from a snack when overlooking the coast near Guerrero Negro, a bowl of fish stew in La Bufadora on the *Peninsula de Punta Banda*, and stops at a few gas stations, they had now been on the road continuously for almost ten hours. And yet, when they lost connection with the Internet again, the further fifty miles to Tijuana seemed almost as long.

"The last time I felt this tense," Giles quipped as they were racing past Campo Lopez, "was when I was in Gunnar Eriksson's study while the Nobel ceremony was in progress, watching the image of Steve's screen while Conrad followed my instructions to find the incriminating evidence. It wouldn't have been half so bad if I hadn't fabricated the first lot in Conrad's villa. Never felt so shit scared in all my life. But this is just as bad. In fact, I think the waiting almost makes it worse."

At the risk of getting motion sick, Fiona kept her eyes on the screen, praying for the Mercedes to reappear. And then what? Would it be in Mexicali or Tijuana? If the latter, would it remain there or cross the border to Steve's daughters' house in Ja Jolla, just north of San Diego? Prompted by Fiona to speculate, Giles thought the latter destination was unlikely.

"I've been thinking more about that one," he said, "and I now reckon there's not much chance. After all, they've probably got something in those two boxes that the US Border Patrol would find very interesting, haven't they? So I'm putting my money on a lab in Tijuana, and a very well equipped one at that. There's a lot of highly sophisticated genetic engineering in those bugs. The big question is what they're planning to do with them."

"Perhaps nothing for the moment," Fiona suggested. "Perhaps the trip has just been to transfer pupae, eggs, or whatever from the farm?"

"I wouldn't think so," said Giles. "I can't imagine Steve would be so personally involved if it were something as routine as that. This has been one hell of a journey. Surely, they'd have couriers? No, I think this must be something special, Fiona. A mission of some sort. Perhaps another trial run."

"But if so, where? Surely not in the US... or around here, so close to the border?"

In the long silence that followed, each knew what the other was thinking. Fiona spoke first.

"You don't suppose it could be for something much bigger than a trial run? Has Ted Crabb been threatening anyone lately?"

"He's always threatening one country or another... sanctions, missiles, tariffs. But I can't believe..."

"Giles, I feel scared. I've a horrible feeling something really terrible is about to happen. You remember that feeling of fear and foreboding I had when we were looking at the mountain?"

"Let's not start speculating too wildly. They could be up to anything. Any sign of the Merc yet?"

"Oh, yes!! Wouldn't you know it? I did exactly what I said I wouldn't do. Took my eyes off the screen."

"Where is it?"

"In the city. Tijuana. And it's stationary."

"Where exactly?"

"Let me see... It's a collection of buildings in the north of the city, right on the border. What are they? Let me see..."

Fiona was quiet for a few seconds while she studied the screen.

"Oh, you were right, Giles! It's the Autonomous University of Baja California. And it looks as if the car's in the car park."

"Brilliant! How do we get there?"

"We stay on this road into the city, until we come to a big junction, where we take the right-hand road, which is labelled *Lib Sur*, presumably an abbreviation for something. Then we keep going until we reach an area called *Buena Vista*, when we head for a road called *Tomas Aquino*. The campus is on that road. Don't worry, I'll give you plenty of instructions as soon as we reach that junction. The institute is only about a mile from the USA-Mexico border crossing, and the same distance from the city's airport. I wonder if that's by design?"

"Believe me, Fiona, everything Steve does is by design. You can bet your bottom dollar he's chosen that location very carefully. This is getting very interesting."

By the time they'd got to the campus, it had started to rain. Fiona had watched the Mercedes move to a position closer to the entrance of the main building. As they neared the open gates, Giles switched off all the lights and reduced his speed to a crawl. One of the few vehicles in the car park, the Mercedes was clearly illuminated by a lamp that hung outside the building's entrance. Keeping his distance, Giles drove slowly to the other side of the building and parked against the wall.

"Are you sure that was a good idea?" Fiona whispered.

"What?"

"Switching off the lights like that. There would have been less chance of being seen, of course, but if we had been spotted, it would have looked pretty suspicious."

"Good point. But too late now. Did you notice there were lights on in a room in the centre of the building on the ground floor, but nowhere else?"

Fiona nodded.

"Apart from the entrance, the only other lights seemed to be in a corridor," continued Giles. "I didn't see a security guard. Did you?"

"What do we do now?" Fiona asked, shaking her head. "I'm terrified."

Giles squeezed her hand reassuringly before quietly opening his door.

"You stay here. No…move to the driver's seat in case we have to make a dash for it. And leave the ignition key in. I'm going to sneak round the other side of the building and have a look in those windows."

"But it's pouring down now! You'll get soaked. Wait until it stops."

"It wouldn't be the first time. This is too important.""

"If you insist. But be careful. And before you go, give me your phone."

"Why?"

"You'll see."

"But I might need it to call you."

"Unlikely. And anyhow, what I have in mind is more important."

"But what…?"

"You'll see. Off you go!"

Keeping as close to the wall as a pile of rubbish bags, an old refrigerator, and several discarded items of laboratory equipment would allow, Giles made his way from their side of the building to the other. As he turned the second corner, he could see the Mercedes clearly. It seemed to be empty.

"Thank God for that," he gasped. "And now for those windows."

Peering between the slats of the Venetian blinds, he could see that the room was a spacious and well-equipped laboratory. From the types of equipment on the benches and along the walls, there was no uncertainty in his mind that it belonged to a genetics unit. If there had been any doubt, it would have been dispelled by what was written on the whiteboard – several strings of letters that could only be representations of a genetic code. Furthermore, it was unmistakably Steve's handwriting, the only person Giles had ever known who habitually wrote DNA and RNA in joined-up lower case letters instead of separate capitals. Suspended from the ceiling over one of the stainless steel benches, a large mosquito net flapped in the current of air from two ceiling fans. A plastic box that looked identical to the ones from Tabasco sat in the centre of another bench. But Giles could see no sign of the second box. While this was troubling, much more so was what occupied a glass table at the far end of the room, next to the open door of what he gathered from the filing cabinets inside was an office: a drone painted in matt black.

Expecting somebody would soon return to switch off a heavy centrifuge that evidently had been left running, given its vibrations and flashing red light, Giles remained huddled below the aluminium window frame, every now and then raising his head cautiously to scan the length of the room. After five minutes or so, Steve entered through a door at the far end to collect one of the boxes before disappearing with it into the corridor. At that moment, the sound of an aircraft on its final descent towards the airport prompted Giles to look up. Noticing that the upper branches of a nearby oak tree, previously in the dark, were now softly illuminated, he stepped back a few feet from the building and saw that the lights in two rooms on the top floor, each with bright yellow and orange floral curtains, had been switched on.

"Must be bedrooms," he muttered. "Labs never have curtains, certainly not like those, anyhow. Does that mean Steve and his buddy are staying the night?"

On his way back to the car, upon turning the corner of the building, he bumped into Fiona sheltering her head from the rain under a plastic shopping bag.

"Fiona! You gave me such a shock. What the hell are you doing here?"

"Keep your voice down! I've got something to show you."

"What? In that bag?"

"In part. But I'll come to that in a tick. There's something much more important."

After leading him to a spot where they could shelter from the rain, she took their phones out of her jacket pocket and handed one to him.

"Here, hold yours up in front of your face, quite close."

Confused, but conscious that, whenever Fiona got up to something puzzling and unexpected, it was always important, Giles did as instructed.

"That's it," she said. "Now, what can you see?"

"Your face."

"Good. So?"

"What do you mean?"

"That's interesting, isn't it?"

"Why? So, you've got the video camera running."

"Wrong! Now look at the real me."

Giles lowered his arm to see that Fiona was holding her phone to her own face, but with the screen facing him.

"You see, Giles, you jumped to the wrong conclusion," she said. "You weren't looking at me with your camera at all. The image was being taken by camera."

"What's going on?" asked Giles, very confused.

"While you were peeking into windows, I was busy doing something else. Do you remember last year, when we went for a weekend in the Peak District, and I was worried someone might break into my flat because scaffolding had been erected around the house?"

"Yes."

"And before we set off, we each downloaded one of those household security CCTV apps into our phones, which enabled mine to be used as a wi-fi security camera, which I left propped on the sofa, and yours as a remote monitor, which we took with us?"

"Yes."

"Well, by subscribing to an optional add-on service, which I've just done with my Visa card, we can now use them without wi-fi. The image of my face was sent from my phone to yours via the Internet. And, since we cannot see Steve's car from where we're parked, I'm on my way to prop my phone against the building so that we can keep an eye on it from the safety of ours."

"Brilliant!" Giles exclaimed. "But what about the rain? If it doesn't ruin your phone, it will at least fuzz up the lens."

"That's where this plastic bag comes in. Inside it, I've got the cardboard box that contained those chocolate biscuits we bought yesterday. I'm going to use it to create a little shelter, weighed down with some of the stones that are conveniently lying around."

"Even more brilliant."

"Is the Merc still in the light from the entrance to the building?"

"Yes."

"Good! That was my only worry. You go back to the car now, while I set it up. Then, you can get me up to date with what you saw in the labs."

When Fiona returned to the car, her face was beaming.

"Just look at this, Giles," she whispered, prodding him out of another doze. "It's working a treat. Now we can sit in here out of the rain, nice and cosy, and watch what's happening over there."

"Excellent," said Giles, giving her a kiss on the cheek.

"So let's make ourselves comfy," continued Fiona. "How about we play your collection of piano classics, and enjoy some of that wine we bought *en route*? I'm fed up of mineral water."

After chatting for an hour over wine from plastic cups, they took it in turns to watch the small screen while the other one tried to sleep. But the time the sun was rising, nothing had happened of note. The Mercedes was still where it had been, and nobody had appeared from the building. Staff and students were starting to arrive, some by bicycle or car, but mostly on foot, holding umbrellas, pieces of cardboard, or newspapers over their heads.

"I'm starting to feel edgy with all these people around," Fiona whispered, turning her face away from a passing girl who was taking an interest in their vehicle. "I'd suggest we move if it wasn't for the fact we have to collect the other phone. Do you think one of us should sneak out and grab it? I wouldn't like anyone to see it."

"Definitely not! It's highly unlikely anyone will spot it in this foul weather. They're too concerned with getting inside. I think we can relax."

By the time the car park was quiet again, now populated only by a few gardeners gathering branches and palm fronds brought down by the wind, Giles's prediction had been correct. Among several other bags and cardboard boxes from an overturned trash can, theirs had been of interest to only a vagrant mongrel looking for breakfast.

"I hope that dog didn't pee on it," Fiona laughed. "For a second, I thought it was going to knock the whole lot over. Which reminds me, how are you in that department?"

"Pretty close to bursting actually," said Giles.

"Me too. Shall we make a dash for the bushes?"

"Not just yet. Let's hang on a little longer."

By the time both hands of the square concrete clock over the buliding's entrance were pointing to the empty space once occupied by a brass number twelve, Fiona was getting increasingly anxious.

"Unless we've missed him, Steve still hasn't come out of the building. What if he doesn't? If he's got a flat up there, he might be inside for days. What do you think he could be doing?"

"Who knows?" replied Giles. "As he must have a house or a proper flat somewhere, perhaps they're preparing something."

"Or just needs a good rest after that journey."

"Don't we all? What I'd give for a bed right now?"

After a long afternoon enclosed within steamed-up windows, with the constant drumming of rain on the car roof and nothing to eat but chocolate and apples washed down with mineral water, the sky cleared and the shadows of the trees were noticeably lengthening. Stretching her legs as much as the cramped space would permit, Fiona ran her fingers through her hair.

Giles opened his window to put a hand outside.

"Yes, it's definitely stopped… at last. It'll be dark again soon. Then we can go for a walk around the car park before camping down for another night. This time, let's take it in turns to sleep on the back seat. We've no choice but to carry on. Steve *has* to be up to something. He can't have been in bed all day."

Giles was on his second watch when things started to get interesting again. He leant over the back of his seat and gave Fiona a nudge.

"Pssst! Wake up! Things are happening. Steve and co are coupling a trailer to the rear of the Merc."

"A trailer?"

"Yes."

"I wonder if it contains the drone you saw in the lab," she said. "I was thinking about that when I nodded off. Do you remember, the Hawaiians said they'd heard a buzzing noise when the mosquitoes appeared, which we assumed must have meant there was a large number of them. This was puzzling me considering not a single one was caught in the traps that were set up. Well, that might be what they heard. It wasn't the beating of thousands of tiny wings at all. It was coming from a *drone*. If a drone had been used to release a few mosquitoes in precisely the right place, it could explain everything."

"Why didn't I think of that?" said Giles.

"Because I'm smarter than you!"

Giles looked at her over his glasses.

"I'm not going to argue with that one."

"Everything about Ni'ihau's starting to fall into place," continued Fiona, sitting up properly. "Here's my latest scenario. Listen carefully.

"After sailing from San Diego to Hawaii on the *Oosterdam* with a few pupae already infected with the virus, whoever it was got off at Kauai and took them to an apartment they'd kitted out in advance. They popped them into an incubator and waited a few days until they'd developed into grown-ups, which were then allowed mate to produce eggs, which were then allowed to develop into the next generation, most of which would have been carrying the virus. As you know, once mosquitoes have got a virus, they can't get rid of it. It keeps on mutiplying and being passed on from one generation to the next. The next stage was to take them by boat or dinghy across the water to Ni'ihau, just a few hours away. They stopped off the coast, and used a drone fitted for the purpose to release them where the Hawaiians were living. I imagine the houses are clustered together, aren't they?"

Giles nodded while keeping an eye on the small screen.

"How far from the coast?"

"About a mile."

"Well within the range of a drone. After releasing them, the drone flew back to the boat. And that was that. The round trip would be well within range."

"It's certainly an interesting thought," said Giles. "Are you sure drones can do a two-mile round trip?"

"Some can do almost five miles," replied Fiona. "My uncle's a wildlife photographer and uses one around Loch Ness."

"How fast can they go?"

"The best more than fifty miles an hour, I think."

"So the attack could have been all over in a few minutes?"

"Yes."

"The sun will be up soon," said Giles, peering out the window. "As soon as they're in the Merc, we have to be ready to move. Cross your fingers and hope they don't see us. We can't be too far behind them this time."

"Who'll drive… you or me?" asked Fiona.

"As I'm already here, it might as well be me," said Giles. "As soon as I start the engine, you go and fetch the phone. Then, once they're through the gates we'll be off. That trailer should slow them down."

"Let's hope it's not very far this time."

Fiona need not have been concerned about how far they would have to travel on this occasion. Steve's destination was Tijuana International Airport, a journey of less than five miles from the university campus.

After following at a safe distance, Giles stopped under the cover of a bougainvillea near the entrance to the airport's car park, while Steve drove to the far side. A uniformed security guard bearing a semi-automatic walked at a brisk pace towards the Mercedes to shake Steve's hand before pointing in the direction of a road barrier. Once it had been raised, the car sped through and disappeared between two rows of palm trees.

Fiona looked at her map.

"It looks as if they could be going to where private aircraft get parked, Giles. It looks like that sort of spot… away from the terminal building, but with access to the runways. Hold on! I know."

A minute later, she'd confirmed her guess.

"Just what I thought. The Google satellite picture shows several small aircraft lined up over there. They must be going to a private plane."

"If so, I think this must be the real thing, Fiona. It has to be. The trial run on Ni'ihau was so successful, I can't imagine they'd do another one. Why take the risk?"

"I agree," said Fiona. "I wonder where they're off to? What could provoke the White House to use such an awful weapon, I wonder?"

"I can think of lots of people who might be a target for different reasons," replied Giles. "One of the tragedies of our time is that the USA isn't short of enemies these days. Perhaps Ted Crabb has given the CIA instructions to assassinate a head of state somewere, one who's ploughing ahead with a nuclear programme despite economic sanctions, or is perceived to be supporting a terrorist group, or has been threatening American troups? A single mosquito released in the right place at the right time would be enough to kill someone, and the cause might never be detected."

"Perhaps it's not one person that's the target, though, but terrorists or drug dealers… or even an army. Could Ted Crabb be preparing to go to war? If that's the case, they might not be planning to use them immediately, but store them in readiness for battle somewhere. Where has the US army got troops these days?"

"Where haven't they, is more to the point. And where is civil unrest currently threatening American geopolitical influence? The list goes on. We desperately need to find out where they're going, Fiona… and pretty quick."

"But how?"

Giles shrugged his shoulders while Fiona held her head in thought.

"Got it! Got it!" she said. "We *can* do something."

Turning to collect her suitcase, she emptied the contents onto the back seat and jumped out of the car, taking the suitcase with her.

"You stay here," she called through the open window.

"What on earth…?"

"If I'm not back in fifteen minutes, come looking for me."

"But that guy's got an AK-47!"

"I know."

Without another word, she set off at speed across the car park, waving the suitcase frantically to attract the guard's attention. As Giles watched in horror, there was a brief exchange between them before the guard pointed in the direction of Steve's car with his gun. After crawling under the barrier, Fiona disappeared among the palm trees.

Time went agonisingly slowly while Giles waited. To add to his confusion, the guard had strolled back to his hut as if nothing had happened, sitting down on the doorstep to light a cigarette, his Kalashnikov propped between his legs. A few minutes later, he was joined by a second guard who had appeared from behind the trees. Giles ducked as the man appeared to point in the direction of the car while talking to his colleague. The call of a distant owl added to his sense of isolation and insecurity, as if he were the focus of the bird's predatory intention.

He was on the point of calling Fiona from his phone when she reappeared, looking unhurried and relaxed as she paused to chat to the two men. Putting his head out of the window, he could hear her giggling as she shook their hands before walking towards the car at a leisurely pace.

Giles kicked the door open as soon as she was in reach.

"What the *hell* was that about? I was worried to death."

Getting into her seat with a contented self-satisfied expression written all over her face, Fiona closed the door quietly, took a very deep breath, and gave him a sweet smile.

"What did you say, Giles?" she asked softly.

"I said, what the *bloody hell* was that all about?"

"Ah yes, that's right. Well, we want to know where Steve's going, don't we?"

"Carry on."

"So… I had an idea. I used my suitcase to get past the guard. I told him Steve had left it in the university, and I needed to get it to him before they took off."

"He spoke English?"

"Just about… with the help of a little body language… with the emphasis on the body bit, if you know what I mean."

"I'm trying not to imagine. And that's all it took?"

"Of course! He's a Latino, isn't he? I followed his directions and after a hundred yards, that felt like a mile, I saw Steve chatting to a woman and a couple of pilots next to an aircraft. His car was parked behind it and his mate was busy transferring things from the Merc. And we were right. The trailer contained the drone."

"It did? What sort of plane was it?"

"A private business jet."

"Any distinguishing features?"

"It had two engines at the back, and the wings were turned up at the tips," said Fiona. "And… oh yes, the tail fin had two little wings at the top. Apart from that, there was nothing special."

"Did you take a picture?"

"Yes… two… you know me. Here they are."

The first image was of the front of the aircraft, where four people were standing by an airstair below the cabin door. Giles then swiped to a close-up of the tail.

Fiona pointed to a series of letters and numbers on the fin. "See that?"

"Yes."

"That's what I was after. It's the registration number. Every plane, private or commercial, has one, and it's totally unique. It's a plane's DNA fingerprint."

"So we can find out who owns it?"

"Presumably," said Fiona. "But right now, it's more important than that… because, with it, we can track the flight. You know the smartphone apps that enable you to follow commercial flights in real time? Well, normally they don't show private jets. But if you type in an aircraft's registration number, it will track it wherever it goes."

"Where on earth did you learn that?"

"I'll tell you later. It's a long story. So, after they've taken off, we should be able to follow them all the way. I suggest we waste no time finding a hotel around here. Call Teuku to get him up to date, and then see where Steve's heading."

"I've said it before, and I'll say it again," replied Giles. "You never cease to amaze me. By the way, what did you do with your case?"

"Took the label off and buried it in a pile of trash. Sad… it was my favourite. Do I smell of rubbish?"

"No. And I'll buy you a new one, don't worry. Best Italian leather. You deserve the best. Now, let's go."

"Hold on!" said Fiona. "I haven't finished. If you look at that photo again, you'll see that, in addition to what's on the tail, there are more letters and numbers on the engine."

"You're right. It says G650ER."

"The 'G' stands for the manufacturer, which presumably will be Gulfstream, and the '650' will be the model. But the interesting bit is the 'ER'. It stands for 'Extended Range', which could mean they're planning a long flight. And when I say long, I mean *very* long."

"How far?"

"Non-stop, close to ten thousand miles."

"Okay, let's find that hotel," said Giles. "And on the way, you can tell me how you came to know so much about private jets."

He turned to look at her inquisitively.

"You've never had a super-rich sugar daddy, I don't suppose?"

"Giles, how *could* you?"

Chapter Thirty-Nine

As soon as they had checked into the Hampton Inn, just a mile from the airport, Giles called Teuku from the lobby to give him the news. Meanwhile, with her washbag and a carrier bag containing a few clothes dropped at her feet, Fiona had logged into Flightradar24 on her phone.

"It worked, Giles!" she exclaimed, pulling his arm. "They're already up. Here's the plane in red among all the yellow ones. They've gone into US airspace."

"Where exactly?"

"Approaching Phoenix."

"Let's go upstairs."

"What floor?"

"Six."

It was soon clear that Phoenix was not the aircraft's destination. It was going much farther than that... to New York. After an hour at John F Kennedy airport, it took off again and headed out over the Atlantic.

***

By the time the aircraft was over Eastern Europe, the sun had set again in Tijuana. It had been another long tedious day of watching and waiting. But at least they had been in comfort this time, not continuously on the move with the constant bumping and vibration of the car, or stiff and hungry with little to do but listen to the rain on its roof. The room was quiet and spacious, and they could relax listening to Mozart, Bach,

Albinoni, and Vivaldi while the flight made its way among the endless procession of long-haul jets crossing the ocean.

At the approach of midnight, needing some exercise and fresh air to steady her nerves, Fiona departed for a walk around the hotel grounds, leaving Giles to order room service, now almost a way of life. Upon her return, over a seafood risotto and white wine from the local Adobe Guadalupe winery, they considered what action they should take. Fiona felt they had already wasted too much time. They should contact somebody – anybody – immediately and tell them everything they knew. Giles, however, didn't agree. In his opinion, it was too soon. They should sit tight for now. After all, they didn't know where the aircraft was going to land yet, did they? And who would they contact at this point: Mexico's *Policia Federal*, the FBI, the press…?

"Neither of the first two could be trusted," he said, "if it was all part of an international conspiracy. And why should the press take such an extraordinary claim seriously without any evidence? For all they know, we might be hoaxers, having a bit of fun at their expense. On top of which, lifting the lid prematurely might put us in mortal danger."

"What about Interpol?" asked Fiona.

"I don't think they talk to the public, only cops."

Giles glanced at the screen.

"It's over Romania now, heading sort of south-east. Where the hell are they going?"

After finishing their wine, they agreed to take it in turns to sleep while the other one remained awake. But it was not long before the alcohol had its inevitable effect.

When Giles awoke, he found himself fully dressed in one of the suite's easy chairs, an empty dessert bowl on his lap, and his napkin and spoon on the floor. The lighting had been dimmed and the blinds closed. Fiona was prostrate on the bed breathing deeply, her empty glass in one hand, her phone in the other. Moving to her side, Giles peered at the screen only to see it was blank.

"Fiona, wake up!" he screeched. "You're supposed to be on duty."

"Oh, my God!" she gasped, rubbing her eyes. "What's the time? That wine completely knocked me out. And, hold on… what's worse, my battery's flat. Damn! Where's the charger? Oh yes, I know. On the dressing table. Can you fetch it?"

It was several tense minutes before the app was running again.

"There they are, thank goodness!" she gasped. "I was terrified they might have landed and disappeared for ever."

Giles peered over her shoulder.

"But hold on! Look *where* they are."

"Let me… oh my God! What's going on?"

Fiona checked the aircraft's height and speed.

"And they're descending, Giles. They must be landing."

"If they're landing there, what are the hell are they up to?"

"I think we can guess, can't we?"

"You're bloody right we can!"

"How far d'you think the airport is from…"

"By road? An hour and a half, I guess. We need to get Sir Q on the blower… immediately. We can forget about the time. This is urgent!"

Chapter Forty

Comfortably reinstated in the cosy ambience of Magdalen's Smoking Room, with a log fire glowing in the Tudor fireplace and the sunlit snow-covered lawn of the cloistered quadrangle beckoning through the leaded windows, even after so many weeks it was difficult for Giles to grasp the reality of their latest adventure.

As Fiona sorted through the ever-present spread of newspapers and magazines on the long, oak table in the centre of the room, he marvelled at the ease with which she had adapted to the strange double life that had been thrust upon them. As always, the task of returning to their academic routine had been a challenge, but nothing to compare with the two previous experiences. He would never forget that journey from Stockholm, when all sense of accomplishment had been dulled by his sorrow over Steve's tragic foolhardiness, his anxiety about the coming reception at the College, and his growing conviction that there was more to Ahmad Sharif's death than met the eye. The return from Rome and the weeks that followed, plagued by doubts about the wisdom of withholding the presumed identity of Ahmad's assassin, had been little better. The fact that Brigitte Dubois Yusuf's identity card was still where he had hidden it upon his return, in his attic inside a rusting Three Nuns tobacco tin once the property of CS Lewis, was never completely out of his mind.

This time, thank God, there were no secrets, concerns, or misgivings to keep him awake at night. On the contrary, the mission had been an unmitigated triumph. Their unravelling of the Ni'ihau mystery had been a piece of brilliant genetics.

Their pursuit of the Mercedes through the length and breadth of Mexico had been nothing less than heroic. And his call to Sir Quentin to urge him to alert Aqaba airport to the approaching aircraft, knowing that Sir Q had just had a highly publicised meeting with King Abdulla II to celebrate the twinning of the College with the University of Jordan, had very likely have saved many thousands of lives. Who knows how the airport's director would have responded to such a seemingly implausible story if it had come from him or Fiona?

The letter from Rashid Yamani that Teuku had brought with him to Jakarta airport upon their arrival from Mexico, containing an invitation to visit several of Islam's most ancient academic institutions during their journey back to England, had given Giles the opportunity to fulfil his lifelong ambition to visit Cairo's *Al-Azhar* University, the oldest of them all. What an experience it had been as he and Fiona had stood together in the mosque's vast courtyard after a rare shower of rain, its gracious columns, porticoes, and minarets reflected in the marble tiles. Could there have been a better moment to give her the ring he had secretly bought in the *Khan el-Khalili* market, while she had been sampling the coffee in Fishawi's nearby? In every way, their latest sabbatical, if it could be called such, had been a huge success.

"Sorry to interrupt your thoughts, Giles, but which one would you like?" Fiona asked in her soft-mannered way, flicking her red locks over her shoulders as she kneeled before him. "*Scientific American, Time, Newsweek, Nature,* or *The Guardian*?"

"You didn't find a dog-eared copy of the *Eagle* by any chance?" he chuckled. "Quite frankly, I'm more in the mood for Dan Dare right now than serious stuff."

"Come to think of it," replied Fiona, "you'd make a good stand-in for that batman of Dan's. What was he called? The little fat chap from Wigan, who was another devotee of English grub?"

"That was Digby. I willingly admit to sharing his culinary preferences, Fiona, but not the rest of that description! I suppose you fancy yourself as the extremely brainy and curvaceous Jocelyn Peabody, do you, without whom Dan would have been totally bamboozled by the green Mekon?"

"Funny you should say that! Anyhow, as there's no *Eagle* here, or even a *Dandy* or a *Beano* for that matter, what will it be?"

Giles took the only daily newspaper from her hand.

"Thanks. Coffee?"

"Yes, please."

While Giles was busy at the *chiffonier* chatting to a colleague, Fiona rearranged the magazines and journals on the table before taking the stool beside the hearth to run her eyes over the pages of *The Guardian*.

"Here we are, dear," Giles chortled on his return. "Just heard a really good Irish one from Jim Cogan. Interested?"

"Not just now, thanks," said Fiona. "If it's from him, I'm definitely not in a rush! There's something much more important in here. It's about the court hearing in Jordan. It finished yesterday, a day sooner than expected. There's a full page report, complete with a photo of Steve… in handcuffs."

"Ha! I wonder if Jordanian ones are more or less comfortable than Swedish ones? He'll soon be an expert at this rate."

Giles took a sip of his coffee. "So, tell me. What does it say?"

"Haven't read it yet. I suggest we gulp down our coffee and make our way to the library, first floor, where it's sure to be quiet this time of the day."

"Good idea. Then I'll get Teuku up to date."

***

When Teuku received the telephone call from Giles an hour later, he was leaning against the railings of the rooftop terrace of Phnom Penh's Rosewood Hotel, preparing the special lecture he was due to deliver the next morning at the ASEAN Conference of Tropical Medicine and Parasitology. Normally, by now he would have edited his slides and rehearsed his talk, put together a list of questions he might be asked, and searched the journals for any data he might need to answer them. Few of his university colleagues ever went to such lengths. As long as they presented something new from their research, they knew the audience would be happy. The quality of the lecture hardly mattered. Teuku had no objection to any of that. But he was in a very different position to them. As INDOMED operated under the same strict rules as MECCAR, any public presentation of unpublished research from his own laboratory was forbidden. Consequently, he'd had to prepare a very different type of talk, a review of recent progress in his field of new antibiotics. It had to be comprehensive, up to date, and accurate. He also wanted to make it entertaining by including a few anecdotes, a surprise or two, and some humour, as it was going to be late in the day, when many in the audience would be getting tired.

It was a task for which he needed several hours of uninterrupted privacy. A lengthy flight would normally have guaranteed it. On this occasion, however, throughout the ten-hour journey from Jakarta he'd been troubled by the knowledge that Steve's court case in Amman was in progress. As he knew he would hear of the outcome at any moment, he'd placed his phone on the railing by his elbow to be sure it would be audible above the traffic noise. But it was a decision he was to regret. For, as soon as Giles's call came through, the vibration sent it falling to the road several floors below.

Having spotted Giles's initials on the screen before it disappeared, he rushed to his suite on the hotel's tenth floor. By the time he'd picked up the telephone to return the call, Giles had given up trying.

"Teuku! Thank God! Where the hell have you been? I must have tried half a dozen times."

"Just lost my phone, Giles… for ever. But that's another story. Any news?"

"Yes, a lot. And it's not what we were expecting. Prepare yourself for an earthquake… and a few aftershocks. I'll try to be quick. But there's a lot to tell you."

"Hold on then…" said Teuku, sitting down. "Okay. That's better. Now I'm ready."

"It wasn't like we imagined at all, Teuku," said Giles. "As you know, after finding a hotel near Tijuana airport, thanks to the wonders of modern technology we were able to track Steve's flight all the way. Once we'd cottoned on to where it was going and guessed what he was up to, I got on the blower to Sir Quentin in Oxford. He called Jordan and told them what was happening. Within seconds of the aircraft touching down, it was surrounded by police cars… lights flashing, sirens howling. Even the army turned up."

"Yeah, I knew all that, of course," replied Teuku. "Who didn't? But what came out of the hearing? What's the deal?"

"Very good choice of word that, as it happens, Teuku… the deal. First, it was absolutely nothing to do with the Pentagon. We were up a gum tree on that one."

"Up a what?"

"Never mind," said Giles. "The point is we were totally wrong. Everything's reported in an English newspaper that I have before me. The US military knew nothing about it. They were to eventually, but not until it was all over. They were as innocent as lambs. The whole thing was Steve's baby."

"How come?"

"As you know, after being thrown out of the National Cancer Institute, Steve moved in with his daughters in La Jolla Shores, just north of San Diego. His wife had already relocated to San Francisco and started divorce proceedings. He was ruined professionally, and, given the ton of money his wife had brought into the marriage, he was about to be ruined financially, too. There was no possibility of returning to the NCI. Nor could he get a job in a university. He applied to more than twenty without getting a single interview. He also approached several biotech companies, but they weren't interested either. He became desperate, almost suicidal, he claimed. And then he had an idea. After working on it and telephoning around, he arranged to meet three Mexicans in the Barrett Junction Café."

"Where's that?"

"In the middle of nowhere on the road between Tecate and San Diego."

"Why there?"

"It certainly wasn't for the coffee, excellent though I'm sure it is. Sitting on the veranda with a Santa Ana blowing sand into their cups, they discussed a deal designed to solve Steve's problems and much more in a stroke. One week later, after a second meeting in the same place, he was on his way to knock on the door of the dean of the Autonomous University of Baja California in Tijuana, just over the US-Mexico border. A couple of hours later, the two of them emerged to take a cab to the Villa Saverios, one of the city's top restaurants, where they wined and dined into the early hours."

"They had something to celebrate?"

"You bet! Steve had hit the jackpot. He couldn't have made a better choice. The timing was perfect, and what he was offering was too good to turn down."

"Which was?"

"In a word, money. Buckets of it. So much it would cover not just the cost of creating a personal professorship for him in the university, but also give him a first-class brand new genetics lab and all the research expenses he could possibly want for years to come. On top of this, the university would get enough extra cash to construct a new building with more labs, lecture theatres, student accommodation, a health centre, a student clinic… you name it."

"Where was the money coming from?"

"I'll give you a clue. Like most endowed professorships, Steve's would have its own eponymous title."

"Which was?"

"The SLZT Professor of Genetics."

"What do the letters stand for?"

"*Sinaloa-Los Zetas-Tijuana.*"

"Hold on!" said Teuku. "The first two are drug cartels, aren't they?"

"That's right. And so is the third."

"You mean it was drug money?"

"Yes," said Giles. "Those nice Mexicans Steve met in the desert were from the *Sinaloa*, *Los Zetas* and *Tijuana* cartels."

"How on earth did he…?"

"Steve had convinced them it would be a smart PR move to donate money, a lot of money, to a Mexican university. He'd reminded them of how Pablo Escobar had become popular with the Colombians, when he put his hand in his pocket for public housing, street lighting, and a reforestation project. Of how Al Capone had gained influential friends by paying for soup kitchens during the Great Depression. And how, in Mexico itself, one of their arch enemies, the Gulf Cartel, had handed out cookies in hospitals and nursing homes, and given toys to children with messages encouraging them to work hard in school. He'd also told them of surveys that had shown how unhappy Mexicans are with the state of their schools and healthcare. If the cartels put some of their profits into good causes like education, hospitals, and medical research, he'd said, they'd be sure to win the hearts and minds of the people, whose cooperation they could then surely count on. Everyone would win. It was a no-brainer."

"Steve's a clever guy," said Teuku. "Crooked, but very clever. But are you saying the drug guys didn't want any more than that? I mean, good PR's worth a lot, but…"

"Well, as a matter of fact, there was something else," said Giles. "Can you guess?"

"I doubt it. Tell me."

"How about a more enlightened attitude on the part of the politicians and law enforcement agencies towards their commercial activities?"

"You mean the Mexican cops turning a blind eye to their trafficking, murder, and mayhem?"

"Spot on! The less the state interfered with their work, the greater would be their profits; and the greater their profits, the more money there'd be for more handouts to all those good causes. As public services improved, so would the politicians' ratings, thereby ensuring their continued cooperation. There might even be some cash left over to reward those same politicians for their commitment to the good of the country. And meanwhile, Steve could be back at work, doing world-class research that would benefit mankind and enhance the university's reputation around the world. Everyone would win."

"Apart from the American people," said Teuku.

"That's true…" replied Giles, "at least the fifty million, who, for some incomprehensible reason, try heroin, cocaine, or methamphetamine at some time in their lives."

"Did you pluck that number out of mid-air?"

"No. It's a fact. That's the official figure."

"God help us!" said Teuku. "But hold on. What would be the point of the cartels shipping more drugs to the US border, if they were just going to pile up on their side?"

"That's exactly what the cartel guys said to Steve during their first meeting," replied Giles. "The idea would work, they'd pointed out, only if the US Border Control came on board, too. And how could they achieve that? Bribes certainly wouldn't work. They'd tried that countless times. Threats had never worked, either. It was a great idea in theory, but not realistic.

"Never one to give up easily, Steve said he thought he could fix it, and they should meet again in seven days' time in the same place. As soon as he got home that evening…"

"Hold on again, Giles! Why was he talking to *three* cartels? Wouldn't one have been enough? None of them are short of dough. Do you know what the Mexican narcotics trade is worth? More than twenty billion dollars a year."

"Obviously, there would be more of that cash available from three cartels than from one. But that wasn't the issue, Teuku. Between them, those cartels cover the length and breadth of the country, from Tijuana in the north-west corner on the US border, to the borders with Guatemala and Belize in the south."

"Okay. Carry on."

"When Steve got home that evening, he called the White House. The following morning, he flew to DC. The next afternoon, he was in the Oval Office – the same office where, not so long ago, Ted Crabb had given him such a torrid time with a despairing Hank Weinberg prostrate on the couch. He presented his proposal to Crabb. He loved it and the next day summoned the Chief of Homeland Security and the CIA Director to the White House. And the rest, as they say, is history."

"What are you saying, Giles? That the President agreed to relax the border controls to let more drugs through… and those two went along with it?"

"In a word… yes."

"Impossible!"

"Not so, Teuku. Not only was it possible, it actually happened."

"But this is crazy, criminal," said Teuku in disbelief. "And just to help *Steve*? I didn't think he and Crabb got on together?"

"They don't. But they have one thing in common."

"Which is?"

"A deep-seated hatred of MECCAR. Being in the top job, when the NCI was beaten to the *Achilles* gene, was a national humiliation from which Crabb had never recovered. He'd also been living in terror that the nightmare would happen again; that another blockbuster breakthrough by Rashid Yamani's team was round the corner. The wounds inflicted on Steve had been even deeper – the same humiliation, plus the shame of his arrest in Stockholm, the ruination of his career, the breakdown of his marriage, the financial loss…"

"Okay, they both hate MECCAR. Message received. But what's that got to do with what Steve was up to?"

"Everything, Teuku. More than anything in the world, Steve wanted revenge. He'd become obsessed with the idea. It had been devouring him. Knowing him, I'd be surprised if it had been any other way. He said during the hearing that he'd brooded for weeks over what he could do to make Rashid Yamani pay for his suffering. And eventually he'd come up with the perfect answer."

"Which was?"

"He'd murder him and everyone else in MECCAR."

"What! How?"

"With their own discovery."

"What do you mean?"

"He'd use the *Achilles* gene as an instrument of mass murder. He'd take a natural virus that's known to be transmissible from mosquitoes to humans, but usually fairly harmless; modify it to contain *Achilles* in a permanently active form; infect hundreds of mosquitoes with it and then release them over MECCAR's gardens."

"You're having me on?"

"Nope. It's in front of me in black and white."

"What did you mean by a permanently active form?" asked Teuku. "I thought *Achilles* can become active only in cancer cells? And, even then, only after it's been given an artificial DNA switch, like Steve's *Deidamia*."

"That's true," replied Giles. "Although all our cells have *Achilles* genes, they don't work because nature hasn't given them a switch. If they're given an artificial one like *Deidamia*, they work a treat. Then, if a cell ever becomes cancerous, *Achilles* wakes up and forces the cell to kill itself by producing a protein that knocks out its batteries, the mitochondria. But, of course, as with all genes, there's an intermediate step. *Achilles itself* doesn't cause the cell to make the protein. What it does is to make it synthesize a messenger, a molecule of RNA, with the same genetic code. This leaves the nucleus to enter the cytoplasm, wherein it instructs the cell's enzymes to manufacture the protein by joining the right amino acids together in the right order. Unlike genes, RNA doesn't need activating. It's always active. As I say to my students, think of the cell as a building construction company: the gene's DNA is the managing director; the RNA is the site foreman; the enzymes are the workforce; and the amino acids are the bricks. The protein is the end product – in this case, one whose completion tips the company into bankruptcy and liquidation."

"Cute! Must remember that one. Go on."

"Steve realised that, if he engineered an RNA virus to contain *Achilles* RNA, or at least the most important part of it, *any* normal healthy cell in the body that the virus infected, whether in the skin, brain, heart, lungs, gut, liver... anywhere, would die. A single bite from a mosquito carrying such a virus would produce a terrible illness as one cell after another got infected and died. It would be a death sentence, and nobody could do anything about it."

"And this is what he was planning to develop in his lab?" asked Teuku.

"Yes. He would engineer viruses to carry *Achilles* RNA. Then he would infect mosquitoes with them, then release hundreds of females after they'd mated over MECCAR's gardens from a drone launched from an SUV in the desert."

"And Ted Crabb went along with *that*?"

"Went along with it? According, to Steve's testimony, he *loved* it."

"Did the cartel guys know about the plan to attack MECCAR?"

"Yes."

"And the university?"

"No. As far as the dean knew, Steve's lab would be modifying mosquitoes as part of a programme to reduce their numbers in Africa and the Middle East."

"Clever! And the virus he chose was the West Nile?"

"Yes," said Giles. "He had to use an RNA virus, of course, not a DNA virus, and the West Nile ticked all the boxes. It can be transmitted to humans by several species of mosquito. In some of them, it's passed from the females to their eggs. And, as it's not very common and no vaccine's been developed... except for horses... very few people have immunity."

"As you say, it ticks all the boxes."

"However, as much as Ted was taken by the idea, he wanted more than mere gratification and peace of mind. Recognising its potential for warfare, he insisted that, once it was all over, the

Pentagon would be given exclusive ownership of the intellectual property. Steve would also have to ensure all genetic material, viruses, mosquitoes, computer records, documents, the whole lot, would be destroyed. Nothing would be left, except for one thing – a single batch of infected pupae that Steve would personally deliver to one of the Pentagon's labs after the big event. These would be the only such pupae anywhere in the world. And, even the Pentagon would be in the dark until Steve arrived on the doorstep with a letter from Ted. Apparently, the Pentagon has a network of shady labs around the world… in places like Georgia, Iraq, Afghanistan, Tanzania… supposedly for defence purposes, if you want to believe it. They're financed by the so-called Defence Threat Reduction Agency. Americans working there have diplomatic immunity."

"But the 'Big Pee' would…"

"The what?" interrupted Giles.

"My pet name for the Pentagon," replied Teuku. "Even though it hadn't developed the virus, the mere fact of harbouring those pupae would put it in breach of the Convention on the Prohibition of Biological Weapons, I'm sure."

"You're right," said Giles. "But do you think Crabb would care about that? For one thing, nobody else would know. It would be a state secret."

"Quite," said Teuku. "So how was Steve going to organise all this? Did Ted just take his word for it and sign off?"

"No. He insisted Steve remained in DC until he'd worked out the practicalities. And that's what he did. It didn't take him very long, because he'd already started."

"And what were those practicalities?"

"He'd create the killer viruses in his new lab from normal West Nile viruses isolated from local birds, their natural reservoir. He'd grow them in cultured insect cells and modify them to contain part of the *Achilles* gene's RNA… not all of it, just enough to do the job. He'd then check that the modified virus was lethal to human cells such as fibroblasts, nerve cells, and so on, but not to bird cells. By the time he'd done all this, he'd have set up the mosquito farm you know about in Tabasco – basically, just a secluded area of mangroves in which some of the local mosquitoes and birds, specifically grackles, were kept together under nets. He'd also have set up a lab on-site in a campervan."

"Why go to all the trouble of going to Tabasco?" asked Teuku. "Why not in the north, somewhere near his lab? It would have been much simpler."

"Two reasons," replied Giles. "First, the *Los Zetas* chap insisted on it. And you don't argue with them… at least, not for very long. Somewhat predictably, Steve didn't trust the other cartels. He didn't like the idea of everything happening hundreds of miles away in the north. He wanted to keep an eye on things. Second, of the thousands of mosquito species on the planet, Steve had decided to use *Aedes sollicitans*, the Eastern Saltmarsh, and the biosphere reserve in Tabasco is one of its natural habitats."

"Why that particular species?"

"Again, two reasons. He needed one that's known to transmit West Nile viruses to its eggs. Not all of them do. The Eastern Saltmarsh does. And, to avoid sowing the seeds of a humanitarian disaster, he wanted a species that would not be able to breed around MECCAR. The Saltmarsh is unusual in that it can breed only where there is rising and falling brackish water, like a shallow tidal estuary with mangroves or a salt marsh. He reasoned that, if he used Saltmarsh mosquitoes, any eggs the females laid around MECCAR wouldn't survive.

"So, to get back to where I was. Steve explained that once his killer viruses were ready, he'd take a batch to Tabasco and inject them into those captive grackles. Why did he choose grackles and not other birds? Because there are plenty down there and, second, studies have shown they're the best for amplifying West Nile viruses. From then on, whenever a hungry female Saltmarsh bit one of them, it would pick up the virus and pass it on to its developing eggs. And, in that way, in next to no time, Steve would have all the infected mosquitoes he could possibly want, thousands if necessary, given the number of eggs that mosquitoes lay.

"All this explains why the viruses that we isolated from the Hawaiians' blood samples didn't just contain *Achilles* RNA, but were also hybrids of two strains – the Tecate strain, which is common in the north, and the Tabasco strain, common in the south. This hadn't been part of Steve's plan. It had occurred by accident."

"How come?"

"Not surprisingly, as it's the major one around there, the viruses Steve used in his lab in Tijuana were of the Tecate strain. But, when he injected his engineered version into the grackles in the south, at least one of the birds must already have been infected with the Tabasco strain. Consequently, the bird's cells synthesised both strains at the same time, resulting in hybrid viruses containing bits of both. As you know, this sort of thing can happen with viruses. Other mosquitoes then picked this up from the bird and passed it on to their eggs. And that's what Steve ended up using."

"And if it hadn't been for that, you might never have solved the mystery?" asked Teuku.

"Quite possibly."

"And the virus didn't make the birds sick?"

"No," replied Giles. "The killer protein has no effect on bird cells. As I said, they'd checked that out in the lab."

"Okay," said Teuku, "so now he'd got a bunch of infected mosquitoes driving those poor Tabascan grackles out of their little avian minds. What did he tell Ted Crabb he'd do next?"

"Enter Ni'ihau. He reckoned this would be the ideal place for a trial run – a tiny island, out of bounds unless you have a permit, very dry so any eggs couldn't develop, and inhabited by just a few people living close together, none of whom had ever been exposed to West Nile virus."

"How could he have been so sure?"

"It's never been known on any of the Hawaiian islands. They have some mosquitoes capable of transmitting arboviruses,

Aedes aegypti and *Aedes albopictus* for example, but the only arbovirus that's ever occurred there is dengue.

"So, using a false name, Steve bought a ticket for a Pacific cruise on the *Oosterdam* from San Diego, and took along a few infected pupae packed with ice, the standard way of arresting their development. Unlike most passengers, he disembarked at the first port of call, in Kauai, which also happens to be the nearest island to Ni'ihau. Someone had flown ahead with some simple lab equipment and rented a villa in Waimea on the west coast. Steve joined up with him for three weeks or so, during which time they incubated the pupae and mated the resulting grown-ups to produce the number of offspring they needed."

"How did he feed them?" asked Teuku. "Not on themselves, obviously?"

"You can feed mosquitoes most of the time on sugar lumps," replied Giles. "When the first lot of females had mated and needed blood, Steve used a small piece of equipment that's common in insect labs. He didn't need it for the next generation of females, of course, because he wanted them to be hungry, very hungry, when they arrived in Ni'ihau. He took them by boat to the west coast of the island, stopped a few yards from the beach opposite Puuwai, where the islanders were living, and used a drone to release them over the houses."

"Boy! And the lady, who died on the cruise ship…?"

"It was more or less as we guessed. Steve admitted in court to having had an accident with the box of pupae when he was waiting to disembark. After putting the box on the deck, a passenger inadvertently kicked it. He hadn't realised any pupae had fallen out. But at least one male and a female must have done, and the resulting adults mated while the ship was touring the islands. The female then flew into the lady's cabin, bit her, got swatted in return, and you know the rest."

"All of which explains why she became ill many days *before* the epidemic."

"Precisely… because Steve had to wait until the eggs from the first generation of adults, the ones grown from his original pupae, had matured into a second generation and mated. Otherwise, he wouldn't have had enough to release over Ni'ihau."

"Mind-boggling stuff, Giles," said Teuku. "Would make a great movie! So, what next?"

"Hold on a tick. My mouth feels like sandpaper."

Fiona, who had been listening to the conversation, opened the bottle of Evian she'd brought from the Smoking Room and pushed it across the table. Giles took several gulps, swilling the last one around his mouth with evident satisfaction.

"So…" he continued, "according to the repoprt in *The Guardian* here, after returning to San Diego on a commercial flight, Steve stayed with his daughters to plan his attack on MECCAR. But he wasn't in a hurry. He'd worked hard to put everything in place, and now he wanted to enjoy the prospect. He went to his favourite spot in Wyoming to be at one with nature, as he put it, while putting the finishing touches to his plans.

"He would need a private jet, capable of flying from Tijuana to Aqaba with just one stop for refuelling – and, of course, a couple of pilots. He'd need a pretty big SUV waiting for him at the airport in Aqaba to drive to Wadi Rum village, and from there into the desert to get as close to MECCAR as possible. And he'd need the best drone available, which he'd fit with the same system he'd used for Ni'ihau – a light cage made of fine wire netting, the floor of which could be opened in flight by releasing a spring-loaded catch remotely.

"I'll now read to you what the article says. Where is it? Are… here we are. 'As he worked on the project in his rustic cabin in Jackson Hole and admired the view of the Grand Tetons across the meadow, so different from the parched mountains of Wadi Rum that occupied his mind, Dr Saloman chose the date for his great occasion. Why not the evening of the anniversary of MECCAR's opening? he'd thought, when Rashid Yamani and all his staff will be partying in the gardens? He had known this choice of date would mean delaying the attack by several weeks, but felt the added pleasure would be more than worth it. He pictured the drone's lights in the starlit sky as it wheeled away after releasing its lethal cargo over the celebrations, the confusion on Rashid Yamani's face as he struggled to comprehend, the ensuing panic as the invaders swarmed, dispersed, and attacked, each tiny bite delivering its deadly injection.

"'He planned everything meticulously. His helper at the mangrove swamp in Tabasco would collect a few hundred pupae, and put them with some ice cubes in an insulated box. A second lot would go into another box, eventually to be delivered to one of the Pentagon's labs when it was all over. He would pick up the precious cargo himself, and take it by car to Tijuana.'"

"Hold it there please, Giles," Teuku interrupted. "As you and Fiona know too well, that's one hell of a journey. Did he say why he didn't get one of his buddies to do the donkey work?"

"He said he didn't trust anyone but himself," replied Giles. "If he was to launch his attack on MECCAR at the precise moment he'd planned, he couldn't afford any accidents or unexpected delays in the run-up. Once he'd collected the pupae, the farm and campervan were to be sprayed with gasoline and torched. So if anything were to happen to those boxes during the journey, it would be a disaster. And the only way he could be sure it didn't happen would be to do it himself."

"So now we know the reason for the cloud of black smoke you saw when you went after the Merc?" asked Teuku.

"Precisely."

"But why use a car, anyhow? Between them, those cartels own hundreds of planes for carrying drugs and cash, more than the national airline Aeromexico. It would have taken only a few hours to get from Tabasco to Tijuana."

"Apparently, the cartels had refused to use their aircraft as it would have meant revealing the whereabouts of their airstrips to each other," said Giles.

"What about the one that took Steve to Aqaba?"

"It was a new one they'd bought for the job, delivered directly to Tijuana. Money was no object."

"Okay," said Teuku, "so let's move on to what happened after you followed him to the university."

"Unbeknown to us," replied Giles, "during the last day of the journey, Steve had started warming up one of the boxes by removing the ice cubes. Inside it, the pupae were contained in a cage of the type I mentioned earlier. Upon arriving in the lab, he transferred the cage from the box to the underside of the drone. By the time they were ready to leave for the airport, the adults had emerged, a mixture of males and females. They took the drone with the cage attached in a trailer to Tijuana airport, about a mile away, where the aircraft was waiting. And oh, yes … before doing so, they'd shredded all papers and cleaned anything that might have a trace of DNA or RNA on it. So, apart from the box of pupae in the fridge, no material evidence was left behind. The only written records of Steve's work were on an encrypted memory stick he took with him.

"When we got to the airport, Fiona left me in the car, while she charmed the guard into thinking Steve had left his suitcase in the hotel. Hiding behind bushes, she watched Steve chatting to a few others waiting by the plane – the guy who had accompanied him from Tabasco, a couple of pilots, and a woman whom she took to be an Arab at the time, but was actually a cartel member fluent in Arabic. Steve was…"

"Sorry, Giles, me again," Teuku interrupted. "I'm sure she was going to be very valuable when they got to Aqaba. How was she going to explain away a drone and a bunch of mosquitoes trapped inside a cage? It was going to look a bit strange to customs, wasn't it? Especially arriving in a fancy private jet from Mexico, of all places?"

"Well," said Giles, "they had fake documents purporting to show Steve was a professor in the Department of Biological Sciences, University of California San Diego, and his side-kick a young researcher at the university in Tijuana. They were supposedly collaborating with the University of Aqaba to develop a new type of mutant mosquito to combat malaria in the Middle East – places like Afghanistan, Yemen, and Saudi. They'd been developed in San Diego, and the drone's software had been written by the Mexicans as part of an international collaboration. In the unlikely event the authorities would want to check their story, the telephone and fax numbers of Steve's office given on the papers were actually his daughters', who would have answered any calls."

"They were in on it too?"

"That much of it, yes."

"But that story wouldn't explain the private jet," said Teuku. "It's not the usual mode of transport for university researchers, is it?"

"They were going to say they hadn't been permitted to carry the insects on a commercial airline, as they were infected with malaria," replied Giles. "And the flight had been paid for by an American company that was helping to fund the project – all supported by another fake document."

"No stone unturned, I see," said Teuku.

"Not even a pebble," replied Giles. "Now… where was I up to?"

"Steve was outside the aircraft, preparing to go."

"Ah, yes. Well, as you know, Fiona and I then went to the hotel, from where we kept a bleary eye on the flight path. They flew first to JFK to refuel, then continued across the Atlantic. It was a long, long wait, but once we saw they were descending towards Aqaba we knew we had to act. And, as you know, that's when I called Sir Quentin. As he didn't know the number of the airport, of course, he went straight to the top and called the Prime Minister, whom he'd met during his visit to Amman to celebrate the twinning of the university there with Magdalen."

"It always pays to know the right people," said Teuku. "And thank goodness he did!"

"Absolutely," replied Giles. "According to *The Guardian*, what happened next is the stuff of horror movies. Once the aircraft had touched down, the pilot was instructed to taxi to the end of the runway, where police and the Special Forces Brigade of *Al-Khassa*, the Jordanian Army's elite anti-terrorist unit, were waiting. As the plane was coming to a halt, one of them focused his binoculars on the flight deck as there seemed to be a lot of movement going on inside, arms waving around and so on. Puzzled, he walked to the nose of the aircraft. And what he found was staggering."

"Which was?"

"The front windows were crawling with mosquitoes, the pilots frantically swatting them off their faces and hands. Running down the length of the fuselage, they saw the other windows were the same."

"Had anyone got out by then?"

"No. When they were landing, they'd been ordered to remain inside the aircraft until given permission. If they attempted to open a door or a window, the aircraft would be blown up with them inside."

"How?"

"The army had shoulder-launch anti-tank missiles at the ready."

"How had the insects got out?"

"During the plane's descent, it had gone through a patch of severe air turbulence. The drone had been tossed onto the floor, releasing the catch on the cage's door. As the hinges were spring-loaded, all the mosquitoes escaped. By the time they'd landed, everyone had been bitten. Steve pleaded for them to be let out, but the airport would have none of it. Not until the aircraft had been fumigated, they said. Insecticides were sprayed into the auxiliary power unit that draws fresh air into the cabin, and the plane was left for a couple of hours before Steve and the rest were arrested."

"Now I know what you meant by a horror movie," said Teuku. "So how come Steve lived to tell the tale?"

"They were taken to a military hospital, where everyone apart from Steve died. He survived because, unknown to the others, he'd taken the precaution of immunising himself at the very start of the project. As you know, there's no vaccine available against West Nile virus – not for humans anyhow, only horses. The only way you can become immune is if you get infected naturally. But, as he'd known that adding *Achilles* RNA to the virus wouldn't alter its surface proteins, the only part to which antibodies develop, he reasoned that, if he injected himself with the natural virus, he'd probably become immune to his engineered one, too. So that's what he did. He injected himself with the natural virus – three times, actually. He knew there was a chance he could be one of the people who get seriously ill from it, but as they're usually over the age of sixty, the risk was very small – less than one in a hundred to be precise. And that was a risk he was prepared to take."

"So he experienced no effect at all from being bitten?"

"He did develop ulcers where he was bitten and was unwell for a few days," said Giles. "But, unlike the others, he survived."

"Nothing like looking after yourself, is there?" said Teuku. "And now it's Ted Crabb's turn to face the music?"

"And Steve's daughters, too, as accomplices."

"This is mind-boggling, Giles," said Teuku. "Many congrats… you too, Fiona, if you're there. This is awesome, truly awesome. And it's certainly going to do me and INDOMED a power of good. Can't wait to hear Rashid Yamani on the other end of this phone thanking me for saving his life!"

"Well, on that note, I'd better get off the phone now, Giles. Thanks for the call. You two go and enjoy yourselves. Go to a fancy restaurant on me. You deserve it."

"Thanks," replied Giles. "Fiona here played a big part, by the way, a very big part. In fact, I'd say her contributions were the most important. Anyway, bye for now, Teuku. Keep in touch."

"You bet!" said Teuku. "Cheers."

Just as Giles was about to end the call, he heard Teuku's voice.

"Oops! No… hold on! Still there, Giles?"

"Yes."

"What happened to the box of pupae Steve left in the fridge?"

"Ah, yes! When the police went to collect it, it wasn't there. The fridge was empty – unlocked and completely empty."

"WHAT! Steve had left a key behind?"

"Apparently not. He claims there were only two and he took both with him. On top of that, he'd had a padlock fixed to the door. But that was unlocked, too."

"Did they search the lab?"

"For the box? Yes… but couldn't find it. It was nowhere. Nobody in the university even knew of its existence. Or, at least, if they did, they weren't letting on."

"Did the locks have any sign of damage?"

"No. There were also no fingerprints on the fridge."

"Sounds like a professional job to me."

"One theory is that it was the US military. Perhaps, when Ted Crabb got word of what had happened in Aqaba, he got in touch with the Pentagon and they sent someone to the university masquerading as a cleaner or a technician visiting the lab to service some equipment. They're always coming and going, as you know. Nobody takes much notice. Another is that…"

"Hold it there!" said Teuku. "I think I know what you're about to say. That one of the drug cartels got there first, yes? That *they* sent a supposed cleaner or technician?"

"Afraid so… or someone with a gun."

"Right. And, of course, there's no way of knowing which of the three it could have been?"

"Correct."

"My God!" said Teuku. "I hope Steve spends many years behind bars."

"I'm sure he will."

"There's only one good thing you can say about him."

"What's that?" asked Giles.

"At least he chose those Saltmarsh mosquitoes, and not another species, to prevent the possibility of a worldwide epidemic."

"That's true. Although, in fact, it might not have worked."

"Why do you say that?"

"He hadn't done his homework quite well enough. He

didn't know that Eilat, in Israel, next door to Aqaba, was built on what used to be a vast salt marsh. The area's a staging post for hundreds of thousands of birds on the Eurasia-East Africa flyway, one of the busiest bird migration routes. As Eastern Saltmarsh mosquitoes are much stronger flyers than most, it could have been within their range from Wadi Rum."

"Wow!" said Teuku. "So the two of you could have saved millions of lives. That could be a very good reason for the Nobel Peace Prize, Giles. Seriously. I've no doubt Rashid would agree with me on that. Anyhow, I need to finish. If you hear anything new, let me know."

"Of course," replied Giles. "Bye for now."

As Giles placed his phone on the table, he looked at Fiona, now on the other side of the room, her eyes fixed on the library's famous barrel-vaulted ceiling as if to distract herself from the reality of all that had happened. Leaving everything where it was, he walked at a measured pace to the tall windows and gazed at two crows chasing a squirrel across the snow in the Longwall Quad.

"So, where do we go from here, Giles?" she called.

"I know where I'm going," he replied. "To the Turf for a D 'n' S. And a bloody big one, at that. Coming?"

"Try and stop me!"

Lightning Source UK Ltd.
Milton Keynes UK
UKHW012353210421
382416UK00001B/128